POMEROY

An American Diplomat

Gordon Williams

reinkarnation

This edition published in 2016 by reinkarnation
Cover design: Marina Esmeraldo

First published in Great Britain by Michael Joseph 1983
© Gordon Williams 1982, 1983

ISBN 978-1-908390-35-6

Gordon Williams wrote *From Scenes Like These* (Booker short list),
The Siege of Trencher's Farm (filmed as Straw Dogs), *The Upper Pleas-
ure Gardens*, *Big Morning Blues* and *Walk Don't Walk*.
Other works by Gordon Williams from reinkarnation:
Big Morning Blues
The Camp

For information about the author and his books see

www.reinkarnationbooks.com

The elimination of Gussie Pingree's virginity took place on a horse blanket in the old harness room. It was her twenty-first birthday, also the day she came into thirteen million dollars.

Outside, on that dark September afternoon, it was raining fit for the second Flood, which might have been a sign of God's disapproval but didn't bother Gussie any — let the gale shriek, let the deluge swamp the whole eastern seaboard, now she could get on with the business of being a woman!

Pomeroy had not realized his cousin twice removed was still a virgin. Not that he had any scruples about assisting a big healthy girl pass a wet afternoon, but he knew how grudgingly any Pingree parted with an asset, and when Gussie freed herself abruptly from his naked embrace to drag on her cotton drawers in the sitting position, her mood seemed a little less than rapturous. Still, in his experience, and he knew something about women, a smidgen of gallantry *afterwards* usually went a long way.

'That sure beat a ten-mile trot in a rainstorm,' he murmured.

Gussie snorted. 'Least it kept the horses dry.' She knelt with her back to him and fastened her stays. Her shoulders and arms were thick with freckles. He leaned over and kissed her hip. She pushed his face away.

'What's the hurry, Cousin Gussie?'

'I have my dance to prepare for.'

'The custom among adults is to engage in a little small talk after the event,' he drawled.

She gave him a fierce look. 'You're only twenty-eight.'

He tried to kiss her shoulder. 'You're a rhapsody in skin, Cousin Gussie —'

'You don't need the banana oil now.' She elbowed him sharply. 'You've done your duty —'

'*My duty*? That's a funny way of putting it. My pleasure — my privilege!'

'Horseshit. It was me dragged you in here, remember?' He grimaced as if deeply wounded. 'You were being so goddam gallant I didn't think you'd get around to it this side of Christmas.' She stood up to drag on her riding breeches. He lay on his back, smiling up at her. He was slim and hard and white except for his red arms and so startlingly nude she averted her eyes. The male body was so *flagrant*. 'Put your clothes on. Don't you feel cold?'

'Cold? This isn't cold. Up there in the Yukon it was often fifty below. A man had to —'

'I suppose you had intercourse with all those dancehall whores and Eskimo squaws,' she said gruffly, with what might have been a hint of jealousy. He reached out to caress her not-quite-slim ankle.

'You remind me of a poem, Cousin Gussie ... *"There once was a man from Nantucket, who kept all his cash in a bucket"* —'

'I don't care for rudeness,' she warned.

' —*"but his daughter named Nan ran away with a man, and as for the bucket, Nantucket!"* '

In her growly voice he found so strangely entrancing, she put his mind at rest. 'Don't worry, Cousin John, I'm not running away with you, and don't move out of here for fifteen minutes after I've gone, you hear me? If anybody finds you in here, say we went out riding and your clothes got wet — what kind of small talk anyways?'

'Oh, little pleasantries ...' She pulled her white polo sweater over her stiff red hair. 'I guess it wasn't so painful as I expected.'

His old man had always cursed the Pingrees as mean and grasping; all he could see was an awkward, vulnerable girl hiding her shyness behind a gruff voice. He gave her his most sincere smile.

'Next time — '

'Next time we'll be married and I won't be worrying about some straw-chewing stable-hand bursting in.'

Caught off guard, he frowned up at her. 'We'll be ... *married?*'

'Well of course we're getting married — would I have let you deflower me in a stable if we weren't going to be married? I'm legally of age as of today, Mama can't do a darned thing about it. That's why we don't have to run away, silly.'

Wind and rain beat on the stable roof tiles.

Her face had the handsome Pingree symmetry that would have been truly beautiful but for the absence of smiling muscles. His brain did a lot of fast work in a few seconds that lasted longer than the Ice Age. He smiled. Maybe it was more of a smirk. 'Love at first sight, eh?'

'Not exactly — I didn't *really* make up my mind till you called me a rhapsody in skin .. .'

Pomeroy, who knew how to swallow without moving his adam's apple, reached casually for his flannel combinations. They were inside out, undeniable evidence of a mad passion now slipping like a predawn dream from total recall. He met her grey-green eyes with a look of poignant yearning and got into his long johns as fast as possible short of looking like a man in a hurry to be somewhere else. 'You're the sweetest girl I ever knew, Cousin Gussie, but what do you really know about me?'

'Well, you could be an inch taller, but you're awful handsome.'

'Your mother called me the bad apple of the family — '

'She called you worse than that!'

'And I'm afraid she was right. I'm just a drifter, I don't have any money or career, you wouldn't want to hear some of the things I've done — '

'All real men go through a wild stage.'

'I bet there's hundreds of rich, eligible, good-looking young — '

'The richer they are the more they're only interested in getting richer. Cam Cadenhead — the one I told you about Mama wants me to marry? He got down on his knee and begged me to marry him because he worshipped the ground I walk on! The hell he does, he worships papa's railroad stock because he wants to be a director of the trust!'

He took a deep breath. 'Gussie — did I say *once* I loved you?'

'If you'd given me any bullshit about loving me I wouldn't be here with you now, stupid. All I ever wanted was a man who lusted after my body, not my money. Love is for the birds!'

'Is lust going to endear me as a son-in-law to Aunt Harriet?'

'I'll handle Mama.' She gave him a playful punch on the biceps. ' This was all ordained, Cousin John. Fate sent you. Don't be scared of Mama, she can't dislike you any more than she does now.'

' That's *very* reassuring.' Sometimes the sneaky thing was also the gallant thing. He sighed like a man with a hurting heart. Sometimes the truth was the sneakiest thing of all. 'Fate didn't send me, Gussie ... I went home to Knoxville last week for the first time in a year. My old man took the time before he kicked me out again to say John Law had been around twice asking for me. I'm on the run, Gussie; once I get hold of my money in a bank in Arkansas, I'm heading south — Mexico maybe, or Venezuela ... I could cut my tongue out for deceiving you, Cousin Gussie.' He sighed.

'I know about you running away from the army — '

'Who told you that?' he snapped.

'Quint Pepperday — '

'He's a damned liar! I resigned my commission — who the hell is Quint Pepperday anyway?'

'He's married to Lucy McFarlane Pingree, you'll meet him tonight, most likely he'll try to inveigle you into drinking and playing cards to win money off you, but just you ignore him, you hear me? I'll choose you for my first dance tonight, then we'll make the formal announcement don't you touch a drop. I hate liquor on a man's breath — '

'Ye gods! Aren't you interested in what I'm wanted *for*?'

She stamped her bare feet down into her riding boots. 'Uncle Marcus is a federal judge, Billy Taylor Pingree runs the state Republican Party, Uncle Fletcher is the biggest lawyer in Baltimore: they can fix most anything — '

'Can they fix a murder rap?' Thinking she was speechless through shock, he took the opportunity to pull on his right sock. 'Five years ago in the Alaska panhandle, in a slice of hell on earth masquerading as a town called Skagway, I took the life of the Moonfaced Kid, a vicious young grifter who — '

'Oh *Alaska?*' She snorted contemptuously. 'Uncle Fletcher got Quint off two attempted-murder charges right here in Baltimore; he crippled two immigrant German hands for trying to unionize the brick works — nobody cares about Alaska, even if it isn't just another of your tall stories — '

'It isn't a tall story! I killed a man and the law's catching up with me!'

She opened the sliding door to check the stables. She looked back at him standing there in his long johns and one sock. 'You do *want* to be married to me, don't you?' Those grey-green eyes now had all the naivete of a cat wondering whether to play with the fluttering bird a while or eat it now. 'Or would you rather I tell Mama and Uncle Fletcher and Uncle Marcus you took cruel advantage of me — an innocent young virgin on her twenty-first birthday? Why, Cousin John, I be-

lieve they'd have you castrated.' Years of training kept his face free of all expression, but she wasn't stupid. 'Don't worry, you big scaredy cat, I wouldn't let them cut your balls off, I think you're going to make just the *most perfect* husband! Bye!'

She blew him a kiss.

'Gussie!'

But she was already striding past the part-Arab hunters in their box stalls. He ran as far as the big white automobile on its new section of cement floor but caught only a last glimpse of her shapely rump ducking under a half-door out into wind and rain.

He came slowly back to the harness room and located his left sock. The impulse was there to jump into his clothes and hightail it but he was, after all, a Pomeroy. Anyhow, it was too damned wet. For another thing, who was this bastard Quint Pepperday?

McGraw, the automobile expert, had just run the steam-driven, wheel-steered limousine into a ditch past Druid Hill on the Baltimore-Pikesville road. Boden, who'd been coaxed into the expensive foolishness of hiring the goddam car, remained out of the driving rain behind the glass windows of the high tonneau bodywork while McGraw checked the semi-flash boiler and the controls. McGraw had agreed to pay any damage. He came back and rapped on the window. Everything was okay, he shouted, just that the front axle seemed to be broken.

'What's a hundred dollars to you, bigshot?', Boden shouted.

'Horses break their legs, don't they?' McGraw yelled back, as if that made it all right.

In the three hours it took Gussie's maid to get her ready for her twentyfirst-birthday ball, thoughts of Pomeroy's hard, slim body kept Gussie's courage up as she faced the problem of telling Mama. She was painfully reminded of his attentions in the harness room by the coloured girl's struggles in back to lace the long stays that pushed up her bosom and elongated her hips and crushed her midriff into a twenty-three-inch waist. Well, if she'd survived *that* ordeal, she could surely face up to Mama.

Automobiles and carriages were arriving outside in the rain, when into the big bedroom came Mrs Harriet Pingree and Mrs Edward Winthrop Fletcher, Gussie's youngest aunt. Cora was helping her into her new gown ($4,360 from the same New York couturier who dressed leading members of Mrs Astor's 400, and anyway, Uncle Harry was paying for it), a *dernier cri* Empire exclusive in palest grey satin with a daringly low decolletage and long train of dark green velvet. In the full length cheval mirror she saw them frowning.

As Cora fastened a choker of oriental pearls ($11,250 of her own money but an excellent investment, the jeweller had assured her), Mrs Pingree said decisively, 'She still has that blue dress she wore to Ruth Ogden McFarlane's dance.' .

'I should have been with them in New York,' sighed Mrs Edward Winthrop Fletcher, a leader of Baltimore fashion.

'It's *much* too forward for her age —'

'*Far* too revealing in the bust department —'

'Yes, but my bust isn't as flabby as yours, Aunt Fletcher,' Gussie said airily.

Mrs Edward Winthrop Fletcher stormed out vowing never to return. Mrs Pingree dismissed Cora and locked the door. Her small, once-pretty face was ugly in anger. 'That was absolutely the most disgusting thing I ever heard! Your mind is sick — poisoned! You'll get down on your knees and beg Aunt Fletcher to forgive you! I should scrub your tongue and send you to bed!'

Gussie smoothed down her hips in the mirror. How could she ever have been afraid of this dumpy woman who had so totally failed papa as a wife?

'You shouldn't come into my room without knocking and discuss me like an item from Sears Roebuck — by the way, I'm announcing my engagement to John tonight — '

'Your *engagement?* What are you talking about? John? John who?'

'John Pomeroy.'

'Let me feel your temperature!' Mrs Pingree put her palm on Gussie's brow and Gussie did not resist. Mrs Pingree frowned. 'You seem normal — '

'You think I'm too plain and naive for John to want to marry me?'

'He'd give his left arm to marry you — with all your money!'

'It wasn't my money under him in the stable this afternoon!'

Mrs Pingree stared in horror. She'd always had a lurking fear the girl was mentally deranged. 'Don't even say things like that as a joke, child,' she said sternly. Getting through this evening without public embarrassment was her immediate concern; tomorrow she would ask Dr Fralick about clinics she'd heard about for treating the unbalanced.

Gussie fluttered her eyelashes. 'Why, Mama, I've been waiting on you to tell me about the birds and the bees, but there's only one way to learn about sex. You don't understand the new morality, mother, we're in the twentieth century now, your generation was totally repressed. I decided some time back I wouldn't be a silly virgin bride — '

'Gussie!'

'—and I wanted a virile husband, not a wet-eyed slug like Cam Cadenhead. The new woman regards long courtships as very *passé,* all that bussing and holding hands? So let John go

the whole way in the stable to make sure he had what it takes
— '

'Shut your filthy mouth!'

'— which he has, oh my goodness yes!'

Mrs Pingree slapped Gussie a real stinger.

Gussie turned to her dressing table and touched the red blotch rising across her cheekbone. 'Kindly leave my room, mother.'

'Don't you give *me* orders in *my* house!'

Then Gussie proved she had truly come into full Pingree womanhood. 'You think you'll be able to maintain *your* house without my money, mother? John and I will probably travel for a year or so, New York, Paris, London — oh yes, and you and Uncle Marcus better draw up a trustees' account of all my money you've spent on your house — '

'I only spent money to give you a beautiful home you could be proud of!'

'You won't even let me drive the new automobile my money paid for! You've been *stealing,* that's what the law will say.'

'That's not true! I'm your mother! Oh, Gussie — tell me you're making it up about John Pomeroy — '

'He certainly doesn't want me for my money; he called me a rhapsody in skin — '

'Oh, my God! He'll go to jail, I swear it!'

'If you're worried about him getting his hands on my money — '

'Money, money, money!' Mrs Pingree wailed. 'I'd break my heart watching a plausible rascal like John Pomeroy humiliate my own darling little girl!'

'Humiliate me!' Gussie snorted in derision. 'He ever comes within a thousand miles of humiliating me, I'll put the rope around his neck with my own hands!'

At that moment, Mrs Pingree thought it was her late husband glaring at her from the mirror — that handsome Pingree

9

face that never smiled, implacably determined to have its own way, and utterly, terrifyingly, sure of itself.

Rain smacked like bullets against their oilskin slickers as Boden and McGraw mounted by the light of a kerosene lamp. The farmer shouted they couldn't get lost now, just follow the Pikesville road another mile or so and they'd see the Pingree mansion up on their left, lot of smart folks going out there tonight for the daughter's twenty-first, whole place would be lit up. At the corner of the barn, he gave Boden the reins of the spare mount with their bags lashed to its saddle. Ten dollars to hire the three horses for one day — plus a fifty-dollar deposit!

They ducked their heads into the wind and pulled down their wide hat-brims as they came out onto the road, both cursing this lousy assignment. Wrecking the hired automobile, no local trains, strict instructions not to go near the Baltimore police department, now being screwed by this yokel bastard for the last of their per diem allowance — with their luck, Boden fully expected to end up in a bog or in Pennsylvania. And all for some well-connected sonofabitch they were supposed to deliver without a bruise on him?

Four hours, twelve minutes after her induction into womanhood on a horse blanket, Miss Augusta Pingree, daughter and only child of the late Furnifold G. Pingree, manufacturer of bricks and barrels and prominent railroad stockholder, made her entrance into the ballroom, where, on a new dance floor of sprung teak ($29,000 that Mama now owed her), two hundred of Baltimore's best were waltzing to 'A Bird in a Gilded Cage', played by a creole orchestra hired all the way from Washington ($960 and rail fares, but they had, after all, played for the lately assassinated President McKinley).

Uncle Marcus saw her first and waved at the coloured musicians to stop. Some guests launched into 'Happy Birthday', others bellowed 'Twenty-one Today'. Graciously ignoring the vocal shambles, Miss Augusta Pingree, multimillionairess of fifteen and a half hours, accepted a glass of champagne (genuine French, but Uncle Marcus had supplied it), and toasted her wonderful mother, to whom she owed everything, while her grey-green eyes searched the throng for the handsome prince who had kissed her to life.

'Festering doodleoohs!'

'A pair of lousy nines!'

'Christ, I folded with a god dam flush!'

For the second time in half an hour, Lewis 'Loot' Pingree, Quint Pepperday, Henry Pingree, Jr, Charlie McFarlane and old Uncle Harry Chambers Pingree had to watch their Tennessee cousin rake in a big pot of gold eagles and silver dollars and greenbacks and treasury notes, maybe three hundred dollars. This wasn't the plan at all!

Pomeroy gave Loot a reproving smile. 'I'll tell you the mistake you made last time, old man. We were both dealt two pairs, yes? You drew one card for a full hand — the odds against you making it were eleven to one. I had a pair of queens, pair of fours — I discarded the fours and the fifth card because the odds against me making three queens were only seven to one.'

'You charge for these little lectures?' Charlie asked curtly.

'All I ask is a full dinner pail.' Pomeroy's smile took in the whole table. 'You were curious about what I did in the Klondike? I didn't find gold, but I played an awful lot of cards. Poker is for fools 'less you play to the percentages. '

Old Uncle Harry saw Loot blinking slowly.

'Your deal, Charlie,' Quint Pepperday said quietly. He was a big-chested man with wiry ginger hair and bushy mutton chops he habitually stroked with the knuckles of his index fingers. Uncle Harry could *feel* Quint's determination to knock the shine off this good-looking cousin with the big mouth and the reputation for devilment. Henry junior tried to inject a more cordial note.

'Is it true, Cousin Pomeroy, in Alaska if you have a stream outdoors your urine freezes all the way back up and when you walk away your weenie breaks off?'

'Worse things than that, Henry,' Pomeroy said enigmatically. He looked round the big library with its ceiling panels of cherubs and fleshy women, and bookcases almost all the way up. 'Mainly, you learn about life. Out west, up in the Yukon, that's where I got it knocked into me — gaming palaces thrown up so fast you could stand back and hurl a big dog through the cracks in the walls; every mean, vicious human jackal round the table ready to gun you down for a nickel. Who reads all these books anyhow?'

'Our late Uncle Furn heard about the kind of library English dukes have and decided he wanted one just the same, so he forked out ninety-five thousand dollars to have an authentic English duke's or lord's actual library shipped across the Atlantic -twenty-five thousand leatherbound volumes plus cases and the stepladder on wheels. Nobody reads the books; Uncle Furn bought them to be admired, not give everybody headaches.

'Deal the cards, you four-eyed over-educated beanpole,' Loot growled at Henry junior, who was six foot four and bespectacled to go with his Harvard law degree, although he was now going to make a bundle on his own account, not working for Uncle Fletcher's law firm but in commerce.

'My partner and I are in negotiation for exclusive distribution rights in three states for a new line in men's toilet articles, *including* the new safety razor. The modern American male can no longer afford to scorn personal hygiene, the rough frontiersman is dead.'

'I'll see the day I stink of perfume and shave with a tricksy little gadget,' Charlie sneered.

'Speaking as the only one here who's recently been to a frontier, I might just try one of these new shaving gadgets at that,' Pomeroy said brightly.

Henry junior broke the grim silence that followed. 'Cousin John, shouldn't you be going upstairs to change for Gussie's dance?'

Pomeroy looked at the others in their formal evening suits, starched white shirts with wing collars and black bow-ties. He was wearing a single-breasted sack suit of brown cloth with a fine gold thread, brown shirt with thin white stripes, white collar and red silk necktie. 'I didn't realize all you Pingrees hankered to be in the Blue Book,' he said slyly. Henry junior rose to the bait.

'*Hankered*?'

'Hell's teeth, *deal*, Henry,' Quint growled.

Pomeroy cocked his head. ' That band's going at some lick — don't you go in for dancing, Pepperday? You look like you could be pretty nimble in a fox-trot.'

Quint stroked his mutton chops. 'You listen to that caterwauling?' Loot sneered. 'What's the attraction of these god dam coon songs?'

'What d'you expect when that damned cowboy's dining niggers in the White House?' Charlie McFarlane demanded. 'We'll all be raising our hats to Mr Booker T. Washington, yassir!'

'Whole country's goin' to hell, all these millions of wops and bohunks and polacks floodin' in every year. America don't want all these anarchistic socialist atheists and stinkin' jews — '

'I like coon songs, as you call 'em,' Pomeroy said with grating cheerfulness. His head nodded in time to the faint strains of the orchestra -and, to their amazement, he burst into song:

'Won't you come home, Bill Bailey, won't you come home?
She moans the whole day long,
I'll do the cookin', darlin', I'll pay the rent — '

'Is this a poker game or a fucking minstrel show?' Charlie snarled. Pomeroy clicked his fingers in time to the music:

'Come on, honey, 'member that rainy evenin',
I drove you out with nothin' but a fine tooth comb?
I know I'm to blame, well ain't that a shame?
Bill Bailey won't you please come hooooome?'

He made a little bow to stony faces, then old Uncle Harry slapped Pomeroy on the shoulder. 'Jeez, you're Billy Pomeroy's boy all right, you could be your father sitting there, it's uncanny!'

'Two-dollar ante,' Loot announced.

Uncle Harry made a show of looking at his cards. 'Forty years ago this week Billy Pomeroy and me came from Knoxville to join Bragg's buildup for the attack on the Army of the Cumberland under Rosecrans. Boy, that was to be our big moment — September 19, 1863, we attacked the Union army at Chickamauga Creek — Chickamauga means 'river of death' in Cherokee and never was a place better named... forty years ago almost to the day, Billy Pomeroy and me — if Braxton Bragg had got off his backside and followed through, we'd have wiped out that whole Yankee army — '

'How come you were a Johnny Reb anyway, Uncle Harry?' asked Charlie McFarlane.

'Us Pingrees were poor crackers from Georgia originally,' chipped in Henry junior.

Loot winked at Quint. 'Us Pingrees adapted to meet the future. I guess the Pomeroys just went on dreaming they were the flowah of thuh Old South, suh!'

Pomeroy was frowning at his hand. 'If I was setting up to swindle people at cards, I'd do it under the sign of the tiger. Faro's easier for greenhorns, plenty of suckers, you can hire a skilled dealer to handle the crooked aspect.'

Again, it was Henry junior whose nerve broke first in the silence that followed.

'This heah's an honest game, suh!'

'Oh ... ' Pomeroy's smile took in the whole table. 'I always did say I'd prefer an honest game — if there was such a thing between here and the Pacific Ocean.'

'I don't understand,' Quint said evenly. 'Is there some suggestion this game isn't honest?'

Pomeroy went on looking at his cards. 'I was one of the kibitzers the night Goldie Golden and Silent Sam Bonnifield played the biggest game of poker ever seen in Dawson City. The raise was twenty-five thousand bucks — a hundred and fifty thousand in the pot when Silent Sam calls. Goldie shows four queens *but* — that cool son of a gun Silent Sam lets the commotion die down and then he turns over his four kings! Now that was an honest game.'

Uncle Harry saw hate in their eyes. Billy Pomeroy was just the same, joshing and joking with a straight face till people lost their tempers and made themselves easy to beat. Henry junior went around the table, wondering why his guts were on edge. Uncle Harry's eyes closed as he fell into a light sleep among the screams and yells and thundering cannons of the river of death. Pomeroy asked Henry junior for one card and made a low flush. Quint stood pat. Pomeroy pointed to the French windows. 'Some night, huh?'

'See ten and raise twenty,' said Quint.

'This great big mansion is only a tiny pinpoint of light in a great black void,' Pomeroy said dramatically. 'Maybe there's a giant out there holding us in the palm of his hand, peering in at us through tiny windows, just a little bunch of miniature creatures playing a silly game —'

'Just you and me still in, Pomeroy.'

Pomeroy frowned at his cards, then shook his head and threw his hand on the deadwood. 'I guess I'm through playing for tonight, boys.'

The steely Quint didn't explode all at once. 'You've won near on three hundred dollars of our money, now you're through playing?'

Pomeroy straightened out a ten-dollar bill. 'Put it another way,' he said cheerfully. 'I've learned when to quit.'

'Just like you quit the army so you wouldn't have to fight in Cuba?' Quint sneered.

Pomeroy stared at the man. 'I resigned my commission as a lieutenant of the Sixth Cavalry in ninety-seven, a full twelve-month before the *Maine* blew up.'

'It still worked out okay, didn't it?' Loot sneered. 'You chasing gold in the Klondike and the men you soldiered with dying for their country?'

Pomeroy counted his money. 'What were you doing around that time, sonny boy — tending your white mice?'

Henry junior tried to save the situation. As if they were chatting about this and that in a family reunion, he asked, 'Why did you resign from the cavalry actually, Cousin John?'

'I get a rash near horses.'

Quint hurled his cards down. 'All we've been hearing from you is bullshit, Pomeroy — you and your father the famous reb general, you and your bragging about the Yukon, you and your lecturing us how to play poker — now you're piking on us? I think you're full of crap, mister.'

16

Pomeroy nodded slowly, then began to collect the cards. 'Okay, fellows, I hate to cause offence. My deal, I believe .. .'

He tapped the deck on the table and showed them the bottom card, five of diamonds. He did a regular shuffle and showed them the bottom card, five of diamonds. He placed the deck for Henry junior to cut, brought the half-decks together for a ripple shuffle, boxed the deck and showed them the bottom card, five of diamonds. He dealt one card to Henry junior, who turned it up, five of diamonds. He took it back and shuffled again and showed them the bottom card, ten of spades. He gave the deck to Henry junior. 'Is the five in there somewhere?' He sat back and folded his arms and Henry's nervous fingers checked the deck. He shook his head. Pomeroy put his elbows on the table and turned over his left hand, in which was palmed the five of diamonds.

Charlie glared at Quint: 'He's a fuckin' cardsharp!'

'Only when I need to be,' Pomeroy said pleasantly, 'like a game where the fellows are playing footsie under the table and ganging up on me — '

'Nobody accuses me of cheating,' Quint barked.

' — or somebody milks a couple of paints out of the deck to have on his lap for the right moment. Check the picture cards, Henry, if you will .. .' They froze as Henry junior fumbled with the cards. Charlie was crouched forward on his high-backed chair, hands gripping the edge of the table. Henry junior looked up. His voice was almost a squeak. 'I can't find the jack of spades or the king of hearts — '

'I'm willing to be searched,' Pomeroy announced.

Charlie slung his whisky at his face. He swayed and some of it spattered on Uncle Harry.

'What's your problem, Charlie — St Vitus's dance?'

'I'll break every bone in your body, you bastard!' Henry junior got away from the table so fast he fell over his chair and lost his glasses. Charlie was halfway around the table. Quint hauled off his coat.

'Leave him to me.'

Pomeroy tsk-tsked. 'Brawling in the library?'

Quint stood up, holding Loot back.

'We'll go outside, bigmouth.'

Uncle Harry woke up with a little shudder and wiped uncomprehendingly at the whisky on his face.

Pomeroy stuck to his chair. 'It's okay, Uncle Harry, just the boys giving their buttocks a breather.' They came at him from both sides. He reached for the bottle and propped his feet against the edge of the table, balancing back on the rear legs of the chair.

'Get up!' Quint stood over him, right fist drawn back. 'Get on your feet, you asshole!'

Softly, he chanted, *'Won't you come home, Bill Bailey* —'

Quint's big right fist swung at Pomeroy where he sat — but suddenly he was kicking himself away from the table, falling backwards with the chair, legs doubling up as he rolled off the crashing chair and somersaulted. He came up bouncing on his toes.

'I learned that from an Italian acrobat.' Quint kicked the chair away to get at him. From the doorway came an icy female voice: 'Is this another custom among adults?'

Gussie advanced into the library. Henry junior bit his thumbnail. Pomeroy stared at her in disbelief; gone was the freckly tomboy with the growly voice. She was *lovely!*

'Our game dragged on some, Cousin Gussie,' he drawled by way of apology, while his eyes reminded her of their secret. Reminded her too damn well! In a chillingly quiet voice, she said, 'Take him out in the stable, Quint — that's where he tried to seduce me this afternoon.'

The race was on to get to him first.

Mrs Pingree hurried round the edge of the dance floor to confront the two big men in wet slickers. 'Who are you?' she hissed, shooing them back into the hall. 'What do you mean by this intrusion — can't you see we're having a ball?'

McGraw had warned Boden they were due trouble on this one. These stuffy Baltimore fat cats weren't about to hand over one of the family to a couple of no-account Treasury agents with a bit of paper. 'We must apologize, ma'am, we're government agents, my name's McGraw, this is my colleague — '

'We believe you have a party named Pomeroy among your guests.' Boden didn't believe in brown-nosing the rich.

'John Pomeroy?' They both nodded. She led them away from the curious faces at the ballroom door. 'Are you telling me you've come to arrest him?'

Still ready for a battle, Boden loomed over her intimidatingly. 'This is confidential government business. We expect your cooperation, but we're taking him anyhow.'

Triumph in her every movement, Mrs Pingree led them along a corridor. The library doors were ajar. She threw them open, saying imperiously, 'I'm *always* prepared to help the government — '

Pomeroy was throwing over a high-backed chair to stop Loot and Charlie chasing him round the table. Quint, in starched shirt and suspenders, had a whisky bottle in his raised right hand. Henry junior was dancing round on tiptoe, screaming at everybody to remember where they were, for chrissake! Gussie was yelling at Quint to hurry it up as she threw open the French windows to let a slice of slanting rain drive into the library. Old Uncle Harry lay slumped face down at the table.

Quint swung the bottle at Pomeroy's head. Pomeroy ducked. Quint's momentum brought the bottle smashing into the glass of the bookcase. Pomeroy came up in a fast bobbing movement and jabbed his right at Quint's nose. Quint brought up his guard, Pomeroy sank his left into Quint's stomach, Quint began to double up. Pomeroy smashed his right into Quint's face and he staggered back, crashing into the tall stepladder. It toppled against the high bookcase and came sliding to the floor in an avalanche of glass and leatherbound volumes.

Boden cleared his throat. 'Which one of these gentlemen is Pomeroy, ma'am?'

'Which one do you think?' she snapped.

'John Stockley Pomeroy?'

'I have that honour.'

'We're Treasury agents, we have written authority from Secretary of War Elihu Root requiring your attendance at a preliminary hearing into your army status — '

'Lousy deserter!' Loot bawled, still trying to get at him.

'Are you coming with us of your own accord?' Boden demanded.

'Aunt Harriet — would you take it amiss if I leave with these gentlemen?' he asked across the big room.

'Get him out of here!' Mrs Pingree screamed. Henry junior was trying to wake Uncle Harry. Big drops of blood from Quint's nose fell on priceless leather bindings. Loot was in tears.

'I catch up with you I'll tear your head off, Pomeroy!' Quint snarled as they escorted him out.

Boden and McGraw understood it even less when the rich Mrs Pingree became so hot to get Pomeroy out of her house she said her man Venables, who knew the road blindfolded, would drive them in her automobile to Baltimore, her hands would return Haydon's horses in the morning, she would even repay them their fifty-dollar deposit and collect it from Haydon.

Only the red-haired girl of the house seemed to have second thoughts. She came through the big kitchen with a coloured servant carrying his one leather grip. He was standing between the two agents in the porch.

'John ... ?'

He looked at her over his shoulder. 'How's Uncle Harry?'

'He's upstairs, Dr Lamartine says he had a minor heart attack — it could've happened any time ... John, I didn't mean to ...'

Ye gods!

Even now she was giving him that loving Pingree look! Those grey green eyes promised that his sins could be forgiven, his crimes could be fixed, if only ... Into the bright light of the portico lurched the stately white tourer, leather curtains flapping from its flat roof. He took his suitcase from the black houseman. Gussie glared at him.

'John ... say something!'

'Next time keep your eyes open, Cousin Gussie.'

She slapped him and that made him feel a whole lot better.

She was still standing there in the portico as the big automobile pulled away into slanting rain and darkness, with the two agents huddling on either side of him in the shelter of the leather curtains and the Pingree driver, in flat cap, oilers and gauntlets, crouched over the wheel to see ahead on a road that was almost a white river of rain spray. One of the agents cupped a hand against the wind and the roar of a twenty-four horsepower engine and shouted in his ear. 'Sorry we broke up the party, Pomeroy.'

'Who are you. bastards anyway?' he shouted back.

'Secret service.'

'Where are you taking me?'

'That's the secret, buddy!'

Forty years on from Chickamauga, in the third week of September 1903, the automobile taking Pomeroy to Baltimore was one of the first luxury limousines produced by the Peerless

Company of Cleveland at $4,250, fixed roof canopy and glass wind-screen extra. Every detail of that day was to become fixed in his mind, the last day his life belonged to himself.

Forty years on almost to the day since Chickamauga. Seven since George Washington Carmack and his Indian partners Skookum Jim and Tagish Charlie picked up the first gold nuggets from Rabbit Creek, a muddy tributary of the Klondike River. Two years on since King Camp Gillette produced a safe alternative to the cut-throat razor. Two years on since the Spindle top gusher came through at Beaumont, first of the Texas oilfields. Only one month since a Packard took fifty-two days to drive from San Francisco to New York, the first automobile crossing of the United States. The population of the States was around eighty million. Life expectancy of an American male at birth was forty-eight years, fifty-one for a female. Henry Ford had just sold his first Model A. Carrie Nation was distributing miniature axes to members of her growing temperance movement. The new books were *The Little Shepherd of Kingdom Come* by John Fox, Jr, and *The Call of the Wild* by Jack London. Scientists were blaming sunspots for the rain — ten inches on New York in thirty hours, thousands flooded out of their homes in New Jersey. The same bad weather was holding back Orville and Wilbur Wright from making man's first sustained powered flight at Kitty Hawk, North Carolina. Russia and Japan were preparing for war over Manchuria. Breaking off negotiations for a Panama Canal treaty because the Colombian government had tripled its asking price, President Theodore Roosevelt said the United States would not be blackmailed by the 'homicidal corruptionists' of Bogota ... forty years on almost to the day since Chickamauga.

The rain stopped as they passed Druid Hill on their left and came by the big houses on Druid Hill Avenue, past Johns Hopkins University to the Baltimore and Potomac railroad depot in Calvert Street. Boden hurried to speak to a uniformed railroad attendant standing with a helmeted patrolman in the entrance hall; a night in a Baltimore hotel would be another dollar fifty out of their per diem. The chauffeur lifted out Pomeroy's grip.

'Hurry it up, Joe,' Boden shouted, 'we'll make the eight twenty-five.'

Pomeroy carried his grip round a big puddle to reach the sidewalk. McGraw went round the other side of the puddle. Pomeroy waited till the patrolman looked at him and shouted, 'These men are armed!' at the same time turning back towards the automobile.

The patrolman threatened Boden with his billy and fumbled to get at his pistol.

'I'm a federal agent, you bum!' Boden snarled.

Pomeroy saw that Venables was going to grab him, the bastard, and dodged the other way. He got halfway across the street. The barked command came from close behind, too close: 'Stop there or I'll kill you!'

2

McGraw's pistol rammed into his back. Steel handcuffs rapped across his skull. 'Chain your right wrist to my left,' McGraw barked. He snapped the cuffs. 'I'm keeping my gun on you under my slicker so just try it again, mister, just try it.'

'These Pingrees sure draw a lot of water in government circles.'

'Shut up.'

Boden looked sadly at Pomeroy. 'I call that ingratitude after us rescuing you and all. Now you can pay your own fare. That's a dollar twenty.'

'The hell with that.'

McGraw twisted the cuffs. 'Pay the man or I'll break your wrist.' Boden got him a ticket from the window and McGraw yanked on the cuffs to make him run across the Calvert Street concourse. White steam was erupting from the locomotive funnel in big spouts. They hurried past the guard putting his whistle to his lips and raising his green flag. Brakes creaked, carriages shuddered into motion, as they climbed aboard. Boden checked the bags and led them along the train to a car that was almost empty except for a couple of half-drowned drummers and some fancy kind of foreigner. McGraw pushed Pomeroy down into a window seat. He couldn't get his raglan overcoat off because of the handcuffs.

'It'll dry faster on you,' McGraw jeered.

Boden brought out a sheet of yellow paper. 'Let's just check they didn't slip us the wrong Pomeroy back there.' The train was moving out. Boden read from the yellow sheet: 'John Stockley Pomeroy, born Knoxville, Tennessee, 1875?'

Those Pingrees sure work fast.'

'Father, General William B. Pomeroy? Height, five ten? Weight, a hundred and sixty five? Hair, fair? Eyes, blue? Distinguishing marks or scars — '

'Not a mark on him, the bastard,' McGraw growled. 'Not yet anyhow — '

'Graduated West Point military academy, 1896, assigned Sixth Cavalry, went absent without leave — '

'Now wait a minute here — I resigned my commission, I have a copy of my resignation in my grip — '

'Shut up.'

He frowned. 'You mean the Pingrees didn't send for you?'

'Nobody *sends* for secret servicemen — '

'Somebody's pulled a boner here — '

McGraw looked shocked. 'Aw gee, Art, we got the wrong man. Pull the cord, stop the train, we gotta take him back to his friends and beg his pardon. Haw haw.'

'No, he's the right Pomeroy.' Boden folded away the yellow sheet.

'Okay, what's the charge?' Pomeroy demanded.

'Shut up.'

The fancy foreign-looking man came up the aisle and gave them a little formal bow.

'Good evening, gentlemen, pardon my intrusion but would you mind terribly if I sit with you a moment?' He had a birdsong English voice.

' We're busy,' McGraw growled.

The Englishman smiled roguishly. 'You Americans are *always* busy. I find life in your country very stimulating, one perpetual *whirl* of telephones, telegrams, phonographs, electric bells, motors, lifts — elevators as you call them — automatic instruments of every kind. I'm travelling across the United States gathering material for a book. My name's Harrison.' He brought out a notebook. 'I'm trying to meet people from all walks of life; they always start by saying how busy they are and they always end up giving me enough material for ten books! I made some notes from a magazine in New York — '

'You got a nerve, buddy.'

'The dogged reporter, y'know. This is supposed to be factual. I'd like your reactions, gentlemen. The average American male is, I quote — "of British ancestry but with some German blood, is five feet eight inches has three children living and one dead is Protestant, Republican, takes one daily and one weekly newspaper, uses twenty pounds of tobacco a year and seven and a half gallons of hard liquor —".'

'I don't believe this,' McGraw snarled.

'Hear it, then we'll discuss it — "He drinks seventy-five gallons of beer a year, lives in a two-storey house with seven rooms, earns seven hundred and fifty dollars a year and has property worth around five thousand dollars ..." What do you have to say to that, gentlemen?'

'Beat it, buddy!'

The Englishman frowned. 'I'm taking a little while to pick up the American idiom.'

'He means go away, sir,' Pomeroy explained. 'I'd like to help you, sir, but — ' He raised his right hand the cuffs dragging McGraw's left wrist into the air. The Englishman blinked. '— Unfortunately these US marshals are taking me to be hung for mass murder — '

'Scram, buddy!' McGraw yanked Pomeroy's wrist down. The Englishman retreated quickly. McGraw's face was red anyway, with open pores and nostril hairs, now it was congested with blood. 'You like playing games, you sonofabitch? '

'Calm it, Joe.' Boden was amused. 'Looked like a gasser of a party back there in the big mansion, Pomeroy. They said you cheated them at cards — you a general's son and a West Point graduate and all?'

McGraw sneered. 'But you didn't get away with it, did you, big shot?'

'No?' Pomeroy reached into his inside coat pocket. McGraw jerked on the cuffs, but Pomeroy's hand came out holding two playing cards.

'Depends what you mean by getting away with it,' he said, tearing up a jack of spades and a king of hearts. They didn't understand and he wasn't about to explain. Sometimes the sneaky thing was also the gallant thing.

Shortly before ten, they reached the Pennsylvania railroad depot in Washington. Pomeroy and McGraw watched the rain pour down on Sixth Street, while Boden went off to phone somebody they called 'that joker Martin' about transport.

'I need to go the john,' Pomeroy said.

McGraw raised his eyebrows. 'We might be arrested for standing indecently close to each other. Do it in your pants, in this rain nobody'll notice. Haw haw.'

'I could also use a cup of hot coffee.'

'People would stare at you manacled to a law officer. Haw haw.'

'You have my word I won't skedaddle.'

' Which word would that be? Haw haw.'

Boden returned fuming. 'The bastard says to take a hack!'

They were waving at the first horsecab in line when Boden suddenly had his slicker over Pomeroy's head, pinioning it around his shoulders. 'In case you're recognized by your society friends,' came McGraw's muffled voice. Haw haw. They guided him up into the buggy. Horse hooves clipped on stone. Boden and McGraw crushed tight against him on either side.

After a while the horse stopped and they shouted their names to somebody. He heard a gate creaking. The hack lurched forwards again in a tight left turn. When it stopped again, Boden kept the slicker over his head as they guided him down and steered him up some stone steps.

When the slicker was pulled off, they were in a brightly lit vestibule. A marine sergeant was locking an outside door behind them. He went to a side door and called to someone in an office. 'They're here, Mr Martin.'

Out came a broad-shouldered man in a dark blue suit, hair parted severely in the middle, mouth set hard with genial ferocity round a small cigar.

'Pomeroy, as instructed,' Boden said, handing over the warrant and the yellow sheet.

Martin saw the handcuffs as McGraw took off his slicker. Without removing the cigar, he snarled, 'McGraw, you're not delivering some yardbird to Leavenworth!'

'He tried a break for it in Baltimore.'

'They wouldn't even let me use the john,' Pomeroy complained in a whiny voice. McGraw unlocked the handcuffs and he painfully massaged his wrist.

'Can I get a hankie out of my case? '

'Please — go ahead.'

He knelt beside his grip. Martin started giving them a bawling-out for bringing him *here* in handcuffs. The marine sergeant went back into the side office. Pomeroy came up holding his Smith and Wesson double action .38.

'Open that door,' he snapped.

Martin shook his head. 'I realize you've had cause for complaint, Mr Pomeroy — '

'Jack!' McGraw yelled at the office door.

Boden took a dive at his legs. Pomeroy jumped quickly and then turned into a narrow corridor and ran for it. There was only ever one good time to escape — right now.

Seeing somebody ahead in the corridor, he turned right up a narrow flight of stairs, which led him onto a carpeted corridor. Holding the pistol under his overcoat, he went the way he was facing, walking quickly without panic. It was a pretty big building and sure to have other exits; a government building of some kind, he didn't care which — that's what government buildings were for, to escape from. He'd deal with the army when he was good and ready, with a lawyer beside him.

Turning the next corner, he bumped into a pair of wooden stilts on top of which was a small boy in a white shirt. 'You're my prisoner!' The boy made a pistol out of his right hand. 'Stick 'em up, mister, I got you covered. What's your name? '

'John. What's yours? '

'Archie — get your hands up!'

He raised his left hand, keeping the Smith and Wesson out of sight. 'I'm kinda lost, Archie, you tell me the way out of here? '

'Don't move!' The boy cocked his thumb and went bang-bang. He clutched his chest and staggered.

'You got me, Archie,' he gasped, and went on staggering to the next corner. Behind, he heard a deep male voice. He quickened his stride, passing a closed door and turning another corner. It wasn't a corridor but the entrance to a roomful of people in formal evening wear. Two flunkeys thought he was going in and held him.

'Which way out? ' he asked pleasantly.

They both put their fingers to their mouths. Through the open doorway he saw a middle-aged woman who was not exactly singing to a piano accompaniment:

' Evenin' comes I miss you more — '
When the dark gloom's round the door —'

Looking back, he saw the big man Martin. He tried to shake off the flunkeys, but a big hand came from behind to take away the Smith and Wesson. Martin nodded for him to listen.

She sounded like a beloved aunt nobody had the heart to tell she couldn't sing. Her name was Carrie Jacobs-Bond. Widowed and suffering from arthritis and trying to support herself and her young son by running a rooming house in Chicago, she had started writing songs by candlelight on brown wrapping paper, inspired by her distant relative John Howard Payne, who had written 'Home Sweet Home'. She came to the climax of the ballad that had made her instantly famous:

'... but there's sadness in the notes,
That come trill in' from their throats,
Seem to feel your absence, too,
Just a-wearyin' for you .. .'

Exquisitely groomed society matrons and silver-haired gents jumped to it. Through the huzzahs, Martin asked the flunkeys if Mr Gray was in there. They weren't sure. Martin eased Pomeroy back against the wall as people emerged from the concert room. Leading them was a stocky man with *pince-nez* and a heavy brown moustache. He and his wife were having a slight disagreement about the girl with them, their daughter, Pomeroy realized, about nineteen, in a blue dress. She was brazenly smoking a cigarette! In a high-pitched drawl the stocky man said, 'Put out that weed, Alice.'

The girl shook her head. The stocky man saw him standing there with Martin. 'Been out in the rain, young fellow? Never saw rain like it, not even in the badlands of the Dakotas, by Godfrey.'

Martin murmured something in the stocky man's ear. People crushed against them. The stocky man was suddenly pumping his hand.

'Billy Pomeroy's boy? How is the old cuss? I'm so glad you managed along, we'll have a good old chinwag in the morning, I want to hear all the latest about my old pal Billy Pomeroy — we could do with men like him in Washington today, instead of all these animated feather dusters, by Godfrey!'

Pomeroy, who had trained his face against independent action, felt his jaw dropping. The stocky man put his arm around the girl in the blue dress. His voice carried better than that of the guest artiste: 'I can do one of two things. I can be President of the United States or I can control Alice. I cannot possibly do both!'

People laughed. Martin steered Pomeroy in the other direction. Around the next corner he stiff-armed Martin's hand away. 'Look, goddammit, what the hell — '

'President Roosevelt doesn't favour strong language,'

'I don't give a good — '

The boy Archie on his stilts appeared in the corridor, followed by another boy and a girl carrying a parrot. 'He's dead — I shot him!' Archie yelled. 'I claim the bounty on him, Mr Martin!'

The big man gave the boy a salute. 'I'll cut you in for half, Archie. Isn't it about time you kids hit the sack?' To Pomeroy he said quietly, 'Let's go find Mr Gray — '

'Who the — who is Mr Gray?'

'A lot of people are asking that very same question.'

Through a series of corridors and stairways until he lost any orientation that might have got him back to that side door and freedom, Martin brought him to an unmarked door in a corridor without windows.

The old bureau desk should have stood against a wall. Instead, it backed onto empty space halfway down the long room. This end of the long room was freshly colour-washed in neutral cream; on white sheets covering the floor stood a painter's ladder and a trestle table with pots and brushes. The room was lit by electric bulbs in big white bowls hanging from the ceiling. The other end was crammed with old-fashioned office furniture. He didn't see the occupant of the room till they crossed the white sheet to the bureau desk. Mr Gray was reading through an open file. At first he didn't look up. His hair was black, a boyish cowlick in front and a spike sticking up at the back where he'd parted it on the wrong line. He was wearing a bureaucrat's black suit. His legs were crossed sideways because they were too long to go under the writing ledge. When he did look up, he had a narrow face and a big nose. It was a long time since his complexion had enjoyed the benefit of sun or wind. He could have been anything between thirty and fifty.

Martin indicated an old davenport with little fractures sprouting horsehair. 'Sit yourself down, John, get dried out.' The davenport was on one side of a tiled fireplace with a bright coal fire in a small iron grate. Above the mantelpiece was gilt-framed mirror. Mr Gray went back to the file. 'We're just moving in here,' Martin explained, 'they're doing it as a rush job. It should've been fixed last week.'

He didn't sit down. Sitting down was an admission you intended to stick around. In the mirror, his face was a shadow with a nose. Mr Gray went on reading.

' Those dingbats Boden and McGraw had Pomeroy here in cuffs with a slicker over his head,' Martin said. 'I know we said to bring him here in secret but hell — he didn't even know he was in the White House.' He put the Smith and Wesson on the writing ledge beside the file and explained what had happened. A long white hand pushed a pencil at the Smith and Wesson.

Mr Gray silent belonged in a pulpit.

Mr Gray when he opened his mouth wasn't a whole lot louder than Mr Gray silent, but he didn't sound so Christian: 'Pomeroy, could be you're the man for a little job the President needs done.' The long white hand tapped the file. 'I believe you're qualified. Pay's reasonable. You interested?'

'What kind of job is it you drag people to the White House in handcuffs?'

Mr Gray spoke with a slight lisp but no change in tone: 'Having read all this stuff, I'm inclined to believe you're an unmitigated rascal, but that's okay. The job calls for a man who can lie, cheat, swindle and maybe even blackmail, only this time you'll be doing it for your country, Pomeroy.'

3

Mr Gray uncrossed his long legs. His grey wool socks hung in folds without garters and that made him seem younger, although death wasn't going to make a *whole* lot of difference to his general manner.

'I can understand you being naturally resentful about the way we had you brought here -and curious, I trust.'

'I stopped being curious about the government.'

'Is that why you quit the army?'

'I get a rash near horses.' Martin smiled.

Mr Gray sniffed. 'I don't have too much time this evening, Pomeroy. This job's worth twenty thousand dollars for maybe three months' work. That make any difference?' He sat down on the davenport. Steam rose from his trouser legs. 'It says in the file somewhere your ambition is to run your own gaming hall, or is that just a pipe dream?'

'Who told you that?'

'We checked you out with various people,' Martin said.

'For the government to payout twenty grand it must be some job.'

'It's undercover work — '

'I play a little poker here and there, nothing that would qualify me for a government fink.' A thought struck him. 'Does my father have anything to do with this?'

'Surely. When your name came up, Roosevelt had me find out if you were the son of General Pomeroy. Believe me, you're the right man, your family background, eleventh in your year at the Point, even your low-life experiences — ' Mr Gray brought a gold watch out of a vest pocket. 'Martin, I have to go now. I'm sure Pomeroy could do with something to eat. There are probably questions you can answer for him. I'll see you again early tomorrow, Pomeroy — '

'What is this damned job?' he demanded.

Mr Gray stood up a long way towards the pale ceiling.

'It's of such a confidential nature I can't give you any specific details until you've signed a few papers, the sort of thing Treasury agents swear to.'

'You mean it's a job you won't tell me about till I've agreed to take it?'

'I guess that's a little hard to understand. I'll speak with you in the morning.'

Martin locked the door and came to sit in a leather armchair that must have been a crackerjack acquisition by the Grant administration. He opened his coat and lit a small cigar. He had a wood-handled pistol in a holster under his left armpit. The elastic harness was tight across his big chest and shoulders. 'Take off your shoes, John, let 'em dry at the fire — '

'Am I under arrest here?'

'Not exactly.'

'Can I get up and walk?'

'Not exactly.'

He took off his black shoes and stuck his argyle socks towards the fire.

'Okay, so you're playing the friendly cop ... I'm listening.'

Martin smiled. 'I'm on your side, John — '

'And I'm from Missouri — '

'I'll tell you how it is, John. Gray was an assistant DA in New York when Roosevelt was commissioner. He helped Roosevelt clean up the New York police. I was a Treasury agent. The President's setting Gray up with this new department to handle unusual stuff the War Department or the State Department isn't equipped for. It's all pretty confidential. Our budget, for instance, comes out of a special fund under direct control of the President. They don't even know about us up on the Hill. That's why you came here in unorthodox style — listen, are you hungry? '

'It can wait.'

'John, I have to be honest — they have you by the balls.'

'So had Gussie,' he murmured.

'Come again?'

'You were going to be honest.'

Martin flicked through the papers in the file. 'They've done a pretty thorough job on you, John ...' He found some stapled sheets of yellow paper. 'Well, stick and carrot, I guess — here's the stick.' He read briskly. 'You're wanted by the state of Louisiana, fraud by gaming, to wit you swindled Frank P. Lavelle of Monroe out of eighteen hundred dollars, April 10, 1901. You're wanted for questioning in connection with a fatal shooting in Skagway, Alaska, 1898 — '

'Knock it off, Martin. I won a few dollars off a bad loser in Monroe — anyhow, it's non-extraditable and I'm not planning a return trip to Louisiana. That Skagway thing? A two-bit grifter got his in a Saturday night brawl — that's what passes for a church social in Skagway.'

'There's other stuff — you have six thousand dollars on deposit with the Merchants and Traders Bank of Arkansas. I don't know why Gray put that in — '

'Maybe just to prove nothing escapes you government boys.'

Then there's your army status, John. You're wanted by the US army for being absent without leave as an officer in the Sixth Cavalry — '

'I resigned my commission!'

'Moot point if an officer can resign by mail ... and now they can nail you for planning to assassinate the President.'

He turned his shoes over on the brass fender. 'You shouldn't ought to dry shoes by an open fire, the leather cracks. The pistol wasn't loaded.'

'We put five bullets in and it's loaded. After McKinley? You're running wild in the Executive Mansion waving a gun? Could be good for ten to twenty, John.'

'Just so I'll take some cockaninny government job?'

'Oh no, John, a special job — they want you real bad.'

'Should I be flattered?'

'They're not joking here, John,' Martin said apologetically. 'I have to tell you this — even if you wriggle out from these other things, there's still your army status. They'll hold you pending a board of inquiry. They'll convene the board hearing or maybe the court-martial in the nearest army post to the town of Monroe. You might be cleared but you'll walk off post into the jurisdiction of the state of Louisiana and be well and truly extradited, John — '

'Railroaded some might say — '

'This is the White House, John, this is where the power is. One telephone call and Gray will be able to tell you the charges, the name of the judge, the verdict, the sentence and whether you'll be doing your time on a state prison farm or the road gang ...'

He turned his shoes over. His socks were almost dry. Facing the coal fire, he might have been in a cosy parlour hearing bedtime stories. Not that he'd ever been a kid at a cosy fire being told bedtime stories ...

He stood up and warmed his backside. 'You say something about food?' He had nowhere to run to anyway. All running away bought you was wet shoes.

He and Martin ate a French dinner brought by a White House waiter to a small bedroom with no windows. Around one in the morning Martin ran out of spiel. 'I guess you must be pooped, John. I've given you the worst end of it, now you should start thinking on the bright side. Have a good night's sleep.'

When he tried the door it was locked. A lot of people would feel honoured. He brushed his teeth in the adjoining bathroom and got between cold government sheets in the buff — they had his balls, they might as well have the rest ...

A walk with the President.

Gray arrived at eight thirty. Pomeroy and Martin were eating sausages and bacon and toast. A valet had taken away yesterday's clothes. Pomeroy was wearing a white shirt but no collar, the trousers of his white seersucker suit, and his other pair of socks. Gray had a briefcase. His hair had been oiled and combed but still stuck up at the back.

'You thought about it, Pomeroy?'

'Yes, I thought about it.'

'You taking the job?'

'Did I ever have any choice?'

'Good.' Gray produced two documents. 'This is more or less the standard loyalty declaration — read it through, you don't get a copy. This one's confirmation from the First National Bank that twenty thousand dollars is on deposit in escrow to your name, releasable on my signature.'

Pomeroy started reading. ' " ... any breach of which confidentiality will be regarded as treason against the United States" ... there's nothing here about immunity for those things you have on file — '

'We don't want you in jail, we'll look after you.'

He buttered some more toast. 'You remind me of Soapy Smith. He ran Skagway on the Chilkoot trail like a private larceny corporation. He had a gang of bunco artists and grifters who robbed people on their way to the goldfields, while they still had money. If you kicked up, two apes called Big Ed Burns and Yeah Mow Hopkins worked you over. This sounds like a deal Soapy Smith would approve. I do this goddam job and you've still got me on the hook? I don't even get my money without your okay? Uh uh.'

'As you say, Pomeroy, you don't have a lot of choice — '

'You can't make me work for you — '

'I can't afford to let you win, Pomeroy. If I have to tell Roosevelt I failed with you I'll need something to save my own ass. Ten years of hard labour for some heinous crime would satisfy him. But I don't want to do that — you're a drifter, Pomeroy, you're going nowhere. I'm offering you a high-paid assignment that could change your life — '

'High-paid? Yesterday I was playing hard to get with thirteen million dollars!'

Gray took his time about bringing out his snuffbox. He sniffed it up but didn't sneeze.

'Jail, Pomeroy, that's the alternative.'

'You'd like me to be enthusiastic, wouldn't you?'

'Naturally.'

'Ten thousand in cash money now — the rest on completion.'

'One thousand in advance.'

'Ten. And what about expenses?'

'Fifteen hundred. Salary and expenses come with the cover job we're putting you into ... I will have some coffee, Martin, plenty of sugar.'

'What job are you putting me into?'

'I can't tell you that till you've signed the oath.'

'How much does the job pay?'

'A hundred dollars a month — '

'Yesterday I could've won that with a pair of deuces — '

'This isn't a game of cards, Pomeroy.'

'Well, there's no deck on the table — '

'You're putting dollars before the national interest.'

'The national interest of this country is the dollar, Mr Gray.'

Martin looked at his watch. 'TR will be leaving in half an hour — '

'Tell the President's office Pomeroy will be joining him — and get him his walking shoes, Martin.'

'I haven't agreed to take the job — '

'Oh yes you have, we're simply haggling .over the terms — '

'You certain about that, Mr Gray?'

'The sovereign nation state lets us all run around on the end of a very long rope, none of us is really free. Just for this moment in history I represent the naked power of the state. You've been brought behind the scenes because the state has a use for you. If you cooperate, you get a reward. If you defy the state, you must be broken — that is the only way great nations are maintained, all else is illusion. I'll make it twenty-five hundred but you buy your own clothes — '

'On top of the twenty thousand in escrow?'

Gray nodded and handed him a fountain pen. 'Go on, Martin.' The big man left. With the gold nib poised, Pomeroy hesitated. 'This has to be witnessed by a notary — '

'That's me.'

'Fine.' Before Gray could snatch the pen back, he wrote *Subject to payment of $2500 in advance* under the typewritten lines and signed with a flourish. 'When do I get the jake?'

Gray signed and waved the sheet to dry the ink. He folded the letter and put it into one compartment of his briefcase. From another compartment he produced a thick bundle of bills and counted off twenty-five hundred in fifties. He put the rest away and then produced a receipt form. He filled in the amount and gave it to Pomeroy to sign. He waved that sheet about as well, then put it away in his briefcase. He smiled. 'I was prepared to go to seven thousand five, Pomeroy. I just bluffed you out of five grand. Maybe I should take up poker.'

'That's okay, Mr Gray, I didn't sign my own name anyway.'

Gray started to dive at his briefcase, then he hissed with exasperation. 'Let's hope your bad jokes are a sign of strength not a weakness. What do you know about international politics?'

'That's the same· as regular politics — jobs for the boys and screw the people?'

'I have a few days to turn you into something that will pass for an undercover agent, Pomeroy. Try to remember how you were as a plebe at the Point — keen, energetic and scared to hell. Particularly *keen* with Roosevelt this morning. He has to believe you're all-fired grateful for the chance to serve your President.'

'I voted for Bryan.'

'Don't tell him that. Don't mock the Rough Riders or San Juan Hill. You quit the army because you were bored in our small peacetime army and when the war started you were iced up in Dawson City; it near broke your heart.'

'It didn't break my heart missing a stupid war for the Hearst papers.'

'And *don't* say that!'

'We won't have much to talk about — '

'He's going to tell you about Andrew Phillips Fry, our ambassador in London. Our information is he's got himself involved with a married titled woman, with the possibility of a messy divorce scandal. He wants you to get Fry off the hook, one way or the other — '

'London, England?'

'Like Skagway, only bigger. I'm going to give you some of it, enough to hold your own in conversation with Roosevelt. Fry is a shipping tycoon. It's just possible he's lost his marbles — on the other hand, there are some indications he may be a victim of blackmail ...'

Gray was still talking rapidly when Martin returned with a pair of walking shoes, size eight with metal studs. They seemed pretty heavy for a short stroll. Martin and Gray found that an amusing concept ...

And so Pomeroy, who had given up on the army and the flag and all the baloney politicians feed the people while they get rich, was recruited into the service of his country, and put on government shoes for a walk with his own Manifest Destiny.

They left the White House grounds in a White Steamer, two presidential bodyguards in front, Martin and himself jamming knees together in back. They waited by the gates till they saw two horses pulling a black lacquered brougham with a cockaded coachman. President Theodore Roosevelt gave them a hearty good morning and they followed the horse carriage across Washington to Rock Creek Park.

'Nothing like a brisk walk to tell you if a man has the right stuff in him. Like walking, Pomeroy?'

'Better than riding, Mr President. I get a rash near horses.'

'That why you left the Sixth Cavalry?'

Did you tell a downright lie to your President?

'Well, sir, I didn't anticipate we'd see action in Cuba — by the time the war started I was stuck up there in the Yukon.'

'But you showed the right spirit getting yourself to the Klondike. Must have been a real adventure. They made me deputy sheriff out there in the Dakotas when I owned my ranch Elkhorn. Along the little Missouri, wonderful country. I took in more than one man who was probably better than I was with both rifle and revolver, but I knew what I wanted to do and I did it first! That's a good rule, Pomeroy. We've both been places where you learn if a man has the right stuff in him, yes sir!'

This close, he realized that Roosevelt — suddenly Teddy didn't seem appropriate — was partially blind in the left eye, where he had been punched sparring with one of his professional boxer friends. It explained a lot about that aggressive way he looked at you through the *pince-nez*. He was five ten,

42

with a heavy brown moustache and strong white teeth. 'What's your philosophy in life, Pomeroy?', he asked in that high-pitched Harvard drawl. Looking back, Pomeroy saw Martin and the other two bodyguards scrambling across big rocks to keep up with them.

'Well, Mr President …' He was out of breath already and didn't have a philosophy. '… Is it true, sir, you were once challenged to a duel out there in the Dakotas and you suggested rifles at twelve paces?'

' That's it, my boy! Never hit if it is honourably possible to avoid a fight, but if you're unable to avoid a fight with honour then never hit soft! When did you last see your father?'

'Last week, sir.'

' That's good. I believe in a family staying close. Think you can manage that steep face? Follow me, I do this regularly.'

He watched in disbelief as the President jumped a deep rivulet onto a sloping rock and went straight up to the top. Oh well, what the hell. He nearly slipped but made it to the top.

'Pomeroy, I'm glad you want to help us. Gray has told you our problem? Good man, Gray, he helped me clean up the New York police, you can trust him. Straight as a die and all backbone. We'll make for that big oak tree. In my last message to Congress I said there was not a cloud on the horizon at present. I meant that there seemed not the slightest chance of trouble with a foreign power. Frankly, son, that wasn't strictly true. It's possible war is coming over there in Europe and I want to stop it. That's one of the reasons we have to be very careful how we handle this situation involving Ambassador Fry. Am I going too fast for you?'

'No, sir, but these aren't my own shoes — '

'You must always have a second pair of good walking shoes already broken in. There's going to be war between Russia and Japan over Manchuria. I'm sure of it. In Europe, Kaiser Wilhelm hates the British Empire, not to mention Czar Nicholas and the third French republic. What's that got to do with us? America is a rising power, Pomeroy, we're going to have to take an ever-increasing share in the larger life of the world, whether we like it or not. Ordinarily, I would not ask a man to do something underhand. Do you find this assignment goes against the grain?'

'I didn't like it at all at first, Mr President — '

'I'm glad to hear you say that, Pomeroy, but don't think of yourself as a spy — you're my eyes and ears over there in London. I simply will not tolerate a situation that at worst might prejudice America's chances as peacemaker and at best bring ridicule on our foreign service just at the moment we're asking the old powers to take us seriously. I will not have it! '

'I did wonder, sir, if this wasn't more properly a job for an experienced diplomat — '

'Don't underestimate yourself, Pomeroy. You're like me, you've seen a deal more real life than all these fancy pants. Would any of them regard tackling a grizzly bear with a knife and nothing else great sport? I believe firmly in the highest, finest and nicest standards of public and governmental ethics, but avoidance of war is a greater obligation.'

Roosevelt was prepared to let him rest for a minute by the tree. Martin and the bodyguards were out of sight. His breakfast was a lump of lead in his belly, but somehow he didn't get around to complaining.

'You weren't always so dead set against war, Mr President.'

Roosevelt gave him a sharp look. The fancy spectacles perched on his nose made him seem even more pugnacious. Then he laughed and slapped Pomeroy on the shoulder. 'That's sneaky, reminding a politician of his old speeches. Yes, in ninety-five I thought we were going to have war with the British over Venezuela. Let the fight come if it must: I said. I don't care whether the British navy bombards our seaboard cities or not, we will take Canada! Ah well, we all become a little wiser.

Not that I'm against war on principle — unjust war is dreadful, but a just war may be the highest duty. We'll go up the creek on the other side, you'll want to see the whole park. I believe we must be just and generous to others, and yet we must realize it is a shameful and wicked thing not to withstand oppression with a high heart and a ready hand.'

'Why don't you just recall the ambassador, sir?'

'Withdrawing an ambassador is equivalent to firing him. Fry would kick up stink and he has powerful friends among the malefactors of great wealth. The muckrakers would look for scandal and the flubdubs and the mollycoddles would believe them. The other powers would make wrong conclusions about American foreign policy from his dismissal. As in so many matters, I have to tread warily — for instance, these homicidal corruptionists in Bogota think they have us over a barrel in the canal negotiations, so in my draft message to Congress I recommended we take over the Panama isthmus without further parley with Colombia. Last night I deleted that recommendation — brute power is best kept in reserve; the less it's actually used, the more potent a threat it is ... provided everyone knows you have it.'

'You walk softly but you carry a big stick?'

Roosevelt's stiff neck turned slowly. 'Walk softly and carry a big stick ... that's good, Pomeroy ... yes. People regard me as an interim President, only in office because McKinley was assassinated. I have strong views on America's destiny, I see so many wrongs that must be righted here at home but first I need the backing of the people ... walk softly and carry a big stick? Mmmm ... ever thought of going into politics, my boy? '

'Never thought I was smart enough, sir.'

'No, you were a soldier, Pomeroy. Pity you missed out on the war. I was with the First US Volunteer Cavalry, y'know. I learned a lot being a soldier. Our own side was often the problem — each of us in the Rough Riders had to show an alert and not over-scrupulous self-reliance in order to obtain *food!* I learned to proceed upon the belief that the supplies will not turn up . That's a useful lesson in life, Pomeroy.'

'You mean I'll be on my own, sir? '

'You don't miss much, my boy. You remind me of Bill Jones, a dear friend of mine back in Medora, he had the right stuff . . . poor Bill, went to pieces with drink and died in a blizzard.'

'Gambling's more my weakness, Mr President.'

Roosevelt laughed heartily. That's right, my boy, stick to pinochle. There's a lot of mud here — jump to the flat stone. You're right, drinking is weakness. If a man can't rely on himself, who can he rely on? Weakness always invites attack.' Pomeroy went up to his ankles in mud and water. 'Never mind, you'll walk them dry. That acute philosopher Mr Dooley said that, in the Spanish war, we were in a dream but the Spaniards were in a trance. He was right, by Godfrey! This is a modern world and we have to be strong and wily to survive. No plainsman needs to be told not to sleep near the fire if there's danger of an enemy creeping up on him . I relied a great deal on information when I was cleaning up the New York police department — an information gatherer can be a most honourable man in the right cause. A government, like a cavalry column, needs scouts.'

'And if the scout meets a war party, sir? ...'

'Make for those big bushes up there. Good to get your lungs cleaned out, isn't it? You'll like London. I married my wife Edith in St George's Church, Hanover Square. I'm partly Scottish by descent — not a drop of English blood in me, thank God.' Roosevelt laughed, at the same time looking back. The other three were struggling over rough ground fifty yards back. His voice dropped. 'I don't know what kind of mess that old fathead's got himself into, but I will not tolerate conduct in public officials that could bring ridicule or scandal on the reputation of the United States. One way or another it has to be stopped.'

'How far do I go, sir — to stop it, I mean?.'

'Ah. I can imagine situations where you won't be able to send telegrams back and forth across the Atlantic. Gray will give you more detailed instructions; there are some things a President should not know too much about. What I do know is that two years ago the German Kaiser told his officers they must be ready day and night to spill their blood for king and fatherland! They're working up to war and Fry's blundering could compromise American neutrality. Take your lead from Gray — anything he tells you has my authority. Now — that way to the road. Everything clear, Pomeroy?'

'An ambassador's pretty high on the scale of things — '

'Generally a party war-horse or a big contributor being paid off. But in time I'll have this country represented by professionals.'

'He's still pretty powerful — '

'All the more reason to take action if he endangers the country's interests. We must exercise the largest charity towards the wrongdoer that is compatible with relentless war against wrongdoing.'

'So you're sending *me* out to tackle the grizzly bear with a knife, Mr President?'

That earned him another thump on the shoulders. 'By Godfrey, it does my heart good, a fine young fellow like you dedicating himself in the ultra-American spirit of patriotism! Now, tell me about my old pal Billy — you must owe your father a great deal ...'

They reached the roadway again. Roosevelt gave him a handshake to lacerate a brick. The other three came running across the park. Roosevelt, who never rode in an automobile while he was President, climbed briskly into the brougham. He raised his hand in farewell:

'*Speak* softly and carry a big stick, Pomeroy!'

Gray came clean by stages.

' The warning sign should have been clear when Fry wrote to the State Department asking if the rules could be changed about American diplomats not wearing finery. He wanted permission to carry a short sword on formal occasions because they kept mistaking him for a waiter at Buckingham Palace!'

They were in the long room. Gray was shifting papers from the old bureau's pigeonholes to a new desk and modern filing cabinets at the other end.

There was a bombing in London this year. It might have been anarchists, but Fry made a speech blaming the Irish Home Rule movement ... only he called them Fenian murderers. That suited the British government -'

'So? We're friends with the British, aren't we? '

'Fry's speech was a spit in the face of every American with a drop of Irish blood. You think Roosevelt wants to lose the Irish vote in next year's election? Fry might simply have forgotten the political realities back here. The British are damned skilful at seducing our ambassadors away from the paths of republican righteousness. Or somebody could be putting pressure on him — the Germans maybe; they would like to cause trouble between us and the British. They would also like to see Roosevelt lose the election — for some reason he detests the Germans.'

'I have to make sure the ambassador's speeches follow the approved line — that it?'

'You have to find out what's got into him. You also have to stop him dragging the good name of Uncle Sam through the divorce courts. Puritan America doesn't understand national representatives who go to Babylon and run with painted harlots.'

'London? Gee — it wasn't like that in *Oliver Twist.*'

'Anyway, that's the job Roosevelt thinks you'll be doing.'

It was his first hint that nothing was simple in Mr Gray's world.

They didn't leave him alone for a moment, day or night. In the long room, in the White House grounds when it wasn't raining, in the new executive wing when it was, in the small bedroom — they put him through it again and again. He went for State Department interviews and processing as a junior secretary in the foreign service, and when he came out Martin was waiting to take him back to Mr Gray.

'For your cover we'll stick close to the facts. Your old man's a friend of the President and you're a privileged son getting into the foreign service as a favour, part-of the spoils system. Over there, you come across as a rich brat, black sheep of a fine old military family, still bitter because the South lost. You didn't want this lousy clerk's job in London, but you're too scared of your old man to hightail it and they'll be too scared of the White House to give you your walking papers.'

'How do I make like a rich sonofabitch on a hundred bucks a month?'

'What would you do stranded with a couple of bucks in Kansas City?'

'You sure about that?'

'I'm not signing you into the Comstock League, Pomeroy.'

'Why am I busted for cash?'

'Your old man's cut your pocket money off. You're due to inherit, but meanwhile you're a high spender with no dough.'

'What's the real reason I'm busted?'

'Somebody in the other intelligence agencies might spot you as a potential traitor and offer you money. We want to know if any other country is trying to get a pipeline into our embassy. In a sense, Fry's a cover for a spot of counter-espionage work.'

'Roosevelt didn't mention that.'

'A President has a lot on his mind.'

'What the hell's going on here, Gray? Who am I really working for?'

'The President of the United States of America. But presidents change. You're working for me and I'm working in the best interests of the United States of America.'

'Why do I have to drag everything out of you like pulling teeth, Gray?'

'I want to see how good you are with the questions, Pomeroy.'

'Andrew Phillips Fry is fifty-nine, married, with one daughter. He's worth thirty, forty million, made his money building ships. He was a McKinley appointment. Roosevelt can't get rid of him because he's very big in the trusts and in the Republican Party. Roosevelt needs their support to get the nomination next year.'

'What's a little scandal to one of those fat bastards?'

'Roosevelt can't fulfil our Manifest Destiny if our ambassadors go around behaving like uncouth hicks spitting tobacco juice on the walls. However, our information is it could be more than a divorce. We hear rumours Fry is making financial investments over there. That could be tied in with the woman — maybe he isn't planning to return home. Some of his investments may be in war industries — that could compromise American neutrality. The European powers will assume he's either acting for the US government or he knows which way the wind is blowing. Get a list of his investments. Identify the woman. If it looks like a divorce scandal, eliminate her. If it looks like blackmail, find out how and why, then eliminate the threat.'

'What do you mean — eliminate?'

'Look it up in *Webster's*.'

'Are you saying I'm maybe expected to kill somebody?'

'You shot a man in Alaska.'

'I'm not saying I did or I didn't, but he fired first.'

'Pomeroy, you're in the secret service now. You were an officer in the US army; this is just a different kind of war. And you won't be dealing with cheap grifters over a penny-ante jackpot. The Russians, the Germans, the French, the Austro-Hungarian Empire all have intelligence branches, so have the British — America's coming late into the game. The German secret service is top class and ruthless as all hell. That's one of the reasons you're sailing on the *Lucania*, October 3. Our information is one of Germany's top espionage experts will be sailing on the *Lucania*. His name is Lang-Gaevernitz. He's been over here contacting German Americans as possible agents. He won't look anything like a secret agent, but he's very, very dangerous.'

'What do I do — chuck him overboard?'

'No, make friends with him. Give him the works. You're the young rakehell forced to work for the government by your father. Let him know you're short of spending money.'

'So he'll stand the drinks?'

'No — so he'll buy *you*, Pomeroy.'

'But I'm not for sale — '

'Oh yes you are, as far as Lang-Gaevernitz is concerned. The Germans want to know everything going on between the United States and Great Britain. You're up for sale as a traitor, Pomeroy, because we want to know what the Germans are doing.'

'Listen, Gray — what the hell's an this got to do with the ambassador's divorce?'

'Let's take it one step at a time.'

They taught him a code. A simple system, Martin called it, coded telegrams based on a book. Gray produced the book — *Oliver Twist.*

'We have an identical copy. Write out your message and find the words in the book. Your telegrams to us will look like financial statements. We'll decipher them by page, line and word number — anybody else would have to know what book we're using. You did say you liked *Oliver Twist,* didn't you?'

'I'm surprised you remember.'

'Pomeroy, you're my first overseas agent, everything about you fascinates me. Why did you like *Oliver Twist* — because he always asked for more?'

'No, his mother died before he — '

He blurted this much out before he could stop himself. It was the first time he'd ever let his guard down about *that.* He felt himself sweating but Gray was already talking about something else. Were they doing a better job of taking him over than he knew?

'Our information from sources in Berlin is that the German espionage departments get copies of all our telegrams in and out of the London embassy. The State Department refuses point-blank to believe one of their people could be a traitor — they'd even try to stop us on this one despite having Roosevelt behind us. That's the job you'll be doing for me, Pomeroy, identifying the German contact in the London embassy.'

'Identifying? Or eliminating?'

'Get the evidence first .. . the closer you get to Lang-Gaevernitz, the more chance you'll have — '

' What if he wants *me* to play Benedict Arnold? They shoot traitors, don't they?'

'It's called playing a double game, Pomeroy — why do you think I picked *you* for it?'

'You got somebody else over there working for you already?'

'I want you to proceed on the assumption you're entirely on your own.'

'Don't you trust me, for chrissake?'

'I wouldn't trust myself if they were giving me the hotfoot and I wasn't wearing shoes. Don't look so shocked — you survived Skagway, didn't you?'

'Soapy Smith and his bunch were Americans, all they did was rob you or shoot you!'

'However, I can tell you that some of our information from the London end comes from a third secretary name of Robert Lyle. He wrote a personal letter to Roosevelt making a lot of allegations — I guess that makes him a patriot. You can pal up with him, sound him out, but on no account do you tell him who you're really working for — you got that? On no account!'

'Just out of interest, Gray — what am I supposed to do if some foreign bastard's burning my bare feet, you tell me that?'

'Grit your teeth and think of Custer.'

They were still holding things back, but he couldn't put his finger on the right questions to ask, and in any case there was something more important he had to know. He saved it for his last meeting with Gray before he and Martin caught the train for New York. They were in the long room, now bright and new and nothing like a cosy parlour. Gray was trying to find the right place for a wire basket on an acreage of shiny desk. Maybe he was having an emotion. He wasn't too sure what he thought of Gray now, but a lot had changed since he first came into this room with wet shoes.

'You conned me, Gray, you know that?' he said cheerfully. 'A little job for the government? I should've taken the easy way out and gone to the pen.'

'No, Pomeroy, you were made for this.'

That dope on me in the file — it mostly came from my father, didn't it?

' We had different sources — '

'He was the only one knew I'd gone to Baltimore. Did he know you wanted me for this job?'

'Nobody knows about your job, only the President, Martin and me.'

'So he did want me in jail ...'

'I guess your father thought he was doing the best thing for you, one way or another.'

'Boy, am I looking forward to telling the old bastard ...'

'Pomeroy, you're *never* going to be able to tell *anybody* about all this, *never.* Write to him, tell him you're in the foreign service, but — '

'We don't write to each other.'

They shook hands. Gray was still holding something back, but then, so was he ...

He walked Owen Martin back from his first-class cabin to the gangway of the liner *Lucania.* All around them people were getting the big send-off. The accents of the English officers announcing sailing time made him feel he was already a long way away. They stood looking down at the hubbub on the pier. Suddenly New York looked like home and the hackies and the baggage handlers seemed like old pals ... Americans.

Owen Martin stood back to admire his new grey suit and matching fedora. 'Big improvement on cuffs and a slicker over your head, huh?'

'I should've given those dumbheads the slip back in Baltimore.'

'Come on, John. It's worked out real fine for you, hasn't it?'

'Oh yeah, sure. By the way, tell Gray to check that letter I signed, will you, the one in his safe?'

'Why, John?'

'Watch his mug when he sees I signed it William B. Pome-roy!'

Owen Martin thought he was joking .

A bell rang. Owen punched him on the chest and went down the gangway. Some English nob with a silk top hat and muttonchop whiskers told his chums that George III had been right in the end: Americans were *impossible.* They took down the gangway. Big ropes were cast off. Tugs hooted.

Oh well, what the hell. On balance it probably beat having Aunt Harriet Pingree for a mother-in-law.

4

Hime yaw stooard, sar, may nymesorton.

The RMS *Lucania* of the Cunard Line, for several years the largest ship in the world, was hardly out of sight of the Statue of Liberty.

'Could you say that again a little more slowly?' he asked the red-cheeked flunkey in the white mess jacket.

'I'm your steward, sir, my name's Horton — '

'Pleased to meet you, Orton.' He stuck out his hand. 'John Pomeroy — '

'No, Horton with an aitch, sir.' They shook hands — reluctantly on the Englishman's part. 'If you tell me whatever you want, it'll be my pleasure to make your voyage as pleasant as possible, sir, What time would you like your tea in the morning?'

He opened his billfold. 'I may need a few things, Horton —'

'I'd prefer any gratuity at the end of the trip, sir.'

He was turning down a tip?

The single-berth cabin had a foldaway bed that turned into a divan, mahogany furniture including a writing desk, a washbasin with running hot and cold, and a square porthole window. While he hung up Pomeroy's three new suits in the wardrobe and put away his new shirts and collars and underwear and socks in the drawers, Horton told him proudly that the *Lucania* had been built on the Clyde in 1893. It weighed 12,952 tons and had twelve main boilers, eight corrugated furnaces and twin-screws powered by a triple-expansion engine that could do up to twenty-two knots. The old icehouse had recently been replaced by what Horton called a refrigerating machine. It —

'Well, isn't that something?' Pomeroy said quickly when Horton took a breath. 'Say, is there a German fellow called Lang-Gaevernitz on board, would you know?'

'What class is he travelling, sir?'

'I dunno.'

There were 526 first-class passengers in cabins or suites, 280 second-class passengers, 300 third-class and 1,000 steerage. The crew was 61 officers and sailors, 195 engineers and firemen, and 159 stewards. Sir would have noticed the heating system —

'First-class, I guess.'

'I'll make inquiries, sir. You'll probably get to know all your fellow passengers, sir, once they get over being seasick. Do you get seasick, sir?'

'Hell no, Horton! I sailed up to Alaska from Seattle and all the way up the Yukon on a leaky steamboat, never got seasick once, no sir!'

' That's nice to know, sir.'

'Which way to the deck, Horton?'

'If sir would follow me — '

He started feeling queasy before he reached the rail. New York was fading in the distance. The sea was grey and choppy — and a long way down. The few other passengers on deck were all pretty old, nobody in the least like a German secret agent. His stomach felt funny. He wanted to watch America until the very last, but suddenly he knew he was going to throw up.

The wind took it away from the side of the ship. He got his arms over the rail and hung there, draped.

'I say — fella's bein' sick already!' growled a voice behind him, an English voice, but it wasn't so much the accent he heard but the sneer.

Then he heard another voice: 'Shouldn't we call a deck steward, father?' It was English too, but female.

He gulped to fill his lungs. 'I'm okay,' he mumbled, taking care not to give them a look at his face.

Even through the wind and the roaring in his ears, her voice was a soft caress. 'Are you sure? We can call a steward — '

'Wait till he gets a taste of the big waves,' said the sneering voice. 'Americans, y'know, damn bad sailors .. .'

When he looked around, they were heading along the promenade. She was wearing a big white hat with a band of chiffon holding it under her chin. Her long white dress was tight at the waist and then flowed over a bustle of petticoats to the deck. He was much older, in a brown tweed suit and black hat. She was holding his arm. When the wind caught the floppy brim of her hat, he saw chestnut hair in a bun and a slim white neck. She might have looked back at him when she raised her hand to hold her hat, but he wasn't sure. He made his way back to his cabin. What the hell was he doing on a big boat full of strange people speaking funny English?

He pulled his bed down and got out of his new grey suit and shoes and climbed in. He was shivering. With his eyes closed, he seemed to hear the great engines churning, walls of steel cutting through water, decks on top of each other swarming with people he didn't understand, people who knew him for a fool.

Even when he felt warm and the shivering stopped, it didn't get any better. What did he know about ambassadors and foreign countries and international politics? He'd allowed himself to be conned into it and threatened and then flattered by a walk with the President. A maniac who thought great sport would be taking on a grizzly bear with a knife! All that crap about ethics and peace and America's destiny and the right stuff in a man. America was all Pingrees getting their tight fists on the dollar, saloon keepers who screwed you and the faro guys who screwed you and the grifters and the bunco men and the panhandlers and the politicians and the big trusts, that was the America he knew, the big swindle. The hell with it, soon as this floating palace hit Liverpool he was on the next boat back home ... move fast, leave no traces, no ties, no traps, no gear you couldn't shove in one bag and just *go*.

Knock knock.

'Would you like a nice cup of tea, sir?'

A naice kip ov teesar.

When Horton came in, Pomeroy was in his underwear at the washbasin.

'Just to let you know luncheon is in twenty minutes, sir — unless sir is feeling a little queasy — '

'Me? No, I'm fine.' Hpdfe splashed his face and almost believed it.

'By the way, sir, that German gentleman you asked about? He has cabin twenty-two, sir, on the other side. His steward told me he's having his meals alone.'

He dried his face. He felt embarrassed, but Horton's expression indicated he was used to seeing first-class gentlemen in all states of undress. While he got into the pants of his white suit, he described the father-and-daughter couple he'd seen on deck.

'Ah yes, sir, that's a Colonel Dalrymple and his daughter Catherine I'm pretty sure they're travelling incognito, sir.'

'Incognito?'

'Just between you and me and the gatepost, sir. I rather have the idea they're titled people, sir; it's quite common for people of a certain class to travel under other names — '

'Like an alias?'

Horton chuckled. 'Not exactly, sir — we are talking about the aristocracy. People in that class have to be careful, you know.'

The first-class dining room was one hundred by sixty-two feet, with a high ceiling panelled in white and gold, and a frieze figured in red. The middle section towered up to a curved dome of stained glass. Down the length of the room ran three tables with heavy swivel armchairs bolted to the floor so diners could take their places without bumping each other. The upholstery was velvet. Down each side were individual booths that could be curtained off.

Bumping into people was not a problem that first meal. The chief steward told him they could seat 430 first-class passengers, but he was early and many people were probably a little under the weather. He took a place near the door on the middle table. He was looking forward to a little snack. He glanced at the menu.

MENU

Consomme à la Princesse

Salade de Filets de Sole

Petites Mayonnaises de Homard

Quenelles de Crevettes en Aspic

Petites Caisses de Volaille en Aspic

Jambon de York braise au Madere

Bouchées de Langue de Boeuf

Chaud-froid de Pigeon à la Castillane

Faisan de Cresson

Mauviettes en Aspic en Caisses

Galantine de Dindonneau aux Truffes

Pate de Faisan en Plumage

Boeuf Presse à la Gelee

Aspic de Foie Gras à la Belle Vue

Salade à la Russe

Crème à la Fraise

Gelée au Noyeau

Gelee à la Macedoine de Fruits

Petits Fours Glaces

Fruits Glaces

Meringues à la Creme

Glaces Napolitaines

'I'll have the beef,' he told his steward.

The wine steward put the list in front of him and stood there looking snooty. The temptation was to stab his finger halfway down the list but how did you pronounce *Clos Vougeot?* 'You're having beef, sir,' said the wine steward. 'If I might make a suggestion — ?'

'I wish you would,' he said fervently.

All snootiness gone, the wine steward recommended a half-bottle of claret, Château Desmirail Margaux, the 1899 vintage. 'The most expensive is not necessarily any less pleasing to the palate, sir.'

'You're the expert.'

Most of the other diners were the same bunch of oldsters he'd seen on deck. Some of them were pushing seventy, a couple of old gents were brought in wheelchairs and had to be lifted into their seats, but they all ate like starving huskies. The precise English use of knife and fork simultaneously, with special ways of holding the fingers, made them look like pecking chickens. He finished with a red apple and asked for his check. Naturally they called it the *bill;* but there wasn't one anyway; the ship was a floating hotel run on the American plan.

Hardly able to walk for the amount he'd eaten, he was heading for the door when in came an important-looking man, Italian maybe, surrounded by officers in uniform and guys with notebooks and not exactly first-class suits.

'No no no, I have gone beyond the experimental stage,' the big noise was saying in English as the little crowd almost knocked him down.

He found the deck again. America was out of sight. What the hell did he do now? Well, since New York he'd heard *one* voice with a touch of kindness in it ...

The ship's library had carved mahogany walls and amboyna panelling, tasselled armchairs and banquette seats round carved pillars, all the upholstering in rich blue velvet. There were writing tables with *Lucania* notepaper and pens and ink. And books, of course, thousands of them behind leaded glass. She wasn't there.

The first-class drawing room was sixty by thirty feet, with a huge brass fireplace surrounded by Persian tiles, a grand piano and an American organ. She wasn't there either.

The smoking room was done up in what they called Scottish baronial style, dark oak, a place for men to drink and smoke and be free of female delicacy. It had tables against the wall with banquette seats and tables in the middle, plus a bar with a steward. By this time he knew the English did not speak to strangers without formal introduction, and was surprised when a burly man in a Norfolk jacket and knickerbockers waved him over to his table. He stuck up his hand.

'American? Jesse Hudson Marchbanks of Austin, Texas.'

'John Pomeroy.'

'Glad to know you, John.' Toe Texan had wide shoulders and a big chest. His hair was gingery, brushed flat against a tendency to curls. What really distinguished him, however, was an absence of anything resembling a neck, so that his big head looked like Humpty-Dumpty sitting on the wall. 'Hey — boy!' The steward came over. 'What'li you have, John old buddy? I asked for bourbon and branch but they never heard of branch water, you believe that? Name it, John .'

'Thanks, but I'm a little out of sorts right now — '

'Would you like some coffee, sir?' asked the steward.

'Well , that would — '

'Coffee my ass, you have some of that fine old cognac, that'll settle your stomach, boy.'

'Black, no sugar,' he told the steward.

'What's your line, John?' Marchbanks demanded. 'I'm in beef. Yessir, I have one of the choicest little spreads in the sovereign state of Texas, twenty thousand prime beeves and dang me if they ain't struck black oil in the east section that wasn't no damn good anyhow. What line did you say you were in, John old buddy?'

'Well, for a while I was in the army — '

'You fight in the Spanish war? Didn't we give those dagos hell? That'll teach 'em to blow up American ships, yessir! I curse the day they told me I was too old to fight, I was just *aching* to get in on it, yessir. Where'd you say you're from, John? You travelling for business or pleasure?'

'I was born in Knoxville, Tenness — '

'Now that is a beautiful state — hey boy, hit me with another shot of bourbon and some of that stuff you call water.'

'Yes, sir,' said the steward, pouring Pomeroy's coffee. His neat English face had no expression on it whatsoever, but there was something going on behind his eyes. A few people came in and went out again. He sipped his coffee and let Jesse Hudson Marchbanks inform him about the world.

'Let me tell you, John, this being your first trip — this here is class! I know a director of this line personally and he told me no expense was spared, no sir. I mean *no* expense. I quote: "We wanted to suggest the stately chambers of a palace rather than accommodation within the steel walls of a ship." Isn't that something? You have to hand it to the limeys, they know all about *class* ...' He leaned over and used his confidential tone, the one that didn't reach all the way back to New York. '... but they don't know nary a single damn thing about making money, no sir.' He winked and tapped his nose. 'I travel for pleasure *and* business, John, only I like to make the latter pay for the former, if you follow. I have to, the amount of dough I lose gambling. Why, last year I took a nice little cruise to Europe ...'

The man in the brown suit came into the smoking room. The girl wasn't with him. He was in his fifties maybe, very lean and tanned. He wore a monocle in his right eye. He had a stiff moustache and his hair was stuck flat on his skull.

'Whisky and soda,' barked that hard English voice. He took a table nearby but ignored them. His skin was taut across his cheekbones. Jesse Marchbanks gave him the once-over.

'There's a lot of 'em like that in England, think they own the whole damn world — '

'They own enough …'

'The future's in America, John, you take my word for it, those old countries are dying on their feet. The only ones they've got with any business initiative are the Jews, not that I like Jews but …'

The girl in the white dress did not come in. Then he realized there were no women in the smoking room. Colonel Dalrymple took his whisky like bad medicine, glared round the room, wiped his moustache with the back of his big bony hand and stood up. A young fellow at another table seemed to recognize him.

'I say — don't we know each other?'

Dalrymple gave the young fellow a stiff look. 'No,' he barked and walked past their table. He was buttoning his coat. Something fell to the carpet. Dalrymple walked on and out of the door. Pomeroy and Jesse Marchbanks craned over their table. The pigskin wallet had fallen open when it hit the floor. They could see money. Pomeroy was nearer; he picked it up. 'I'll run after him — '

'Now, just a moment, John — how do we know it's his?'

'You saw him drop it, didn't you?'

'I saw him drop it,' said the young fellow. He was already halfway to their table. 'You ought to give it to the steward — '

'You might be stealing it,' Jesse Marchbanks protested.

Pomeroy gave him a hard look. 'Say that again?'

He hurried back to his own cabin area and met Horton carrying a coffee service on a silver tray.

'Was luncheon to your liking, sir?'

'Unbelievable — which number did you say for those people, the girl with her father?'

'The Dalrymples? Suite eleven, sir, if you go that way and — '

'Thank you, Horton.'

He took a deep breath and knocked. 'Yes, what is it?' She was asking as she opened the door. The light was behind her. She was still wearing the long white dress. Her thick chestnut hair was pulled back off her forehead and twisted tight in a high knot at the back. Her face went with her voice, brown eyes, straight nose, a full mouth and strong white teeth. The severity of her hairstyle went with her serious expression, yet there was a smile lurking somewhere behind those brown eyes.

'My name's John Pomeroy, I'm in cabin twenty-five. I was in the smoking room and — '

'Where did you get that?' she demanded, frowning at the wallet in his hand.

'Colonel Dalrymple — he's your father, I understand — he dropped it in the smoking room and I thought I'd return it.'

'Oh.' She seemed confused. Then she did smile. Briefly. 'That is kind of you, thank you very much indeed.'

'You want to check there's nothing missing?' was the best he could come up with to keep her talking.

'I'm sure it's all right, I'll tell my father you returned it. Thankyou very much again, Mr — ?'

That voice! If roses could talk ...

'John Stockley Pomeroy. And you're — ?'

'Thank you again, Mr Stockley Pomeroy — '

'Well actually, the Stockley is — '

65

She had the pocketbook out of his hand as the door came to meet his face. He listened for a moment, for some reason thinking she was crying in there. People came along the corridor. With nothing better to do, he headed back to the smoking room. Those sad brown eyes, that shy smile — he felt breathless.

In the now-crowded smoking room, Marchbanks was drinking champagne with the young English fellow, name of Francis Holborn. His voice was a languid drawl — *house* became *hise, Francis* became *Frawncis* in his kind of English. He was good-looking, dark, older close up when you saw the lines round his eyes, something of a boozehound by the look of him. When the steward came with a glass and lifted the champagne bottle from its ice bucket on a stand, Pomeroy turned his glass upside down.

Jesse Hudson Marchbanks gave him a mocking smile. 'Did you catch up with the old boy?'

'No, I gave the wallet to his daughter. Their name's Dalrymple — that ring a bell, Holborn?'

The languid Englishman shook his head. 'No, should it? '

'I thought you recognized him. My steward did say they ' re travelling incognito. Why would that be?'

'Sometimes one finds that people react rather *clammily* to a title. I suppose you could say I travel incognito in that sense. I'm. actually Viscount Holborn of Seaton Delaval.' He grimaced. 'You Americans are right, it's all frightfully silly — '

'Hell no,' Marchbanks protested. He raised his glass. 'Great honour to make your acquaintance, Viscount — '

'Francis, *please.* Come on, John old boy, have some bubbly, I'm paying.'

He shook his head. 'It's not the paying that stops me, *old boy.'*

'Oh dear, I didn't mean to —'

'Well, will you look who's here?' Marchbanks hissed. He nodded urgently. A dignified, dark-faced man was going towards the bar. He had a blue suit with a red handkerchief sticking out of his top pocket. His hair was black, oiled flat with no parting. He spoke to a steward, who found him an unoccupied table.

'Somebody famous?' Holborn asked.

'Either of you two gambling men?'

Holborn smirked. 'Not much. My father's been dunned so often to cover my debts he's threatening to pack me off to Australia.'

'I've played a little faro here and there,' Pomeroy said. .

Marchbanks snorted. 'Faro? I'm talking about high-class gambling, not skinning rubes in the Midwest. That man over there is none other than Charles Devoy!'

He sat back and waited for their exclamations.

'Charles Devoy, eh?' Holborn looked impressed, then he asked, 'Should one have heard of him?'

'He's just about the most famous sporting man in Europe, that's all. Why, I once saw him win close to a hundred thousand francs in Monte Carlo! Baccarat, vingt-et-un, any form of poker you name — he is the king! Oh boy — and he's on this ship? Been my ambition for years to sit down with Charles Devoy —'

'Anyone here seen a wallet by any chance?' came that gruff, sneering voice. Pomeroy looked up at Colonel Dalrymple. This close, the face was almost without flesh under parchment skin.

'I took it back to your cabin — '

'What? What d'you mean my *cabin*? I'm not in a *cabin* — who the hell are you, sir?'

'My name's Pomeroy, I gave it to your daughter — '

'Damn you, there's a procedure for lost property, donchya know? I don't want any Tom, Dick or Harry sniffin' round my private quarters. How did you know it was mine anyway? Looked through it, eh? My God, it's a bit hot when people go sniffin' through a man's private belongin's — American, are you? Thought so.'

67

Francis Holborn wasn't about to let his new buddy be insulted. In his most languid, insolent tone, he drawled, 'I don't know your name, sir, but you've a bloody peculiar way of thanking Mr Pomeroy for doing you a good turn. Bloody peculiar.'

'And who the hell might you be?' barked Dalrymple.

'Viscount Holborn of Seaton Delaval, as it happens. Pomeroy here did you a good turn and all you do is kick up a bloody fuss? Bit of a bad show, I'd say.'

Dalrymple coughed and humphed. 'Damned silly of me to drop it in the first place.' He growled something that might have been 'thanks'. To the steward he barked, 'Give these gentlemen whatever they want; put it on my bill, Colonel Dalrymple.'

'Yes, sir.'

'Why don't you all take a seat, colonel?' Marchbanks moved his bulk an inch or so along the banquette. Dalrymple glared down through his monocle.

'Okay by me,' Pomeroy said. Dalrymple sat down. 'Matter of fact, we met already.' Dalrymple frowned at him. 'I was the party being ill over the side this morning? What was it you said — Americans made bad sailors?'

'I don't recall sayin' any such thing. True, though. John Paul Jones was Scottish, wasn't he?'

The steward stood patiently by the table. At first they looked nauseatingly servile, these white English servants, but after a while you noticed subtle clues in their impassive faces, just a hint about the eyes, an infinitesimal variation in the tone of voice. This one was in his thirties, good shoulders on him, too manly-looking for kowtowing to rich boozehounds. But it was there all the same, behind the politeness, like that same expression coloureds often had when serving the white man, yassuh massa suh, and all the time laughing at him in a way he couldn't pin down but knew damn well was happening. Maybe this guy was one of these radical socialists — no, it was not so much hatred behind his eyes, more like contempt, a suggestion he knew all about them, they didn't *fool* him.

'You anything of a gambling man, colonel?' Marchbanks asked.

Dalrymple's upper lip curled. 'I have played baccarat with His Majesty the King of England,' he said down his steep nose. 'When he was Prince of Wales, that is. I spend part of every year in Deauville or Biarritz, Monte Carlo, Baden-Baden. I think I can claim that I am not unknown in all the better gamin' rooms of London and the Continent.'

Marchbanks nudged him and nodded for him to look down the crowded smoking room. 'You see that party in the blue suit — sitting by the door on his ownsome? You know him?'

Dalrymple narrowed his free eye as if to squint across a hundred miles of sun-baked India. 'Can't say I recognize the fella, some kind of dago, is he?'

'That is Charles Devoy, the famous gambler!'

Dalrymple took out his monocle, rubbed it on his shirt cuff, and screwed it back into his eyesocket. 'Really? Heard of the man, of course, bit of a scurrilous johnny by all accounts.'

'Another bottle of bubbly — make it a magnum,' Holborn said with an expansive wave of his arm that knocked over a glass. Pomeroy and the steward caught it together off the edge of the table. For a moment their eyes met and he got the impression the steward was trying to tell him something.

'Whaddya say, Dalrymple?' Marchbanks was agog about something. 'We'll probably lose a bundle but it would be something to tell about afterward, wouldn't it?'

The snooty Englishman shook his head, looking down the smoking room. 'I don't know — fella's a damned professional after all.'

'What are you two up to?' Francis Holborn demanded. Marchbanks pursed his lips and sucked in air. 'Me and Dalrymple here would dearly love to say we'd sat down with the great

Charles Devoy — nothing you two young fellows would be interested in. Say, Dalrymple, I'm just a hairy-assed cattleman from Austin, Texas, so don't take this as an insult but — well, I'm loaded and it's the only reason I make these here trips, to have a little sporting recreation. The money ain't important; why, I have a hundred thousand dollars tucked away in the purser's safe, spending money for this trip to Europe, money I don't intend to bring home again — let old Jesse cover the losses, whaddya say?'

'Of course not,' the colonel barked. 'Funny thing if a gentleman started behavin' like some damned Jewboy!'

'But you'll do it?' Marchbanks was almost begging him. 'You know he only plays with the *creme,* he wouldn't waste spit on *me.'*

'Well, I don't mind speakin' to the cove,' Dalrymple announced. Holborn said he wanted to be in on it, whatever it was. Marchbanks shook his head. Locking horns with Charles Devoy was for men who knew gambling — sure they might lose a bundle, but in some circles that would be considered almost as good as having played with the King of England.

'I fancy I've lost enough money at the table to claim some slight knowledge of gambling,' Holborn drawled. 'Perhaps my title would make him more amenable, eh, Dalrymple?'

'Holborn may have a point there, Marchbanks,' the crusty colonel conceded.

Marchbanks relented. 'Okay, Francis, no offence intended — '

'I wouldn't be averse to a little flutter myself,' Pomeroy said innocently. 'I haven't played too much poker, but I can afford to lose a dollar or two.'

'No reflection on you, Pomwhatever your name is,' Dalrymple said gruffly, 'but I'm not in the habit of playin' for pennies with a bloody beginner.'

'He's right there, John old buddy.' Marchbanks put a consoling hand on his shoulder. This wouldn't be any game for you to start learning the rudiments, no sir.'

'Right, then.' The colonel adjusted his monocle, wiped his moustache, stood up and squared his shoulders. 'I'd wager he's a thunderin' . braggart, but let's see if I can cut him down to size, what?' He marched off down the smoking room towards the sallow man in the blue suit. Pomeroy looked at Holborn's eyes bright with champagne, listening avidly to whatever bullshit Marchbanks fed him, a born sucker if there ever was —

Hell's teeth! In Skagway, he'd have been wise the moment the wallet hit the floor —

Con men!

What had confused him was being on a famous British liner, travelling first-class with snobs and toffs. He watched Marchbanks laughing uproariously at some joke of Holborn's. The young Englishman's cheeks flushed with pleasure, as though nobody had ever laughed at his jokes before. That's why they didn't want any beginners, they already had their pigeon!

Dalrymple was talking to Devoy at the other end of the smoking room, then he came striding back to their table. 'Just as I expected — a typical lounge lizard, but I soon had his measure. Bloody man has a high opinion of himself — he says he'll meet us after dinner when he *might* be in the mood to discuss the possibility of a game. Bloody cheek, what?'

'Man like that can't be too careful,' Marchbanks assured them. Francis Holborn, eyes hot with anticipation, said he'd better get some wherewithal out of the purser's safe. 'How much do you suggest, Jesse? Five hundred? A thousand?' The lamb was in a hurry to be fleeced.

Pomeroy said he had some work to do and nobody minded him leaving. One pigeon at a time, that was the rule. Maybe now he understood the sadness in her eyes.

Unable to face an eight-course dinner, he had Horton bring him cold beef and pickle and two bottles of beer in his cabin. With all his other charges dressing for dinner, Horton had time to chat. 'Oh yes, you'll have a most enjoyable time in London, sir. For those with money, London is the place. Everything your heart desires is there, sir. Some even call it the modern Sodom and Gomorrah.'

'If you don't have money — ?'

'Ah. A very stony-hearted place, London, if you have no money, sir. I know. I'm from just outside London, a village called Staines. We were very poor. My sister's in service with Lord Hednesford in Belgrave Square. We've been very lucky, as it happens.'

'I sure hope I can get to grips with all these titles. How do you get a title, Horton?'

'They're usually inherited, sir.'

'That Colonel Dalrymple — you say he's really a titled aristocrat? He struck me as one of the rudest bastards I ever met.'

'Oh yes, he's the genuine article, sir. you can tell. I have an idea he's like so many others of his class today, sir, a long pedigree and not enough money to go with it. '

'My family came from England way back — maybe I can claim a title? Who gives them out, the King?'

Horton hesitated. 'I shouldn't really say this, sir, but ... well, standards have declined, sir — titles can be *bought.'*

'Yeah? How much? Could I lay out a few dollars and call myself Lord Pomeroy of Knoxville? The Viscount Stockley of Pomeroy?'

Horton found that very amusing. He liked Americans. 'After all all, sir, you're almost the same as ourselves, lot of line gentlemen these days are marrying young American ladies. Let me see now — Lord Randolph Churchill's widow is an American, so is Lady Essex and Lady Lister-Kaye and Lord Curzon's wife

— and the Duchess of Marlborough. Then there's the Marchioness of Dufferin and Ava — '

'Is it illegal to kid that you have a title?'

'I don't actually think it is, sir — but most people would soon spot that you weren't the genuine article.'

'Only, in Dalrymple's case, he's the genuine article pretending he's a bum army colonel? Why would he do that, Horton?'

The steward sighed. 'You never know with titled people, sir, they're not like you and me.'

It had to be crooked some way. First the pocketbook being dropped, then Marchbanks making a big thing out of this Devoy fellow being on board, all leading up to a little friendly game. Even the way they pretended not to want Holborn in on it, letting him persuade them. That was classic, getting the mark frothing at the mouth. Working the tubes, grifters called it; conning people on boats ... disappointing, somehow, to meet up with it on a swell British liner.

He put on his raglan overcoat and left his cabin. It happened that he passed her door on his way to the deck, but she wasn't looking out and he couldn't come up with another excuse to knock. Out on the open deck it was blowing hard. Looking down over the rail , he could make out white foam from the bow. It was one of those nights when a silver moon and towering clouds make the sky into a vast cathedral. He felt very much alone yet not lonely, the only person privileged to see the moon and the clouds and feel the power of the wind racing across huge spaces in the dark. Was that what Gray had given him — a meaning for his life? He'd walked with a President, a man who knew all the secrets, a man whose name would be in the books long after all the grifters and the boosters and the wiseguys were dead and forgotten ...

He was shivering. Back in the warm passageway, he heard the steady hum that permeated the whole ship, all the way up from the mighty engines and the roaring furnaces. Stewards and officers and sailors with CUNARD on their chests greeted him respectfully. He was waiting for one of them to sneer, 'Cut the crap, Pomeroy, you're only a drifter and a vagrant who's scuffled in ratholes all the way across America and up to Dawson City with all the other bums and dreamers, you don't belong here.' But no, they saluted him. They asked if there was anything they could do for him. A first-class ticket, that's all it took.

Again he passed her cabin door. Probably she was at dinner. Approaching the drawing room, he heard somebody playing the piano. He went in. The long room had satinwood walls, cedar mouldings, a pine ceiling with ivory inlay and gilding, a Persian carpet, ottomans, rich drapes and upholstery. The piano was at the other end. Through the angle of the raised lid, he saw blond hair cut short and a clean-shaven face. He sat on a velvet chair by the big brass fireplace. Flames from the coal fire glistened on Persian tiles.

At first the music sounded heavy and out of key. Classical, he supposed, no tune his ear could pick up. Then it began to make some kind of sense, deep notes for tragedy, a lighter theme for contrast. He'd never heard music like that. The sound began to create pictures; the deep notes came from somebody in despair, the light theme rippled like a waltz from long long ago, from a dream maybe, as if somebody was telling you that tragedy was inevitable, that happiness was way back in the past when you could still believe it. The music stopped. The blond man came to the fire. He was wearing a black cardigan jacket with silk sleeves and black trousers. He was very straight, not too tall.

'Don't stop for me, I was enjoying that.'

The blond man spoke precise English with a slight accent. 'Ah. Thank you. You like Liszt?'

'I don't know a thing about classical music.'

'Ah — that is why you enjoyed it. I am not a good player. That is why I wait till they are all at dinner. It is not a published work of the composer Liszt. My mother knew his pupil Gollerich. It was written during that time in the Abbe's life when everything seemed tragic, his late period — *Sunt Lacrimae Rerum,* a line from Virgil's *Aeneid* referring to the fall of Troy. Liszt had in mind the collapse of the Hungarian revolution many people find it disturbs them.'

'Well, it sure isn't "Come into the Garden, Maud", but I thought you played it pretty well — '

'Only because you know nothing about classical music.' They both smiled. The movement of the blond man's cheeks made visible a dull white scar roughly parallel to his jawbone. 'You will have a drink with me, yes?'

'Why, sure.'

He had a bottle of cognac, which he fetched from the other end of the room. His back was as straight as a board and he walked with a slight roll, like an old-time horse-soldier. He was around forty. He rang for the steward to fetch another glass. He poured from the bottle, then shook his head.

'Ach, how disgraceful of me.' He brought his hand down from the high mantelpiece, clicked his heels together and bowed slightly from the waist. 'Uwe Lang-Gaevernitz, of the Imperial German diplomatic corps.'

Pomeroy, who knew how to swallow without moving his Adam's apple, didn't even risk swallowing. He stood up. 'John Pomeroy ...' They shook hands. He hesitated. '... of the United States foreign service.'

It sounded stupid to him but Lang-Gaevernitz didn't laugh.

'A fellow diplomat! *Wunderbar* — wonderful! So. This is a coincidence. Would you care for a cigar?' He had them in a special pocketcase.

'Thanks, I don't use tobacco.'

'It relaxes me. Ah — the English with their coal fires, no? We have even copied them on our German liners now. The whole world copies the English style; they are the masters, no?'

'I guess they think that.'

'Ah — but you got them off your back, yes? The Boston Tea Party! I learned that at school. Did you know you Americans almost decided to adopt German as your native language? Yes, that's true. Many, many Germans live in the United States. I have been visiting my brother, he lives in New York State, Poughkeepsie. Is this your first posting to Europe?' .

'It's my first posting to anywhere! Third secretary at the London embassy — '

'Ah. So — London. That is where I am the cultural attache, a minor official. Imperial Germany, I regret to say, does not place great importance on culture. He shrugged. 'For me it is ideal, however. I have no interest in the hypocrisy of orthodox diplomacy and. international politics. As a young man I wished to become a concert pianist, but I come from an old Prussian military family ...'

He could hardly believe this was Gray's dangerous master-spy. The most pleasant fellow he'd run into for years?

'... no, I was shoved into it by my father, he's an old buddy of President Roosevelt's.' Lang-Gaevernitz looked impressed. 'That's how things work with us, the spoils system they call it. My daddy didn't want me marrying this girl I got involved with in Baltimore so he had me enlist in the foreign service. He wants to improve my character — I'm supposed to live on the goddam salary. A hundred bucks a month — wouldn't pay for a night in a Kansas City cathouse! I don't know how the hell I 'm going to get by in London, England.'

Lang-Gaevernitz gave him serious look. 'I think you are going to be In the most terrible danger in London, Mr Pomeroy.'

'What kind of danger, Herr Lang-Gaevernitz?'

The German's broad pink face smiled suddenly, as if a switch had been thrown. 'A handsome young American diplomat? Unless, of course, you are married — ?'

'Hell no!'

'London is a mad whirl, a truly scandalous place, capital of the greatest empire the world has ever known. By comparison, Rome was a provincial market town, but the same pagan attitudes are there — so with pride and arrogance — '

'I hear they kinda look down their noses at us American hicks.'

'The English look down their noses at everyone! Imperial Germany they refer to as Our Dear Gretchen! But these decadent English snobs are finding life harder in this new modern world. Money is opening many doors, other nations are challenging their industrial and military supremacy — '

'I don't think my lousy salary's going to open many doors...'

'A poor American?' Lang-Gaevernitz smiled at this paradox. 'I am sure you will be a great success and perhaps I can help you. Get in touch with me when you settle down. I would be honoured to introduce you to my own modest circle — '

'You know any of the staff at the American embassy?'

'Oh yes. Ellington Fairbairn, the second secretary, is a man of culture. I have met Ambassador Fry at social functions.'

'So — tell me about them.'

Lang-Gaevernitz hesitated, waving away cigar smoke. 'It is not for me to make personal comments on your superiors — '

'That bad, are they?'

'Oh no. Ellington Fairbairn is a professional diplomat of the highest ability — in many ways. They say he knows everybody worth knowing in London society. The junior members I am not so familiar with ...'

Pomeroy gave him a nudging look. 'Never mind the juniors — what's the dirt on Fry?'

'Well ... shall I merely say that yours is a young country still learning the essential purposes of diplomacy? Its choice of ambassadors seems based on principles that are not always clear to those of us in the more traditional mould of — no, it is not correct for me to make judgements that might prejudice your attitudes to your own superiors.' The German frowned. 'One thing, Mr Pomeroy — for your own guidance. They may not like you having a friend in the German embassy, better perhaps you don't inform them that we have become acquainted. The diplomatic world is very small and very suspicious.'

'Is that because there's going to be some kind of war?' he asked naively. The German raised his eyebrows. 'They kept talking about war back in Washington.'

'Russia and Japan are mobilizing for war over Manchuria — is that the war they were talking about?'

The question hung in the air just as tangibly as the blue cigar smoke. He was being pumped! He shrugged indifferently. 'All that stuff reminded me of boring old lectures at West Point — anyhow, America is a neutral country, we don't want to be involved in Europe's wars.'

(Was that a straw in the wind Berlin would hear about? When did the foot burning start?)

Lang-Gaevernitz gave him an appreciative look. 'So, you were at the famous military academy?'

'Another of my daddy's schemes. I made it to lieutenant in the Sixth Cavalry, then I resigned one jump ahead of a court-martial. Boy, did I hate the army!'

'That is a coincidence — my father, too, wanted his son to be a military hero. I was in the navy.' The German sighed and passed the cognac. They raised glasses. 'Oh yes, there will be war, it is inevitable. Why should we delude ourselves that a new type of man will emerge in the twentieth century? Nobody ever *wants* war but ... there is a war party in my own country — in England, Sir John Fisher of the Royal Navy talks openly of war with Germany — always the call is for bigger warships, bigger guns ... to keep the peace, of course, that's what they tell us. I try to delude myself I can escape the savage fantasies of the warrior caste; I occupy my life with music and paintings and literature but . . . none of us can really escape, Mr Pomeroy. Liszt knew it, in the end it is all music for the grave ...'

Pomeroy stared at the fire. He remembered that first night in Gray's office. His feet were wet, he'd been hauled in out of the rain, after that it was too late to escape ...

There was no blinding moment of revelation. The elation came on him gradually, far beyond anything he'd ever known. This wasn't some jingled bullshitter sitting across a back room poker table. They d both told lies, but he knew it, Lang-Gaevernitz didn't. A different kind of war, Gray called it, fought with smiles and lies over cognac in first class comfort ...

You didn't want to escape, Pomeroy, all your life you've been looking for this kind of war ...

' ... but surely you people over there in Europe are always slaughtering each over some goddam thing or another?'

Lang-Gaevernitz lost a little of his geniality. 'Americans are different? Crossing an ocean is enough to change human nature? America may be a young nation, but your Civil War may have given us a vision of the future. I read military history as a cadet in the Imperial Navy. Total destruction as a strategy — that was what Grant and Sherman gave the world. If Americans could do that to each other over black slaves, subhumans, what are they capable of when the issues are national survival — or national supremacy? I saw no reluctance on America's part to use armed might against Spain and to hell with moral considerations! What will happen when America realizes the real issues in the world we are facing — not trivial bickerings over trade and frontiers but the forthcoming struggle between the advanced races and the teeming millions beyond the ramparts of civilization! Race survival for those destined to —' He threw up his hands and shrugged in apology. 'I told you, none of us is immune to the infection, Mr Pomeroy.'

'John, please.'

'Ah, yes, of course. Uwe. Yes, I like American informality. And *your* enthusiasm for new ideas, all these inventions from Mr Edison. Amazing. I daresay you are keeping an eye on this Italian fellow Marconi they have on board —'

'Oh, that Italian guy I saw in the dining room With a bunch of bigwigs in fancy uniforms?' . . .

'He is doing experiments with telegraphy, sending messages Without a cable —'

'How the hell can you send messages without a cable? Who's he goldbricking?'

The German brought out his pocket watch. 'It's later than I thought.' He stood up and raised his glass. 'Let me give you a toast. To your enjoyable discovery of Europe and your successful career as an American diplomat.'

'Gee — what can I say? Thanks, Uwe.'

Lang-Gaevernitz clicked his heels, bowed and left.

He came to attention. Clicking his heels together, he raised his glass to the empty room. 'Gentlemen, a toast. To John Stockley Pomeroy, an American diplomat!'

Next morning he was up before seven. Horton had fixed him up with deck shoes. In old pants, blue shirt and towel round his neck, he went out onto the open deck. A blustery wind caught his hair. Smoke from the two massive funnels streaked away under dark clouds. The sea was grey with white horses flecking the crests of the big swells. Making sure nobody was watching, he found a sheltered spot and started his routine by touching his toes one hundred times. He then did one hundred knee bends, ten minutes' running in place, fifty backsprings from a standing position, one hundred pushups, five minutes' shadow-boxing. During the night, in shame and embarrassment, he'd remembered telling Gray why he liked *Oliver Twist* . He could've cut his tongue out. As punishment, he forced himself to do another fifty push-ups. Checking again that he was alone, he finished his workout by going forward smoothly into a handstand. He walked on his hands from one rail to the other. Hearing somebody clapping, he flipped onto his feet. Huddled against the funnel to escape the wind was the young English aristocrat Francis Holborn. He was still wearing evening dress. His good-looking features weren't nearly so pretty with a stubble and muddied eyes.

'Late night, old man?'

'We've just this minute stopped playing poker. I say, you don't have anything in the way of drink in your cabin, do you?'

'What you need's black coffee, old man.' He took Holborn to his cabin and rang the bell for Horton. 'Coffee for two, Horton. I'm just going for a quick wash.' He put on his robe and left Holborn flopped on his foldaway bed that turned into a divan. In the bathroom he sluiced down with hot and cold water and scrubbed himself all over. Coming back to his cabin, he found Horton putting down a tray with tea and crackers — what they called biscuits. The two Englishmen didn't speak to each other across the social barrier. Pomeroy threw his robe on a chair and began to lather his shaving brush. The young Englishman shuddered.

'Need you flaunt all that rude health in my face?'

'How did your game go?'

Holborn cheered up. 'I don't know about my liver but by some miracle I actually won about a hundred smackers.'

'Smackers?You weren't playing for money?'

'You know — a hundred quid ... pounds.'

'What's that — about four hundred dollars? I thought this Devoy fellow was going to eat you alive according to Jesse Hudson Marchbanks, your Texas buddy.'

Holborn looked pained. 'That voice of his! He must've been down about seven or eight hundred and you'd've thought it was prizegiving day! Where do you Americans get all the bloody energy, that's what I'd like to know.' Pomeroy opened his razor and held his jaw to one side. 'Oh well , one is going to hell in several directions, which road one takes is immaterial, I fancy. Don't brandish that razor quite so enthusiastically, it's making my skin twitch!'

He shaved his throat and around his mouth. 'Close your eyes, old man. Devoy as good as Marchbanks made out?'

'By jove, isn't he just! Sooner this floating gluepot reaches Liverpool the better — '

'You don't have to play, you know, there's a good library.'

Holborn laughed through his pain. 'You're not a man of God by any chance?'

'Hell no, Francis, I'm an American diplomat. I take up my post at the London embassy October ten.'

'A diplomat, eh? Yes, Marchbanks thought you were a kill-joy of some kind.'

Pomeroy finished with a few delicate touches under his nose and splashed his face in hot and cold water alternately. 'My old man would sure be amused by that.' He got into white pants and a clean white shirt and sat down . He poured himself some black coffee. 'So — you 're going to hell in several directions at once, huh?'

Holborn was almost proud of his own decadence. 'Wine, women and song, that sort of thing.'

'And playing cards with strangers on a boat?'

'I've lost enough to my damn friends. This can't be any worse!'

'Still, you blue bloods aren't short of a smacker or two, eh?'

Holborn found that amusing. 'If only that were true, John old boy.' He was laughing, then coughing. 'Oh God .. . half the time I wish I were dead. My dear chap, what you have to understand is we're basically parasites, we have no real place in modern society. The French did their aristocrats a favour shoving them under Madame la Guillotine. We have to live on, clinging to our estates, pretending we've some reason for our existence — we're useless! I'm not fit for any sensible occupation. It would be unthinkable for Viscount Holborn of Seaton Delaval to do anything resembling *work*. D'you know, my father has never read a book in his life and he's proud of the fact! Books? Demned rubbish for shiny-arsed clerks and sex-starved spinsters! Now my younger brother, different for him, not being the heir to the title. He was lucky, went into the army, did awfully well against the bloody Boers. He's at the War Office now .. . and I do the rounds and pass the time till my father dies — not that the old devil's going to oblige me in the near future. He's still drinking and hunting and whoring in his seventies, he looks good for another thirty years — by which time the money'll have gone and some bloody grocer will own the land. I'm boring you, old chap — '

'Not at all.'

'What about yourself?'

'Me? Here I am working for Uncle Sam and hearing people think I'm a killjoy! General William B. Pomeroy of Knoxville, Tennessee, would be greatly surprised — '

'Oh? Your father's a general?'

'He fought for Dixie; it didn't payoff too well. He shoved me in the army, but I upped and went to Alaska to look for gold, didn't find any. Moved around some, California, Kansas City, St Louis, New Orleans, you know, just drifting and looking for something, then this job came up because my old man's a pal of Teddy Roosevelt.'

Holborn tried to look suitably impressed, but like all his kind he was wrapped up in his own drama. 'That's most interesting, old chap, yes indeed. Anyway, I'm pretty well flaked out, better be toddling along to my hammock.' He got up with a nice display of hung-over heroism. He was at the door when he hesitated. 'John, when you said that about playing cards with strangers on a boat ...'

'You planning to play some more with them?'

'What else is there to do in the middle of the bloody Atlantic? You know anything about cards, John?'

'I've been cleaned out a few times.'

'My father has had to settle my debts once already this year; that's why he sent me to America — moral regeneration on the open plains, that sort of thing. John — how can you tell if people are crooks?'

'Generally because they do all the winning. All you have to do is say no, Francis.'

'That's the one thing I find quite beyond me!' The young Englishman, whose face was already looking old before the rest of him had grown up, tried to mask his despair behind a mocking smile. 'Oh well, a short life but a sordid one. Sorry for boring you, old man.'

Why waste pity on his kind? They brought all they needed with them.

He missed lunch that day and did a little reading in the library, books that Horton suggested might answer some of his questions. When he wandered into the smoking room around five, he got a cordial greeting from Jesse Hudson Marchbanks. He ordered tea, to the Texan's continued amusement. Something had changed, however.

'John, I surely didn't mean to offend you yesterday, when I said you were too green to play with us? Matter of fact, it's a very friendly little game and if you're in the mood tonight you'll

84

be most welcome, I assure you. We're meeting up after dinner, whaddya say?'

' Thanks, Jesse, but I have a whale of a lot of work to catch up with. Maybe some other time.'

She came into the dining room that night in a shell-pink dress with a high neckline. Colonel Dalrymple gave him a stiff nod but led her farther up the table. It was a simple meal of ten courses during which English toffs on either side of him exchanged gossip about London society while treating him as invisible. Smart people attended cockfights in the Mayfair home of somebody called Frank Lawley of the *Telegraph* . The Portuguese minister to London was nicknamed the Blue Monkey because he had a blue chin and chased everything in skirts. When Thellison, a Swiss financier, cut his grown-up children out of his will and left six million pounds to his grandchildren, his sons used his portrait in oils for pistol practice. He tried to copy their English way of using knife and fork simultaneously and immediately felt all eyes on him, yet when he looked up he became invisible again. He couldn't see her face from where he was sitting. The accents got easier to follow all the time. One old gent with a belly that started under his chin horrified everybody by telling how a lady of his acquaintance had been at a certain shooting party in the country and, bored one morning, had gone down to the library for a book. There she found Lord Desborough giving his loaders some practice in secret. Damned bad form, what? Some sneered, some found it hard to believe of Lord Desborough.

'There something wrong about practising, sir?' asked the naive American.

The fat old party glared at him and humphed. 'S'pose you load your own damned guns in America, eh?'

'Well, sir, you don't have too much choice when those pesky Comanches come whooping down on your wagon train.'

One minute he was invisible, the next he learned the truth of what Price Collier, the American journalist, said — if you cannot be a duke with a large rents roll in England, by all means be an agreeable American, for to one and the other all doors are open. He answered with authority all these questions about the Wild West, his father being General Billy Pomeroy, famous calvary hero of the Indian wars. They were thrilled to hear about blazing six-guns in the sudden-death saloons of Skagway. When he told them he was being posted to the American embassy in London, he saw glances being exchanged. He threw in the name of Andrew Phillips Fry and, sure enough, after a brief display of tact and good manners, a whiff of scandal entered the gossip. These upper-crusty English viewed your average American as a pretty rough customer, and who better to share the jokes with than an agreeable young American who didn't at all mind them laughing at his abysmal ignorance of cutlery protocol? Through the humming. and hawing and hints, he was given to understand that Andrew Phillips figured in London gossip quite a bit. He also heard two names for the first time, those of Sir Oscar Betts and Lady Crediton — close friends of the American ambassador, it seemed. .

Next time he looked along the table, she and her father had gone.

Twenty minutes later, he found Dalrymple and Francis Holborn in the smoking room. The crusty colonel gave him a stiff nod. Holborn maybe regretted having bared his soul that morning and said indifferently, 'Weren't thinking of joining the game, were you?'

'Well, I do have some stuff to write. I guess I could be through in a couple of hours — '

'You stick to your scribblin', Pomeroy,' Dalrymple growled. 'We'll be playin' long past your bedtime. '

'I sure hope so, colonel! '

This time when he knocked on the door of suite 11, she opened the door without looking to see who was there and turned back into the stateroom. 'Shall we play rummy tonight?'

'Miss Dalrymple — '

She looked around quickly, and blushed. 'Oh. I'm sorry. I thought it was — '

'I have to speak with you, Miss Dalrymple,' he said quickly, before she could close the door. 'I believe your father is about to be robbed.'

'*Robbed?* What are you talking about? How could anyone rob him on the *Lucania?'*

'He was playing poker with three men last night and he's gone off to play with them again tonight. I'm pretty sure they're crooks. I thought I should warn you and you could get him out of there before I go see the captain. It'll obviously create one hell of a scandal and — '

'For God's sake!' She leaned out to glance up and down the corridor. 'Must you blare it out for the whole ship to hear?' She gestured urgently for him to come in. He resisted the impulse to walk across her threshold on his hands.

5

'So all you have are vague suspicions?' she said coldly.

'It has all the signs of a gaff, Miss Dalrymple. I guess you're not too familiar with how these grifters operate — '

'Grifters? Shills? Working the tubes? Gaff? It's your American expressions I'm not familiar with, Mr Pomeroy. Aren't you being a trifle melodramatic over a harmless game of cards?'

She was still standing between him and one of the bedroom doors, the one that was open when he came in. Before she closed it, he caught a glimpse of a brass bed and the trimmings of a lady's boudoir. The high-ceilinged stateroom was furnished in satinwood and mahogany, with the usual divan that folded down into a bed, and two armchairs. On the table was a book with a kid-leather page mark, an open bottle of wine and two glasses.

'I've seen men losing a hundred thousand dollars or more in these harmless little games, Miss Dalrymple. '

She was as tall as himself, slim in proportion to her height but by no means frail under the silk that sculpted the contours of her bosom and hips. She came to the table and picked up her book. Face on, her pulled back hair suggested someone slightly severe, but in profile the delicate wisps of chestnut under her chignon made her look younger and vulnerable. 'Have you read this, Mr Pomeroy? It's *The Four Feathers* by A. E. W. Mason, very popular novel this year in London, full of intrigue and adventure and romance — '

'You think I'm making all this up, Miss Dalrymple?' His little bow owed a lot to Lang-Gaevernitz. 'I apologize for bothering you, I see you're expecting company.'

She let him get to the door. 'At least let me offer you a glass of wine, Mr Pomeroy — '

Thanks, but I have to catch the captain before he hits the sack — that's American for going to bed.'

'I'm expecting my *maid* — how on earth do you think one could get in and out of these ridiculous clothes without help, Mr Pomeroy? '

He made like a man learning something new. 'You drink alone at night with your coloured maid? Gosh, and I thought America was democratic. Well well well.'

'She isn't coloured, Mr Pomeroy — we're that much ahead of you in democratic habits. She's travelling second-class; she sneaks up here at night when daddy's out of the way. We're very good friends, Letitia and I—'

'Letitia? I love your English names. My cousin Augusta — the Baltimore brick heiress? Her maid's called Cora, she is coloured and they don't drink wine together in the evening but I'll drop her a line; she likes to keep up with all these English fashions. Mind you, it's going to be a shock for Aunt Harriet — '

'You're laughing at me, Mr Pomeroy.'

'Why not at all, Miss Dalrymple. I'm wondering why you're so scared of me going to the captain ... it is Miss Dalrymple, isn't it? Daughter of Colonel James Dalrymple?'

'Are you insinuating something?'

'I believe the term is incognito in England. In America it's more usually alias. The last time I saw that dodge with the wallet to hook a sucker it was an old bunco artist called Doc Baggs. You probably aren't familiar with the Soapy Smith gang of Skagway, but Doc Baggs was a genius. You know he invented the goldbrick game? Doc Baggs and the colonel would have a lot in common, if they could understand each other's lingo and Doc was out of the pen. In the end it all boils down to the monte man's tripe and keister. I guess I'm insinuating that you and the colonel are strictly phonus-balonus. I don't know what would be called in England — '

She'd listened all through without any change of expression. Now she came right up to him and slapped him on the face.

'That would be called a foul calumny.' The second time she really belted him. 'What do you say to that, Mr bloody Pomeroy?'

'I'd say you struck the first blow, Catherine — '

He got his arms around her silken waist and kissed her. She did better than struggle; she didn't move a muscle. Her body was firm and supple and she smelled of flowers. With a pleasant smile that was so goddam English and insolent and killingly polite, she said, 'Is that your seduction technique, Mr Pomeroy?'

'Forget it, I — '

Somebody knocked at the door.

'It's Letitia,' she hissed. 'Quickly, get in there.'

She was pulling him towards the bedroom door. He resisted. 'I don't want to hide — ' She pushed him through the door into the luxuriously furnished bedroom and gestured fiercely for him to keep quiet.

He listened at the door but heard only the constant hum of the ship. There was a lock with a brass key. He eased the key out and got down on one knee. He saw a flash of pink silk and then another skirt was coming straight towards the keyhole, a brown skirt with folds. He jumped quickly. The doorknob turned. The wardrobe! He took one step and his knee cracked like a rifle. He froze.

He was still standing there, back to the door, when it opened.

'You were saying, Mr Pomeroy — ?'

He rubbed his knee. 'Okay, so you drink with your maid. What are you, some kind of rich eccentric?'

'No, I am a socialist. I also campaign for women's emancipation. In America I met Susan B. Anthony and Samuel Gompers. I tried to meet Carrie Nation but — '

'You should've tried the saloon.'

She made no move to let him out of the bedroom. 'You look positively scared to death. Is that because you think my father and I are crooks? Frightened I'm packing a derringer under my garter?'

'Who else did you meet — Chicago May?' He made to pass her.

'Oh no, I want an explanation. Or would you prefer me to scream for help?'

'Why don't you? And I'll tell them to look up that book in the ship's library — the one with all the names of British officers?'

'The army list? Ah — you looked up Colonel James Dalrymple and he wasn't in it?'

'I checked every goddam regiment and the retired list.'

She burst out laughing!

It went on for some time. Just as he had visions of her turning hysterical and crewmen smashing down the door to rescue her, she flopped on the bed. Her long skirt rose over her white satin shoes. She was wearing purple cashmere stockings that clashed with her pink dress. More of her thick chestnut hair was coming free in little wisps. Finally she got her breath back. Her sides were sore from laughing. He sat down beside her on the bed. 'You're very lovely for a socialist, Catherine.'

He had her flat on her back before she knew what was happening. She looked up at him defiantly. His fingers caressed her rose-petal cheek.

'What are you doing, Mr Pomeroy?' she demanded.

'The sea air has stimulated my imagination, Miss Dalrymple.'

'I could scream — '

'From you it would sound like a rhapsody — '

'Will you leave this bedroom immediately?'

'What will you do if I don't?'

'I'll have you arrested for indecent assault — '

'How do you feel about a decent assault?'

He pinned her down and kissed her ear and her cheek, and her chestnut hair. There was some resistance, as you would want from an English lady.

'You had this in mind all the time, you swine,' she hissed.

'Right from that first time on deck! That white dress, that big hat, your hair all tied up at the back — that voice! Shoodent we coal a deckshtard, fahtha?'

'Don't make fun of the way I speak, you bloody American. What kind of bloody diplomat are you anyway?'

'I'm studying protocol — '

'What's wrong with you? Jesus Christ — '

'This administration doesn't favour strong language, ma'am — '

'—will I have to call for Letitia to get this bloody dress off?'

An English lady. A rose-petal complexion. Purple stockings under pink silk. So demure, so delicately coarse. Frilly white drawers. Smooth white shoulders. All smelling like flowers. 'There are certain things a lady must take care of first — all I expected tonight was a game of rummy with Letitia.'

He went to lock the outside door and waited. And waited.

Just as he was remembering that the bedroom had another way out into the passageway, she opened the door. She was in her blue satin stays and long purple stockings. She beckoned him inside and locked the door. When she saw that he was hesitant about undressing, she came to peel off his coat and suspenders. 'It's all right,' she assured him as she began to unbutton his trousers at the waist, 'I was married, you know.' It wasn't his concept of the way a man should behave but he had never been with a woman like her before. She sat on the edge of the bed and eased off her stockings. Her slimly muscled legs were lightly downed by soft brown hair. She unhooked her stays and let them dangle from her upraised hand before flicking them across the room. They came into each other's arms, stretched full length on the cool, silken bedcover. Her arms encircled his neck as he pulled up her nainsook chemise. An English lady. He kissed her face and her neck and her shoulder and she brought up her firm thigh and white knee to rest on his hip. He stared at her lips as she stroked his hair. 'I've never been with an American man before ... are you very rough?'

'No, I won't be rough — '

'Yes ... be rough, I want you to be rough, be rough with me! Oh God, yes, yes, it's been so long, I want all of you, be rough, be rough, yes, yes, you're so hard, crush me, be rough with me, you bastard, you're so hard. Oh God yes yes *yes!'*

There is a low humming noise throughout the ship. It must come from the big engines way down there below the decks where all the people are. Out through the square window with the velvet curtains are the endless waves of the huge ocean. Fish swim down there in the deep, dark water.

His fingers stroked her knee. Her thick chestnut hair was all over her face and shoulders. He smoothed it back with tender fingers. He kissed her eyelids and her nose and her lips and her neck and her breasts. She sprawled out on her back to let him kiss her stomach and her thighs. He kissed all the way back to her outflung arms. He kissed her arm, her elbow, her wrist, her hand, her fingers. Gussie had jumped free at the first chance. The English lady felt for his head and brought him back to her breasts and face. Her hand stroked down his chest, down his flat belly, stroking and then nipping and teasing and then gently fingering his maleness, her hand coaxing him back to life, her lips nibbling at his ear and his cheek and his nose, her movements becoming more urgent until her legs and arms wrapped around him and they rolled over and she was straddling him, her thick shiny hair brushing across his face, little noises coming from her throat, her eyes hidden by a curtain of hair, enmeshing him, pinning him down, challenging him to accept her control. He had never let himself go like this, never known the absence of guilt and triumph and resentment. This wasn't a contest; he had never known what it could be like when the only memory was of touching lips, when the mind was blank and the eyes saw only her. To please her, to love her, moving at her touch, wanting what she wanted ... my darling, my lovely darling, yes yes ...

She lay on her back, looking up at the ceiling. He studied her in profile. Her forehead was almost straight, her nose had a little bump halfway down, her lips were moist, her white teeth glinted, her throat moved: '... you were right but you were wrong ... on my passport it says I am Catherine, Lady Cameron ... my husband was a lieutenant in the Scots Guards. We were married in the Guards Chapel when he was twenty-four and I was eighteen. He was killed fighting the Boers at Magersfontein, December 12, 1899, making me a widow at the age of nineteen. You don't have to say anything trite, the time for condolences is long past — '

'I was going to say my arm's gone to sleep ... thanks.'

'Colonel Dalrymple isn't my father's name but I swore on the Bible I wouldn't tell anybody on this trip who he really is. He had a breakdown, you see, and we thought a trip right across America and Canada would do us both good. He's always been a bit silly about gambling but he can afford it, anything that provides a diversion and takes his mind off things is a blessing. He is quite important — if you go to the captain and kick up a stink about their game it would be disastrous for his reputation. I can't tell you any more than that — do you believe me?'

'It's a very touching story.'

'You cynical bastard. Go away.'

'You mean that?'

'Don't be laconic. Talk to me properly, hold me, tell me I'm young and lovely and desirable — '

'You're lovely, Catherine — '

'No, *Kate,* call me Kate — '

'You're young and lovely and desirable, Kate, you're the — '

'Don't be tender with me, you bastard! I don't want any bloody pity! If you want me take me, be rough with me. I'm not a lady, I'm a crook and a fake and a trollop who picks up men on ships — I'm a common whore! What do you say to that?' She bared her teeth. 'What's wrong, John? Have I shocked you? Gosh, you Americans, you're really quite prudish and — '

He silenced her with his mouth and her legs were around his waist again and her nails were ripping down his back but he pushed her arms down and when she screwed her eyelids tight shut and clenched her fists and started to struggle violently from side to side he hardened all his muscles and made his body as impervious as stone and she became his soft English lady again and he came into her without pity or tenderness and she gasped and quivered and held onto the runaway stallion for fear of being thrown off and broken, until their bodies were one creature locked tight in a frenzy to devour itself ...

When his eyes opened, her lovely white arms had his head in a gentle embrace, his face at her breasts. She smiled down at him. There was somebody moving about in the stateroom.

She put her finger to his lips. 'It's my father.'

They lay together trying not to laugh out loud as they heard him banging about and cursing. Then another door slammed. She stretched and yawned until her jaw was so extended he could see her tonsils. 'I'm battered and bruised all over.'

'Let me kiss you better all over.'

'It's six o'clock. Shouldn't you be going back to your own cabin?'

'You want me to go?'

'As you please. Daddy will be asleep till lunchtime ...'

He propped himself on his elbow and gazed at her lovely body. The inside of her raised thigh was like satin. She watched his face, making no attempt to hide herself. Even on her back, her breasts were firmly outlined. He kissed them both.

'What about Letitia?' he murmured.

Her hand moved quickly to take hold of his erection. She twisted against him. 'If you're frightened of a lady's maid, I don't think you're going to have much success in London.'

An English lady. A rose-petal complexion that was a little rougher now. Demure eyes that dared him to violate a lady.

'This time I'm going to lie back and close my eyes and think of England,' she said. He guessed it was some kind of joke.

When he had his clothes on and had used her brush to straighten his hair, she checked the passageway and signalled that the coast was clear. He got his hands under her flowing robe and held her naked and kissed her.

'You still think it was a mistake?' he whispered.

'Not while we're at sea — ' and she steered him through the door. He started worrying about that last remark of hers on his way back to the other section. Apart from a few stewards carrying trays, he met nobody in the passageways — the English stewards didn't seem to find anything unusual in a gentleman still dressed for dinner at seven in the morning. Did she mean —

A door behind him opened and he heard the unmistakable voice of Jesse Hudson Marchbanks:

'— I can do that, sure ...'

He looked around. Marchbanks had his back to him, talking to somebody in the cabin. He made it to the next corner without hearing his name called. He saw a door to the deck and stepped out into the wind. His back was stiff and his eyes were bleary. Did she mean it could only happen on the ship? Please, God, don't let us ever reach Liverpool!

When he opened the door again, the passageway was empty. He walked back round the corner and identified the cabin Marchbanks had been leaving... What was Jesse Hudson

Marchbanks doing at seven inß the morning visiting with Uwe Lang-Gaevernitz of the Imperial German diplomatic corps? Getting in on that game suddenly seemed like a duty.

6

On that third day out, she was already lunching with her father but the seats all around them were taken and the best he could manage was a view of her lovely neck from halfway down the next table. The old first class people were now eating against a coming famine, shoving away the pigeon pie and quails packed with *foie gras* and *galantine* of tongue. He had cold chicken in aspic with salad and they asked if he was ill. He saw March-banks on the other side, eating in a booth with a bunch of noisy toffs. The Italian inventor guy arrived with his usual entourage and got a little round of applause from those who appreciated that only that morning, October 6, the *Lucania* had become the world's first ship to have its own daily newspaper. Using a syntonic 'tuned' circuit operating on a 100-metre wavelength, Guglielmo Marconi's wireless telegraphy transmitters at Cape Breton, Nova Scotia, Sagaponack, Long Island, the Nantucket Lightship and Poldhu in Cornwall, were keeping in contact with the Cunarder all the way across the Atlantic. The first news item was the resignation of the Duke of Devonshire from Prime Minister Balfour's government in London. This seemed to excite the oldsters. The duke, they explained, had quit the Conservative cabinet over the freetrade question. He kept his eye on Kate. Joe Chamberlain, they told him, wanted to tighten Britain's bonds with the empire nations by discriminatory taxes on imports from non-imperial countries, which basically meant higher food prices. The Duke of Devonshire believed in open trade — cheap food. First Joe and now the duke had resigned to fight out this momentous issue. Asked where President Roosevelt stood on this matter, the tactful diplomat said the White House Was keeping a careful eye open. 'Where Britain leads, the rest of the world follows.' They liked him for saying that and enjoyed giving him more gossip about people he would meet in London. Ambassador Fry, it seemed, was prominent in a *certain section* of society. Subtle English tones said more than words Fry's friends were not quite top drawer, was the implication. Innocently, he asked about Sir Oscar Betts, learning that he was a big-time financier and industrialist who'd started life as Oskar Beitz.

'The King seems to enjoy the company of these colourful chaps,' somebody said. The merest twitch of an eyebrow told him that the King was playing unfair, making friends of these rich cosmopolitans who, if they weren't actually Jewish, were of European origin and therefore *dubious,* to put it mildly. He excused himself when he saw Kate and her father walking down between the tables.

He caught up with Kate in her stunning white dress as she and her father were deciding whether to go out on deck. She gave him a little frown, but he spoke anyway.

'Colonel Dalrymple — Miss Dalrymple — am I wrong or does this ship seem to be rolling some?'

'Some what?' Dalrymple barked.

'It's an American turn of phrase, daddy.' That voice!

'Whose bloody language is it, I'd like to know,' Dalrymple snapped.

'You worried by this news about your Duke of Devonshire, sir?'

Daddy growled and grunted. 'Time the old buffer went. He was best described as a statesman in the last stage of ossification. Joe Chamberlain's the man — if that means anythin' to you, Pomeroy.'

'I'm catching up on British affairs pretty fast, sir.'

Her eyes narrowed. Dalrymple said he had to see a man about a dog. She said she would be on deck. Pomeroy followed her out into the open passageway under the bridge. The wind gusted against her long white dress, outlining her hips and legs. She held onto her hat, the sauceboat style with feather wings. The sea was in a turmoil, white foam lashing off the crests of rolling troughs. Even this high he felt spray on his face. Little wisps of loose hair lashed delicately against her neck.

'Aren't you cold?' he asked.

'Not at all. I'm glad you're catching up on British affairs.'

'What's wrong, Kate?'

Two gents in thick tweed overcoats came along the passageway. They raised their black derbies to her. The wind billowed up her dress. She slapped it down and led him to the comparative shelter of a lifeboat on davits. Another gust forced her to turn her back on him. The moment she felt his hand on her waist, she turned sharply. 'I want you to promise you won't come to our suite tonight — or any other night.'

'Why not?'

'I am not one of those smart society sluts who indulge in clandestine affairs to defeat boredom. I have a very busy life. Some of us are meeting in Manchester this month to launch a proper movement for women's emancipation .. .' Stronger gusts made them move closer against the clinkered planks of the lifeboat. 'Last night was a mistake. I will not let it deteriorate into a habit. Give me your word you won't come anywhere near my cabin tonight.'

'You have my word.'

She frowned suspiciously.

Dalrymple came on them huddled in the shelter of the lifeboat. She gave him a sweet smile and took her father's arm. He watched the.wind pushing the white dress against her willowy body. English ladies, it seemed, were not permitted to shiver. Then the wind moved her skirts and he saw that she was wearing black ankle boots and woollen long johns as well, under the white summer dress. No wonder the sun never set on the British Empire.

Marchbanks was taking champagne in the smoking room.

'Wet your whistle, John old buddy.'

'I didn't sleep much last night, I'm going to get my head down — '

'Yeah — then you'll be bright-eyed and bushy-tailed for a little action tonight, huh?'

'Well . . . I'm not much of a gambling man — '

'You'll have a fine old time! See me at dinner. Devoy likes to keep it kind of quiet. Oh yeah — we use British money. Now, whaddya say, John old buddy?'

'Looks like I'd better rob the piggybank.'

Marchbanks caressed his shoulder with the fat hand of friendship. 'Don't you all worry about the money, your old pal Jesse will look after you.'

He changed two thousand dollars into an assortment of British bills and gold coins at the purser's cabin and spent half an hour having Horton teach him about British money. At $4.86 to the pound, his two thousand bucks came to just over four hundred pounds, fifty of it in small gold sovereigns with the head of King Edward VII. The Bank of England bills were big and white, with black lettering and a Britannia seal, important looking stuff to remind lesser breeds just who owned a quarter of the world and didn't rate the other three quarters. He had had fifty pounds in fives, one hundred fifty pounds in tens and twenties, one fifty and one hundred. Horton said they also had bank notes for two hundred, five hundred and one thousand pounds. The average British worker earned around one hundred pounds a year.

Horton gone, he laid out the coat of his dinner suit. From one of his suitcases he got a leather tobacco pouch containing scissors, sewing needles, black thread, thimble, and a little nickel-plated box with two compartments. Each compartment had a lid with a small hole. He cut open a few stitches at the hem of his coat. The box had small flanges to take a thread. He inserted it upside down under the coat lining and stitched it firmly in position. When he put on the coat and stood before the

101

wardrobe mirror, the bulge was hardly visible. Casually fingering the hem of the coat, he brought up his right hand. There was an oily blue daub on the tip of his forefinger. He wiped it off on a towel and this time when he touched the box, his fingertip had a small red daub.

Up there in Dawson City, One Eye Riley the mad gambler was asked, 'Is it true you regard poker as a matter of life or death?'

He replied, 'Hell no, cards is serious.'

From the first time his fingers caressed a deck and found the *perfect* shape, real life, so-called, became stuff that interrupted the Game. Life and Death were not yours to control but with the cards in your hand Fate became your own business. The real world so-called was that shadowy void at your back and nothing obliged you to look over your shoulder. Sometimes you stopped to sleep and change your clothes and get yourself a new bankroll, but real time so-called had no other meaning you could ever discover. Along the way you sometimes met a woman who tempted you to admit it was only playing cards for money; love so-called. It never seemed to last; maybe it was too dangerous.

7

A strong whiff of death ...

He arrived at suite 40 a few minutes before eleven. Following instructions, he let some noisy diners clear the passageway before knocking; Marchbanks wanted to protect the steward whom he'd tipped for the key of an unoccupied suite so they could play discreetly without interruptions, each free to come and go as he pleased.

(Just as bunco artists usually pick an anonymous hotel room to clinch the deal — no witnesses, no traces.)

Marchbanks let him in. Dalrymple and Holborn were standing at a side table with bourbon, Scotch whisky, brandy, chilled Rhine wine in an ice bucket, a tray of neat sandwiches under a stiff linen napkin. He asked for bourbon and water.

'I knew you weren't one of these temperance fiends we read about. I *knew* you were a regular sport, John old buddy!'

Momentarily shielding the drinks table, he checked the gleaming folds of linen, an obvious place to stash a rigged deck for the old switcheroo. He didn't find one. Maybe they were counting on lavish booze to do the job.

He raised his glass. 'Nice of you fellows to ask me in on your game.'

Dalrymple, stiff and gaunt in an old-fashioned dinner suit with tails, his starched collar so high and tight it looked set to slice through his scrawny neck, grunted something. (Colonel James Dalrymple, who wasn't a colonel and wasn't called Dalrymple but who travelled with a lovely daughter, who also had a fake name, even if she was his daughter.)

'Our old buddy Jesse was telling us we're due the most frightful shellacking from the great Devoy,' Holborn drawled. He looked a deal sleeker this time of night, Francis, Viscount Holborn of Seaton Delaval, who was going to hell in several directions. (It was a lot of name for one guy, but it was listed in a library reference book recommended by Horton, *Debrett's Peerage.)*

'Devoy's something of a mystery man,' Marchbanks said, with just the right touch of melodrama. 'He's from Australia but the rumour is he's the illegitimate son of some titled personage, maybe even of royal blood. I happen to know — '

'The bugger drove young Milconna to suicide, didn't he?' Dalrymple growled. Marchbanks was quick to the defence (Jesse Hudson Marchbanks, just a hairy-assed cattleman from Texas who happened to be on calling terms with one of Imperial Germany's top secret agents.)

'You'll hear a lot of stories about Devoy in the fashionable casinos and hotels of Europe. Sure, Lord Milconna, the young Irish blueblood, cut his throat in Monte Carlo after losing fifteen thousand pounds to Devoy in a private game of ecarte — he was already in deep with the moneylenders.'

'Trust an Irish aristocrat to take the easy way out,' drawled Holborn.

'Milconna's family tried to bring a case against Devoy in London, but he was cleared completely. Fifteen thousand is nothing to Devoy. I happen to know he has real estate in New South Wales worth twenty times that. Man like that, professional gambler, he lives by his reputation or he's finished in the circles that count. Sure, we may all lose a bundle to him, but we'll have been beaten fair and square by a king among gamblers!' (Good old Jesse. Your pal. Even warned you against the Man, what could be fairer? First he steered you to the game, then his creepy little tale had you believing Devoy was unbeatable before a card was dealt but think of it as a privilege.)

Holborn was obviously the prime pigeon, but Lang-Gaevernitz wasn't involved with a cardsharp gang for a cut of the jake. Gray said that cooking up scandals was a favourite blackmail ploy of these secret intelligence agencies. Maybe Holborn as an English aristocrat was worth something to the

Germans. As for himself, no puzzle there: they'd only asked him into the game when he let it be known he was with the US foreign service. All he had to do now was let them clean him out, then see what Lang-Gaevernitz had in mind for him. That was all, play to lose!

They waited five minutes or so before somebody knocked. Holborn got there first and made a little bow: 'Gentlemen — Charles Devoy, esquire!'

A whiff of death.

It came into the stateroom along with the famous gambler. Like a delicate chill, it hovered above the red damask where five gentlemen in formal evening wear made the closed circle of the table.

He was a dignified man of average height, dark skin that bordered on the swarthy, deepset brown eyes, age around thirty-five or maybe a little older when you realized his hair was too black to be natural. Under expensive tailoring, he was built for heavier work than dealing cards around. The deepset eyes looked out from a fixed smile and told you that all your secrets were known. .

Marchbanks did the honours. 'Charles — my very. good friend John Pomeroy of our American diplomatic bureau.'

'A pleasure to meet you, Pomeroy.'

'Likewise, Devoy.'

The connection with Lang-Gaevernitz began to make sense just looking at him! Marchbanks produced three decks and they took their seats. Marchbanks asked Dalrymple to pick which deck. (It never occurred to suckers that *all* the decks could have been doctored and the seals replaced. Some of these high-class operators had their own printing plates.)

Being the naive diplomat, he sat with his back to the stateroom's only mirror. Marchbanks was on his left, Dalrymple facing him, then Devoy with his back to the curtained window, then Holborn on his right. There was a lamp above the table; the rest of the stateroom was in sombre shadow. Dalrymple broke open the seal. The cards were blue-backed, fancy scroll-work around naked goddesses.

(Intricate scrollwork gave plenty for scope of sections of line to be painted in or coloured over. You couldn't detect these without a fast ripple through the whole deck, then the altered bits would leap about in front of your eyes like those little stickmen kids draw in the corners of school books.)

'Last night we made it a five-pound ante, fifty-pound limit. That may be too steep for you, Mr Pomeroy,' Devoy said politely.

'I don't require special treatment.'

(Insinuating the square john was out of his depth usually provoked him into rash bets to prove his virility.)

When he saw how much the others were laying out, he grimaced. 'I hope I can come to grips with this British money. A pound's about a fin ... ' He picked up a gold sovereign. 'One pound, right?' He twisted the small gold coin between his finger and thumb. 'So that's King Edward, eh? Back home we call him Edward the Caresser — it true he has the old roving eye, colonel?'

'Vulgarity comes easily to you bloody Americans.'

Holborn had no reverence for his monarch. As they cut for deal, he said, 'Edward the Caresser, very apt. Y'know, at his coronation the old bugger had so many mistresses present in Westminster Abbey their pews were called the royal loosebox!'

'Cut it out, Holborn,' Dalrymple growled.

'I'm not blaming old Bertie, the Queen's as deaf as a post and none too bright — '

'Runnin' down the royal family in front of foreigners is not my idea of conduct from a gentleman!' Dalrymple pointed at Holborn. 'I won't have it, y'hear? His Majesty is known to me personally.' (A shill claiming to be friends with the Kind of England, now that was a touch of class, yessir.)

Devoy twisted off his big gold ring. 'I make it a rule not to wear this during play,' he explained. 'I might accidentally get a reflection off the underside of a card during my deal. I've learned to be meticulous about such things.'

(Now, what could be more honest than that? Except that he placed the big shiner on the tablecloth slightly to his left, an even better location for a mirror.)

Holborn won the cut for deal. From the start, their styles were clear. Holborn was mad to bet and showed no common sense — but maybe, like a lot of his type, losing gave him more pleasure because people were sorry for him. Devoy played the way you'd expect from a professional: doing nothing rash without a reason — namely, to keep them guessing. Dalrymple was so anxious to win that he telegraphed the strength of his hands by the opening and closing of his free eye. Marchbanks was just a cattleman on a spree, wanting the excitement of it all more than the small change. As for himself, he played the Stonewall Jackson game, establishing himself as a nervous tightwad who only bet on sure things.

On his own first deal, he shuffled amateurishly, giving himself time to establish there were no strippers in the deck, high cards shaved at one end or in the middle to guide expert fingers at the cut. Neither could he see any daub smudges on the backs of the cards.

That time around, Dalrymple drew one card and couldn't wait to raise. Everybody else folded, leaving Holborn in. Dalrymple was furious when the other Englishman called him sooner than he wanted, and banged down a full house. 'I could practically see those aces flashing at me from your monocle,' Holborn drawled.

'Anybody ever told you you're a confounded smart aleck, Holborn?' Dalrymple snapped. Marchbanks gathered the deadwood and loose cards for his deal and said, 'Just a friendly little game, boys.'

With Dalrymple and Holborn tangling, and Devoy lighting a black cheroot, only Pomeroy was watching as Marchbanks picked up three aces from the table and calmly put them together at the bottom of the deck. (That, of course, was when rabbits and pigeons and square johns were too busy kicking up about the last pot to pay attention, the key moment when the card-sharp selected high cards for stacking.) He watched the Texan's fat hands shuffling them, and it stood out like a burning barn on a high hill, milking 'em off top and bottom to get the aces placed for the deal. Then the ripple shuffle that interlaced the cards at one end only, the two half-decks being forced apart again when he boxed the deck exactly as it had been.

'Cut if you will John,' Marchbanks said. Reminding himself he was here to play pigeon, he cut as square johns always did, halfway down the deck. He left the two half-decks for March-banks to pick up.

The Texan got the top stack in his left hand at the edge of the table and pulled in the bottom stack with his right hand. To the innocent eye, the bottom stack now went on top, but — if you knew what to watch for, you saw a quick movement of his left thumb turning the top stack over in his palm so that the bottom half went back on the bottom again.

If there was any doubt, the way the Texan's left hand held the deck for dealing proved it; thumb on top forcing the cards slightly askew, forefinger controlling the top end, the other three fingers completing the lock. The mechanic's grip, the one you needed to control the cards and deal second card or off the bottom.

Devoy was the man — Marchbanks was the worker!

(Suckers would watch the famous gambler for fancy stuff, but he could play a straight game, because his agent had given him the cards. Like any other bunco dodge, it all hinged on making sure the suckers never suspected they were partners.)

There was a lot of betting and straddling before the draw. Dalrymple asked for one card, meaning he had two pairs, or a bobtail hand needing one for a flush or a straight. Devoy drew four cards and sucked his teeth. Holborn stood pat, already choosing which bill to open with, which was no surprise at all. Pomeroy was holding a pair of nines. The kicker card was an ace. He kept it and asked for two cards. He found himself looking at the pair of eights from Dalrymple's last full house. There was maybe four hundred pounds, in the pot, coming on for two thousand dollars, almost three years' earnings for the average American man when Holborn spread out his three aces; the same three from Dalrymple's last hand.

'That beats two pairs, I guess,' said the naive diplomat, showing his cards. Dalrymple put down a flush in diamonds one at a time and started to recite poetry!

'Ye mariners of England!
That guard our native seas;
Whose flag has braced, a thousand years,
The battle and the breeze!'

Marchbanks whistled. Holborn stared at the five diamonds. Dalrymple's big bony hand dragged in the gold coins and the white bills. Holborn kicked back his chair and slouched to the liquor table. He looked shaken. He kept looking at Dalrymple and frowning as he poured himself four fingers of whisky and came back to the table,

'Fond of poetry, are you, Dalrymple?' Then he, too began to recite:

'Stormed at with shot and shell,
Boldly they rode and well,
Into the jaws of Death, Into the mouth of Hell,

Rode the six hundred.'

"The Charge of the Light Brigade" by Tennyson — thought you'd know that one, Dalrymple?' '

'Don't be ridiculous, man, course I know it:'

Pomeroy saw Devoy's mouth going tight. Marchbanks said, with mock severity, 'I'm an uncultured sonofabitch. Let's cut the poetry crap, Francis.' '

Holborn's eyes were still on Dalrymple's gaunt face. 'Perhaps you don't like being reminded of our heroic military follies, Dalrymple. You see, John, we English absolutely glory in our military incompetence. We call it muddling through.'

'You talk a great deal of rot, Holborn,' Dalrymple growled.

They hit Holborn again around one thirty. Marchbanks's deal of course. Holborn had maybe learned something; he let them do the raising and once or twice squinted at his cards to see if he was risking too much on a bad hand.

Pomeroy stayed in till he had less than one hundred pounds left in fives and tens and gold sovereigns. He was holding three of a kind but folded. He went to the liquor table and fixed himself more water than bourbon. Passing behind Holborn, he saw his hand, two aces, two jacks. Dalrymple passed. Devoy raised again. Holborn saw eighty pounds. Marchbanks saw eighty and raised fifty. By now there was close to six hundred pounds in the pot. Holborn flicked through his remaining bills. I'm running a trifle short here, pity the damned purser's cabin is closed.'

Marchbanks was already pulling a big bundle of hundreds from his inside pocket. 'What do you want, Francis? Five hundred?'

'Make it the round thou, there's a good chap.'

'I'm sorry, I don't play against borrowed money.' Devoy put down his cards. 'It's one of my personal rules. I believe everybody should stand or fall by what they bring to the table. Borrowing money is a temptation to lose more than you can afford.'

'What damned business is it of yours what I can afford?'

Devoy looked at him steadily, The rest of the world might be impressed by these high muck-a-mucks, but his rules applied here. 'No personal imputation, Holborn. Gambling is my business — the slightest suggestion of irregularity and people will balk at sitting down with me. People of distinction I mean, people like yourself.'

'Would it be okay if Francis gives me his cheque, Charles?' Marchbanks asked anxiously, as if it was all his fault. 'I know he's good for it. I was in the purser's cabin with him when he put his money in the safe.'

'I have no objection to people cashing cheques with each other. That's a closed transaction; it isn't the same as borrowing.'

As he watched Holborn write a cheque for one thousand pounds to the order of J. H. Marchbanks, Pomeroy began to feel angry. When they turned over and Devoy beat them both with a low straight, he couldn't take any more. He got out his wallet and grimaced.

'I've already lost more than I can afford. I guess I'm calling it a night.' Dalrymple fixed him with the monocled eye. 'Sick again, Pomeroy? Needs a strong stomach, this kind of thing.'

The passageways were deserted. Through the steady hum of the ship he could hear the gale. Laughter came from behind a cabin door. He'd been forced to sit there passively and watch the Game and that was where the anger came from . It wasn't crooks at work, or a sucker begging for punishment — he'd been in those kind of games all his life. What he had seen for the first time were things as they really were — illusions, phony bravado, phony triumphs. He'd spent most of his life thinking he was a winner in the Game when he'd only been playing cards with losers, and winners who couldn't win anywhere else!

He hammered a couple of times before he heard her muffled voice.

'Who is it? What do you want?'

He stiffened his jaw. 'Forgot me bloody key,' he growled.

It didn't sound much like the colonel to him, but she opened the door and he was inside before she could close it again. She was in a white cotton nightgown with bare arms. Her hair was all loose. 'Get out of here,' she said calmly.

He closed the door. 'Do you want me to — 'She kicked him where it would have hurt if he'd stood still.

He moved quickly and yanked her off her bare feet. She was already trying to tear his hair out by the roots before they reached the bedroom door.

8

As he dumped her on the bed, she kicked out at his crotch. Her nightie pulled up over her slim white legs. He hauled off his coat and thumbed off his braces. She jumped off the bed and tried to get her fingernails into his eyes. He caught both her wrists and shoved her back onto the bed. He stooped to get his shoes off and she came at him again, sliding forward off the bed so that her nightie pulled all the way up to her slimly mus- cled thighs. He caught hold of her heel and capsized her back onto the bed, and this time he was on top of her to smother her violent struggles.

'Hold still or I'll paddle your backside.'

'I'm not a bloody canoe!' He struggled out of his pants. Still in his starched white shirt and black socks held up by garters, he held her wrists down on the pillows. She glared up at him.

'You bastard,' she hissed, 'you'll go to prison for this.'

'Don't you want to hear how daddy's doing at the poker game?' She twisted her neck to get a bite at his arm. He forced her wrists farther apart. 'Tell me again about your gallant hus- band dying a hero's death in the far-flung empire — '

He let go of her wrists and buried his face in her neck and she twisted and fought and tore at his hair and tried to bite his face. He forced his head up against her jaw. She scratched at his neck and ripped at his scalp. He got his teeth around her nipple through cotton and let her feel how hard he could bite if she didn't stop tearing at his hair. They were locked in vicious combat and nothing changed except that she let his right knee force her thighs apart and her nails were digging into his back and her legs were trying to crush his midriff and her teeth were biting to spur him on and he came into her, all the way in and she was still cursing him and mauling him as he thrust deeper into her in a madness to conquer her and she went on gouging and scratching and snarling 'I hate you! I hate you! ' as they fought each other to a shuddering agony.

They lay locked in each other, rigid, devastated, afraid to let go. His eyes moved up the firm contour of her jaw, the downy outline of her cheek. Her mouth was wide open, saliva on her white teeth, her head thrown back beyond the pillow, her eyes hidden by soft chestnut hair. He put his face against her breast and felt her heart beating. He tenderly kissed her nipple through cotton.

'That ugly old bastard never produced anything as lovely as you. He's your husband, isn't he?'

'My *what?'* She pulled away from him. 'My *husband?'* She held him off and got to her knees and shook him by the ears. That's *disgusting.'*

'He has to be your husband. Why else didn't you tip him off I was wise to their gaff? You couldn't tell him without him finding out about us.'

She tightened her grip on his ears. 'So that's why it excites you so much — you think we're a couple of crooks and I'm his wife! You're *perverted,* Pomeroy!'

She scrambled off the bed, the white nightgown falling out of its tangle down her bare buttocks and legs as she went to her dressing table. She was looking for a gun! He catapulted off the bed and got to her in a couple of strides to pinion her arms from behind. 'I want to show you something,' she snapped.

'Show me what?'

'I can't show you unless you let go ...'

She reached down into a drawer of lingerie and stockings and brought up a framed photograph. A wedding group. She was the bride in white. She was on the arm of a young officer in a fancy British uniform. It was a big group. Dalrymple was standing beside her in a frock coat, holding a silk hat. Her forefinger stabbed on glass at another front-row guest.

'Recognize that gentleman?' The stout party was bald, with heavy lidded eyes, a long nose and a pointed beard. That's Bertie, as intimates know him,' she said mockingly. 'He was Prince of Wales then, you probably know him better as King Edward VII. Admittedly, he has some peculiar friends, but do you seriously think the heir to the throne of England would attend the wedding of a cardsharp's daughter — in the Guards Chapel?'

She left him gaping at the photograph and went through the stateroom to the other bedroom. It was the King all right, just like on the gold coins. She came back with a flat wooden box. She turned a little brass key in the lock and directed him to look at medals and ribbons laid out on blue velvet. 'A few trinkets awarded to my father for services to Queen and empire. *This* is the medal and clasp from the Zulu war. *This* is the medal and clasp from Tel-el-Kebir. *These* are from the Nile campaign. He was also mentioned twice in dispatches — Queen Victoria, of course, not the queen of bloody hearts.'

He looked at the medals and the photograph and then at her.

'Could be I've pulled a boner here.'

'Could be you're a fool, Pomeroy.'

'You going to tell me who he is?'

'You know too much already.'

She took the box back to the other bedroom. He tried to remember everything that had gone on during the game. A shill who spouted poetry and had his photograph taken with the King of England? A shill who was a hero?

'Well?' she demanded.

'What did he tell you about dropping his oakus — his wallet?'

'He wasn't going to tell me, then you returned it. I — why is all this so important to you?'

'They had me lined up as a mark.'

'A mark of what?'

115

'A sucker — a victim.'

She took the photograph out of his hands. He stood there frowning at her in the mirror as she slid the photograph under her lingerie and stockings. She straightened up. 'You look like a sucker now, standing there in your shirt-tail and socks — '

'Okay.' He hauled off his shirt.

'No! Put it on again!'

He stooped quickly and yanked her nightgown up from her ankles, all the way up her slim white legs and peachy buttocks and firm white back, entangling it around her shoulders and arms as he pressed her towards the bed. She got her hands free to claw at his face, but he was already forcing her legs apart and flattening her on the firm mattress. There was no single moment: she was fighting him off, then she was biting and scratching and prodding him to a greater frenzy, not of love, not of hate, not pain, not pleasure-beyond pain or pleasure to blinding·oblivion.

When she was properly asleep, he slipped off the bed. The box of medals was under some starched shirts and collars in the dressing table of the other bedroom. Under the box was a crocodile-skin writing case. He slid it out and clicked the brass fastener. He saw tickets, letters, two British passports. One passport belonged to Catherine, Lady Cameron, the other to Sir Walter Freese Tennyson, Bart.

Tennyson?

One of the letters was in copperplate handwriting on stiff parchment paper with an embossed heading:

The Admiralty

Whitehall London

On behalf of His Majesty's Government, the undersigned, Admiral Sir John Fisher, Second Sea Lord, requests and requires all persons in the United Kingdom of Great Britain and Ireland, India, the Colonies and Protectorates, and the officials and servants of all powers friendly to His Majesty's Govern-

ment, to accord diplomatic courtesies and privileges commensurate with his status as an envoy extraordinary of His Majesty's Government to the bearer of this letter, Sir Walter Freese Tennyson.

He remembered Holborn's languid drawl, reciting 'The Charge of the Light Brigade' — by Tennyson! Holborn, who thought he recognized Dalrymple that first day in the smoking room ...

She was stretched out naked, arms flung wide as if to embrace him, one foot dangling over the edge of the bed. He got dressed and used her brush on his hair, then kissed the creamy skin of her instep, then her shin, her knee. His lips were touching her smooth white thigh when her eyes opened. She grabbed the silk coverlet up to her neck.

'My father will be back at any moment — '

They're still softening him up for the kill. They won't be through with him yet awhile.'

'You talk like something straight from a penny dreadful.'

'Forgive my penny-dreadful ignorance, but what does *Sir* signify before someone's name?'

'That he's a knight or a baronet. Why?'

'Sir Walter Freese Tennyson the knight or the baronet?'

She yawned. 'What are you talking about now, John?'

'It's the name on his passport — '

'You bloody sneak!' She swung her legs off the bed to attack him, then realized she was naked and clutched the coverlet around her shoulders. He caught the loose end and wrapped it around her, pinioning her arms. 'Let go of me! Who the hell are you?'

'I'm an American diplomat — '

'You're a bloody spy!'

The United States does not use spies. You expecting somebody to be spying on him? Why? What was he doing in the States?' 'Let me go!'

'I don't think these guys are ordinary cardsharps. I think they're planning to blackmail your father — '

'How the hell can they blackmail him over a simple game of cards?'

'It isn't a simple game of cards. When did you book your passage?'

'Go to hell!'

'You want me to ask your father?'

'Our itinerary was arranged weeks ago, before — '

'So they knew well in advance you'd be on the *Lucania.* That figures. Why was he in the States?'

'He had a nervous breakdown — '

'He'll have a worse breakdown if Devoy and Marchbanks get their hooks into him. Come on, Kate, that's all crap about a breakdown travelling under a fake name with official accreditation from some admiral called Fisher?'

She hung her head in horror. He let her sit on the edge of the bed. She looked like a squaw woman with the coverlet draped around her shoulders. 'He'll kill me,' she moaned.

'If he finds out ... you can trust me, Kate — '

'You cold-blooded American bastard, I wouldn't trust you' if — '

'If they're planning blackmail on him, they're sure as hell planning the same for me ...'

'Oh God! All I know is it has something to do with oil supplies for the Royal Navy. There's a big argument about whether our warships should use coal or oil. Jackie Fisher is the Oil Maniac, he's known my father for years — I don't really know much about it apart from what I overheard. He doesn't confide in me because he knows I *loathe* Jackie Fisher and this *obscene* passion for armaments and war ... how can you help him?'

'I get him off the hook. I also get myself off the hook. I need to get back into the game only I'm short on dough now — '

'I have fifteen pounds — '

They're betting in hundreds in there.' He got out his pocket-book. He had around eighty pounds left from the game, two hundred dollars of his advance, and in his cabin he had a few gold eagles he'd copped from the table in the Pingree library. It was enough to get him into the stateroom at least. 'Maybe I'll hit it lucky.'

She looked at him doubtfully. 'You won't tell him about us, will you? Please don't, I beg you!'

'Scared of your own daddy, eh? Out of interest, what would he do if he found out about us?'

'He'd take a horsewhip to *you.*'

He kissed her on the brow. 'You seem to be a pretty violent family all around.'

The *Lucania* was steady as he made his way through the deserted passageways. Behind each door he seemed to hear mutterings and furtive movements. At night the lighting in the public areas was dimmed and spooky. He was heading back to his own cabin to pick up the gold eagles when he heard the piano ... music for lost souls at sea ...

At four in the morning, Lang-Gaevernitz looked pink and newly shaved. He was wearing a tweed jacket over a white shirt with no tie. He smiled and went on playing. Pomeroy pointed to the bottle of cognac on a silver tray. The German nodded. Pomeroy poured himself a drink and stood by the big brass fireplace. Fine white ash covered the dying coals. Wherever he looked he saw power and wealth, the ivory and gilding on the pine ceiling, the satinwood walls, the huge Persian carpet, thick velvet and rich fabrics, all of it designed to make wealthy people forget they were being carried across a huge ocean at night in a storm. The music stopped. Lang-Gaevernitz brought the bottle to the fireplace. He filled his own glass. His nails were manicured. He filled the glass to the brim and held it up in a toast.

'Liszt again?' Pomeroy said.

'Schlaflos — Frage und Antwort ... why can't we sleep, the question, the answer.'

'What's the answer in your case, Uwe?'

'Oh, I can only ever sleep well in my own bed. Travelling alone is romantic only for the young.'

'I'd have been better feeling romantic. I was playing poker and I ran out of scratch.'

'Scratch?'

'Dough. Money. I didn't start off with enough. Jeez, it's killing me thinking of those guys sitting in there just *waiting* to be taken — they're lousy poker players, dammit. If I had *just* a few hundred pounds — I'm a pretty good poker player, you know.'

Would he take the bait?

'John, I wonder .. .' Lang-Gaevernitz put his glass on the high mantelpiece. He frowned, hesitating, wondering if he was doing the right thing. His hand strayed nearer his hip pocket. 'John, would you be insulted if I offered to lend you some money? We are both members of the *corps diplomatique,* no? We are friends — I hope ...'

Pomeroy grinned. 'Insult me all you like, Uwe.'

Lang-Gaevernitz brought out a thick black leather wallet. 'I have British money from my official allowance, I didn't spend much in America. How much would you need, John?' He brought out a wad of one hundred pound bills.

'Five hundred would be great, Uwe! Mind you, I could blow the whole goddam lot and I wouldn't be able to pay you back before London — '

'We'll be seeing each other, won't we?' Lang-Gaevernitz pushed the bills into his hand. Let us drink to your success.' They toasted each other, then the German frowned at some passing thought.

'What is it, Uwe?'

'No, it is nothing. We Germans are famous for being an obsessional people, the Teutonic anxiety for order ...'

What he wanted, and what Pomeroy had known he'd want, was his signature for the money. He went on apologizing as he unfolded some sheets of lined paper from his wallet. On these he listed every penny he spent, with dates and abbreviated annotations in German script. He said he envied the casual way Americans treated money and gave Pomeroy his fine new American fountain pen to write out an IOU for the five hundred pounds. Pomeroy wrote it, dated it and signed it *John S. Pomeroy, US Embassy, London.* Lang-Gaevernitz apologized again as he waved the ink dry and said he hoped he was acting like a friend and not doing Satan's work for him, encouraging a young man in the paths of temptation. A Teutonic joke, no less.

'See you in hell, Uwe,' Pomeroy said solemnly, shoving the bills into his own wallet. 'I don't want to appear rude, but — '

'I am happy playing the piano. Good luck.'

What really puzzled him then was the feeling that the German really did like him as a young man out in the wide world for the first time. Acting wasn't all of it. If anything, he was just an good as actor as Lang-Gaevernitz. No, underneath the acting, the guy really did like him. In this game, the players didn't shuffle cards, they shuffled their own emotions and laid them out as required. For all his sophistication and culture, Lang-Gaevernitz had the soul of a whore. (Eventually, of course, he was to realize that liking the enemy paid off better than hating him; liking the enemy helped you understand him. You were looking for his weaknesses but you could still like him. You only hated people you were afraid of.)

Devoy opened the door of suite 40. His smile was instant, automatic, like one of those fiesh-eating plants that ooze sweet nectar at the buzz of a fly. He was delighted to hear that Pomeroy had found some more money.

'Marchbanks is getting some fresh air,' he said quietly. 'The smoke made him feel sick, he said.' Devoy smiled. 'Losing probably helped to make him feel sick.'

Holborn and Dalrymple were facing each other across a reasonable pot. Holborn looked a little drunker, a lot less sleek with his coat off and the beginnings of a dark stubble. Dalrymple sat ramrod straight, seeing every raise and upping another fifty. Finally, Holborn looked up at Devoy.

'Where the hell's Jesse got to?' he asked irritably. Holborn was running low but his banker wasn't there. He went in another hundred, leaving him with fives and tens and gold sovereigns. Dalrymple saw, and raised. Holborn didn't have enough for his next bet.

'We'll have to wait for Jesse, I need to cash another cheque,' he said.

Dalrymple thought he had him by the balls and raised again.

'If you can't bet, you're beat,' he barked .

'I hardly think that's fair, Dalrymple,' Devoy said firmly. 'It's not Holborn's fault Jesse isn't here.'

Dalrymple humphed and grumphed, then said he didn't mind winning a cheque as part of the pot. 'Make it payable to cash.'

Holborn got his chequebook out of his coat and wrote a cheque for one thousand pounds, which he took in hundreds and fifties from the middle of the table. His obvious intention to go all the way with it made Dalrymple think again and he called him. Smirking triumphantly, Holborn turned over three kings. Dalrymple stared at the cards. The eye behind the monocle was unwavering, the other eye blinked rapidly.

Holborn pursed his lips in a silent whistle of triumph. Dalrymple turned over four aces. Holborn moaned theatrically and hung his head, but in a moment he was slashing another four fingers of the nearest stuff into his glass and draping himself across his chair for another joust with the bitch goddess of fate — his expression. Dalrymple picked up the cheque in his fingertips as if it might carry leprosy, then folded it away and sorted out the bills. They waited a couple of minutes. Holborn wanted to start again without Marchbanks, but Devoy didn't like the idea. Pomeroy volunteered to go find Marchbanks.

The Texan was standing by a door open five or six inches to the outside walkway. Gusts of wind moved his gingery hair.

'How you feeling, Jesse?' Pomeroy asked.

'A little better, I guess. Thought you'd quit the game, John.'

'I broke open my piggybank. They're ready to deal back there. You want us to deal you out this hand?'

Marchbanks took a deep breath and let his chest expand. 'I'm okay now. Who won last time?'

'Dalrymple. Between you and me, Jesse, I think Holborn's getting plastered. He doesn't show it too badly, but maybe we should stop him playing, don't you think so? '

'It's not losing money you'd have to save Holborn from, you'd have to save him from himself. Inbreeding, that's what it is, John. These English aristocrats have been marrying each other for a thousand years, the same goddam blood's in all of them. They're finished. Don't lose any sleep over Holborn, John.'

Picking up the loose cards for his first deal, Pomeroy got a nine and ten of diamonds together. These went south off the edge of the table onto his lap. Before he shuffled, he got out his wallet and produced Lang-Gaevernitz's five hundreds. The two cards went back into his inside pocket with the wallet. He didn't quite know what he was going to do just yet, but he wanted to be ready when the right moment came. Daubing the aces was ruled out; in this game they were all accounted for. He palmed the six of diamonds from his own discards at the draw and held it against the underside of the table with his knee until he could switch it to his pocket. For the next few hands, he took it very carefully, good old Stonewall Jackson again. For some reason, Dalrymple's run of luck was over. When Marchbanks dealt, Holborn won. Dalrymple took his setbacks like his triumphs, a growl and a glare. Holborn was getting soused by the minute. Marchbanks had to tell him to keep his voice down. When he drew the jack of diamonds on Devoy's deal, he couldn't palm it without leaving himself four cards in hand, so he took off his coat and hung it over the back of his chair. This gave him a chance to press the little nickel-plated box and when his hand came up there was a spot of blue daub on the tip of his forefinger. While studying his cards, he smudged the jack top left and bottom right.

(The marking paste in the little box was a concoction of dye, camphor and glycerine; a smear on the card's blue backing left a slightly darker smudge nobody would notice, or take for a minor printing fudge if they did. It could easily be rubbed off again.)

Just before five there was a knock at the door. Marchbanks gestured for them to keep quiet and cautiously opened the door. It was only his tame steward. Marchbanks brought him into the stateroom. Nobody was hungry. 'Fix us a pot of coffee, George,' Marchbanks said over a couple of gold sovereigns.

'Be a pleasure, Mr Marchbanks.' The steward had another weird English accent. Marchbanks locked the door again.

Marchbanks who went missing just when Holborn needed money? Marchbanks who looked as delicate as a Brahman bull suddenly turning queasy because of the smoke? Marchbanks who felt a lot better as soon as he heard that Holborn had lost? Marchbanks who had cashed Holborn's first cheque because he knew Holborn had plenty of money to cover it in the purser's safe? Pomeroy thought back. It was Dalrymple's deal when he brought Marchbanks back to the game, which meant Marchbanks had dealt the hands for the big pot, hands that would get them both betting heavily, with Dalrymple bound to win on his four aces. Dalrymple, who was really Sir Walter Freese Tennyson, an envoy extraordinary of the British government? Who was now holding Holborn's cheque for one thousand pounds? The cheque, it had to be the cheque. What did you do with a cheque? Cash money left no footprints, but a cheque was undeniable proof you'd taken money from the man who signed it. They wanted it on record that Dalrymple had taken big money off Holborn, that had to be it!

The arrival of the coffee gave him a chance to palm the eight of diamonds. The daubed jack was in Devoy's cards at the next deal. When it came to his own next deal, he saw the seven of diamonds among the discards and that went south as well. He started betting a little more bravely and got them used to his tightwad's nervous habit of bringing out his wallet to keep tabs on his money.

He noted that Devoy was winning a lot now, at least when Marchbanks was dealing.

Something else came back to him. That first day out from New York in the smoking room. Dalrymple had dropped his wallet,. a grifter's standard ploy. That was what had confused him. But, Just before Dalrymple dropped his wallet, Holborn had spoken to Dalrymple ... *I say — don't we know each other?* ...

Francis, Viscount Holborn of Seaton Delaval, who was going to hell in several directions ...

Marchbanks had just won a pot of maybe one hundred forty pounds when Devoy concealed a yawn that would have gone unnoticed if he hadn't put his hand to his mouth. Marchbanks was gathering the cards for his next deal. Devoy pulled out a gold watch on a chain across his black velvet vest. 'Mmmm, five to seven? I think I've had enough for tonight, gentlemen.'

'Now just a moment!' Holborn's voice was slurred now, his eyes dulled, but he sounded a lot less indolent. 'Some of us have lost a fair bit of money in this session.' He looked to Pomeroy for support. 'Frankly, I'd consider it a damn bad show on your part to call it a day before we have a chance to recoup, Devoy, a damn bad show — you agree with me, don't you, John?'

Pomeroy looked uncomfortable, being too inexperienced in these matters to risk taking sides. Dalrymple growled that he'd be glad to get to bloody bed.

'Oh yes,' Holborn sneered, 'run away with your winnings, you mean?'

'Aw, come on Charles,' Marchbanks pleaded. He was already chopping and riffling the cards — and from that moment Pomeroy didn't take his eyes off the Texan's fat but so very, very nimble fingers. This had all the sound of a fast shuffle. Sure enough ...

Devoy nodded seriously. 'If Holborn feels he's having a slight run and nobody else objects, I'm willing to play one more hand at an increased limit — a hundred pounds say?'

Suddenly it was back in the gloomy stateroom: the whiff of death. Maybe this time it was more like the scent of a kill. These last-hand-of the-night wheezes were a favourite ploy among cardsharps, when even Stonewall Jacksons were tempted into recklessness. He watched the cards dance all ways in the Texan's dukes, all varieties of fancy shuffling, ending with a natty threeway cut that would have fooled an old monte man. Marchbanks placed the deck for him to cut. The Texan had been out of the room long enough to stack another deck according to their seating positions. It was no coincidence that Devoy had announced last hand when Marchbanks was due to deal. But if the deck had been switched, his palmed cards were no good .

He let his fingers caress the edges of the deck, but it wasn't enough to tell if it had been switched.

(How did you tell if they'd worked the old switcheroo? The new cards felt colder in your hand, simple as that, the old cold-deck trick everybody talked about but few knew the meaning of)

He watched the deck disappear again into Marchbanks's hands. If getting Dalrymple to take Holborn's cheque was their first objective, what was their angle now?

They were crooks, weren't they?

Marchbanks started the deal, very fast, impossible to tell which end of the deck they were coming from. He picked up his cards as they fell. Pair of queens, pair of sixes, three of spades. Then he saw it — in Devoy's cards the daubed jack of diamonds. They were still using the old deck!

As usual, everybody was going to bet a storm on this last go-around. They always did, the last flingding. They were raising by tens and twenties before the draw. Marchbanks went around with the deck.

Dalrymple, one card. Devoy, one card. Holborn, no cards. He discarded the pair of sixes and the three. Marchbanks gave him three cards. He was looking at a full house, three kings, two queens, a very strong hand .. . but not aces.

Frowning at his cards, Pomeroy chewed his lower lip, looked to the ceiling for guidance, then tapped them together and put them down on the table. He reached into his coat for his wallet. His fingers pressed the palmed cards against leather. While the wallet was below the table edge, he checked that the cards were facing the right way. He put down the wallet on the table, the palmed cards underneath. He opened the wallet without picking it up, the left flap coming down on the cards. Marchbanks had dealt. He took out the five one hundred pound bills he'd borrowed from Lang-Gaevernitz.

Marchbanks raised his pig's bristle eyebrows. 'Having a rush of blood to the head, John old buddy?'

'Could be I've been fooling you fellows,' he said slyly.

He closed the wallet right to left, leaving the palmed cards in view. He slid his fingertips under the wallet and dragged it and the other cards of the table and down into his coat pocket. Easy, really, when they weren't watching you for fancy tricks. He glanced at Devoy, who looked more than ever like a merchant of doom and death.

They'd discover he was a cheat when it was too late: Whatever happened, it was going to be too risky going ahead with their blackmail scheme on Dalrymple. No, they wouldn't complain, they might try to kill him, but they wouldn't complain .. .

Dalrymple folded when the raise got to forty pounds. Being an English gentleman he didn't brag about how much he was ahead on the night's play but put his money away in that same wallet he dropped in the smoking room. Gruffly he said, 'Can I get anyone a drink?'

'I'll have a stiff Scotch, old man,' said Holborn. Nobody else wanted to break concentration. Devoy and Marchbanks didn't seem unhappy about Dalrymple folding . . . which meant *he* was the prime pigeon now.

Maybe they signalled, maybe they didn't have to, but around the time Pomeroy was running out of money, Devoy saw the last bet and didn't raise. There was enough money on the red damask tablecloth to feed a small-size town for a month.

Marchbanks had an ace high flush in spades. He looked at Devoy and sucked air between his teeth. 'Not enough, is it, Charles?'

Devoy tapped his black cheroot in the cut-crystal ashtray and turned over each card with a flick of his forefinger. 'Four kings.' The master gave them a little insight into his methods. 'I had them before the draw. I asked for one card to make you think I had a bobtail hand.'

Holborn slung down his cards. 'One lives to fight another day,' he said defiantly. Marchbanks leaned across to press Pomeroy's shoulder. 'You went all the way, John old buddy, you ain't short on nerve, no sir.' 'Does a straight flush beat four of a kind?' he asked nervously, turning over his ten-nine-eight-seven-six of diamonds.

Dalrymple broke the silence. 'I'm off to bed. Been an interestin' evenin', what?' The naive diplomat stuffed away his hundreds and fifties and twenties and tens and fives, then the scattered gold coins. Wait for me, colonel! At the door he gave them a nervous smile, some of which nervousness wasn't faked.

'I still can't believe it myself. Good night — or is it good morning?'

Marchbanks looked ready to open him up starting at the heart. Holborn was staring vacantly at the wall. Devoy was just staring.

Walking along the deserted passageways, Dalrymple turned the monocle on him. 'When you've played more poker, you'll realize just how bloody lucky you were there, Pomeroy. Take my advice, man, stick to deck quoits in future.'

'You suggesting there was something *fishy* about the game, colonel?'

'No, I'm suggesting you're a damned awful poker player. Good night to you, sir.'

He'd been in his cabin twenty maybe thirty minutes when somebody thumped on the door. He shoved the money among his clothes in a suitcase. The knocking became more violent. He unwrapped the Smith and Wesson from his black swimsuit. He shoved the suitcase back into the wardrobe and held the Smith and Wesson down his thigh in his right hand as he opened the door.

Francis Holborn burst past him into the cabin. 'Lock the door!' he hissed. He was carrying a bottle. 'Will you lock the bloody door, man? Marchbanks is going to kill you! '

Looking along the corridor, he saw Horton coming out of his pantry. The steward gave him a little wave and called,

'Ready for a nice cup of tea, Mr Pomeroy?'

9

Wind battered on glass. The Englishman's face was a ghostly blur against a faint grey light from the cabin window.

'I don't know why I bothered warning you, you're a worse crook than them!'

'Just because I won a hand at poker?' He put the pistol on the table. 'Lots of Americans carry guns, Francis — '

'It's not *Frayncis,* damn you, can't you bloody Americans learn to speak the language properly? Anyway, I've told you, I'm going now — '

'Siddown, Francis, tell me about that cheque you landed on Dalrymple.'

'None of your bloody business!'

'I'll be a witness when he goes to the captain. I'm pretty sure he'll go to the captain when I tell him it was a rigged game, Francis. How do you think you'll come out of it, Francis? Pretty important man, Tennyson . . .'

'Oh no .. .' Holborn's mouth met the brandy bottle coming up and he let Hennessy's Three Star slurp down his throat. 'Oh God .. .'

Pomeroy stayed by the door, listening for anybody approaching. 'How come you're friends with people like that, Francis?'

He didn't know all of it, but what he did know was scaring him to death and at last he could spill it. Marchbanks and Devoy had got their hooks into him in New York. His father had sent him on a sea voyage for his health — well, not exactly his health, his father thought a change of scenery would get him off the booze. They'd picked him up in the Windsor Hotel on Fifth Avenue near Grand Central; they'd shown him the town, taken him to fancy joints, introduced him to lovely girls who just loved his cute accent and his wonderful manners, taken him to juice joints, taught him about craps, showed him the action.

Next thing he knew, when he sobered up, they were holding his paper for around nine thousand pounds, which he didn't have. They told him he could have his cheque back and earn a little money if he helped them set Dalrymple up for a squeeze — Marchbanks made it sound almost like a jape. Dalrymple was a well-known cheat in London gaming circles, who got away with it because of his connections. He'd vaguely recognized Dalrymple that first day in the smoking room, the name had come to him during the game. He knew then they'd been lying, but when the last hand proved that Pomeroy was wise to them, he thought they'd give up on Dalrymple.

'Not a bloody bit of it! As soon as we're back in London and Tennyson's had time to put my cheque through his bank, I'm supposed to accuse him of cheating at cards on the *Lucania*! He won't be able to deny that he won a lot of money — he'll be finished!'

'On your say-so? Backed by a couple of crooks?'

'It won't have to be backed up, you dolt — why do you think they got me into it? Because of my title! If I publicly accuse him of cheating, he'll be blackballed from his clubs, his regiment will shun him, the whole of London society will cut him dead — it's a question of *honour,* man!'

'What are you going to do about it?'

Holborn took another drag at the brandy bottle. His voice dropped almost to a whisper. 'They've got my cheques, John, they can accuse me of swindling them ... unless I commit perjury to blackmail Tennyson ... I wish I was dead ...'

'Maybe I could help you, Francis .. .'

'Nobody can help me — '

'If I got your cheques back you'd be in the clear, right?'

'How the hell could you get my cheques back?'

'I managed to get my money back at poker, didn't I?'

'Why would you want to help me?' .

'I don't want to be dragged into all this — what were they planing for me anyway?'

'I don't know, they didn't tell me. Would you really help me, John?'

'You got a pen? There's plenty of writing paper under the table. Why don't you just write it all down, Francis. Confession is good for the soul,   isn't that what they say?'

Holborn thought about it during another pull at the bottle. Then he stood up. 'I'm not writing any bloody confession for you to blackmail me.'

'Siddown, Francis. I don't want to blackmail you — ' He shoved Holborn in the chest and he flopped down again. 'I want it on paper before you change your mind. Or do you want me to go to the captain right now? He has powers of arrest, I believe.'

He stood there by the cabin door while Holborn alternately drank brandy and wrote feverishly on *Lucania* notepaper. He could hear the scratching of the fountain-pen nib through the noise of the gale on the other side of the window. It hardly seemed thick enough to protect them from that huge ocean out there.

'Make sure you put in that I was to be a victim as well,' he said.

Finally, Holborn capped his pen and picked up the bottle. He tried to get up but Pomeroy stood over him while he read the neat handwriting.

Only the sloping lines gave an indication it had been written by a drunken hand.

That's okay,' he said. 'Now why don't you go and lock your cabin door and hit the sack, Francis? And stop drinking, for pete's sake.

' I might as well be dead now,' Holborn said thickly.

When he woke up it was dark again. Half past seven. He washed, shaved and dressed and went around to Holborn's cabin. He knocked but there was no answer. The door was locked. Most likely he'd awakened with a parched throat and gone looking for another drink; lushes usually did. On his way to the smoking room , he saw a seaman standing like a sentry at one of the doors that faced the deck .

'Something wrong?' he asked. 'We're requesting passengers not to go out on deck in this gale, sir, turned a bit blowy, as it happens.'

Holborn was not in the smoking room. Marchbanks was at the bar, but he didn't spot him. Holborn wasn't in any of the public rooms. When he reached the door of Holborn's cabin again, he heard a voice inside and sighed with relief. He knocked. The door started to open.

'Well, old buddy ...'

'Yes, sir?' said a ship's officer.

There were two of them. They were packing Holborn's clothes into a suitcase. They tried to tell him that Viscount Holborn was in the sickbay, but when he said he would go there right now to see his good friend, one of them got between him and the door. Both were wearing naval caps with stiff peaks down to their eyebrows.

'Had Viscount Holborn been drinking heavily last night, sir, to your knowledge?' asked the one at the door.

'I'm not answering any questions till I know what's happened to him.'

They looked at each other, these fresh-faced, clean-cut English officers who clearly didn't have much respect for the rich guzzlers and boozehounds they were forced to sail with when they should be following Nelson's footsteps on the deck of a warship.

'This is in the strictest confidence, sir. A seaman on the bridge saw a passenger on deck about an hour ago. The passenger was wearing evening clothes. The wind got up so the first officer sent somebody to tell the passenger the deck might best be avoided. They couldn't find him. A steward said he'd seen Viscount Holborn heading towards the deck in evening clothes. I'm afraid he must have been blown overboard, sir.'

Pomeroy gave him a steady look. 'Or jumped.'

Again they looked at each other.

'We would be grateful if you wouldn 't voice that thought to anyone else on board, sir.'

'We don't want to cause his family any more distress than is absolutely necessary, sir.'

'Why didn't the ship turn back?'

'By the time we'd established he wasn't in his cabin or in any of the public rooms there was no point in turning back, sir. We're making twenty knots and he would have been in the water for almost half an hour.'

'He couldn't have survived five minutes in that sea.'

'In this light we wouldn't have spotted him right under the bow.'

'You won't be discussing this with anyone else, sir?'

'You know how nervous elderly people can be.'

'I won't discuss it.'

'Sir, did you have any particular reason for thinking that he might not have been *blown* overboard?'

'No, I guess not .. .'

'Can we tell the captain we have your word you won't talk about this to any of the other passengers, sir?'

'You have my word.'

Even in the dark, he kept seeing the neat handwriting, the sloping lines, his eye always drawn to one word ... *honour* with the *u,* the English version. Listening to the gale, he imagined what it would be like back there, floating up and down in the deep troughs and the wind-whipped waves, the bright lights of the huge ship getting smaller and smaller. Maybe with enough booze in you —

There was a gentle tapping at the door.

Kate!

He jumped naked out of bed, pulled on his robe and went to the door in bare feet.

'Well, hi there, John old buddy.' Marchbanks was smiling. His formal coat was hanging open like a gunfighter's. On his feet, he looked like a boxcar with a head on top. He made a little tsk-tsk noise and his meaty hand came up holding a blue-backed playing card ... the daubed jack of diamonds.

Pomeroy shook his head. 'Sorry, I've brushed my teeth.'

'It's not an invitation card, John old buddy. It's a pledge you are about to redeem. Thanks, I will step inside for a moment.'

He took a step forward. Pomeroy didn't move. Marchbanks's eyes were too small for the big ruddy moon of his face. They were smiling as his right shoe began to press down on Pomeroy's bare toes.

His left hand jabbed into the Texan's nose and upper lip.

Marchbanks brought up his fat hands, his face contorting in a snarl. Pomeroy sank his right fist into the Texan's big belly, way below the line and moved close, left-right, left-right, deep into the lower abdomen. Marchbanks began to double forward, mouth stretching like a beached fish, then he sagged and slumped onto his knees, his big head going down towards the carpet as if in prayer.

Pomeroy turned back into the dark cabin and reached for the whisky bottle on top of the wardrobe. He put his bare foot against the Texan's shoulder and gave him a shove. Marchbanks toppled sideways.

Pomeroy tilted the bottle between his teeth. A throat fighting for air sent whisky down the airpipe and Marchbanks convulsed violently, short legs kicking across the carpet, making retching noises through the gurgling.

He poured some more whisky over the Texan's shirtfront, dropped the bottle beside him and went back into his cabin.

It took a couple of minutes before the bell rang in the steward's pantry down the corridor. When he heard Horton's voice, he tousled his hair and opened the door, blinking sleepily.

Horton was bending over Marchbanks. The Texan convulsed in slow time, letting out the most disgusting noises. 'It's all right, Mr Pomeroy,' Horton assured him, 'this gentleman's had a drop too much to drink, that's all.'

Another steward came hurrying along the corridor. Horton put the bottle in the pocket of his white mess jacket. A silver-haired gent poked his head out of a cabin on the other side. He watched the two stewards wrestling to get Marchbanks upright. 'Some people have no consideration for others,' was his pronouncement. The stewards got Marchbanks's arms around their necks and hauled him away, toe caps dragging on the carpet. The other passenger shook his head . 'I know that fellow — American, of course, no idea how to behave.'

'You're doggone right there, buddy.'

Something caught in the silver-haired gent's throat and he closed his door. Pomeroy stooped to pick up the jack of diamonds from under his bare foot.

On Friday morning, their last full day at sea, he had an early breakfast in the dining room. After breakfast he went outside. A seaman warned him against leaving the safety of the open gangway as the deck was being swept by a gale. Two English gents were not about to be bossed around by a deckhand or intimidated by a little breeze. While they were cutting this sailor down to size, one of them lost his black derby to the wind . It rolled out onto the open deck and the wind spun it up in the air and over the side. Give them credit for sense of humour: they both laughed heartily. He watched the hat floating in a smooth trough, then dancing and disappearing in churning white foam at the crest of the big waves.

Lang-Gaevernitz stared at him in horror. 'John — this is terrible! I don't know what to say, it's ... I can hardly believe it!'

He looked genuinely shocked, this man of culture who hated war and played classical dirges at night to ease his anguished soul, sitting there so solid and pink and honest-looking in a collarless white shirt fastened at the neck with a gold stud. The five one-hundred-pound bills lay on the blue tablecloth beside the silver coffee service. Lang-Gaevernitz shook his head in bewilderment.

'But John — you knew these people were card cheaters, criminals yet you went back to the game?'

'Would you have loaned me the money if I'd told you, Uwe?'

'A man is dead, John. Am I being humourless and Teutonic when I say I don't see any joke in it?'

'I'll tell you something else pretty damned funny, Uwe. Holborn came to my cabin just after the game broke up and told me some cock-eyed yarn about Devoy and Marchbanks being blackmailers. He was soused to the gills, mind. Anyway, he said they were setting up Dalrymple for a bunco operation .. .'

Even now the temptation was there to blurt *all* of it out, that he knew who Devoy and Marchbanks were working for, who Dalrymple really was — maybe Uwe would admit it was a game that had got out of control, that he'd never intended anybody to die, and they could be genuine friends together against scum like Devoy and Marchbanks. But the temptation didn't match the kick he got out of putting one over on the bastard; that was a real pleasure, that made his balls tingle.

When he finished, Lang-Gaevernitz folded his arms. He frowned. 'But, as you say, John, the man was drunk and full of self-pity, he would make up any story to save his self-respect.'

'That's what I said.' He saw a little flicker in the German's eyes. 'I don't think we should go to the captain, do you, Uwe?'

138

'We?' The one-word question came a fraction too quickly. Of course it was the one thing Lang-Gaevernitz had to know. He remembered a high-pitched drawling voice ... *weakness always invites attack ...*

'Dalrymple wants me to tell the captain everything. They could have those two buzzards arrested when we reach Liverpool. But I don't want to have to admit I cheated in the game, I might get dragged in over my head — '

'Yes, that is a serious possibility, John — '

'—on the other hand, you could tell them I had to borrow the money off you to get back in the game. That would prove I wasn't in cahoots with Devoy and Marchbanks, wouldn't it?'

He said this with a straight face and Lang-Gaevernitz took a long breath through his nose. Quite noisy it was too.

'John, that would not be the act of a friend,' he said sharply.

Pomeroy smiled. Slyly. 'You mean you don't want people to know you financed a dirty, low-down cheat in a crooked game that drove one guy to suicide?' Give him his due, the German managed a pained smile. Maybe he did see a certain grisly humour in this naive young braggart having some kind of hold on him, although there wasn't much else he could do but smile, was there?

Oh yes there was.

Ruefully, he said, 'You have an unusual sense of humour, John. In the service of the Imperial German diplomatic corps even a hint of scandal would be disastrous for my career. That reminds me ...' He got up from the table and went to his wardrobe. He reached into his coat and brought out his black wallet. 'A trivial matter compared to these dreadful things you've told me about but ...' He unfolded a sheet of lined paper and held it out for Pomeroy to see the handwritten IOU for five hundred pounds. 'In a treacherous world we cannot be too careful even of our friends — I must destroy the evidence!' He laughed. 'See, you have me making jokes like an American now.' He tore up the sheet, once, twice, three times, then opened his cabin window and let the gale whirl the bits of paper against the side of the ship. 'Now, John, you must be serious. I think you underestimate the ruthlessness of such criminals. One of them has already tried to attack you — '

'He only wanted the dough back — '

'I don't think so, John. Dalrymple cannot make any accusations against them without you as a witness, correct? If they thought you could send them to jail, what lengths don't you think they would go to? You could be in danger, John, you must stop Dalrymple going to the captain or to the police — '

'He won't take orders from me — '

'John — think of your career! A crooked game of cards, a society gentleman committing suicide — and you in court as a witness, when you would have to admit *you* cheated as well? John — what would your superiors in Washington say?'

'I think they'd say I wasn't too much of an asset to the foreign service. But you don't know Dalrymple, Uwe. He has the hide of a rhinoceros and he despises Americans. How can I stop him?'

Lang-Gaevernitz pulled back his lips and tapped rhythmically on his front teeth with his fingertips. Maybe he was playing one of those tunes without a tune. 'John — this is a serious situation for you. I think you are justified in protecting yourself with any means at your disposal ... you agree?'

'Sling him overboard?'

Lang-Gaevernitz winced. 'John, you *must* take this seriously. My advice to you is to tell Dalrymple that if he makes any accusations against those two men, you will say that he *was* cheating in the game.'

The last bit came quickly. Pomeroy's eyes widened. 'Uwe!' Then he puckered his lips in astonishment. 'Gosh darn it, Uwe, you diabolical swine, that's brilliant! Yessir! Boy, that's just too clever for words would I like to see his face?' He slapped his thigh. 'I'll go and see him right now! Where in tarnation did you think up a wheeze like that, Uwe?'

Those square-set blue eyes appraised the naive young American bigmouth who was so easily manipulated. He uttered a few words of caution, of course, then he wasn't sure if it was good advice, the decision had to be his alone. 'Be careful, John, this is a more complicated world than you realize.'

Maybe some of his concern was for real. Maybe — but you were right, Gray, he is the enemy. That wasn't my IOU he scattered on the ocean, was it?

On the other hand, I lied in my teeth about Dalrymple being wise to all this, didn't I? Thanks, Gray, you cold-blooded bastard, you didn't have much time but you taught me well.

In the dining room at lunch, the oldsters were having their last six course blowout before the seven lean years. He couldn't see her or her father. The latest news from Marconi's telegraph without wires was the steel trust's declared dividend on common stock. 'Wireless telegraphy will soon lose its novelty value,' announced an English gent. 'All it can do is bring you news you don't want to hear faster.'

Nobody mentioned a missing passenger. Gossip was the staple fare here. Some *nouveau riche* bounder called Reuben Sassoon had built stables on top of his house in Belgrave Square, had even installed an elevator to take the horses to the roof. 'Why is it all the wrong people have the money nowadays?' demanded a big-bosomed British lioness who'd just put away enough food to see Dawson City through a bad winter. 'Standards have dropped disgracefully. My very close friend Lady Wills was persuaded recently to spend a weekend with that dreadful little man Carnegie — not a friend of yours in America, I trust?'

'Andrew Carnegie the steel magnate? I never met him personally —'

'You showed good taste. He has this ridiculous castle; only a ragtag from the slums of Scotland and my friend Lady Wills says he has eighty-five servants, not to mention a library with twenty-five thousand volumes, and his guests have to endure bagpipes screeching at eight in the morning! Organ music during breakfast as well! I should have thought America a much more appropriate place for such a man — why did he leave, Mr Pomeroy?'

'He got kind of unpopular with the workers.'

'Really? Is one obliged to be popular with the workers in America? How very quaint.'

He got a table to himself in the smoking room after lunch and, sure enough, five minutes later in strolled Marchbanks wearing his Norfolk jacket and the knickerbockers that made it obvious he had the legs of a smaller man. There was no fat hand of friendship. The Texan sat down and told a steward to bring him bourbon and water.

'Well, you bastard ...' Marchbanks looked around to make sure nobody was eavesdropping. 'Why didn't you tip me off? One worker meets another all you have to do is say you're in the rabbit business. We could have come to an arrangement. Jeez, you pack a punch. Where'd you learn to use your dukes like that?'

'Up in Dawson City they had a projectascope thing, you know, moving pictures flashed on a white bedsheet? I saw Gentleman Jim Corbett, one of those fights he was trying to get his title back — '

'Glad it wasn't some *rough* fighter you saw! You don't blame me for trying to get my dough back, do you? Hell, I was madder'n a tomcat with mustard up its keister last night, but I'm not sore now; I'm big enough to recognize when another fellow's been smarter than me.' He waited till the steward had gone away and swirled the bourbon in his glass. 'You intending to give me a chance to get even, John?'

142

'Uh uh.'

'I lost a lotta money!'

'Never trust a square john who isn't sure of the rules.'

'You frenchy bastard! You really are something, John old buddy.' He lowered his voice. 'You hear about Holborn?'

'Tough.' . .

Marchbanks hunched forward. His eyes were too small for his slab of a face but they made up for it in cunning. 'You going to tell them he was playing poker?'

'Not unless I have to.'

'Nobody knows, only you, Dalrymple, Devoy and me. It wouldn't do none of us any good for it to come out. John, you owe me a chance to get my dough back, it's the code. Come on, would there be any gaffing now we all know the score? Just you, me, Devoy and maybe Dalrymple?'

'You'd be watching me too close next time.'

'John, I'm an American like you, I can ride with life's ups and downs. Devoy isn't like us, John, he's a *mean* bastard. I think it would go a long way to making things right between us if you was to turn up tonight and play poker with the man.' Pomeroy shook his head. Marchbanks looked around again. 'Believe me, John, that man scares me and I am his partner. He'd break both my arms if he knew I was talking to you like this. Now wouldn't it be a whole lot easier just to sit down with the cards and — '

'Forget it, Marchbanks. See you around.'

That left only one piece of unfinished business on this ship he'd thought was going to be so dull and English and starchy.

He was changing for dinner when Horton came to make up the bed.

'Your friend say if he delivered my note, Horton?'

'Oh yes, sir, he gave it to the young lady in person, just as you wanted.'

'I appreciate that, Horton, I wish you'd let me — '

143

'Now now, Mr Pomeroy. If you feel my efforts deserve any reward, I'll be happy to accept a small gratuity when we reach Liverpool tomorrow.'

'Sorry. What're they saying about that guy who was blown overboard, Horton?'

The steward hesitated. 'You know about that, do you, sir?'

'Sure, two of the officers questioned me. I had a few drinks with him that night.'

'Yes, they do say he was a heavy drinker. Of course, they'll keep it very quiet. There's his family to think of and it would also create a bad impression. These big liners aren't doing as much business as everybody expected, a lot of competition from the German lines. A thing like that might give the ship a bad name.'

She sat only a few places away from him at dinner. Dalrymple, or Tennyson, gave him a curt nod, but when he signalled urgently she looked right through him. He sat through ten courses and coffee to make sure he was right behind when they left. He caught up with them on the corridor.

'Colonel Dalrymple — Miss Dalrymple — '

'Not playin' cards tonight then, Pomeroy?' Dalrymple growled.

'Not after what happened to Francis Holborn, sir — you did hear about that?'

'Keep your voice down, man, you want the whole blasted ship to know we had a hand in the wretched fellow's suicide?'

She had been looking this way and that, apparently bored by men's talk. She turned on her father. 'That isn't true. You mustn't say things like that.'

'I've been wondering,' Pomeroy persisted, 'you don't think by any chance those other two are kind of suspicious?'

Dalrymple prodded him in the chest with a stiff finger. 'My daughter is absolutely right. Your mouth could very easily get you into trouble, Pomeroy. Now, good night to you, sir.'

Again, he had to watch them walk away, arm in arm; she didn't look back. That neck, those delicately voluptuous hips ... he went back to his cabin but there was no note from her. Nothing. His whole body craved for her. He went walking, and would have hammered on her door but for knowing Dalrymple was in there with her.

He was passing the smoking room — again — when he saw Dalrymple sitting with three other English toffs. A steward was lighting a big cigar for him. Somebody finished a yarn and Dalrymple threw up his hands and heehawed so much he had to take out his monocle to wipe his eye. He didn't look like a man preparing to hit the hay.

Have a swell time, colonel!

She was in a long white robe when she opened the door. Her hair was loose, such loveliness, such depravity. Her eyes widened in horror. He clicked his heels. She slapped him hard.

He grabbed her around the waist and knees and hoisted her into his arms. She kicked and struggled but he pushed her against the door, burying his face in her bosom to protect his eyes from her clawing hands. Inside the cabin, she stopped struggling. He lifted his face and found himself looking into the astonished eyes of a girl with lustrous black hair and the brightest red cheeks he had ever seen.

10

Kate slid down from his arms. Calmly adjusting her cotton robe, she said,

'You haven't met Letitia, have you? Letitia, this is Mr Pomeroy, he's an American.'

That seemed to explain everything. The girl smiled. There was a giggle behind her strong burr. 'Very pleased to make your acquaintance, sir.'

Vurry playeezed, was she?

He gave her a little bow. 'Likewise, Letitia.'

'Praps I should be getting back to my own cabin, ma'am,' the girl suggested, proving how smart she was. He'd imagined a woman in her forties. Letitia was around twenty. Her eyes were very dark, with a glint. The light shone on her thick black hair. Treacherously, his eyes insisted on returning to the curves beneath her stiff grey skirt. Treachery was suitably rewarded.

'Letitia's staying with me tonight, she tends to get sick when it's stormy,' Kate said firmly. She was careful not to brush against him when she opened the door. 'Goodbye, John — '

She closed the door on his face and he didn't see her again on the *Lucania.* Next morning the bustle was on for landing, stewards carrying luggage, bosom buddies swearing eternal friendship over more last drinks. He went on deck for his first look at England. The wind came in squalls, with driving rain. Liverpool looked black and bleak and low on the horizon. Tugs were hooting around the *Lucania,* one of them coming alongside to let a party of men wearing derbies and homburgs and raincoats climb aboard. With nothing better to do and no bosom buddies to hoist a last drink with, he followed them behind a ship's officer to the dining room, where they joined the officers and newspapermen who'd made the trip along with the Italian inventor. A ship's officer distributed copies of the *Lucania's* news sheet, the last issue still hot with the imprisonment of the King of Serbia.

'Apart from keeping ships' passengers amused with the novelty of news at sea, what practical application does your invention have, Signor Marconi?' asked a fearless newshound.

Guglielmo Marconi smiled patiently.

'I have got quite beyond the experimental stage. My experiments through the whole voyage have been entirely successful. We have never been out of touch during the trip. I shall be opening up my business commercially very soon.'

'Is one voyage adequate proof that wireless telegraphy works, Signor Marconi? What about all the ships that take a different route across the Atlantic? And they'll still need underwater cables when there's thick fog, won't they?'

Marconi, who had remained in Britain even after Queen Victoria described him as an electrician, was prepared to strain his tolerance for these cretins. 'You may depend upon it, there will be no question of messages going astray. They will pierce thousands of miles of wind and fog and rain between the two continents with just as much assurance of reaching their destination as the sun's rays reach us!'

'Not much sun getting through today,' quipped a British Journalist. Pomeroy headed back to his cabin against a flow of oldsters squawking for umbrellas to keep them dry down the gangway. Horton was not in his steward's pantry. Along the corridor, stateroom doors lay open to show wet towels strewn on carpets and unmade beds. In five and a half days, the *Lucania* had become almost a way of life — not just a big ship crossing the Atlantic but a place in its own time. He felt older than when he'd waved farewell to Owen Martin on the New York pier, older and more sure of himself. Putting one over on the Imperial German secret service, that was something, wasn't it?

147

Leaving his cabin door open, he put three ten pound notes on the table for Horton and knelt to strap up the last of his three suitcases. He was singing softly, '... with nothin' but a fine-tooth comb — ', when a man's black shoe came down on the carpet beside his knee.

'Say, Horton — '

A white towel came in front of his eyes and strong hands pulled his head and the towel together, smothering his yell. The sweetish tang of chloroform reached his nose and mouth. He fought desperately to pull the towel off his face and then he was struggling into oblivion.

From a dream of floating face up in warm waves, he woke half an hour later on the cabin floor. The money was gone from the table. His wallet lay open on the carpet — oh no, even the gold eagles from his vest pocket! The bastard had chosen exactly the right moment, with everybody crowding off the ship, stewards all running every which way. Cursing himself for underestimating the Texan, he splashed his face repeatedly in cold water. The thought of that bastards fat hands poking into his pockets ... if anything, that was what he resented most.

Bastard. . . Horton was having a quiet smoke and a glass of beer in his pantry. He frowned in disbelief. 'Say, Horton, about your gratuity — '

'Did you come back on board to give me a tip?' Horton looked quite moist about the eyes. 'I'll say this, Mr Pomeroy, people talk about Americans but — '

'Horton, how would you feel about lending me some money?'

11

England in the rain ...

Last passenger off the *Lucania,* unlucky with a hotshot British customs officer who searched everything twice (but missed the Smith and Wesson stuck down the back of his pants), Pomeroy put up that night in a cheap hotel near Liverpool's Lime Street railway station. England was damp sheets, an iron bath with a grease ring, and drunks bawling Irish songs all night in the rainy street below.

Horton had believed him about falling asleep after farewell drinks and then finding he'd lost his wallet — it took a lot of persuasion to stop him having the ship searched end to end. Taking ten pounds off the guy was bad enough. What made it really embarrassing was Horton trying to lend him his wages as well because he was a gentleman and shouldn't have to travel in reduced circumstances.

He caught the first London train next morning, after a breakfast of lumpy oats dished up by a waiter with dirty fingernails and a gumboil. He knew he was in a foreign land for sure when he saw the train. The London and North Railway carriages were maroon and pale blue, with doors in the middle and wheels below the platform level. Instead of the regular type of carriage, he found himself in a little cabin with facing seats and sliding doors. There was no restaurant car ... England on a wet Sunday rolled by the steamy, rain-spattered window, miserable cows huddling against hedges on pocket-handkerchief fields, trees, slummy backyards in black towns, trees, quaint villages with church steeples and no people, seagulls swarming on lakes with hedges that marked off the flooded fields, trees, an untended horse plodding alongside a dirty canal pulling a barge on a rope, trees, small towns of red brick and stone and not a single wooden building, the turrets of a castle sticking up

149

among thick trees on a hill as smoothly contoured as a breast, ducks and geese in a muddy farmyard, all of it small and wet and populated only by huge horses and sad cows that were so well trained the loco didn't need a cowcatcher. America was all space and distant horizons and people passing through. England was a completely different place every time white steam and brown smoke cleared the windows. But England wasn't going anywhere, it had arrived. The train stopped at villages and small towns and big towns, but if anybody got on or off it was at the other end. Maybe he was still in a chloroform dream, maybe this was limbo, stuck all alone in a little cabin compartment with mesh luggage racks and brown photographs of mountains and rivers. He relieved his frustration by using the wooden bars of the luggage racks as parallel poles for a gymnastic workout that ended with his soles against the carriage ceiling. At Euston terminal, he was whistling up a porter through the window before the loco reached the buffers. Following his grips being pushed on a trolley, he handed over his ticket at the gate, watched by the pale, pasty faces of people meeting the Liverpool train. He was following his porter through the crowd when he caught a glimpse of Francis Holborn.

It took him a couple of seconds to recover from the confusion between what his eyes thought they'd seen and what his brain told them they could not have seen, then he pushed sideways into the crowd. A woman carrying an infant in a shawl turned angrily when he bumped her. 'Watch where you're going, will you?' she snapped. People jostled around them. He came out on the other side of the little crowd, but there was no sign of the man in the homburg hat. They all had their backs to him now, pushing forward to meet passengers at the gate. No, he'd imagined it, a trick of the brain, anybody could be spooked into imagining things under the gloomy vault of Euston terminal, particularly on an empty belly.

He walked quickly to catch up with his baggage. Reaching the line of two-wheel horsecabs under a big wrought-iron awning, the porter lifted his grips into the first cab in line.

'The American embassy,' he told the hackie, who looked like a walrus wearing a derby up there on his roof seat, he had so many coats under his rubber slicker.

Wareszatguv?

The porter and the hackie went into native lingo. The second hackney in line pulled away, and so did the third. The driver of the fourth cab in the line was taking away the leather feedbag from his horse, a solid black mare with a white blaze down between the ears. Bits of chaff dribbled from the mare's mouth onto wet stone.

'He doesn't know where it is, guv,' said the porter.

'He doesn't know the American embassy?'

'He didn't know America had an embassy.'

Opin guv, alawska bobbee.

Hop in, governor, I'll ask a bobby, meaning a police constable, meaning a patrolman. To leave the rank, the driver pulled the reins hard left and the horse came around in a semicircle. Through rainwater cascading down glass he saw the silhouette of the passenger sitting down inside the other cab. He was taking off his homburg hat — Francis Holborn, no doubt about it!

LONDON

The paradise of the rich. The purgatory of the poor. The hell of the wise.

12

Rain blurred his view of the other cab. Little eddies of water became rolling waves. a few bubbles turned into wind-lashed foam. a grey cab window blurred into a vision of the endless ocean and through the blur he seemed to see the mutely pleading face of Francis Holborn.

'No!'

He screwed his eyelids tight. He heard the clopping of horse's hooves. the creak of an axle, the steady squish of rubber-bound wheels on stone, the drumming of rain on the roof. He opened his eyes. The cab window was streaked with warm yellow tints from London's gaslights. He quickly rationalized his moment of hysteria; he was hungry, in a strange foreign city under a sky dark enough for the end of the world, delayed shock at Holborn's death, maybe even a hangover from the chloroform — sure, that was it. He sat nearer the window. Rain was spooky stuff. everybody knew that (and that weekend London was having its heaviest rainfall in living memory; in the outlying village of Perivale in the country of Middlesex, only the chimneys of the little houses were visible that Sunday above floodwater). This was the Old World, where the ghost stories came from. He peered up at the darkly looming buildings whose high nooks and crannies looked like places for hobgoblins to live. Rain bounced off the tall helmet and rubber slicker of the bobby who knew the address of the American embassy. Rain sprayed white on the sidewalks and flooded the gutters with little rivers on which he could imagine a lead soldier standing one-legged on a paper boat. Rain shrouded the instantly recognizable outline of the Houses of Parliament and the clockface of Big Ben at five after two.

When the hackney stopped. he opened the door but didn't get out. He'd imagined an embassy to be a smaller version of the White House this wasn't even a separate building but one entrance in a block the length of the Lucania.

'You sure this is the place pal?' he called to the driver. NE

'A hundrid'n twenny-free, guv, 'at's wot the bobbee said. wunnit?' Pulling up his collar. Pomeroy ran across the sidewalk into the doorway of 123 Victoria Street. On one side, sure enough. was a dull brass plate:

Embassy
of
The United States
of
America

There was a bell push, but it felt slack when he tugged it. He tried the handle and the heavy wooden door scraped across a stone threshold. He came into a shadowy vestibule with a doormat worn almost smooth. A glass door opened into a dark hallway. Coming down a dimly lit staircase ahead of him was a woman wearing a black straw hat, a long waterproof coat and black ankle boots. She was unfastening a brown umbrella. He raised his fedora.

'Pardon me, ma'am, I'm looking for the American embassy?' She had dark stuff around the eyes. Her cheeks were bright with rouge and her lips even brighter with red paint. Her accent was halfway , between Kate's upper-class English and the hackie's cockney: 'First door on the right, dear — lovely day for the ducks, innit?' She opened her umbrella and ducked out in the street. Deeper into the dark lobby, he knocked on a big brown door. He heard footsteps. The man who opened the door had bright red hair in stiff waves that started too low on his brow, too much hair for a small round face with wary eyes and a stubby nose, a short, dapper man in a bureaucrat's black coat, white shirt with a wing collar, bunchy cravat fastened with a gold pin, light grey trousers and white spats over patent-leather shoes. 'Yes?'

'Sorry, I'm looking for the American embassy — '

'We're closed — it's Sunday don't you know?'

'This is the American embassy?'

'Well it isn't Buckingham Palace.'

Pomeroy stepped past the little man into a dingy hallway. 'You fellows ever think of buying a pot of paint?'

'We failed to get an act through Congress. Now, if you will — '

Pomeroy went along the narrow hallway, looking into a windowless kitchen, coming to the door of the first outer office, a small crammed room with a high ceiling and one window looking out into a dark well of brick walls festooned with pipes. The little man was close behind him.

'I want to see the head man around here.'

'I'll have to ask you to come back tomorrow — '

'And who might you be, mister?'

The dapper little man had a funny way of seeming to bounce up and down on his toes without actually moving. He inclined his head as if to bow: 'Ellington Fairbairn, second secretary, United States legation in London.'

'Oh .. .' Pomeroy made the kind of face that goes with 'aw shucks'. He grinned sheepishly, then threw up a snappy salute: 'John Stockley Pomeroy reporting for duty, sir!'

Shaking the hand of Ellington Fairbairn, the man with the permanently pursed lips, was like tug of war with a tulip.

'Welcome to London, Mr Pomeroy, I'll see you here at eleven tomorrow, good day to you.'

'Don't I get a look at the place?'

'Far be it from *me* to quench a raging *prairie* fire of enthusiasm for our great task ...' He emphasized prairie in such a way as to cast doubt on the rumoured existence of a faraway land called America. He walked quickly, on his toes. 'This is the room we keep the locally hired English staff in ... through here we have the wide-open vistas of the third secretaries' room ... my office is up here — am I going too fast for you?'

The third secretaries' room had all the imposing grandeur of a four-track streetcar terminal, yet it contained only three desks, each with its own window onto the same dark well, and a nice big fireplace. Fairbairn pointed at each desk in turn, two cluttered with files and papers, one bare. Here sitteth your colleague Mr Mitchell Dean Spence ... Mr Lucius Menifee Sleath ... and Mr Robert Lyle, who is ill. Now, if you would care to trot along behind me ...'

Fairbairn bounced on his toes to the far end of the long room and opened two tall doors into a kind of antechamber hardly big enough for them to move around an oval table to reach another pair of tall doors. Fairbairn threw them open and stood back like a flunkey.

'The ambassador's room, holy of Holies.'

Pomeroy looked into a square office with one big desk in front of curtained windows looking out on a small walled garden, a bookcase full of shabby brown tomes, a table with a globe of the world on it. Their eyes met. Pomeroy sniffed. Fairbairn's dinky little mouth tightened against any urge to smile.

'That, Mr Pomeroy, is the odour of congressional stinginess. Twenty-nine years of dust and darkness ...' Somewhere back in the gloomy regions of the embassy, a telephone was buzzing. 'If you would seal up this living tomb again, I'll attend to the telephone.'

Pomeroy closed the doors and came through the antechamber. He could hear Fairbairn's voice from the farther outer office. Gray said to look for any member of staff spending more than his salary warranted or making excuses to work odd hours when documents could be copied out in safety. He turned left into Fairbairn's office. On a big mahogany desk with two wooden trays and a brass tortoise that was really an inkstand, there were several foolscap sheets covered with tight copper-plate handwriting. spread on a tooled-leather blotting pad. He went around the desk. Sheet One, so marked, was headed *Ellington Fairbairn, Second Secretary, to His Excellency Andrew Phillips Fry*:

MINUTES OF MEETING. BRITISH FOREIGN OFFICE. OCT. 7.
SUBJECT NEGOTIATIONS RE EXTRADITION TREATY COVERING
BRIBERY

When he reached the cramped outer office, Fairbairn was standing by a four-line switchboard. 'No no no, chief inspector, no trouble at all, it's *living* Americans one finds oneself slightly reluctant to become involved with. St Mary's Hospital? Yes, I'll have one of my assistant secretaries meet you there in the morning ... goodbye.' He replaced the telephone. He sighed and shook his head. 'I come in here to catch up with my paperwork on Sundays because nothing ever happens on Sundays. Well now, Mr Pomeroy, if you'll excuse me — '

'Say, Ellington, can you spring me a few bucks? I don't even have the price of a hotel room.'

'You had an allowance albeit pitiful from the State Department, didn't you?'

'That all went on the boat. Boy, did I have a wingding time!'

'Unfortunately, Mr Pomeroy, advances require the ambassador's authority — '

'Okay, where is the old coot?'

'In the country — '

'I should think he is too in the country if he's the goddam ambassador to it!'

Fairbairn might look like a man who preferred candy to steak, but he was no pushover. ' "In the country" is an English expression, it means "out of town" — '

'If you mean "out of town" why not say "out of town"? '

157

'Being a diplomat in a foreign country, I take the view that a smattering of the local language aids communication.'

'You remember any American expressions? I have a hackie waiting out there, you want me to panhandle on the London sidewalks to pay him off?'

'It wasn't me *wingdinging* across the Atlantic, Mr Pomeroy.'

He was a feisty little guy even if his tight waist was probably in men's corsets, but it was time to let him know the score. Pomeroy appraised the jumble of rolltop desks and tables and filing cabinets. 'I sure as hell didn't expect to be working in a closet like this when Teddy Roosevelt took me for a stroll in Rock Creek Park. Teddy goes way back with my daddy. This cockaninny job is something they cooked up together to keep me out of mischief ...' Fairbairn tried not to show it but his dinky little mouth was twitching. Pomeroy treated him to the warm smile of a handsome bully. 'What's your suggestion, Ellington old man — I should wire the White House collect for the price of a hotel room?'

Fairbairn acknowledged defeat with a little sniff. He brought out a lady's change purse, selected some gold sovereigns and half-sovereigns and dropped them finger and thumb into Pomeroy's travel-grimed palm.

'That's six pounds, almost thirty dollars, a personal loan you can repay out of your first salary cheque.'

'That's white of you, Ellington old man.'

'I'm only thirty-seven and junior staff address me as Mr Fairbairn. I do not have the patronage of the President, but I have devoted my life to the foreign service of the United States, fourteen years in Europe, ten of them here as second secretary, basic salary two thousand dollars a year, on which I couldn't live but for private money. Being a professional, I am, of course, ineligible for an ambassadorship. Early in my career, a State Department assistant secretary wangled the top position in the diplomatic bureau for his son-in-law, a man described as unread, uncultured and altogether undesirable. In other words, Mr Pomeroy, I am *au fait* with the realities, hence this little loan you have gouged out of me. However, while you may be President Roosevelt's protege, I know that he is anxious to raise the professional standards of the foreign service, and has even advocated selection by merit, wildly radical as that may sound. I can't dismiss you or even discipline you, but I can put in such shocking reports on you that President Roosevelt will have to disown you if only to save himself from public embarrassment. Do I make myself passably clear?'

'Yes, Mr Fairbairn, all too clear.' Pomeroy snapped off another salute. 'Orders received and understood, sir. I won't sneak on you and you won't sneak on me, right?'

'Try not to slam the door.'

The rain had stopped. Victoria Street was almost empty of traffic. His hackie was wiping down the horse's flanks. As he crossed the sidewalk, he saw another two-wheel hansom cab standing about forty yards along on the other side. 'You know a good hotel in the downtown area, respectable but not a funeral parlour, know what I mean?'

'Sure, guv, 'op in.'

His cab did a wide turn and they went back in the direction of the Houses of Parliament and Westminster Abbey. He wiped condensation from the rear window. The other cab was following right behind him. The horse was black, with a white streak down its forehead. A doubledecker horsebus came out of a side street between the two cabs and he lost the other cab.

Outside the Excelsior Hotel in the Strand, within sight of Lord Nelson's statue on its gigantic column in Trafalgar Square, a massive flunkey in a green top hat and matching uniform with medal ribbons threw open the cab door. 'Good hafternoon to yew, sah, sun peeping through, can't be bad, may I henquire, sah, are yew booked? The 'otel is packed to the rooftops I swear. Jolly farmers, yew know.'

'Sure, I have a reservation — '

'I'll 'ave a portah take your luggage hinside, sah.'

Always get yourself into the hotel that's full up, it's generally the best one in town. He went up the steps and waited under the marquee for his hackie.

'Wiv wytin toime attulbee five bob, guv.'

He fished out Fairbairn's coins. The big doorman made the hackie stand back and said, confidentially, 'Yew being an hamerican gentlemun, may I 'elp 'ere, sah? These rascals would nick the pennies off of a dead nun's eyes, I swear.'

'You handle it, would you?' He gave the doorman a half-sovereign. The cab with the black mare had pulled up about thirty yards back. The driver sat there holding reins and whip. Watery sunshine had brought crowds onto the sidewalk and he couldn't see if anybody was getting out of the cab. He came down the steps and headed towards it against the flow of flat straw hats and umbrellas. The driver suddenly flicked the reins and the black mare pulled out into the traffic. When it passed him he couldn't make out if there was anybody inside.

Seeing him through the swing doors, the big flunkey gave him his change. 'I gave 'im thruppence tip, sah, generosity is a commendable himpulse, sah, but hit's spoiling these rogues, I swear.'

He was liking the Excelsior before he reached the desk. The lobby was busy with people of all shapes and sizes and both sexes. He saw his first Indian — not redskin but Indian from India, wearing a long skirt instead of pants. From the rear he heard an orchestra. He stood by his cases at the desk. A clerk in a brown suit was telling a middle-aged man and his younger woman companion there wasn't a vacant room in the hotel because of some big agricultural show. The couple left hurriedly.

'My name's Pomeroy, you have a reservation made for me by the embassy of the United States.'

The clerk checked his book. An assistant manager in a black suit checked the book and a file. 'I'm terribly sorry, sir, but we don't seem to have a reservation under the name Pomeroy, and I regret that the hotel is full — '

'Let me see the manager.'

'However, sir, I'm sure the mistake is entirely ours, sir, if you'd care to take a seat?'

He nodded curtly and strolled back towards the street entrance. Outside, it now looked like high summer. None of the men sitting on big sofas under palm trees in pots looked anything like Francis Holborn. The cab tailing him from the railway depot was no hallucination, however. Who the hell could be tailing him? Detectives, maybe, something to do with Holborn's suicide? What did a British detective look like? English clothes weren't too different, it was the faces and the voices that were foreign to him — fat faces, crimson faces, pasty faces, a few big bony faces, no two the same, none of them what you'd call a regular face, noses that were too big, eyes too far apart, hardly any suntanned faces and then one that some far-flung sun had cooked to leather. He could spot the farmers now, burly men as wide as they were tall in thick, hairy suits, faces so red they were almost bleeding, bowed legs you could see the carpet between when their heels were touching. And the voices, quiet and burred, squeaky and merry, not so loud as American voices, but that somehow made you pay more attention to what they were saying. Not that he could understand some of the accents

'Mr Pomeroy?' He came to the desk. The assistant manager was most apologetic. 'The best I can do for you tonight is a single room on the seventh floor, but tomorrow I'll be able to move you downstairs presuming you still wish to stay with us after this regrettable mistake.'

Weakness always invites attack. President Roosevelt said that.

'The embassy was also supposed to have some cash waiting here for me, I only got off the Lucania at Liverpool yesterday and I don't have any cheques. Goddammit, what a foul-up!'

'I could always get our cashier to draw some money from the safe and put it on your bill. Would twenty pounds be enough, sir?'

'It'll do, I guess.'

Miss Busby the cashier was a smallish girl head to toe, but not stunted back to front, with black hair piled in plaits and dark blue eyes. He was liking the Excelsior better by the minute. 'Miss Busby will have the money here for you when you come down to dinner, sir. I can thoroughly recommend our restaurant. Porter!' Ping went the bell and up to the desk loomed the lankiest, saddest, oddest boy he had ever clapped eyes on.

'Toms, Mr Pomeroy to 316 and look lively, boy.'

Toms was around five eleven with a downy moustache, one big red pimple on his virgin chin and very little in the way of a chest. He wore a green shirt and a white apron over brown pants that didn't make it to his ankles. His skull was cropped to the bone except for the stiff brush on top. He got one suitcase under a long, thin arm and picked up the other two. He staggered slightly as if his long legs were stilts. His voice had only recently broken and wasn't too sure where it had broken to.

'Please follow me, sir,' he rumbled, *basso profundo* with a squeak.

They crossed the marble floor to the golden portals of the elevator-lift, they said. The attendant was a young guy with the shirt sleeve of his missing right arm pinned across his chest, on which he had some medals and ribbons. Nobody in the busy lobby seemed to be paying any attention. Toms backed into the elevator, caught his heel on something and began to topple. Pomeroy steadied him. His arms felt like sticks in linen. Two farmers coordinated their shoulders to get in and the one-armed attendant slammed the gate and pulled the brass lever.

The farmers got out at the third. 'Mangelwurzels,' murmured the one-armed attendant. 'Aaarrr, tis your swede-bashers up in Lunnon for the bright lights and the painted wimmin, aaarrr.' He winked at Pomeroy and nudged the blushing Toms. 'Stay away from painted wimmin,lad!'

'South African war?' Pomeroy said.

'Rifle Brigade.' The elevator attendant wiggled his right shoulder stump to make his empty shirt sleeve flap against his chest. 'Lost this in the siege of Ladysmith — wasn't shot off, me and my mates got fed up eating rats and cats. I said I'd give my right arm for a decent bit of stew.' He winked at Pomeroy and nudged the boy. 'Ever had an elbow sandwich, Naunton?'

The boy went red in the face.

'I was in the army — Sixth Cavalry,' Pomeroy said, for no particular reason. The boy gave him a quick look.

'Better money in the American army,' the elevator attendant said.

Pomeroy followed the boy along one corridor, up a short flight of stairs, along another narrow corridor that turned right onto a landing, with stairs twisting down into darkness and an iron stepladder up to a frosted-glass hatchway in the roof. Even as he was looking up at it, hailstones began to crack against the glass. 'Where does that go to?' he asked the boy, pointing down the stairs.

'Down to the kitchens, sir. Actually, this is supposed to be staff quarters.' He contorted his question-mark body to get the key in the door of 316, still holding the three cases. The little bedroom looked out onto black slates and chimney stacks bouncing white hailstones. There was a washbasin in the corner, a big wardrobe, a little table and one big easy chair. The boy let the cases slide down his legs to the floor and knelt in front of a tiled fireplace already set with paper, kindling sticks and coal in a small black grate. He struck a match. It broke in two. The flaring head hit the rug. He snatched at it and hissed as it burned his fingers. He had to put it out with a brass shovel. Sticks began to crack. 'There's a bathroom back along the corridor on your right, sir.'

'Thanks, Naunton.' He flicked a half-sovereign across the bed. The boy missed it, ducked down, hit his shoulder against the bed and fell on his side. His pale face that had yet to meet a razor was a deep crimson when he came up. He held out the half-sovereign.

'This is too much, sir, the correct tip for a porter is sixpence.'

'How old are you, Naunton?'

'I'll be fourteen in January, sir. We're not allowed to use Christian names with guests, sir.'

'Why, don't I look like a Christian?'

'It isn't allowed to discuss personal matters with guests, sir.'

Pomeroy did a fast head roll over the bed and sprang onto his toes in front of the boy. Naunton Toms went red again. Pomeroy stuck out his hand. 'I've never known a boy could give me an inch — John Pomeroy, pleased to meet you, Naunton.'

'Pleased to meet you, sir,' the boy said gruffly. His hand was surprisingly hard.

'Want to earn that half-sovereign, Naunton?'

'You don't have to pay the porter for service — '

'Maybe this isn't regular service, Naunton. Listen. You hang around the lobby being a bellboy, you must know everything that happens, that right? When you go downstairs, could you quietly find out if anybody's been asking for me at the desk? Or if anybody comes asking about me? Just a little private favour to me, huh? What's bothering you, Naunton?' The boy shook his head. 'Spit it out, kid.'

'Were you really in the United States Cavalry?' A sad face was suddenly alive, although in Naunton Toms's case that didn't mean anything so frivolous as a smile. 'Did you fight red Indians? I'm joining the Guards as soon as I'm old enough — did you know General George Armstrong Custer?'

That nut Custer was famous among London bellhops?

He had been born in the year of the Little Big Horn but, if it made Naunton Toms amenable …

'… and that's really all I can remember about being on Custer's knee, all that yellow hair.'

'Cripes.' Naunton Toms looked at him in awe. 'I'm going to join the Coldstream Guards, but if I can't get into them I'm going to join the Khyber Rifles and fight Pathans up the Khyber Pass.'

'Well, you have some years to think about it, kid. Now — you going to do that little thing for me?'

The lanky boy nodded. 'Is somebody after you, Mr Pomeroy?'

'Naunton, all I can tell you is — cross your heart and cut your throat and hope to die if you breathe a word of this to anyone else.' The boy's hand moved quickly across his chest and throat. 'I'm with the American government, a confidential assignment, I believe that London is full of foreign spies …'

He was coming out of the Excelsior restaurant into the crowded lobby later that afternoon, feeling a whole lot better after a bath and a steak dinner, when he saw Francis Holborn again.

13

Some noisy farmers had just crossed in front of him on his way to the desk. The sleek, dark head was moving towards the front entrance. He didn't have to see the face, that was Francis Holborn!

He let a group of men and women dressed for some fancy occasion shield him as he came down the lobby. Holborn was wearing a brown chesterfield overcoat with a black velvet collar and carrying a black homburg hat. He didn't look so languid now; his shoulders were straight and his stride was brisk, but there was no mistaking that sleek head of dark hair. As soon as he was through the revolving doors, he put on his hat and turned left, walking away quickly.

Pomeroy got into the doors before a couple of ecclesiastics in short coats and gaiters and ran down the steps to the curb. He waited for a break in the flow of buses and cabs and ran across the Strand, dodging vehicles coming up from Trafalgar Square. He drew parallel with Holborn at the forecourt of the Charing Cross main-line railway station and kept pace with him skirting the barricades around the construction site for the new Hampstead underground railway.

When Holborn turned left at the comer of Trafalgar Square and Northumberland Avenue Pomeroy ran back across the street. A brisk walking pace kept him maybe twenty yards behind Holborn: he could have caught up with him easily but ...

His death had been a fake, something to do with the blackmail set-up for Tennyson, but how come he'd got the Cunard officers involved? Unless he'd fooled them as well, Devoy or Marchbanks could have hidden him in either of their cabins and smuggled him ashore at Liverpool.

He didn't notice Holborn look but he was quickening his pace down the wide street of massive buildings. There were fewer people here to dodge behind but it was almost dark, so he quickened his own stride to keep up. Why had Holborn tailed him from Euston to the embassy and the hotel? Obviously, to find out where he was staying in London. Which meant he was still part of their blackmail scheme — but why risk the chance of Holborn being spotted when they'd gone to so much trouble to fake his suicide?

At the bottom of Northumberland Avenue, Holborn slowed down, as if deciding where to go next. Before he could look around, Pomeroy dodged into a doorway. When he looked out again, Holborn was gone. He ran to the corner. Across the street was the Thames embankment, to his left a railway station. Seeing nobody wearing a black homburg under the embankment lamp-posts, he hurried to the tiled station entrance, Charing Cross on the District underground railway. He saw the black homburg moving away from the ticket collector's gate on the other side.

'Ticket, sir?'

He shouldered the man aside and ran to the top of the stairs.

'Here — come back you!'

He ran down the stairs, into the gritty smell of the London subway system — tube, they called it. A dark red steam locomotive with an oil lamp in front and a funnel and brass boiler dome on top was coming towards him out of a dark tunnel. The driver and fireman standing on their open footplate both looked at him as the engine passed, slowing down. Gatemen positioned on open platforms between the carriages called out the station name and opened little iron gates to let the people off, most of them in their Sunday best. Other people surged forwards to make little crowds around the gates between each pair of carriages. He moved quickly along the platform, peering between the hats and the heads for a sight of Holborn. Each gateman leaned out to signal to the guard when all passengers were inside the carriages. The guard waved his green flag and whistled to the driver, and the coal-burning locomotive got up steam again and pulled towards the next dark tunnel. Pomeroy peered in the windows of each carriage as it passed but didn't see anyone in a brown overcoat.

'Just a moment there, sir,' snapped the ticket collector. 'You're the party who barged past me without a ticket — '

'I'm sorry, I was trying to catch my friend — '

'American, are you?'

'Only got here today, I thought I could pay on the train — '

'This is London, sir. We don't adhere to that system on the District Railway. Missed your friend, did you?'

'I guess so. Do I owe you anything?'

'Give my regards to Buffalo Bill!'

Walking back up to the Strand, he was passing the barricades around the shafts being sunk for the Charing Cross — Hampstead underground line when it came to him — the written confession! Holborn was the weak member of the outfit. He'd written out a full admission against a threat of being hauled before the *Lucania* captain. When Devoy and Marchbanks heard about it they would have hit the roof — a signed statement that could put them in jail! Marchbanks must have been looking for it as well as the money when he used the chloroform. Now they were scared and desperate to get it back, but they'd put the burden on Holborn, let that poor dipso take all the risks ... he wished now he had grabbed hold of Holborn instead of tailing him.

'If you would just sign here, Mr Pomeroy.'

The pert Miss Busby, cashier, had an accent he recognized from some wild bastards he'd known in Dawson. 'You're Scotch,' he said, taking his twenty pounds. She smiled patiently. 'You know Davie McDonald and Donald McColl from Paisley, Renfrewshire?'

'I'm from Aberdeen actually — '

'You'd know Mad Murdo Minty and Big Don Emery then. They were from Aberdeenshire, I knew them in the Yukon.'

'They don't sound like my type, sir.'

'What's your type, Miss Busby?'

'I'm walking out with a police sergeant, sir. Tall men are my type.' She liked saying that. He gave her his narrowed-eye look. She smiled cheekily and flounced her saucy behind back into the cashier's office. He sauntered across the lobby to a big divan under a palm tree and picked up a magazine. He hadn't imagined the cab with the black mare. Somebody had picked him up at the railway terminal and followed him to the embassy and then the hotel. He flicked through the pages, just a man on his own in a hotel lobby, killing time. His eye caught the word 'American' and he thumbed back through the pages.

American quick lunches NOT served at
GALT'S RESTAURANT
66 Cheapside
Real turtle soup from turtles alive the same day
A four course lunch 1s. 9d

When he was certain that nobody in the lobby was watching him, he strolled outside. It was dry and chilly. The big doorman saw he wasn't wearing a hat or overcoat.

'Going to 'ave frost tonight, Mr Pomeroy, yew should wrap up well if you're going hout and habout —'

'Floods, sunshine, hail and now frost — all in one day? How do you people know what clothes to put on in the morning?'

'That's the benefit of being poor, Mr Pomeroy. Only one lot of clobber to choose from. Can I call you up a cab?'

'I guess I'll just stroll around tonight. I don't know your name — '

' 'oare, sir. H-O-A-R-E, and I've 'eard all the jokes — '

'You're too big for me to make jokes about your moniker, Hoare. Listen, I was expecting the American embassy to send somebody around — anybody been asking for me?'

'Not to my knowledge, Mr Pomeroy. If somebody does henquire, shall I say where to find you?'

'I don't know where I'll be, Hoare. Maybe you can direct me to the bright lights and the action. There much gambling going on in London.

'Mainly in private 'ouses and gentlemen's clubs, Mr Pomeroy. Anything else is illegal; steer well clear of any strangers who invite you to a little friendly game of cards, oh yes. The devil's work 'as many willing 'elpers in this town I swear.'

A man leaves his hotel in a strange town and somehow each turning takes him inevitably to the bright lights — that was a rule of nature. Knowing nothing about London that wasn't in *Oliver Twist*, Pomeroy crossed the Strand — not a beach but a wide street running from Trafalgar Square to Fleet Street. In that direction he would .have come to St Paul's Cathedral, but instinct guides the strange man in town away from places of worship. Following the general drift, he reached Leicester Square, taking his time, giving anybody tailing him every chance, then arriving at Piccadilly Circus, into the full maelstrom of people and traffic, buses automobiles, 'growler' cabs and hansom cabs and private carriages, the rumble and roar at the hub of the British Empire.

Treat your hair kindly —
ROWLAND'S MACASSAR OIL

Under the streetlights and in the glare of shop windows, the sidewalks were jammed with slow-moving crowds, the Sunday night promenade, all drawn to London's West End by that staunchest of all human attractions the crowd itself, people flocking to see other people. He sauntered aimlessly, attracting attention only because of his fair hair among all the straw hats and flat caps and homburgs and bowlers. Inevitably, the shuffling mass brought him to the brightest of all the lights, a street called the Haymarket, where the lovely ladies paraded in their finery, so haughty, so grand — until the mascaraed eyes fluttered and the lovely behinds just happened to wiggle saucily. under his nose.

Hello, handsome, feeling naughty tonight?

They winked in the bright light from shop windows, they brushed past and smiled coyly, they called softly from doorways.

Looking for a good time, darling?

Of course, the brighter the lights, the darker the shadows. Here, at the lower end, the paint and powder were thicker and the voices harsher — old women flaunting what used to be, young girls taunting a man with their precocious understanding of his own secret desires, some of them children. Not the Haymarket so much as the Fleshmarket. Clutching hands, ravaged faces, divine faces, puppy-fat faces, soft words and alluring smiles and the same anxious plea in all the eyes: buy me, don't send me back hungry to that other world beyond the bright lights. This was the heart of the world's greatest imperial power that claimed it ruled by Christian decency. He hadn't expected it to be a place of whores and beggars, old men in rags, maimed veterans with rows of medals and ribbons, blind men selling matchers and jumping beans off trays, freakish men with painted faces dancing like drunken braves in the gutter for pennies, fast-talking men offering to sell diamond rings and gold watches, organ grinders with wise little monkeys on chains, whores and beggars and hustlers and drunken crones and little girls and Cleopatras with cockney accents. And everywhere the shuffling crowds looking for a little excitement on a Sunday night when their proud and haughty rulers weren't needing them for any particular war.

171

Money.

He was in a big corner pub at Piccadilly Circus drinking Worthington's East India Ale, and wondering whether a simple American drifter could plunder some dough out of this historical city, when he saw a face he'd seen in the last bar on the other side of Piccadilly Circus. He remembered the thick eyebrows and the hard lines down the cheeks, a square-shouldered man in his thirties, drinking alone and trying to look like a man who enjoyed drinking on his own. He stared until the man caught his eye and looked away quickly, then he moved round a bunch of young fellows playing some game with pennies in their hands.

'Say — do we know each other?'

The man with thick eyebrows looked at the clock and tipped up his glass.

'Not me, old boy, sorry, got a train to catch,' and he was heading for the door. Pomeroy was going to run after him, then he remembered Gray's advice: if you can spot a tail, they're either incompetent or they're giving you a sight of one of them to test if you're expecting to be tailed. Either way, you don't let on you've spotted it, which leaves the initiative with you. It's the tail you can't see you worry about.

One of the young guys playing the pennies game smiled at him, a happy fellow in a flat straw hat and slick brown suit, red shirt with .a white collar and a flower in his lapel. It was a game where they put their hands in their pockets and shoved out closed fists in a circle. They each guessed a number in turn and, when they opened their fists, the one who'd guessed the correct number of coins on display dropped out. The young fellow in the straw hat stepped back from the ring.

'Fancy a game?'

'What's it you're playing?'

'Only spoofing for drinks — are you Australian?'

'Hell no, I'm an American .'

'Really? My brother lives in San Francisco. He's done ever so well in America, fair coining it in he is. What's your poison — my name's Harry Smithers.'

'Quint Pepperday. Pleased to make your acquaintance, Harry.'

An American called Quint Pepperday from Baltimore over here to see the old country where his great-grandpa hailed from originally was a novelty item and soon he was in the circle with the fellows. He guessed wrong every time and took their joshing in good spirit as he gave Harry a half-sovereign to buy the drinks. While Harry was at the bar, he learned that these other fellows had never met Harry until that night. 'He's a tout,' one of them said. They were all smiles again when Harry came back with the drinks. Harry, however, nudged him and muttered that he was bored, why didn't they try some places he knew with cracking girls? They bowed out of there in high spirits. Harry, the slick-salesman type with oiled hair parted in the middle, said he usually 'came up west' on a Sunday night for 'a bit of skirt'. Of course, if you wanted to get into 'the right places' you had to pay a bit 'on top', particularly in the Piccadilly and Soho area.

'What's a tout, Harry?' his new American buddy asked naively.

'That what those berks back there told you?' Harry asked defensively. 'They're just twats from Camberwell, what do they know?'

His new American buddy punched him playfully on the biceps. 'Where do you steer a high-rolling gambling man in this wonderful friendly city of yours, Harry?'

Didn't Harry just happen to know the best 'spieler' in town — Tosher Delaney's near Blackfriars? Of course, you couldn't just walk in off the street. Tosher ran a high-class place and they didn't play for coppers, which meant pennies, halfpennies, farthings.

173

'I have a few sovereigns to fling around, Harry old bean. Lead me to it!'

They caught a cab on Shaftesbury Avenue. The sidewalk was too crowded to make out anybody who might be watching him, other than all the pale faces rubbbernecking at the noisy American slapping his pal's back into the cab.

On the journey back down through Trafalgar Square and then onto the embankment street alongside the river Thames, Harry advised his new buddy Quint that getting into Tosher Delaney's might require him to bung the geezer on the door a couple of sovs. 'Bung' meant 'bribe'; 'geezer' meant 'bloke'. Harry seemed to relax with two gold sovereigns in his hand and Pomeroy wondered what kind of steerjoint Tosher Delaney was running if the tout was so anxious to get his rake-off in advance. The cab passed a bridge over the Thames on their right and entered an area of darker streets with wharf buildings and big warehouses, the sort of place a Smith and Wesson might be a comfort.

Tosher Delaney's was a big pub in a gloomy street of dark tenement buildings. Harry told him to wait while he cleared things inside. Pomeroy paid off the hackie.

'This a good place for a little enjoyment, mate?'

The hackie sniffed at a drop on the end of his nose. 'Oh yeah, you'll enjoy yourself, guv. Great fun, picking up yer own teeth, innit?'

The cab drove off quickly. He saw other vehicles farther up the street, then Harry came out and took him by the elbow. 'I've fixed it, you'll be all right, Quint mate.'

He looked back along the street. 'This looks like the sort of place Jack the Ripper did his terrible deeds, Harry old bean.'

'That was the bad old days,' Harry said, pulling him inside. 'You do know Jack the Ripper was a member of the royal family, don't you?'

Skagway by the Thames! The clothes were different and the accents were pretty weird and they served liquor strictly by the shot, but Tosher Delaney's establishment was otherwise the same. old saloon mothers from here to the Pacific Ocean warn their sons against. Sporting gentlemen, lively ladies, crowded bars, a jangly piano somewhere, the kind of barkeeps who had tattoos above the elbow and kept billy clubs under the counter, and here and there biggish guys in stiff collars and slick suits, not drinking, just watching. The muscle. Harry's say-so took them deeper into a rabbit warren of crowded rooms and private booths until a big fellow stopped them at the bottom of some stairs.

'It's all right, Billy, this is an American friend of mine,' Harry explained. Billy had a good look at Quint Pepperday's face under a gas mantle and gave them the okay to go on up. In the narrow corridor at the top of the stairs, Harry said, 'Tosher's got to be very careful, y'see. The rozzers want to close these places down so they try to slip narks in, know what I mean, just to stop geezers having a bit of malarkey?' He knocked on a door marked PRIVATE. 'Lucky you bumped into me, Quint, you'd never have found this place on your jack jones, would you?'

They were playing a simple game called three-card brag. An American friend of Harry's? Wonderful. Tosher himself was a belly with a colour blind tailor. They had a green baize cloth over a big round table. Of .the eight men sitting around it, five at least he spotted straightaway as shills, with two suckers. The room had heavy curtains on the windows, two doors at opposite ends and a low ceiling with wooden laths showing through the plaster in a couple of places.

'You played brag before, have yer, Quint old chap?' Tosher asked:

'I pick up any game in five minutes,' Quint assured them all. The shills were the ones who asked questions and wanted to make him feel at home. The two straight johns were itching to get on with their punishment. The cards were greasy, and daubed. Tosher explained the rules. Three-card brag was a kind of dog soldier's poker.

'A dollar ante,' Tosher announced.

'You play with American money?'

'Nah, a dollar's what we call five bob — five shillings. Bettin's double if anybody don't look at their cards an' goes blind.'

'We soon will have American money the way Pierpont Morgan and Yerkes are taking over,' complained one of the straight johns. Morgan, it seemed, had bought several British shipping lines and was now moving into power companies and·public transport in London. Yerkes struck a bell in connection with public transport.

'Not Charles Tyson Yerkes of Chicago?' he asked.

They told him Yerkes was head of the syndicate that had got Parliament's approval for the new underground railway being built from Charing Cross to Hampstead.

'Charles Tyson Yerkes? Your government's given him the railway contract? Why, he's one of the biggest crooks we've ever had in the States! He was a banker in Philadelphia till they jailed him for fraud, then he moved to Chicago and bribed every alderman in sight to get control of public transportation. He got out of Chicago in 1890 when citizens came with guns and ropes to string him up! They say he stole twenty million dollars out of the Chicago traction tangle! And your Parliament's doing business with him? You know his business motto — "Buy up old junk, fix it up a little and unload it upon the other fellows"!'

'Never mind, he's got things movin' — so can we get on wiv the game?'

Skagway by the Thames went by universal rules. Somebody fetched him a drink — gin and water was the favourite tipple. He took it easy for the first couple of rounds, just feeling his way. On the third deal, he blew a silent whistle at his cards and brought out the four five pound notes Miss Busby had given him. Just as in Skagway, Tosher and his shills were going to make sure the sucker started off with a nice win to give him confidence. Around and around the betting went at five shillings and then ten shillings a time, a simple game with one vicious difference here — there was no turning up till only two players were left in, which meant you either had to fold and lose what you'd put in the pot, or let two house agents milk you dry before one of them dropped out. There was around sixty pounds in the middle when the remaining player, a silver-haired fellow who at his age should have repented a life of crime, put in two sovereigns to see him. He turned up a pair of fives, a lousy hand even in brag. The old fellow let out a moan and stacked his hand without showing what he had.

Tosher rewarded his American guest with a playful punch on the arm. 'Gotta 'and it to yer, Quint. Come in 'ere pretendin' not to know the game an' you takes the first big kitty? Cor blimey, you Yanks'll 'ave the shirts off of our bleedin' backs!'

'Call me Pierpont Morgan,' he said with a smug smile and raked in the pot, bundled the notes, dropped the coins in his coat pocket, stood up and said, 'Thanks for the game, fellows.'

Caught by surprise, they let him reach the door before chairs scraped on wooden planks.

'Where the fakk you fink you're goin', you bawstard?, Tosher barked.

There wasn't time to get the key out and lock them in. He ran along the narrow corridor. From behind, hoarse cockney voices yelled to Billy to stop him. Big Billy was there for that very purpose. He stood at the bottom of the stairs, hands on hips.

'Doin' a runner, are yer, Yank?' he sneered.

He came dancing down the wooden steps and kicked Billy in the face, at the same time getting both hands on the rails and vaulting over him.

He made it to the first bar before shouts from behind had two or three bouncers converging on him. He went left into a hall and then into a dark bar room packed with people at tables and many others standing around big wooden pillars. A piano was playing.

'Stop 'im!' roared a bouncer from the doorway behind.

'Git that thievin' bawstard, Wally!'

He started shoving into the crowd. Two barkeeps were coming down from the high bar counter backed with big wooden kegs. Somebody grabbed at his arm. He jerked his elbow back at face level. 'Don't hit me, Pomeroy,' growled an upper-class English voice, 'I'm your one hope of getting out of here.'

The tall man was wearing a black homburg hat and a brown overcoat. He had a stiff moustache, in his twenties. Gesturing for Pomeroy to follow he led the way through the crowd. From the back, he became Francis Holborn again!

14

He let the Englishman push ahead through the Sunday-night revellers, rakes and gay young dogs and mashers trying not to look like Monday morning's city clerks, good-time girls and brazen doxies pretending not to be shop assistants and type-writer girls counting the minutes before the dash to catch the last electric tramcar south of the Thames. The pianist changed tempo and the crowd sang to the piano's bittersweet jangle:

'Tell me that you love dear mama,
Lying in that cold cold room,
That you don't love your comrades better,
Cursing there in that saloon...'

Pale blob faces swayed in time to the raucous but sentimental heartbeat of their ancient city as everybody started bawling the chorus:

'Don't go out tonight dear father,
Please think how sad 't would be — '

'Oy!' came a brutal yell. 'Grab 'im, Wally, the bleeder wiv the fair 'air!'

'When the angels come to take mama,
But papa isn't there to see ...'

The Englishman grabbed his arm. The door by the piano!' Both barkeeps saw where they were headed and changed direction. The Englishman was forcing his way behind a bunch of youths clambering onto chairs. Pomeroy jumped onto their table and ran with his head ducked to miss the big wooden beams, kick-ing through bottles and glasses. As he vaulted down between two startled girls with Spanish kiss-curls, somebody hurled a bottle after him. It smashed on the wall beside the piano. The woman in the red dress went on thumping the ivories, smiling dreamily:

'Heavenly Father, please forgive him,
Reunite us all up there …'

He crashed through a door marked GENTS and ran along a narrow passageway between dirty plaster walls. Hinges ripped out of rotten wood as he hit another flimsy door.

He was in a small stone yard. On three sides black buildings went way, way up to London's sulphuric night sky, on the fourth was a lean-to shed against a high brick wall.

As the Englishman came dashing down the narrow passageway into the yard, Pomeroy jumped from a crouch. He got his elbows onto wet timber, then swung his feet up onto the shed roof. From the passageway came a hoarse cockney voice: 'He won't git far — stoopid caant's gorn to the carsi, hunney?'

'Give me a hand,' the Englishman hissed.

'Why don't you stay and talk with them?'

He went sideways up the sloping roof of the carsi — the men's john.

The black brick wall went up another six feet or so. The Englishman's head and shoulders appeared against the rear windows of Tosher Delaney's emporium.

'Don't go out tonight, dear father …'

Feeling the shaky roof sag under the Englishman's weight, he did a jackin-the-box spring to get himself up on top of the wall. The hoarse cockney voice came from the yard below. 'Fakk me, they're only up onna fakkin roof! Git rahnd the front — Tosher wants this caant's balls!'

The Englishman was trying to drag himself up the brick wall.

'Give me a hand, Pomeroy — '

'I thought it was you saving me, pal.'

Pomeroy dropped into the black void and hit slimy stone. A running figure came in silhouette against the gas lamps at the end of the narrow alley. Pomeroy pulled back against the wall.

'Come on dahn, you fakker,' the bouncer snarled up at the Englishman. Out of darkness, Pomeroy smashed his right fist into the bouncer's face. The Englishman dropped to the ground on all fours.

'There's the caants!' came a brutal roar.

They ran up the narrow alley into a wider lane, along a dark tenement wall under the windows of noisy rooms, then into another dark cleft. Pomeroy skidded on something soft and pulpy. Yowling cats scattered in the dark. The Englishman steadied him.

'Don't panic, old boy. I'll see you out of this.'

'Who the hell are you?'

'A friend in need.'

Hugging the walls of a narrow entrance, they looked down St Andrews Hill. Coming up from Victoria Street was a brewer's wagon piled high with wooden barrels. The drayman was standing up, singing lustily to encourage his two giant horses:

'Land of Hope and Glory, Mother of the Free,

How shall we extol thee, who are born of thee?'

About thirty yards behind the wagon, four or five men in shirt sleeves came running out into the street, looking in all directions.

'Wider still and wider shall thy bounds be set,

God who made thee mighty, make thee mightier yet — '

Pomeroy jinked out into the street and ran ahead of iron hooves crunching and scraping on wet cobblestones. The Englishman caught up with him 'You're quite nippy, Pomeroy — '

'How do you know my name?'

'You're scarin' the 'orses, you berks!' The drayman slashed his whip at them over the blinkered heads of his mighty chargers. 'Fakkin toffs, git out ovvit, go on, piss orf back to yer poncy fakkin wineshops!'

His shouts alerted the bouncers. Pomeroy and the Englishman veered left into Ireland Yard and ran deeper into the warren of alleys and courtyards north of the Thames at Blackfriars, through narrow stone tunnels that rang with the echo of their pounding feet. Passing a doorway, he glimpsed ragged children and a woman screaming abuse at a cowering boy.

'Try to keep up with me, Pomeroy,' the Englishman snapped.

'I'll try my damned hardest, mister.' He accelerated into a murderous sprint that took him yards ahead into a wider alley that turned right at the last moment against a blank wall, then left towards a well-lit street. The Englishman was blowing hard as he caught up. 'How am I doing?' Pomeroy asked.

'Not bad. This is Ludgate Hill, we may get a cab coming down from St Paul's.'

Pomeroy was looking up the hill at the great black dome of the cathedral against the orange glow of London's night sky when he heard a dull boom. They both felt the shockwave. 'What the hell was that?'

'A bomb, I should say — '

'There's the fakkers!'

They sprinted diagonally across Ludgate Hill. The Englishman pulled him right into another side street. 'The Old Bailey might scare 'em off — '

'What's the Old Bailey?'

'The Central Criminal Court ... where the judge puts on a black cap and ... sends you to the gallows. I think I'm getting a stitch ...'

The Englishman was holding his side. He was panting and grunting. They made it past the court and came level with the demolition site of grim Newgate Prison, symbol of terror for generations of Londoners, now being consigned to history along with the Roman wall found underneath it. Running easily, Pomeroy looked back. Three bouncers in shirt sleeves were still coming after them. 'Keep moving,' he snapped. The Englishman stumbled and came to a halt.

'It's no good ... we can handle three common hooligans ...'

'The hell with that, you handle them!'

Pomeroy ran on towards the brighter electric lights of a street junction, thinkng to force the Englishman to keep going. He looked back. The Englishman was squaring up to the advancing bouncers. They rushed him, he grabbed one of them and they danced around and around.

Pomeroy raised his hands and came back. 'Okay, okay — you can have the money.'

With one bouncer wrestling the Englishman, the other two faced Pomeroy, giving themselves a moment to get their breath back. One of them had a face like a muddy shovel, the other wasn't so good-looking.

'That's decent ovvim, innit, Jim?'

'American, innee? Should ov brought yer mustang, Yank.'

He was reaching into his hip pocket, still holding his left hand up. 'I give you the dough back — no hard feelings?'

'Course not, mate. we all gits a bit naughtee at times — '

His right arm pistoned up and out without any pullback. Into a dark grinning face. Knuckles on thin bone. Crack. The other one had something black in his right hand. He swung it at Pomeroy's face. Pomeroy swayed inside the scything arm and jerked his head in a savage butt. Dancing back, he ducked as the first one swung his life preserver in a short arc. The little club of lead shot in leather hit the angle of his shoulder, right on the point. He caught hold of the one he'd butted and swung him round as a shield, at the same time jerking up his knee into the man's privates. As he danced around, he saw the Englishman swinging punches at his bouncer. Pomeroy feinted left, right, came forward on both feet and started hammering punches into the first bouncer's face lefts and rights, knuckles on bone and skin and flesh. The one he'd kneed was sinking forward, clutching at his groin. The big one was trying to protect his face with his arms and fists. Pomeroy moved in close and his fists hit deep into a solid belly. The one on his knees tried to hug his legs. He did a little fast run on the spot, his knees hammering into the guy's face. Somebody came running at him from behind. He went down in a crouch at the last moment and the third bouncer toppled over him. Pomeroy came up between his legs, grabbed his ankles and yanked them up in the air to sink his shoe into an upside-down stomach then let him drop face first on the cobbles. He stood there for a moment: hearing his own breathing; his eardrums were popping; cold air scoured his tongue and throat; three men, one retching, one crawling, one weeping .

The tall Englishman was out cold, spread-eagled across the gutter on his back. Through the rasping in his throat and the cracking in his ears Pomeroy heard people shouting and jabbed the Englishman with his toe.

'I don't know who the hell you are, buddy, but I'm not losing you now!'

15

He hauled the Englishman off the ground. ducked his shoulder against the taller man's midriff and hoisted him into the air. The deadweight on his right shoulder helped ease the numbing pain in his left shoulder. At his first step, his foot kicked against something soft and light. It was the Englishman's hat. He let his knees bend, still balancing the tall man over his shoulder, crammed the hat on his head and started toward the brightly lit street junction.

People were standing under the lamp-posts. Faces came looming towards him. Mouths gabbled at him. Hands tried to touch him. Forced into a staggering jog to keep his balance, he made it across the wide three-way junction and turned down into a steep dark alley on the other side. A whistle started blowing.

Halfway down the alley, he heard feet pounding up the slope. He got into the dark shadow against a wall before a helmeted constable came running past him up the slope.

He staggered on through the alleys around Smithfield meat market and Farringdon railway station until the deadweight of the Englishman threatened to drag his shoulder out of its socket. Coming to a silent corner under a wall gaslight, he let the Englishman slide forward to the ground, jamming him upright against a tinplate advertisement showing a happy couple driving a dinky little automobile in the glorious English countryside:

CLIPPER BRITISH MADE MOTOR TYRES TAKE THE ROUGH
WITH THE SMOOTH

The Englishman began to moan a little as Pomeroy felt inside his overcoat to the inside breast pocket of his tweed jacket. He eased out the pigskin wallet and leaned against the Englishman to keep him up while he held up items from the wallet to the gaslight. Money, calling cards, tickets, photographs, receipts, and an official War Office identification card with a photograph, made out to Captain The Honourable Holles Holborn, Me, Coldstream Guards ... *honourable* with a *u*, the English way...

Now my younger brother, different for him, not being the heir to the title. He was lucky, went in the army, did awfully well against the bloody Boers...

'Why are you wearing my hat?' was Holles Holborn's first coherent remark.

They crossed a wide street with dead shops and offices. Holles Holborn looked in either direction. 'How far have we come?'

'About a half-mile — keep moving.'

'Ouch — I've got the most frightful headache! That bugger hit me with a bloody cosh. This must be Farringdon Road — how much did you steal from them anyway, Pomeroy, just out of interest?'

'Sixty pounds or so ... *won.'*

'I couldn't help noticing that you're obviously no stranger to violence — '

'I don't like violence — '

'You're rather good at it though.'

' Thanks be unto God for his unspeakable gift, Second Corinthians chapter nine, verse fifteen.'

'I see. Bible quotations. First you steal their money, then you beat the living daylights out of them — '

'Let's turn in here, get away from the lights.'

186

'I'm surprised you didn't go into that brawl singing a bloody hymn.'

They turned left into Charterhouse Street and down some steps into a narrow alley that immediately started up a slope.

'I take it you know I'm Francis Holborn's brother. This may come as a shock to you, Pomeroy, but I've been following you all day, ever since you got off the train at Euston.'

'You have?'

Walking up the dark alley, under a narrow slice of London's sulphuric night sky, night without darkness, sky without stars, the drawling voice had echoes of Francis Holborn — without the self-pity. Holles Holborn's story sounded plausible enough. He'd gone to meet Francis off the *Lucania,* he didn't believe the wind could blow a man off the topdeck and, being an aristocrat and not easily brushed off, he'd insisted on asking questions.

'It's amazing the loosening effect a five pound note has on the tongues of the servant class. You recall a steward called George?'

'George?'

'The one your friend Marchbanks bribed to use an empty stateroom for the poker game. He brought you coffee. There was you, Francis, Marchbanks, a man called Devoy and some English chap — Dalrymple. You played all night for big stakes. Francis was drinking heavily. You cheated him and the others out of a lot of money. Next day Francis disappeared, presumably drowned.'

'You got all this from a steward who brought us coffee? '

'Oh no. I was on the boat train. I managed to have a little *tête-à-tête* with Marchbanks. You're a diplomat, I believe ... mmm, no wonder American foreign policy tends to the rough and ready.'

'Look, Holborn, I'm very sorry about Francis.'

'Oh. Good.' Holles Holborn grabbed his shoulder and swung him around. 'Don't get unctuous with me, you bloody ruffian!'

187

For the first time in his life, Pomeroy did not hit a taller man who'd laid hands on him. 'I understand how you feel — '

'I want the bloody truth out of you!'

He twisted away from the taller man's grip and kept him at distance with a straight left arm. Holles Holborn kept coming forward. He backed away, out of dark shadow into a dim light where the steep alley was crossed by a lane. 'Take it easy, Holborn — '

'I'll wring your neck, you American blackguard!'

Pomeroy backed into the continuation of the alley on the other side of the lane. Suddenly Holborn rushed at him and a big hand crunched into his windpipe. He had his fists coming up when a light shone in their faces and a deep voice growled at them. 'Wot's going on 'ere then, *eh?* '

At the advent of a police constable, Holles Holborn's grip on Pomeroy's throat changed to a friendly arm around his shoulders and an angry voice became a languid drawl. 'Ah, good evening, officer, you come like the answer to a maiden's prayer. My friend and I seem to have drifted off course rather — '

'Having a bit of a barney, were we?'

'A minor navigational dispute, officer. We started off with a few noggins at the Dorchester, my birthday y'know. How we arrived in this dreary backwater I cannot possibly imagine. Oh, pardon my hiccup. Not to put too fine a point on it, wine has been taken.'

The oil lamp sank to a more respectful level, illuminating black boots on round cobblestones. 'You have wandered off the beaten track, sir. Nasty little place this at times, things aren't wot they used to be, no hooligans brawling openly in the street, bombs going off — '

' That frightful bang we heard?'

'Tried to blow up the Bank of England, sir!'

'Anarchists, was it?'

188

' Them or Irish Fenians, sir, murdering swine. I'd hang the lot of 'em, only langwidge they understand. Now sir, your best bet for a cab is up Clerkenwell Road, just keep on 'ere up Saffron Hill to the very top...'

Saffron Hill?

He could even remember the page with little rusty spots ... A boy sitting on an iron cot reading by a kerosene lamp and imagining a yellow street of higgledy-piggledy witches' houses and wishing he was with Oliver and the Artful Dodger ... This was it, this dark alley?

Holborn waited till they were waving down a hansom cab going back to the West End. 'Sorry I lost my temper back there, Pomeroy, inexcusable of me. Guards Club, driver.'

'Francis told me you got a medal in the South African war and they've put you on the staff, is that right?'

'Good Lord, Francis did talk the most frightful tosh at times.' Holles Holborn shuddered at the vulgar suggestion he might be anything so *flagrant* as a hero. 'I picked up a gong, they were chucking 'em at anybody who didn't actually faint at the silky breath of a Boer Mauser. Now they're given me the most frightfully boring desk job at the War House, bit of charity really while I make up my mind what the hell I'm fitted for.'

His explanation sounded more plausible all the time. Marchbanks knew that Pomeroy the cheat was coming to work at the US embassy. What more natural to assume he'd be off one Liverpool train or another? Marchbanks had given Holles Holborn a pretty good description but he wanted to be sure he'd picked the right man at Euston. These were pretty serious allegations. 'I followed you to the American embassy, then to the Excelsior and then to Tosher Delaney's looking for the right moment to confront you.'

The cab lurched along Theobald's Road and then down Shaftesbury Avenue towards Piccadilly Circus; the bright lights were dimmer now and the crowds had mostly gone home; drunks and vagrants and demented crones fought and screamed in shadowy doorways.

'Gee,' Pomeroy said when Holborn had finished. 'That was some job of shagging me you did — '

'I beg your pardon? '

'You shagged me all around London — '

'My dear chap! Not to be too squeamish about it, in this country *shagging* is the vulgar term for sexual intercourse!'

Army bullshit shone off every inch of wood floor in the snooty Guards Officers Club, 70 Pall Mall, worse than the American version, but these people had been at it longer by maybe a thousand years. On their way in, Holborn introduced them to a couple of stiff-necked Brigade of Guards officers, six-footers called Boy and Paddy. They'd heard some talk about a bloody bombing, hanging was too good for the rascals. What else did you expect with all this accursed socialism on the rampage and jumped up tradesmen getting into the Jockey Club? On the other hand, meeting an American with no hat and a few bruises amused them no end — anything went if you were in the club.

Holborn took him to a private room and ordered bacon and eggs. Beer came in silver tankards. They ate silently until he realized Holborn was obeying some code about asking direct questions. Trying to strangle you in an alley was one thing — he was a guest now.

'Your brother was drinking an awful lot on the boat,' Pomeroy said. 'I didn't get in on the game first couple of nights, then he said to me he thought they might be crooks. I've played a little poker — first hand I spotted Marchbanks dealing them off the bottom. Francis got cleaned out, afterward he told me how much he'd been losing to Marchbanks and the other man, Devoy. Obviously, I was next sucker in line — the next night I got cleaned out. If you'd spoken to my steward you'd know I had to borrow ten pounds from him for the rail fare. My first overseas posting and I have to tell the second secretary I lost my salary advance to cardsharps? When this fellow I met in a bar wanted to steer me to a gaming den, I was just desperate enough to take a chance — there's always a moment when they let the sucker win some bait money.'

Holles Holborn frowned — in admiration. 'You've a lot more nerve than I'd expect from a diplomat — even an American diplomat.' He smiled — a jest — and was still smiling when he slipped in the question: 'Know anything about the other fellow in the game — Dalrymple, wasn't it?'

'An English gent, a colonel I believe. He won quite a bit, maybe they were saving him up for next sucker ... unless, of course, he was. part of it .'

Holborn almost frowned at that, then shrugged as if it were irrelevant. 'Francis didn't get blown overboard, did he? He jumped, of course ...'

'I guess so. He lost a lot of money, he was pretty low, but naturally I didn't take him seriously about wishing he was dead ...'

Holborn sighed. 'Poor Francis. Drink, you know. Father was pretty severe with him. However, that doesn't stop one taking a rather dim view of the blackguards who battened onto his weakness. Marchbanks said he was staying at the Savoy, I may just take a stroll round there tomorrow and have a man-to-man chat with the bugger. You'd be not at all unhappy about getting your money back I expect?'

'Uh uh. I'm through brawling. The Roosevelt administration takes a rather dim view of people who drag down the good reputation of the United States.'

'Is that a fact?' Holborn said pleasantly, with his exquisite English way of using a raised eyebrow to mock the notion that the United States had a reputation to protect. All in all, he was a pretty good compendium of upper-class English mannerisms, but behind the stiff little moustache and the by Joves there was a young guy needing to grow up. 'Anyway, now I'm *au fait* with what actually happened on the boat I'm in a better position to convince this Marchbanks johnny of the error of his ways.'

'Frankly, I think he'll be handing you back your teeth, Holborn.'

The young Englishman made a pompous show of ignoring this aspersion, pulling out a gold fob watch on the end of a chain across his tweed vest. 'Good Lord, it's half past one in the morning. Let's whistle you up a cab,eh?'

On their way out they met two more lamp-posts with hair under their ice-cutter noses, a couple of majors called Buffy and Jock, jolly eccentrics who just happened to have come by the greatest empire in history. They found the night's bombing highly amusing and Buffy did a little Irish jig with his head at an angle under Jock's hand holding an imaginary hangman's noose.

Coming through the polished vestibule, he said, 'You people think it's a joke — terrorists bombing your capital city?'

'Hysteria comes easier to your average Frenchman, old boy.' Out on the pavement it was cold enough for frost. 'Ah, there's a cab.' Holborn raised an indolent arm, where common men would have shouted and yelled. 'Driver, take my friend to the Excelsior if you will and don't overcharge him, y'hear? Been most interesting evening, Pomeroy. Possibly bump into each other again, what?'

'If you keep shagging me, we will.'

Holles Holborn strode back up the steps into his upper-crust cantina, where the blood ran cold and blue and the upper lips weren't so stiff they couldn't curl at the ghastly American notion of ketchup on bacon and eggs; Captain The Honourable with a *u* Holborn, who had a boring fill-in desk job that entitled him to a War Office pass signed in person by Field Marshal

Earl Roberts, commander in chief of the whole British army? You're a bigger liar than me, Holborn, by three inches at least …

All that concern about a brother he hadn't seen for months and cared so little about he let him travel the Atlantic alone knowing he was a suicidal dipsomaniac with a gambling fever? One man on his own meeting every Liverpool train and then tailing him halfway across London, on his own, to find the polite moment for a talk? No, there had been three men at least needed to tail him on foot and by cab as far as Tosher Delaney's.

Why?

The casual way he slipped in the question about Dalrymple was the key. Dalrymple, who really was Tennyson, a secret envoy of the British government. They were worried about that.

They?

Was there any doubt? As the cab went around Trafalgar Square, trying to see Horatio Nelson way up there in the cold and the dark, he heard Gray's voice, back in the long office: 'The British secret service is very efficient in India and the East but they've only recently become interested in Europe and they've a long way to go to catch up with the Germans and the Russians and the French. Don't make the mistake of assuming they're friends of ours, Pomeroy. There's a lot of influential people in Britain hostile to the United States. Your main advantage will be they don't know we have a secret service in Europe. Your handicap will be that you are our secret service in Europe …'

The prim Miss Busby came out of her cashier's office as the night clerk was giving him his key. The lobby was noisy with happy farmers carrying pals whose legs were full up. Miss Busby saw his grazed cheek.

'Been out for a wee stroll, Mr Pomeroy?'

'I bumped into a lamp-post. Can I have an early call for seven?'

'You won't have very long in bed, Mr Pomeroy.'

'How long does one need, Miss Busby?'

'That depends how tired you are, I suppose.'

'Good night, Miss Busby.'

'Good night, Mr Pomeroy.'

Up there in his little room under the roof, all muscles aching after a hot bath in a cold bathroom, he opened the suitcase with all the books Gray said would hide which one they were using for the code. He found *Oliver Twist*. The coal fire was almost out, but the bed had a rubber hot-water bottle. He threw his bath towel over the chair and got between warm linen sheets. The grazed skin on his knuckles was white from soaking in warm water. He found the page:

As John Dawkins objected to their entering London before nightfall it was nearly eleven o'clock when they reached the turnpike at Islington. They crossed the Angel into St John's Road; struck down the small street which terminates at Sadlers Wells Theatre; through Exmouth Street and Coppice Row . ..

All his life he'd imagined the yellow street of higgledy-piggledy houses and tonight it turned out to be a dark alley. The big point was — did the British know Marchbanks was tied in with Lang-Gaevernitz of the German secret service?

... down the little court by the side of the workhouse; across the classic ground which once bore the name of Hockley-in-the-Hole; thence into Little Saffron Hill; and so into Saffron Hill the Great; along which the Dodger scudded at a rapid pace, directing Oliver to follow close at his heels ...

'You and me both, Oliver,' he muttered. There was a soft knock at the door. He jumped out of bed and shoved Oliver Twist back in the case and dug out the Smith and Wesson. He got against the wall beside the door.

'Yeah? Who is it?'

'It's me, Mr Pomeroy,' came that cute Scotch voice.

He had the bath towel wrapped around his waist when he opened the door. The prim Miss Busby averted her eyes from his bare torso and delved into her purse — handbag, they said. She brought out a little brown bottle. 'I was going off duty anyway, I brought you some iodine in case your cuts turned septic.' He closed the door behind her. She uncorked the bottle.

'This is most kind of you, Miss Busby.'

'You'd better sit down.' He chose the edge of the bed. She stood in front of him. Her hands were plump, very white and smooth.

'Hell's teeth!'

'Sssshhh.' She poured brown acid onto his other hand.

'Jesus H. Christ!'

'Keep your voice down, I'll get the sack. Let me see your cheek.' Her thighs touched against his knees and her starched grey bosom came level with his eyes as she tilted the brown bottle against his grazed cheekbone. He hissed air between clenched teeth. 'Men are such cowards,' she murmured. She corked the brown bottle and put it on the bedside table, then sat beside him on the bed. Her hand rested on his thigh. 'This towel's damp, you'll catch your death of pneumonia, Mr Pomeroy.' Her other hand moved across to tease at the stiff hairs on his chest. 'Don't say you're shy, Mr Pomeroy. You don't look like a Uranian — '

'What's a Uranian?

'Mary Anne — what do you call homos in America?'

'I knew one called Wilbur — '

'How well did you know him?'

'He didn't scare the pants off me if that's what you mean.'

'So I don't need to call for help — '

'Depends what you've got in mind, Miss Busby.' '

'I mean for these bloody buttons!'

He stood up. His chin was level with her plaited hair. 'I thought you were walking out with a tall police sergeant.'

She pulled at his bath towel and it fell to the rug. 'What he doesn't know won't hurt him, will it?' She turned her back to him and he undid the row of buttons and started to unpeel the grey dress off her plump white shoulders, but she pushed him back on the bed and eased the dress down over her hips. She stepped out of it and threw it at the chair. Next came her lace-trimmed camisole and her black moirette underskirt. Her black lisle stockings were held up by Velvet Grip suspender straps with brass fittings. She put each foot up on the bed to untie her dumpy-heeled Glace Gibson shoes. Her legs were white and smooth. Her brocaded coutil corset unhooked down the front. 'You wouldn't call me a loose woman, would you?' she muttered. Under the corset she was wearing a chemise of pink crepe de chine and matching drawers — knickers, she said. Shyly, she crossed her arms over her plump white breasts.

'You sure we've time for anything before you need to start dressing again?' he murmured. She sat in his lap and put her arms around his neck.

'I've plenty of time, as long as I'm back on the staff floor before daylight.' She bit his ear and they fell back together. She snuggled her buxom body all over him and he dragged the sheet and blankets up over her buttocks and back. 'I suppose you think I'm fast', she said when she stopped kissing him. 'Everybody says American women are very fast. Is that true?'

'Over short distances.'

'Do American women shave their legs?'

'Sure, they have special barber shops with very high chairs.'

'You don't even know my first name — it's Arabelle. Can I call you John?'

'Shouldn't somebody introduce us?'

'You're shy, aren't you? What do you do at the embassy, John, are you very important? Tell me about yourself, you're the very first American I've ever done this with, my spine started tingling the first moment you looked at me, you've got the devil's eyes, you know that? Are you going to be in London long?'

'How long is this going to take?'

'It's better if I'm on top, you're much taller than me.'

That excited him. Plump white arms cradled his face up against her bosom. Her plump body was all promise, her knee was rubbing into his groin, but boy, did she want to talk? 'What does a diplomat actually do, John? I suppose you sign treaties and keep state secrets and — no, kiss me, John, we've plenty of time. I don't know anything about you — no, just you lie there and do what I tell you or I'll pour more iodine on you! I suppose you go to lots of diplomatic balls and have intrigues with fabulous beauties . . .' All this in her cute Scotch voice with the rolling rrrs while her hands were everywhere and her knee was prodding into him and he was getting ready to explode .

If they get to Marchbanks first you're in trouble, Pomeroy. This turns into a public scandal you'll be of no use to me. Get out there and find Marchbanks and scare him out of England.

It's the middle of the night over here, Gray!

He threw her over. and pulled himself up until his face was on the pillow higher than her plaits and she squirmed plumply under .him and the talking stopped as she gasped her way to a climax.

What were you saying, Gray?

Out of warm darkness, her voice was a soothing lullaby. ' … soon as they saw I was pregnant they sacked me, they didn't do anything to him, oh no, perfectly all right for a married butler to have his way with one of the maids … are you sleeping, John?'

'Whassat?'

197

'My father and mother never spoke to me again, they're very hard on sin in Aberdeenshire, as far as they're concerned I'm dead .. . it's all right, I won't get pregnant this time, I just wish somebody had told me what precautions to take when I was seventeen — och no, it turned out for the best, I'd still be stuck in a big house polishing the silver — I wouldn't be here now, would I? Was it all right, John? John — don't go to sleep on me, I want to hear all about you ...'

He was a loud snorer. Nothing could wake him. Very gradually, she eased out from his arms and got off the bed. He flopped onto his stomach and snored disgustingly against the pillow, his mouth wide open. She dressed by the soft light from the bedside lamp. 'I'm going now, John,' she whispered, shaking his bare shoulder. He went on snoring. The key turned in the lock, the door opened and closed quietly.

He went on snoring, and then he jumped off the bed and got between her and the door before she could shove his wallet back into his pants.

'I was looking for a card to write you a wee note.'

'Who put you up to it?'

'What are you talking about, John? I told you — '

'I'll count to five then I'm going to open this door and holler. Just being in my room will get you canned, isn't that what you said?'

'Let me out of here!'

'One — '

She tried to fight her way past him. He swung her around and pushed her back into the middle of the room.

'Two — '

'I'll say you tricked me into coming up here — '

'Three — '

'Please, John!' Her face was contorting into tears. 'You'll get me in terrible trouble — '

'You're already in trouble. Four.'

'Do what you like, I don't care.'

'Five.' He started to turn the handle.

'All right, I'll tell you — don't open the door, I'll tell you ...'

16

Dawn was pink among the London chimney stacks. Brown smoke rose in straight lines from the terracotta pots like a plantation of wispy saplings. He smashed cold water into his face.

'Bit taters this morning,' boomed Naunton Toms. 'Taters in the mould -cold! Fancy a pair of Jack the Rippers for your breakfast? Jack the Rippers — kippers!'

He'd already been informed his minces were looking a bit dodgy. Mince pies — eyes. *Dodgy* didn't have a rhyme, but it sounded right for the bleary orbs in the mirror. The hot tap sent a shuddering noise back through the piping system.

'Naunton — you have any pals at the Savoy Hotel?'

'Billy Marsh, we were in the Barnardo's Home together. He's a porter, thinks he's real flash 'cos they get kings and millionaires.'

'You trust him?'

'We're blood brothers; you know how Apache braves cut their wrists and let their blood mingle and — '

'Sure, I've seen them do it. I have to know if there's a party named Marchbanks checked in at the Savoy, maybe not under that name, built like a barrel, red hair, comes from Texas — '

'There's a story in *Boy's Own Paper* about the Texas Rangers!' The lanky boy pulled out a folded paper from under his shirt. 'You can borrow it if — '

'Thanks. This guy's dangerous, Naunton, he doesn't have to know you've been asking about him — nobody has to know, you hear? Get his room number, you could also ask if there's a man called Devoy staying there.' He started stropping his razor. 'Take some shillings from the table — '

'You don't have to tip me,' the boy protested.

'I know that, Naunton. It's for your pal Billy Marsh. If he's curious, tell him it's a police matter and he'll get in bad trouble if he talks. The Savoy, that far from here?'

'Just down the Strand a bit. I'll say you've sent me out for a magazine or something. I'll leave *Boy's Own Paper* for you — there's a good joke in it. Hear about the archaeologist whose career was in ruins?'

'Don't make me laugh, Naunton, my head's splitting. Oh and Naunton you do know I'm not officially allowed to operate in this country, don't you? What would you do if the British police asked about me?' '

'I wouldn't tell them a sausage, cross my heart, cut my throat and hope to die!'

'Good. Also, don't tell anybody at the desk you're running errands for me, okay? I think those kind often work for the cops on the sly ...'

They'd used her before to get close to men they wanted investigated. They paid her five pounds each time. Usually it was foreigners of some kind — she was never told why, just to pump them and search their things and pass it all on. Once only, she'd helped them get in a position to blackmail somebody, a French diplomatic courier who was in bed with her when a policeman pretending to be her husband burst into the room. She didn't know why they wanted to blackmail the Frenchman. She didn't like doing it, but they said they would frame her on stealing charges if she didn't cooperate and the money meant she could keep her illegitimate son at a boarding school in Dorset. Holborn told her to get friendly with Pomeroy. She didn't know Holborn's name. She took it for granted he was a Special Branch policeman. He had three or four colleagues.

'He told me you were a confidence trickster who blackmailed important people. He thought you might have an address book or something that would put them onto your associates. I'm very good at memorizing things. I only have to read a sheet of paper once and I can remember most of it.'

'Nobody else in the hotel works for them?'

'No, just me. They're very clever. They got a policeman to pretend he liked me; he took me to music halls and theatres and restaurants. It started with small things, tipping him off about suspicious guests, then they wanted me to search somebody's room .. . now I can't get out of it.'

'How do you contact them?'

'I can't tell you that. Honestly, if they even suspected — '

' All I have to do is holler — '

'That would only mean getting the sack. They'd kill me if I told you — '

'I'll holler, then I'll make an official complaint. You'd be a severe embarrassment to them if it looked like a diplomatic scandal. What do you think they'd do to you?' .

'Oh Jesus ... you don't know what they're like!'

'I'm beginning to get an idea.'

There was a man here I had to get friendly with; he said he was Swiss. I think he was Austrian. I gave them his wallet — and he just disappeared! I had to tear the page out of the book and do another page without his name, they gave me the money for his bill — I mean, he just vanished! They're bastards.'

'Okay then — how do you contact them?'

'Christ, I thought the English were hard — '

'You don't like the English?'

'In Scotland they say an Englishman has all the attributes of a poker except its occasional warmth. I have a telephone number, Westminster 121. I have to ask for Mr Brodie. That's just a name they all use, there's four or five of them.'

'Arabelle, did you mean that about emigrating to the United States?'

'America wouldn't let me in — a single woman with a young son?'

'I could maybe fix you up with an American passport under another name.'

'Oh, aye? What would I have to do for it?'

'Tell me whatever it is they ask you to do. String them along, say you're getting to know me but I'm very cagey. Tell them things I want them to hear.'

'Are you a spy?'

'The United States does not use spies. I'm a third secretary at the American embassy. I want to know why they're curious about me — the real reason. Any of them sleep with you?' She nodded. 'What's his name?'

'I told you, they're all called Mr Brodie. He's the one who drinks a lot, he's married with five children, I know that much. He comes from Yorkshire, he snores as well.'

'Find out anything you can from him.'

'Do I have to sleep with you as well?'

'That isn't the American way.'

'You could have fooled me — you knew why I came up here, didn't you?'

'I wasn't a hundred per cent sure — '.

'At least you didn't make me feel dirty ... how do I know if I can trust you?'

'Consider this, Arabelle — I've promised you an entry visa, the worst I can do is let you down. But you tell *them* the truth about tonight they won't reward your loyalty, all they'll care about is me knowing you work for them. You'll be a serious liability to them — *alive.*'

Twenty-five before eight. In the mirror his blue suit bought in Washington looked very American, too American. He walked down seven floors for the exercise. All told, he had eighty-nine pounds, of which he had to return ten pounds to Horton's sister in Belgrave Square. He needed English clothes to make him less conspicuous.

Her instructions to sleep with him had come from Holborn by telephone — *after* they'd said goodnight at the Guards Club. That sounded as if they were in a hurry about something. The

Germans wanted to set Tennyson up for blackmail; it would have worked out fine but for a naive American diplomat who turned out to be a cardsharp. Now British intelligence was interested in him. Roosevelt was worried about a war coming in Europe. Maybe it was already under way. A different kind of war, that's what Gray called it ... an American diplomat who was worrying both the Germans and the British because he might know too much ...

He was having coffee and toast in a dining room of farmers easing their hangovers with kedgerees and sausages and bacon and eggs and fried tomatoes and fried bread and black puddings, bawling table to table like spooked steers, when the lanky boy came to his table under the window and put down a shiny magazine and two silver coins, a shilling and a sixpence.

'Your change, sir.' Then, out of the side of his mouth: 'No Marchbanks at the Savoy. I gave Billy Marsh sixpence.'

'Well thanks, Toms,' he said loudly, pressing the two silver coins into a big white hand on the end of a thin red wrist. Blushing for whatever reason, the boy touched his forehead and stumbled over his own feet, dodging a sour-faced waiter who gave him a snarling rebuke.

He beckoned the sour-faced waiter.

'Yes, sir?'

'I see you treating the boy like that again I'll have the manager fire you, buddy,' he said coldly. The waiter pretended not to understand.

Twenty after eight. He took the magazine through to the lobby and asked a male desk clerk where to buy good-quality clothes.

'I can recommend several good tailors, sir — '

'I need them today. Ready-mades.'

'Ah, off the peg, sir. Of course, one of the best places for you would be the Army and Navy Stores, quite near your embassy in Victoria Street — '

'Fine, I think I saw it yesterday.'

'Unfortunately, you have to be an officer or a senior NCO in the armed forces to shop at the Army and Navy Stores, that's why it's such good value, they run it for the benefit of the members — '

'We'll be moving you down to a much nicer room today, Mr Pomeroy,' said the assistant manager.

'No, I like that room just fine. I'd prefer to keep it. Is that all right by you?'

'Your wish is our command, Mr Pomeroy.'

'I guess your big department stores would open at nine o'clock, wouldn't they?'

'Not as early as that , I'm afraid ...'

He sat in the lobby under a palm tree and looked through the *Illustrated London News.* Eleanora Duse was playing Hedda Gabler at the Adelphi. A national convention of women's suffrage societies had collected two thousand pounds as an election war chest to oppose new laws removing the few political rights women had in Britain. The convention was held in Holborn Town Hall. He looked up quickly but saw nobody who might be watching him. The new novel was *The Ambassadors* by an American writer, Henry James. The new Duchess of Roxburghe was to be an American girl, it said in the gossip column. His Majesty the King was breaking his journey from the Continent to Balmoral for the start of the shooting season to attend a ball being given by the American ambassador Andrew Phillips Fry for his attractive and popular daughter, Miss Amelia Fry. He worked out the date and realized it was that night.

FOX'S PATENT

SPIRAL PUTTEES

Are so shaped as to wind on spirally from Ankle to Knee and to Fit
Closely to the Leg with Even Pressure without any turns or twists.
Can be worn under Trousers to keep the Leg Dry In Wet or Snow.

———————————

Czar Nicholas of Russia, Emperor Francis Joseph and Arch-duke Ferdinand of the Austro-Hungarian Empire had gone shooting chamois together in the Styrian Alps. Russia was postponing evacuation of Manchuria, making war with Japan inevitable. Despite the Colombian government's rejection of an agreed deal, President Theodore Roosevelt was adamant about the Panama route for his canal, although a Nicaraguan route would not need locks; critics alleged there was a secret deal between influential Americans and the shareholders of the French Canal Company, which owned the Colombian canal franchise and stood to make millions.

Maybe Charles Tyson Yerkes was about to teach them over here about good old American graft — was it really true he'd put the fix into the British Parliament to get his underground railway concession? Anyway, maybe graft was better than war. Every page of this fashion-and-society magazine had a drum-beat. The British Royal Navy had finally abolished training un-der sail — there was a photograph of Nelson's *Victory* being taken out of service as the admiral's flagship to go on public show, eighty-eight years after defeating Napoleon's navy at Trafalgar! There was also a photograph, however, of the Royal Navy's new 1A-type submarine boat. It had a periscope device with a retractable mast to see above the surface without the submarine boat coming up. An even more modern submarine type derived from the American Lake's *Protector* design was being developed in secret by the Bradstock shipbuilding com-pany for sale to the major powers. There was big money in submarine boats.

On Wimbledon Common, British soldiers had just tested a mobile searchlight for warfare at night, as if the day wasn't long enough. War seemed a lot closer than in Rock Creek Park, war after dark and war under the sea ...

At the desk on his way out he asked where he might pick up a street map and they gave him a Philips' pocket atlas guide to London, mustard and green maps and a street index. He was taking a quick look for Saffron Hill when he heard one of the desk clerks say two Fenian terrorists had been arrested in Camden Town for last night's bombing.

Outside, it was sunny but cold. Hoare the doorman gave him a snappy salute. He went left along the Strand to Trafalgar Square, passing the wooden barricades around the diggings for Yerkes's underground railway. He waited for a break in the rush of four-wheel growler cabs, hansoms, buses advertising Schweppes Dry Ginger Ale, Hudson's Soap, Gullick's Coal, Lipton's Tea — 'The Finest the World Can Afford' delivery wagons, and even a smart Panhard Levassor automobile with a uniformed chauffeur and two fur-clad ladies sharing a rug in back. He crossed to the fountains under Nelson's Column. Only the pigeons and the vagrants camped between the big stone lions seemed interested in him as he did a little gawking. He crossed again and walked on down Whitehall, past the entrance to Downing Street into Parliament Square, past the Houses of Parliament and Westminster Abbey into Victoria Street. All the time he felt sure he was being watched and not just by the people who glanced at him in passing, obviously spotting him for a foreigner. Gray had said that being alone in a foreign city might make him jittery and overly suspicious of people. What he hadn't expected was the first slight twinge of excitement at being alone in a foreign city on a secret mission; why had he ever taken to gambling if not to beat boredom?

At the entrance to the massive Army and Navy Stores building, 105 Victoria Street, he was saluted at the top of marble steps with brass rails by a doorman in a red uniform. 'Good morning, sir, turned out quite nice after all that blinking rain. Can I be of assistance, sir?'

'Well, you see, I'm the new military attache´ at the United States embassy — Lieutenant John Pomeroy, Sixth Cavalry, now assigned to the foreign service. I was dining at the Guards Club last night and my friend Captain The Honourable Holborn, Coldstream Guards, said I just might be accepted here as a patron ...'

A guide took him to gents' tailoring on the fourth floor, top of the building. The sale clerk knew he was American before he opened his mouth. His manner suggested absolution for the Boston Tea Party. 'Yes, sir, I have noticed that the better class of American gentleman appreciates English tailoring.'

'Give us the clothes and who knows.'

'Pardon, sir? Who knows what, sir?'

'That's what I'm hoping to find out.'

As with so many English people, the starchiness went out, dealing with an American. Soon the problem was to stop them talking to get your business done. He chose a worsted lounge suit, dark grey with a cutaway coat. The pants were taken away to be shortened a half-inch by the store tailor so they would 'break' over his shoes. 'That's the correct length without turn-ups, sir, of course, if sir was having turn-ups the appropriate length would be to the top of the shoes.'

'Cuffs, you mean — '

'Oh no, sir, cuffs are what one has at the end of one's shirt sleeves.' The sales clerk had more or less taken over by then. Sir would obviously want an overcoat to go with the suit. He tried on a grey vicuna chesterfield with a black velvet collar, then a much shorter covert coat In waterproof Venetian cloth. The chesterfield made him look important, the covert coat made him feel rakish and ready for action. The hell with it, Tosher Delaney was paying: 'I'll take 'em both.' The sales clerk recommended a black, stiff felt bowler hat with a curly brim to go with the chesterfield. The guide then took him down to the first floor, where he chose three cream shirts in spun silk, a couple of broche silk Windsor neckties, suspenders they called braces in white kid leather, and some Irish cambric handkerchiefs. He'd always maintained in the past that clothes didn't interest him too much but that wasn't precisely true; now he felt his inhibitions disappearing, like being told a secret vice had just become commendable — he even picked up a swanky black umbrella in glace silk with a rhinoceros horn handle. Back on the fourth, he stopped to admire a rack of jackets — by *coat* they meant overcoat. 'Those would be for more casual wear,' the sales clerk said. The slight suggestion in his voice, real or imagined, that an American might not know the difference between formal and casual was enough. 'I need some casual duds, of course,' he said and they started over, a pearl-grey wide-awake hat in soft felt with the brim turned up, a navy-blue reefer jacket in vicuna, double-breasted with eight buttons, striped cashmere trousers, narrow cut, grey to match the hat ... each time he looked in the big mirrors he felt less familiar with what he saw and happier with how he felt. All his life he'd been covering up for his own sense of emptiness, but if this was covering up he had a good reason; he was an undercover man, wasn't he? Trying on his suit pants for length, he asked the sales clerk, who decided these rules about length and style.

'Tradition and custom, sir. For instance — ' the sales clerk undid the bottom button of his vest — 'we leave the bottom waistcoat button open because King Edward tends to the portly. His Majesty found it more comfortable to leave the bottom button undone and everybody followed the royal fashion.' He wanted to laugh — His Majesty was too fat to fasten his vest sorry, waistcoat — so an open button became *de rigeur?* — but this store for an empire's military men was no place for levity. While the sales clerk called for a minion to parcel up his American clothes and all the extra items for delivery back to the Excelsior, he looked through the store catalogue. In the weapons section was the heading, *Cheap Guns for the Use of Natives on Expeditions, etc.,* — scatterguns that couldn't kill the sahib bwana while he was busy winding on puttees to keep his legs dry. He could've laughed at that, too, until he remembered a prim girl who made love to strangers on instructions, and Naunton Toms, a kid aged thirteen who worked the legal maximum of seventy-four hours a week for a dollar's wages and didn't like big tips because already he was thinking like a soldier; that's how you got an empire, by following *all* the rules

The sales clerk let out a little gasp: 'We've forgotten *gloves, sir!*'

'My hands get too hot in gloves — '

'Not wear *gloves,* sir? A gentleman would as soon go out in public without his trousers!'

Black kid gloves-completed his transformation.

'Now all I need's elocution lessons, eh?'

'We have a wide variety of books on proper English grammar and pronunciation on the third floor, sir — '

'I'll pick it up by ear.'

The bill came to thirty-five pounds eighteen shillings, around one hundred sixty dollars. The sales clerk mentioned it almost as an afterthought and looked forward to the honour and pleasure of serving him again.

Out on the busy sidewalk, nobody jeered at him for a damn-fool American idiot; in fact, hardly anybody looked at him, in fact, it was downright disappointing — not a single admiring glance? Copying the English way of swinging an umbrella, he strode briskly along Victoria Street, checking his British bowler and rakish covert coat in every available window; it felt like playing a kids' game, dressing up, but maybe that was the secret to undercover work, treating it like a game … the kids' game he'd never played as a kid. Reaching number 123, he turned in out of the sunny street, to see the reflection of a smart young

Englishman about town in the glass door. Through the glass door, he took a few steps into the gloomy lobby, then turned and stood in shadow; people passed the entrance in either direction, nobody looking inside; intermittent gaps in the two-way flow of horses and vehicles gave him separate snapshots of the opposite sidewalk; at that range, looking through sunshine into shadow, it was hard to tell but he had the impression he saw the same brown overcoat and tweed hat two or three times …

He stood unnoticed for a few moments in the doorway of the small outer office watching the locally hired English staff, two male clerks and a dark-haired girl in a white blouse working at a typewriter. The younger clerk was poking the small coal fire — if he'd hoped to see or overhear something significant, all he got was a sight of the older male clerk, a haggard man in his fifties with yellowing hair, methodically picking at his ear with a match in a handkerchief.

'Hi there,' he said, doffing his bowler.

The girl got up from her rolltop desk and found a way through the jumbled desks and cabinets. She was in her twenties, brown hair in two loose waves at the front and pinned up at the back, not exactly beautiful but with prominent cheekbones that gave her a certain austere handsomeness bordering on the gaunt.

'Do you have an appointment with anyone, sir? Embassy business is conducted between eleven and three in the afternoon.'

'That sounds like a working day I approve of.' He took off his right glove and stuck out his hand. 'John Stockley Pomeroy. We're going to be colleagues — '

'Oh yes, somebody telephoned for you a few minutes ago. I made a note of the name, he's going to call back.' Finally she shook hands and did the introductions. 'I'm Miss Willoughby — Mr Kennedy ... and Mr Hitchings ...'

Hitchings, the young one, had white teeth and darkish skin, Italian looking, like a lot of Londoners he'd seen. Old man Kennedy and his white shirt had both seen better days and his handshake was like an apology for the way he was now. Miss Willoughby said she would take him through to meet Mr Spence and Mr Sleath, then remembered his call and picked up a small notepad by her typewriter. 'It was a Mr Charles Devoy — this way ...'

He didn't have time to ask her any questions before she ushered him through the doorway for his first sight of Mitchell Dean Spence and Lucius Menifee Sleath, cream of the junior diplomatic corps. 'This is Mr Pomeroy,' she said. 'I'll get you a cup and saucer.'

Like a couple of guilty kids, Spence and Sleath were hastily swinging their feet off a desk on which was a china-tile tray with a coffee service and a plate of buttered scones. 'Don't stand up for me, fellows,' he said cheerfully. They hesitated a moment, curious about his bowler and umbrella, then got their feet back on the desk.

'Welcome to the slough of despond, Pomeroy — do you play bridge?'

Grissom, the steamship tycoon, had called American diplomats 'the parasites of society', and he spoke with authority, Grissom junior being in the foreign service. Back in the White House, Roosevelt might be gunning for the Colombian government to get his canal that would link two hemispheres and help launch America onto the world stage as a major power; war might be threatening millions in Asia and Europe; here, in the London embassy, the big issues were finding a bridge foursome in the absence of the other third secretary, Bob Lyle, and whether Miss Willoughby had unnatural leanings.

Lucius Menifee Sleath, twenty-six, now so reclined he had his saucer balanced on his shirtfront, was from Bristol, Connecticut, conveniently dumped nephew of a New Hampshire mill family; lank black hair with oil to hold the dandruff and mama's big dark eyes, a sulk hiding behind a smirk.

Mitchell Dean Spence, thirty-two, was another spoils-system product, from Flint, Michigan; tall and slackly built, sandy hair and freckles already tinged with the greyness to come. Neither of them looked to have enough energy to fart against a mild breeze, but the arrival of a newcomer stirred them to a recital of grievances, sneers and gossip that quickly had him realizing he was a patriot after all. The more he listened, the more he felt inspired to kick their butts all around the room, but that was another twist to undercover work — the ones you liked least were generally the most use to you . In other words, who else should a sneak make pals of but creeps?

'We do some work, y'know, we transcribe embassy correspondence and telegrams into the permanent record books, we issue passports — '

'But only between two and three on Tuesdays, Wednesdays and Thursdays — '

'We hold custody of the seals, codes and archives. We stand in as *charges d 'affaires* when Nellie Fairbairn is all taken up introducing prominent American socialites to London society — '

'Nellie is more English than the English; he never *mentions* Chicago in the salons and drawing rooms of Mayfair — '

'It's six months at least since His Excellency Andrew Phillips Fry put a foot in this building — '

'It's so *degrading,* sharing an entrance with immodest-looking women from the cheap apartments upstairs — '

'Fry maintains a mansion in Park Lane. His personal goal is to make himself the most popular man in Britain bar none. You got the engagements book. Loose?'

Sleath stretched a tired arm for a blue-roan leather diary. He blew crumbs off his shirtfront. 'Well now, let me see ... tonight it's Amelia's big ball ... dinner with the Law Society tomorrow night, the Imperial League banquet Wednesday when he's guest of honour, Thursday lunch with Prime Minister Balfour at 10 Downing Street, lunch Friday with the City of London Corporation, then off for the weekend with his pal Betts ... he's also due to speak to the Omar Khayyam Society, the Dante Society, the William Wordsworth Society and the Browning Society. He's down to give an address on Benjamin Franklin to the Birmingham and Midlands Society — they made him their honorary president — '

'Nellie writes the speeches, you understand?'

' — he's listed for prize-day speeches at three public schools — which here means private schools for the rich. I also have invitations from philanthropic societies, workmen's institutes, sporting clubs, foxhunting clubs, literary clubs. All over England they see him as the *only* man to unveil a bust or a portrait — '

'Libraries refuse to be opened without him!'

'Sounds like he's running for office,' Pomeroy said.

'He likes the sound of his own voice — '

'He has this love affair with the British aristocracy — '

'To be consummated by Amelia marrying some titled sprig of an illustrious family — '

'I hear he's having a love affair of the other kind.' They both raised their eyebrows. 'Gossip on the boat coming over. There is a Mrs Fry, isn't there?'

They grinned at each other. Spence flicked ash on the carpet.

'Let me put it this way, Pomeroy — '

'Mr Sleath — have you sent out those invitations?'

Second Secretary Ellington Fairbairn, known as Nellie, came bouncing up the long room on his toes. He was wearing a black morning coat over a black suit and carrying a black bowler hat, black gloves and a black umbrella. Spence and Sleath were already on their feet. Sleath mumbled that he was just about to send Hitchings out with the invitations.

'No hurry, Mr Sleath, the ball doesn't commence until eight o'clock this evening. Mr Spence — have you drafted that letter about the harbour dues in Zanzibar?'

'I'll have Miss Willoughby type it out this morning, Mr Fairbairn.'

Only then did Fairbairn acknowledge his presence. 'Congratulations, Mr Pomeroy. I never expect a new third secretary to get the correct day, let alone turn up at the appointed hour. We'd better fix you up with a desk — you'll have to use Lyle's for now. Have we heard anything from Mr Lyle, Spence?' . .

'Not since his housekeeper telephoned to say he had influenza, Mr Fairbairn. He was also due to start two weeks' vacation today. Shall I telephone him, Mr Fairbairn?'

'Your concern does you proud, Mr Sleath. My office if you will, Mr Spence.'

'Miss Willoughby?' Sleath shouted. He winked at Pomeroy. The typewriter girl came into the big room at one end as Fairbairn and Spence went into the second secretary's room. 'You can clear this stuff away, Miss Willoughby.'

'Allow me,' Pomeroy said, making to pick up the heavy tray.

'I can manage, thank you .'

Sleath crept up on her and put his arm around her waist. 'You want anything, Pomeroy, ask Miss Willoughby. Why, I do believe the whole embassy would collapse without Miss Willoughby. to open in the morning and lock up at night and check the electric lights aren't burning up Uncle Sam's money and make the coffee and type the letters and answer the telephone and maybe one day have dinner with me — '

'Will that be all, Mr Sleath?' His arm fell away from her waist. Pomeroy held the door for her but she didn't even look at him. Sleath waited till the door was closed.

'Trouble with these London office females, if they're not men in disguise they're prudes — their virginity is their sole market asset. I guess. Where the hell did I leave those invitations? Trust that old windbag to have friends turning up from New York at the last moment — '

'Do we wear white ties for the ball?'

'We?' Sleath snorted. 'Cluttering up the dance floor with underpaid American functionaries isn't the idea, old man. Unless you care to volunteer to check the hats and coats.'

'You mean that? We're not good enough to attend a ball given by our own ambassador?'

'Nellie doesn't even get an invite — he'll be there but strictly as Fry's social secretary, you know?'

Pomeroy went to the third desk. Unlike the other two, it wasn't cluttered with files and papers and books. 'What's Lyle like?'

Sleath had found a bundle of gilt-edged invitation cards and was checking names on a slip of paper. 'What's that, old man? Bob Lyle? He's okay, I guess — well, tell the truth, he's a pain in the ass. You'd think he was bucking for an ambassadorship the way he takes this job. Polishes apples for Nellie, know what I mean? Not that I want to prejudice you against him in advance — '

'Mr Pomeroy?' Spence was beckoning him from the door of Fairbairn's office as the telephone rang on Sleath's desk.

'Sleath here ... it's a Mr Devoy calling you, Pomeroy — ' He shook his head. 'Sorry, Mr Pomeroy is in with the second secretary right now, have Mr Devoy call later.'

Perched behind his mahogany desk under the high ceiling with his back to the big window, Fairbairn looked as if he'd come from a smaller world. He nodded and Spence left them, closing the door behind him. The little red-haired man pressed his fingertips together as if in prayer. 'You find a satisfactory hotel, Mr Pomeroy?'

'Sure, the Excelsior.'

'Yes, I could've guessed. Tell me, Mr Pomeroy, did you bring that suit you're wearing from the land of the free?'

'I bought it this morning.'

'The indigenous cockney population of this great metropolis has a typically colourful expression for borrowing money — on the earhole, they say ...'

'Oh yeah, the money I had from you yesterday. I'll settle with you now.' He brought out his wallet and put a five pound note on the desk, then a gold sovereign from his pocket. 'I ran into a little card game last night.'

'You conjure up a vivid picture of your private life, Mr Pomeroy.'

Fairbairn put the coin in his lady's change purse, the bill in a fancy crocodile-skin wallet that was also a cigarette case. 'I'd thank you not to mention our little transaction. Borrowing from the junior staff is totally forbidden and Mr Sleath would want some too.'

'Good of you to help me out, Mr Fairbairn.'

'I was seduced by your charm, Pomeroy.' Fairbairn extracted a cigarette and tapped it on the desk. He reached into a drawer for a box of Bryant and May's wax matches. He lit up and puffed like a kid copying the grown-ups. 'American cigarettes, Mr Pomeroy, Richmond Gems — I haven't totally forgotten my origins. Perhaps I've been away so long America has become an ideal for me to serve rather than the geographical and political reality. Perhaps detachment enables one to identify

217

the nation's long-term interests rather than the erratic impulses of whichever political machine is temporarily in control.'

'That's called democracy, isn't it?'

'I believe. You are, of course, a product of the all too real system as it is — with the President as your patron, you present me with certain difficulties. How would you advise me to handle you, Pomeroy?'

'I guess I'm no different to those two spoiled brats out there.'

'Hardly. For one thing, they wouldn't have the objectivity to describe themselves as spoiled brats. You graduated from West Point and served as a lieutenant in the army — isn't this a bit of a retrograde step for you?'

'What do you want me to say, Fairbairn? I guess I get bored easily. You worried I'll sneak on you to Roosevelt if you raise your voice at me?'

Fairbairn leaned back in his chair. 'Somehow I feel you have a vision of manliness that precludes telling tales, Pomeroy. All right. In time I might hurl you into the maelstrom of international diplomacy, such as rent negotiations with the tightwad London landlord at whose mercy rests the representation of our great nation. In the meantime It's customary for the new boy to handle some of the more mundane chores while he brushes up on his bridge. Somebody has to meet with Chief Inspector Harris of Scotland Yard at St Mary's Hospital in Paddington. They have a dead American citizen on the slab —'

'What do we do about dead Americans, Mr Fairbairn?'

'Inform the old folks back home, take custody of his effects, perhaps arrange to have the cadaver shipped back to the States if they're rich, or buy a very cheap headstone if they're not — ' the little red-haired jack-in-the-box was unscrewing his gold-nibbed fountain pen to scan some typewritten pages — 'call it your initiation into the corpse *diplomatique.* Now, if you'll excuse me — '

'Hey — corpse *diplomatique,* that's very funny, Mr Fairbairn.'

'Save your merriment for the morgue, Mr Pomeroy.'

Why did he get the impression that Fairbairn disapproved of everything about him, yet at the same time wanted to be his friend?

Spence told him to take a cab, then make out an expense chit and give it to Miss Willoughby. In the outer office, she was typing. He eased his way towards her and showed her his street guide. 'I have to go to St Mary's Hospital in Paddington — '

'That's in Praed Street: She took the book. She had what looked like white burn scars on the back of her right hand. Her fingernails were cut short, like a man's. She wasn't wearing a ring of any kind. She found the page for Paddington and he leaned down until their heads were level.

'It's up Park Lane and then up the Edgware Road, it's not far.'

'I hope you don't think all Americans are like Sleath,' he murmured.

'That's nice to know: she said coldly. A little flap dropped on the switchboard and she swivelled away from him to plug in a cord. 'Good morning, American embassy, can I help you? ... One minute, please.' She plugged in another cord, pushed one of four red switches and turned the handle. 'The ambassador's residence on the line for you, Mr Fairbairn ... putting you through now.' She pushed a second cord and swivelled back to look at him. 'Anything else, Mr Pomeroy?'

On his way out, he noticed the embassy keys hanging on a hook by the door. He came to the curb and looked for a cab. A few yards farther along, a lanky man in a tweed deerstalker hat and an ulster overcoat was also searching the oncoming traffic for a cab. When one came along, the man in the deerstalker was looking the other way and he got to it first.

'Eleven Belgrave Square, driver.'

He checked the route against the street guide, along Victoria Street past the Victoria rail terminal, across Buckingham Palace Road into Grosvenor Gardens and up Grosvenor Place, which ran along a high brick wall around the gardens in back of Buckingham Palace. Not that he was sucker for all that stuff, but it did seem a mite peculiar, noisy city traffic this side of a brick wall, a king and queen on the other. Did they wear their crowns picking flowers? Was a princess complaining about another goddam pea under the forty mattresses last night, egad!

The cab turned left on Chapel Street. Belgrave Square, where the nobs hung out, had massive cream-coloured palaces that were actually terraced mansions facing each other across a railed park with tall trees and thick bushes, all of it under a milky sky smeared by brown smoketrails from irregular lines of red and black chimney pots. He paid off the cab and went up a couple of steps under a porch with columns. He pulled a brass bell knob. A couple of hansom cabs and a coal wagon came around the square. He couldn't see which house had a stable on top, but all the roofs looked big enough for horses. A small red-faced housemaid with a starched cap opened the door. Behind her was a big hall with a chandelier and a wide staircase with a red carpet.

'Miss Horton?'

The girl frowned. 'Servants' entrance is down t'stairs in't basement — '

'Is that you, Charles?' came a haughty upper-class voice, to go with a haughty upper-class lady in a black satin skirt to the ground, a short sable jacket fitted tight at the waist and a green satin hat adorned with tasselled cords and furry animal tails.

'He's askin' for Horton, ma'am,' the girl said nervously.

Looking directly at him, the haughty lady, who was about his own age, said, 'What on earth is he doing at the front door then? Inform me when Lord Parkstone arrives.'

The girl closed the door in his face. He went down the outside stairs into the railed basement area. Just before he descended below the level of the pavements he saw another hansom cab coming along this side of the square. Partially shielded by the railings, he watched it go by. The man with the deerstalker hat was peering out of the window.

A kitchen maid with bare arms and straggles of hair over her eyes opened the downstairs door.

'Miss Horton?'

'Have 'ee coom about the boiler? About bluidy time an' all.'

Horton's buxom sister, cook to Lord and Lady Hednesford, was like Horton around the eyes and mouth but with no yen to bend the knee. She received him angrily in a big warm kitchen with an iron cooking range and a stone floor. Maids were peeling potatoes and scouring pots . A young boy was cleaning silver tankards and plates at the long wooden table. Horton's sister started to give him hell about the boiler, until he produced three five pound notes from his wallet and explained he was returning money borrowed from her brother on the *Lucania.* The buxom cook stared at him and the money in disbelief and made him say it all again, then flopped down in a big wooden chair with a lumpy cushion, looking faint. 'Oh my goodness … I thought he was dead … Perkins, put on some fresh tea… oh my goodness …'

He sat quite awhile with Lily Horton in that big warm kitchen while she told him about her brother Tommy who'd run out on his wife and two stepchildren after coming home from the Boer War — otherwise Corporal Thomas Horton VC of the Devonshire Regiment, awarded his country's supreme honour of the Victoria Cross for conspicuous heroism at Elandslaagte, October 18, 1899, when he took part in the storming of a hill under murderous rifle fire and killed five Boer sharpshooters, four with his bayonet and one with his bare hands, while rescuing a wounded officer.

'Oh yes, he always was the quiet one, our Tommy. You're not the only one who couldn't believe what he did in the war. He married too young, you see, she was ten years older than him with two nippers from her first marriage. Proper harridan she was, too, didn't give poor Tommy a moment's peace, so he did a bunk. You've no idea what it means to me knowing he's alive and well, he never was any good at writing, asking you to give me the money is his way of letting me know where he is. I'm ever so grateful, your cup's empty ...'

The little housemaid who had opened the upstairs door to him came down to the kitchen with Lady Hednesford's message that she had changed her mind about going out and there would be six to luncheon. Lily Horton cursed Her Ladyship warmly. 'She's only a jumped-up trollop of an actress. It's them with no background are the worst snobs, believe me. Anyway, come December she can have a hundred to lunch for all I care, I'm getting married, thank goodness — the stories I could tell you about our so-called social betters!'

The great and the grand had no secrets from the downstairs population that served them hand and foot for lousy wages and board. A little gossipy scandal over tea in a basement kitchen with the servants might not have been Gray's idea of secret service work but he picked up a little more background on the notorious Lady Crediton, not least of it that she'd been one of the King's playmates a year or two back.

'I wonder, you ever come across people called Tennyson?' he asked. 'I met them on the boat, Sir Walter Freese Tennyson and his daughter Catherine. I was to look them up but lost the address.'

'Can't say I know of them myself but I can ask for you. Would you like me to telephone you?'

'Now you mention it, I don't know the embassy number.'

One of the maids went upstairs for the London Telephone Company book. Lily Horton gave it to him, saying she didn't have her glasses

Central 6200 AMERICAN Dental Manufacturing Co. 16 Poland St.

Gerrard 1462 AMERICAN Electrical Novelty 102 Charing Cross Rd.

Westminster 397 AMERICAN Embassy 123 Victoria St.

Central 6592 AMERICAN Exploration Co. 86 Strand.

Gerrard 2729 AMERICAN Express Co. Banker 3 Waterloo Place.

American businesses took up most of the page, everything from lead pencils and shoes to phonographs and teeth. Tennyson wasn't listed. He looked through the *W* section but the War Office either hadn't installed the telephone or was keeping the number a secret from Britain's enemies. Lily Horton came to the basement door and watched him put on his bowler. 'I only bought it this morning,' he said defensively.

'Very smart.'

'Thank you. Have your brother call me if he comes through London, won't you?'

'Knowing Tommy, he'll be too shy.'

The same hansom followed about thirty yards back as he came through Wilton Crescent onto the broad boulevard of Knightsbridge. Holles Holborn's people, of course. He crossed and walked alongside the Hyde Park railings as far as Apsley House, bestowed by a grateful nation on the Duke of Wellington for beating Napoleon at Waterloo, before waving down a cab. Holles Holborn obviously didn't believe a word he'd said last night ... or maybe British intelligence kept watch on all foreign diplomats in London. Anyhow, Devoy was his immediate concern. He lost sight of the hansom in the traffic going up Park Lane, Hyde Park on the left, big mansions on his right. He wondered which was Fry's. By the sound of it, breaking into London society for a third secretary was on a par with getting up the Chilkoot trail into the Yukon. But what was the big hurry? A couple of months wouldn't be so big a slice out of his life, would it? And he might as well get some wear out of his fancy English duds, he'd certainly never be able to wear them in Kansas City.

A burly joker with a moustache waxed to spiralled points was poking his forefinger through a smoke ring when a helmeted bobby brought him into a gloomy little yard under the towering walls of the hospital. They shook hands.

'John Pomeroy of the United States embassy.'

'Chief Inspector Alan Harris of Scotland Yard. I always like saying that, don't get enough chance these days.' He blew a perfect smoke ring and speared it with his index finger. He had a gruff voice, semi-educated by English standards. On his chin he had some smooth-topped warts that made Pomeroy wince imagining him shaving. 'I suppose you're used to seeing stiffs of a Monday morning, America being the land of sudden death and so forth?'

'You people have some funny notions about the United States.'

'Maybe it's because we believe all we're told by Americans.' He brought out a pack of Player's Navy Cut, full strength, and lit a fresh cigarette from the damp butt of the last one. He blew another smoke ring, then a second and tried to spear them simultaneously. 'I'm working up to three. Anyway, before our friend calls us in to admire his handiwork, I'll fill you in. Chummy' — he jerked his thumb at the door of the single storey mortuary annex — 'was found hanging in his bedroom at the De Vere Hotel yesterday at 11.50 a.m. Straightforward suicide it looked, tied the rope to a hot-water pipe and kicked the chair away. He'd been drinking, American, only booked in the night before. He had a fair bit of cash in his wallet and his case didn't look as though anybody'd gone through it, which ruled out robbery.' He blew one good ring and one failure.

'I wouldn't have been there, only my wife's brother is the assistant manager. You know what hotels are like, thing like that they prefer it kept quiet as possible. Then our friend sticks his oar in.'

'Our friend?'

'Young bloke at the medical school here, always pestering me to get practical experience of murders and suicides *in situ,* just *loves* a cadaver. He's studying pathology here, assistant student demonstrator they call him. Strictly speaking, he's not actually qualified, if you follow. We'd've had a Home Office pathologist if there'd been the slightest doubt. Anyway, too late to worry about that now, I'm pretty certain Chummy topped himself.'

'Does all this affect me or the embassy?'

'Better if you're satisfied. Families don't usually like suicide verdicts, for insurance and so forth . I daresay it was a *wee* bit irregular turning our friend loose on Chummy — ah, speak of the devil — '

A tall man had come to the door of the mortuary annex, six foot two at least, in shirt sleeves and a rubber apron, in his twenties but long past the age of frivolity. 'Bernard, this is Mr Pomeroy from the American embassy — Mr Pomeroy, this is Mr Spilsbury.' Leading them into a little hall, Spilsbury looked sternly at Harris's cigarette. Harris grimaced but nipped it out and put it back in the pack.

'You'd be well advised to give that habit up,' Spilsbury said.

'Wish I could, price of the buggers nowadays — ninepence for twenty-four!'

The air was suddenly a whole lot cooler inside the tiled morgue. Spilsbury started explaining the difference between suicide by hanging and murder by strangulation.

'In manual strangulation, the ligature groove is usually horizontal round the neck, with cuts and bruises where the victim's fingers tried to grasp the rope or wire. The groove is roughly the same depth at all points ...'

It look a moment for his eyes to accept that they were looking at naked people who weren't about to blink their eyes open and ask the time. Spilsbury led them between the slabs. His eyes tried to escape from misshapen toes, hairy thighs, jutting hipbones. Some of them were women.

'...with suicide by hanging, the ligature is usually positioned between the larynx and the hyoid; the groove has a yellow parchment quality and it's deepest where the rope took the body's weight — of course, there are no fingermarks ... the tongue is forced upwards and outwards and generally gets clenched in the teeth ...'

They came to a slab with a bulky shape under a stiff grey sheet. Spilsbury wheeled around a stand on castors and lifted a cloth off an enamel tray.

' ... neck incisions can cause blood to seep into surrounding tissues and create an impression of bruising, often leading to an erroneous conclusion of manual strangulation. To drain away the blood, therefore, I first removed the heart and the brain ...'

A red heart layered with yellow fat. A whitish brain, a human brain ... Spilsbury took hold of the grey sheet above the bump of a nose. Pomeroy's eyes found Harris's black shoes of magnetic interest.

' ... certainly the indications are of suicide by hanging, except that on closer examination of the neck I discovered that the body of the thyroid cartilage has been fractured, which is *not* an indication of suicide. I'll show you ...'

Pomeroy finally won the battle of wills with his eyes.

There was an open flap on top of a head of reddish curls. A fleshy neck had been sliced open in several places. There was a gaping vent in dense ginger hairs on a burly chest.

Face swollen, eyes glaring up at the ceiling, Jesse Hudson Marchbanks seemed on the point of shouting, 'Look what they've done to me, John old buddy!'

17

'Fracturing of the thyroid cartilage is extremely rare in suicide by hanging. I believe this man was struck a blow to the throat — here probably with a length of metal piping or a heavy stick, and then hung up while he was unable to defend himself ...'

Me, I'm just a hairy-assed cattleman from Austin, Texas ...

'There's other evidence of violence. This bruising — here — was caused by heavy blows to the abdomen, although I have to say it's two or three days' old — '

'It's not relevant then, is it?'

'It throws some light on the kind of life he led.'

John, I'm an American like you, I can ride with life's ups and downs.

'One minor injury which *might* have been caused by a blow to the throat but all the other evidence adds up to suicide? Not much to justify a murder investigation, Bernard — '

'Whoever killed him was *counting* on that kind of attitude, even if anybody bothered to do a post mortem — '

The perfect murder, you mean? Come on, Bernard — '

'No murder is perfect. Very clever. Not a blow to the *head*, oh no, a blow to the throat, which would then be covered by the rope, don't you see?'

Devoy isn't like us, John, he's a mean bastard.

'Are you all right, Mr Pomeroy?'

His eyes found a section of tiled wall and stuck to it. 'I knew him, we came over on the *Lucania* together ... I was only talking to him Friday.'

'Let's get you out in the fresh air, old chap.'

He kept his eyes on the far door and didn't look left or right until they were out in the gloomy little yard. He let his head flop back, and took long deep breaths. The sky was grey, the most wonderful his eyes had ever caressed. A nurse looked down from a high window, the most beautiful woman in the world. Harris's match flared into a flame as big as a bonfire ...

I'm sorry for you, Jesse, truly I'm sorry but you're in there and I'm out here, old buddy, and I'll tell you something — out here *is* better and I sure as hell don't intend to let any bastard rob me of a single wonderful precious goddam moment of it!

Raw elation just at being alive began to subside, leaving him with that one image, of Marchbanks's head topped open like somebody's boiled egg for breakfast. Marchbanks's things were laid out on a table in Paddington Green police station. A young constable packed everything into Marchbanks's big leather grip, including the norfolk jacket and knickerbockers he'd been wearing that first day out from New York. That was creepy enough; among the items checked off by Harris against a police list was a set of women's silk lingerie, outsize, and a pair of purple cashmere stockings with silk stripes.

'Probably a gift for a lady friend,' Harris said with true English tact, although they could all see the lingerie had been worn. 'Now, here's his wallet ... a hundred and ninety-five American dollars, three hundred and twenty-five pounds. I ask you — would any murderer leave that much? He wasn't carrying any cheques or bank drafts — did he say if he was visiting anybody in this country, any friends here?'

'I dunno. He told me he made a trip to Europe most years — gambling seemed to be his chief interest.'

'Mmm, not much money for a gambler to be carrying ... Anyway, if you would just sign this official receipt for his stuff ... good, here's your copy. Young Bernard's very clever, but these airy-fairy theories of his? No jury would ever believe a word of it. Experience and common sense, that's what you need. What does a gambler do his first night in a strange town? He looks for a place to gamble in, doesn't he? Lots of crooked gaming dens in London just waiting to fleece people like him. That's the way I see it. He's lost a lot of money, he's half drunk, all alone in a strange city, not what you'd call a stable character … makes more sense than a murderer with medical knowledge, doesn't it? I'll give you a lift back to Victoria Street — feeling better now?'

'Sure, I'm fine.'

'Must've been a real shock for you, true enough. You might be needed to give formal evidence of identification at the inquest, I'll let you know. The embassy concerned usually contacts the deceased's family in these cases, but there's no home address in the wallet — '

'He said he was from Austin, Texas — '

'Texas, eh? All those trigger-happy gunslingers blazing their six shooters in the Dead Gulch saloon and so forth? Wonder if I'm too old to join the Texas Rangers and see a bit of real excitement … ?'

He didn't see Deerstalker's hansom on the ride back. He did see polite gentlemen raising their hats to handsome ladies in furs, trees with autumn leaves in the park, big houses for the rich, a brick wall around a palace garden, things Jesse Hudson Marchbanks would never see again. Through the traffic noise and Harris's droning reminiscences of better days, he thought he heard deep piano notes ... music for the grave. He kept telling himself it was shock but it felt similar to being afraid. Five men played cards, now two were dead. Two suicides? One-Eye Riley wouldn't give you odds on a coincidence like that. Marchbanks was murdered. He'd have known that even if he hadn't been there to hear Spilsbury explain how it was done; the only question was whether Holles Holborn's people or Lang-Gaevernitz's people killed him.

Holles Holborn? He could have followed Marchbanks from the train to the hotel. He had reason enough, but this wasn't murder for revenge or greed; this was an *elimination* by people who knew what they were doing.

Devoy? He would've known which hotel Marchbanks was at — they wouldn't stay at the same hotel because their victims had to believe they were total strangers. Everything about it seemed to point to Devoy, clever and brutal, a paralysing blow to the throat in the middle of a casual conversation, those big hands fitting a noose around his neck and lifting him onto a chair. Why? Because Marchbanks was an old-time grifter who just couldn't bear losing all that money and risked exposing the blackmail scheme with that chloroform dodge? Or — more likely because Holles Holborn questioned him on the train, proving that somebody knew he'd been involved with Francis Holborn and Tennyson on the boat? Either way, Marchbanks had become a liability. Did you give the word to have him killed, Uwe? Gray said you were dangerous. Maybe I was fooled by all that culture and piano playing. Did you lose any sleep over him, Uwe? Who gets killed next, Uwe? Two dead out of five only leaves three alive. Nice rhyme there, Uwe, kids' stuff compared to Liszt, of course ...

The horrors came on him quickly, in a police cab coming by Victoria railway station in London, England. Images of Marchbanks's swollen face and bulging eyes merged with dark buildings, each blink of his eyes putting him on the edge of a vast chasm in a dark void. He couldn't breathe. Harris's face with his pointed wax moustache grew bigger and bigger ... the horrors.

There was a trick. You're in the dark, scared to hell. Something's stalking you, a monster, an ogre. You scream and run, you smash into walls, chairs, closed doors. The monster follows, slow but sure. But you don't scream and run, you take one step sideways and you freeze. You let your eyes pick up what glimmer of light there is. Shapes come into focus. The monster can't hear you but you hear the monster, only by now it isn't a monster, it's a bullying cadet captain called George Reardon, his little game after lights-out has gone wrong, now he's blundering in the dark and the victim's become the stalking monster who waits there in the dark to smash a flatiron into his head.

All you have to do is take one step sideways and freeze. I am the monster in the dark, you say. It worked then and it worked now.

'Pity I don't have time to take you for a drop of brandy, old man,' Harris said outside 123 Victoria Street. 'I'll bring the case — '

'I'm fine now, but thanks all the same.' He made to get out, then remembered something and sat down. He had to be safe against any investigation Harris might decide on. 'You know, it's just occurred to me, chief inspector. One of the fellows we played cards with on the boat was blown overboard — Viscount Holborn?'

'Oh yes, I believe I did hear something about that.' Now that the cab had stopped there was no draught to spoil Harris's smoke rings. A big finger stained with nicotine speared the drifting halo. 'No connection with Chummy though, is there?'

'I don't think so …'

Harris suddenly pointed at him. 'Let that be a warning to you, young fellow.'

'A warning? In what way?'

The wages of sin is death!' Harris broke into a coughing fit and slapped his chest. 'Let me know if you've any trouble contacting Chummy's family.'

He carried Marchbanks's heavy grip across the sidewalk and again he saw the reflection of a smart young English gent in the glass door. Don't be afraid of the dark, just take one step to the side and freeze and say after me, 'I'm the most dangerous thing around here!'

18

'No, you go ahead and have some lunch, Mr Kennedy, I'm not too hungry right now.'

'If you're sure, Mr Pomeroy — '

'No point in you missing out on lunch when I'll be here anyway, is there? Don't your American colleagues ever take a turn minding the store?'

'Oh yes — well, Mr Lyle does occasionally...'

Still the old cove prevaricated. Pomeroy let something dawn on him and gave him a sly look. 'Why, Mr Kennedy, I do believe you have some little plan for being here all alone — a lady friend dropping by for instance — ?'

'What a ridiculous idea,' the old fellow protested, blushing like a boy. Yet he was flattered. 'I'll plug the outside line through to your room, not that we get many calls during the luncheon hour. If you want to make yourself a cup of tea ...'

When he locked the door behind Kennedy, the gloomy embassy seemed awfully quiet. He found the john through the narrow, cluttered kitchen. Sitting with his pants down was conducive to brainwork, he'd always found. In the dark, the best way to see something was to look at something else.

You were absolutely right, Gray, a different kind of war, that's all. Seeing Jesse Marchbanks with the top of his head sawn off and the yellow groove of a rope around his neck has cured a lot of my childish quibbles. Old men always tell young men not to waste a single day of their lives because it won't be coming around again, and young men scoff because they think it's all going to go on for ever and ever. Maybe all young men should be taken on a tour of the morgue, Gray. Sure you didn't have Marchbanks murdered just to get me wise, Gray? I always suspected you weren't being straight, you bastard. For twenty grand you knew I'd probably take the job anyway, but all that stuff about Fry and a traitor inside the embassy, that was the old flimflam, the free lunch — you knew the dangerous part was getting involved with Lang-Gaevernitz. 'I'll be an amateur up against professionals,' I said, and you said, 'I know but we don't have any professionals and you're a fast learner, Pomeroy.' I was flattered Gray. Now I know why you needed the penitentiary to hold over me as a threat — to stop me from quitting when I found out you'd thrown me in among the wolves. If I get killed, you've lost one amateur, plenty more where I came from. Well, up yours, Gray, make sure you have my twenty thousand dollars ready for me to pick up, you bastard. Seeing Marchbanks on that slab cured me of all that happy-go-lucky crap, Gray. You wanted a professional secret agent, well now you've got one. Never mind if I don't like the work, I like being alive. You pleased about that, Gray? You know what it feels like? Just as if I was cocking a rifle ...

He sat at Miss Willoughby's desk and from his wallet unfolded the three sheets of *Lucania* notepaper. It took him ten minutes or so to get the hang of Miss Willoughby's Remington typewriter and produce a top copy and two carbon copies of Francis Holborn's written confession: 'I have done the worst thing an Englishman can do, lose my honour, without which it is not worthwhile to live ... ' He put each copy in a separate white envelope. The original was his life insurance. He couldn't carry it or keep it hidden in his room because they'd probably strip the wallpaper once they knew he had it. He couldn't trust anybody to keep it for him or even put it in a bank safe deposit box because the British secret service could most likely get into any London bank. His eye travelled around the shabby office ... somewhere he could get at it but where it wouldn't be found accidentally.

To reach the row of correspondence box files on the top shelf, he stood on Hitchings's desk. He chose the 1901 file.

Dust flecked his face. He pulled out the 1901 file and put the crisp sheets of *Lucania* notepaper among letters dealing with Americans taken prisoner during the Boer War. He couldn't see Spence or Sleath taking them down for a little light reading.

Going through Sleath's desk, he found the engraved invitation cards to Miss Amelia Fry's reception and ball at the residence of His Excellency Andrew Phillips Fry, United States Ambassador to Great Britain, RSVP. He made sure the cards were not numbered in any way for Sleath to discover one was missing. Sleath's drawers yielded nothing else of much interest except some French picture postcards of plump women in various states of semi-draped nudity. Spence had his top drawer locked and nothing but stationery, official books, a manicure case and a bottle of hair brilliantine in the others. He was on his way to Fairbairn's room when the telephone rang on Spence's desk.

'American embassy, can I help you?'

'May I speak to Mr Pomeroy if he's in?'

He came around the desk and sat in Spence's chair.

All you do is step to the side and freeze.

'Pomeroy speaking.'

'This is Charles Devoy — we met on the *Lucania*.'

'Yes, I remember.'

'I'd like to meet you again, Mr Pomeroy, if that's possible, perhaps for a drink or dinner.'

'Why?'

'It's something I'd rather discuss in person — could we meet tonight, for instance?'

'I'm tied up tonight.'

'Tomorrow night then?'

'Okay.'

'Say six o'clock in the bar of the Palace Hotel at Piccadilly Circus? Maybe you don 't know where that is — '

'I'll find it.'

'Mr Pomeroy, this isn't something I'd particularly like to discuss in front of other people — you will come alone, won't you?'

'No partners?'

A slight pause. 'I don't have a partner, Mr Pomeroy. I wonder who you had in mind.'

'Marchbanks.'

A slightly longer pause. 'Did he say we were partners?'

'Not this morning he didn't. He's dead, didn 't you know?'

'Dead? Are you sure?'

'They found him strung up on the end of a rope. When I saw him, they'd cut out his heart and his brain. I'm fairly sure he was dead.'

'Suicide?'

'Kind of eerie, eh — after Holborn? Almost make you think there was a curse on our little game.'

A short but emphatic pause. 'I'm sure you don't suffer from superstition, Mr Pomeroy. People generally die for practical reasons. May I ask how you got involved?'

'I'll tell you tomorrow night. Matter of fact, I may have a proposition might interest you but we can talk about that.'

He hung up on Devoy.

People generally die for practical reasons?

All of Fairbairn's drawers were locked. He had a big iron safe in his room, also locked. He sat in Fairbairn's fancy chair and read through his handwritten draft of Fry's speech for the Imperial League banquet on Wednesday night. Most of it read like a petition for America's readmission to the British Empire. The last page wasn't finished — Fairbairn had found difficulty thinking up an appropriate phrase for the vile perpetrators of Sunday night's bomb attack on the Bank of England, that bastion of British financial acumen and probity that was the envy of the world, like British culture and British parliamentary democracy and British justice; *vicious fiends* was scored out; *men of mindless violence cloaking their foul hatreds behind a twisted perversion of Irish patriotism* had a big question mark beside it.

How do I stop an ambassador making a speech, Gray?

It was 2.05 when he came back into the big room. What else should he be attending to?

Money.

He thought about taking the dough from Marchbanks's wallet but Fairbairn or Spence would find it missing when they checked the police list of his effects. What happened to the dough Marchbanks had stolen back from him? Harris was right, a gambler should have been carrying more than that. Not that Marchbanks gambled with any notion of losing, but the old flimflam needed a bankroll to impress the suckers …

The big leather grip had two belts with buckles and a spring catch. He opened it on the floor and tipped everything out onto the carpet. He lifted the case onto Lyle's desk and felt along the side lining and the bottom, then checked the lid and the outside stitching. Nothing. He had to steel himself to touch the norfolk jacket. He felt along the linings, the lapels, inside the pockets, and crumpled the shoulder padding close to his ear for a crackle of paper. Nothing. The underwear he couldn't bring himself to touch and picked it up item by item using a wooden ruler from Sleath's desk. He checked the shoes for false heels, ripped out the absorbent insoles. A travelling man had once told him of a dodge whereby you got a shoemaker to fake up an old scuffed pair no thief would look at twice as a safe place to stash your dough. Nothing. The suitcase filled up again. The last item on the carpet was a cowhide traveller's toilet case, a battered but once-expensive item holding two hairbrushes, clothes brush, soap dish, toothbrush, shaving brush, tin of dental powder, bowl of shaving soap, two razors, scissors, bottle of eau de cologne, cardsharp's nickel daub box, buttonhook, nail file, tweezers for removing nostril hairs, comb and mirror. He removed each of these accessories from the band of chamois leather holding it in place and then held the empty case up by one flap. He shook it but couldn't feel any movement. He put it on the desk and smoothed his hand across the chamois lining. He knelt by the desk and got his eyes level with the stitched seams of the toilet case, turning it slowly. The second time around he got it — the end flaps had a double thickness. He got one of the razors and touched the stitches with bright steel. Two thicknesses of leather peeled apart. When he finished counting the US Treasury bills and greenbacks and British notes, there was $6,500 and £1,885 on the desk.

'I was just having a little snooze — '

She passed him and went into the outer office. 'Where's Mr Kennedy?'

Hanging the embassy keys back on their hook, he said, 'I told him he could go eat, no point in two of us missing out on lunch.' Miss Willoughby must have noticed something different about her desk. Before she could reach it, he said, 'I hope you don't mind, I typed a letter home on your machine.'

She poked around on her desk, still suspicious. 'Have you been looking through my things?'

'I took a couple of envelopes from your drawer — '

'It's official embassy stationery not my private property,' she said huffily. 'You shouldn't have told Mr Kennedy to go out, somebody has to be here to answer the telephone.'

'There's probably a lot of things you better put me right on, Miss Willoughby. I guess you don't have too high an opinion of Americans — '

'What gives you that idea?'

'Watching your face when Sleath was sweet-talking you.'

'Some men seem to think they can fondle any woman who works in an office as if she was a pet dog. I suppose he told you I was a lesbian?'

239

'Either that or a prudish virgin.'

'At least you're honest,' she said. There was a lot more boiling up in her to be said, but she turned her back on him, taking off her overcoat.

He got the keys off the hook.

'Can you recommend me a place to get a quick bite around here?' he said.

'I usually go to the Devonshire Tea Rooms across the street, but you wouldn't like it. There's plenty of places in the area — just for your own information, I'm neither.'

'Nigh-ther, nee-ther, it's really none of my business, Miss Willoughby. I'll be back.'

In the lobby he turned right instead of going to the front door. Beyond the stairs to the apartments above there was a corridor where the carpeting ended, then a bolted door out into a little dirty yard with ashcans and a coal bunker and another door in a brick wall that brought him out into a side street. He crossed over and came into Victoria Street some twenty yards from the embassy entrance, went in the other direction and then crossed Victoria Street and came back along a crowded sidewalk. Sure enough, there was a hansom cab standing at the curb diagonally opposite the embassy entrance. The driver was feeding his horse from a nosebag. Inside there was a man, but he couldn't make out if it was Deerstalker. A friendly London bobby told him there was a locksmith in Gillingham Street off Vauxhall Bridge Road. The friendly locksmith looked at the four heavy keys and said he could have duplicates ready for Wednesday morning ...

'Really — is that the earliest?' he said despairingly. He brought out his wallet. 'I'm willing to pay extra to have them done now.' He brought out a five pound note.

Ignoring the fiver, the locksmith said, 'Is it an emergency, sir?'

'Is it? My first day in the London office and I've mislaid my keys! I swiped these from the old man's overcoat hoping to get them back by two thirty. If you knew that old buzzard…!'

'Well, I could ask Bert if he'd work through his dinnertime.'

'No, I need them before tonight!'

'This is our dinnertime, sir, I suppose you call it lunch. Bert — got a moment? Give him a couple of bob for himself, sir, that'll keep him happy for a week.'

Bert said it would take him twenty minutes. Pomeroy asked which was the nearest bank and used the time to open an account with Lloyd's Victoria branch, putting in fifteen hundred pounds of Marchbanks's money, some of the notes looking like old friends from the *Lucania* poker game. After picking up the keys, he had a roast-beef sandwich and a cup of gamy tea in the buffet at Victoria railway station and got back into the embassy by the rear door before Spence and Sleath were back from lunch. Hanging up his coat and bowler on the hatstand in the outer office, he got the original keys back on their hook and was sitting at Lyle's desk when Fairbairn and then Spence and Sleath returned from their midday meal. Fairbairn was going out again almost immediately to meet with the ambassador at the British Foreign Office and left it for Spence to take him through the various procedures connected with the death of an American citizen. Once he started working, Spence seemed quite sensible — Sleath did a lot of yawning. Around three thirty, Spence took Miss Willoughby into Fairbairn's room to give her some letters. Pomeroy got his feet up on Lyle's desk.

'What d'you do nights here, Loose?'

'Oh, various things — eat out, go to the theatre, concerts you know …'

'Don't these diplomatic circles go in for lots of parties and such?'

'Nellie gets lots of invites to the other embassies' functions.'

'And we don't get invited by our own ambassador? Doesn't that stick in your craw, Loose?'

'That's the way it is.'

'That's the way you fellows have let it be, you mean.'

'You're going to change things?' Sleath sneered.

'I was good enough to spend the night as a guest of Theodore Roosevelt in the White House — why, old Teddy asked me how to stop Alice smoking! Hey — can you do this?' He swung his feet off the desk and did a flip onto his hands. Sleath's upside-down face still looked sulky. He walked on his hands between the desks. 'A man can do anything if he has the right stuff in him, old man. I wouldn't let any twobit ambassador stop me attending a ball if I had a mind to go — '

'Want to bet on that?' Sleath sneered.

Gray called it the lizard's-tail trick.

On his way back to the hotel, he honoured the Army and Navy Stores once more with his custom as a military attaché of a foreign embassy. This time they gave him a ticket entitling him to shop there and he picked up a satin-lined, black vicuna inverness cape for wear over evening dress, a silk top hat, first quality, and a pair of white kid dress gloves. 'I'll have these put on the free delivery van at five thirty, sir. You'll have them by six thirty at the latest.' There was too much traffic in Victoria Street for him to see if he was being followed but he took it for granted he was now under permanent surveillance. In the Excelsior, the orchestra was playing a Gilbert and Sullivan selection beyond the palm trees. He sat with a magazine, watching the desk for Miss Busby to appear. A magazine humorist was having a lot of fun about an American 'business consultant', a man called Martin Killman who had been lecturing British businessmen on their laziness, bad physical condition that left them easily tired, and out-of-date methods. The cheek of these Yankee upstarts!

'Hello, Miss Busby.' His smile was intended to reassure her nothing had changed but she looked tense. He pulled out a sealed envelope with J. S. POMEROY printed in the top left corner. 'I'd like this in the hotel safe overnight, Miss Busby.'

She put on her brisk business-lady's voice. 'The contents have to be verified if you want the management to take responsibility for cash or valuables, Mr Pomeroy.'

'It has no cash value, it's an official document.' Just for a moment the male desk clerk had his back to them. 'You can tell Mr Brodie about it,' he murmured. 'Has he been here?' She nodded. The desk clerk leaned across for his pencil. 'Very good, Mr Pomeroy,' she said. 'I'll write you out a receipt.'

He was struggling with his collar stud getting into his evening suit after a bath when Naunton Toms came up to his room. The lanky boy put his finger to his mouth and didn't speak till the door was closed. There was a man asking questions about you this afternoon!' he hissed. 'He spoke to Bella Busby — he called you "Our American Friend".'

'Good work, Naunton. You help me with this goddam stud. What did he look like? Hey, don't choke me, for pete's sake!' Naunton described Deerstalker and asked if he thought Bella Busby was working for them. 'I wouldn't trust her,' he said emphatically.

'In my profession you don't trust anybody, Naunton. Keep a general eye on her, will you? Not scared, are you?'

To prove he wasn't scared, the boy came out with another of his rib ticklers. 'What lies at the bottom of the ocean for years and years yet never stops moving about and trembling? You don't know? A nervous wreck!'

'Don't make me laugh, Naunton, this shirtfront may crack. You think you're ready for something a little harder than surveillance work?' The boy nodded eagerly. 'Before I tell you what it is, Naunton, you and I have to reach an understanding about one thing — you're doing work for me on a regular basis, therefore you must be paid — let's say one pound a week to start with, that okay with you?' The boy was embarrassed even to talk about money; to him it was all a game, a substitute for the kids' games he should have been playing at his age. Pomeroy assured him that working for the United States government in no way made him a traitor to his own country. 'In fact, Naunton, I can tell you, in the strictest confidence, President Roosevelt wants much closer ties with Great Britain, but there are people who don't want that. They're the ones I'm up against. After all, would you and I be friends if I was a German or a Russian who didn't even speak the same language? Anyhow, this little job is more in the nature of a test — a practical joke, really. Can you make a telephone call at fifteen minutes before nine precisely?'

'Yes, I finish work at eight tonight.' The boy was radiant with excitement and pride at being selected for dangerous stuff. (It was only vaguely occurring to Pomeroy that he had slipped easily into the business of manipulating people, the very thing he had always despised in others.)

'This has to be at a quarter before nine exactly, Naunton. I'll write down the number and what you have to say. Gerrard 773 ... you ask for Mr Ellington Fairbairn, second secretary of the United States embassy they'll say he's busy, but you'll say it's a long-distance call from Washington, DC — '

'You mean in *America*?'

That's right. You say, if you're asked, you're the exchange operator you won't get scared, will you? No, sorry, of course not. Now, you get Fairbairn to the telephone and then you tell him to stand by . . .'

Apparently, a lot of English farmers had never seen a handsome young society gent in an inverness cape, cutaway tailcoat, white vest, starched shirt, white tie and gloves. In the silence that broke out at his progress through the lobby, he half expected a round of applause. Seeing Miss Busby at the desk, he struck a pose, silk hat under his arm. 'You think I look okay for the ambassador's ball?'

Despite the tension his proximity now seemed to cause in her, she had to smile. 'You look far too swanky for the Excelsior,' she murmured.

Outside, he acknowledged Hoare's salute. He put on his silk hat, haughtily ignoring the stares of passersby. Hoare held the cab door for him.

'Sixty Park Lane, driver.'

19

The man who came in with the King.

The lights were on inside and outside the big Regency mansion. Two flunkeys in powdered wigs and knee breeches poised to come down the wide steps. It was only twenty-one minutes before nine on the gold hunter watch he'd bought in Seattle when returning gold miners were starving and poker players were loaded.

'Drive on around, I'm too early.'

They turned off Park Lane into the heart of Mayfair, where every big house seemed to be full of fashionable people under chandeliers, round Grosvenor Square and back again. The second time around it was fifteen before nine precisely; Naunton would be just getting through. The flunkeys were on the sidewalk meeting a large private carriage. He paid off his cab and sauntered towards the wide steps, timing it just right to fall in behind the flunkeys escorting a couple of stout parties in tall silk hats up the steps. Through the big doorway, he could see other flunkeys under a truly massive chandelier. The two stout gents didn't exactly bound up the steps, and he got a little twitchy in case he missed the moment when Fairbairn was called to the telephone. He bumped into one of them.

The face that looked around was astonishingly familiar; long nose, pop eyes with heavy lids, pouting mouth and a pointed beard. The voice was deep and guttural, with rolling rrs. It wasn't pleased: 'Are we obstructing you, young man?'

'I'm sorry, I didn't mean to tramp on your heels, sir.'

It was the face on the coins!

His Britannic Majesty, King Edward VII of Great Britain and Ireland, Emperor of India, Defender of the Faith, ruler of Gibraltar, Malta, Cyprus, Aden, Perim, Sokotra, Kuria Muria Islands, Bahrein Island, India and its dependencies (Baluchistan, Sikkim, Andaman Islands, Nicobar Islands, Laccidive Islands, Labuan), Hong Kong, Straits Settlements (Singapore, Penang, Malacca), the Federated Malay States (Perak, Selangor, Negri, Sembilan, Pahang), Johor, Cocos Islands, Christmas Island, Wei-hai-Wei (China), Ascension Island, St Helena, Seychelles, Basutoland, Bechuanaland, Cape Colony, Central African Protectorate, East Africa (including Uganda Protectorate), Islands of Zanzibar and Pemba, Mauritius, Natal, Nigeria, Orange River Colony, Rhodesia, Somaliland Protectorate, Transvaal Colony, Gold Coast, the Gambia, the Bermudas, Canada, Falkland Islands, British Guiana, British Honduras, Newfoundland and Labrador, West Indies (Bahamas, Barbados, Jamaica, Leeward Islands, Trinidad, Windward Islands), Commonwealth of Australia, self-governing colony of New Zealand, British New Guinea, Fiji, Tonga, Pitcairn Island, Ducie Island, Phoenix Isles, Ellice Islands, Gilbert Islands, British Solomon Islands, Santa Cruz Island and Duff otherwise Wilson Islands, raised his eyebrows. 'Far be it from us to stand in the path of an American in a hurry. After *you*, sir — '

'Oh no, after *you*, sir ... King — Your Majesty.' Pomeroy had very rapidly discovered the power of a real live king at close quarters to make staunch republicans, egalitarians and lifelong scoffers go weak at the knees. The other stout gentleman, almost the King's spitting image, was less inclined to see the humour in it. The King nodded amicably to Pomeroy and led the way inside. A king needed no invitation card — Pomeroy's card was taken by a pageboy with a silver tray, his cape, hat and gloves by a liveried footman. He had no alternative but to follow the King between dazzling banks of hothouse flowers, ferns, palms in pots.

He then had his first sight of Andrew Phillips Fry, New Jersey-born son of a hardware merchant who drank, now hurrying down the staircase to greet his royal guest. Silver side-whiskers framed a fleshy face going bright red with the sheer joy of being host to Edward the Caresser. A substantial waist was forced into a stiff bow.

'We are deeply honoured by Your Majesty's most gracious presence.'

'My dear friend Fry, it is our pleasure,' boomed the King. 'You know Betts, of course.'

'Sir Oscar, how good of you to come. Now, if I may escort you upstairs to meet my wife and my daughter — '

'Mr John Pomeroy, State Department,' announced the flunkey, holding his invitation card. Fry was too excited for this to register and would have ignored him. The king indicated him with a regal gesture. 'This young man came in with us.' .

Fry pumped his hand. 'Very good of you to come, Mr — '

'Pomeroy.'

'Of course. Always a pleasure. Now ...'

Fry led them up the big staircase, laughing heartily at anything the King said. They turned left at the top onto a gallery landing, which led them to the ballroom door.

Mrs Andrew Phillips Fry, daughter and sole heiress of a Chicago glue manufacturer, curtsied in a shimmer of beads and silk, although being a small woman, she did not have far to go. Miss Amelia Fry, twenty-four, a good head and slim bare shoulders above her petite mother, did an elaborate curtsy, sinking so low that in his view of her she might have been naked. When she stood up she did something very daring — kissed the King on the cheek.

'Amelia!' her mother hissed, but old Bertie liked that sort of thing.

As an afterthought, he was introduced by Fry to Mrs Fry and Amelia. The fact that he had come in with the King was credential enough, it seemed. He stood back on the fringe of the royal party. This surely was getting close — but where was Nellie Fairbairn? When the orchestra struck up in Waldteufel's 'Tendresse' waltz, Amelia persuaded the King to take the floor.

248

What she lacked in conventional ideas of beauty — her coppery hair was a little too far back on her brow and her father's eyes and nose gave her a rather domineering expression — she more than made up for in good health and enthusiasm. She was living a fairy tale and she had a ballgown to go with it, a complicated extravaganza in different layers, dull gold sequins and fancy scrollwork on fine net over a matt-gold material with a band of guipure around her feet also encrusted with gold sequins. The titled English were snapping up American heiresses as brides, but if that was real gold she'd be worth marrying for the melted-down value of the gown. Breathless at their temporary posses-sion of the King of England, the Frys were in no state to won-der which of them had invited the polite young American. A footman gave him a glass of champagne from a silver tray.

'You must feel very proud of your daughter, ma'am,' he said to Mrs Fry.

'That's very kind of you to say so, Mr — ' .

'Pomeroy, ma'am.' A slight hint of curiosity in her eyes was forestalled by his smile. 'The man who came in with the King?' He turned to Fry. 'By the way, sir, President Roosevelt asked me to give you his very best regards when I saw him last a cou-ple of weeks ago.'

'Oh? Did he indeed? How is the President?'

'Well, sir, between you and me, he's having trouble making up his mind about the isthmus canal.'

'I believe the sensible location for the canal is the Panama-nian one,' Fry said. 'You see, Mr — '

'Pomeroy.'

'Of course. Now the Nicaraguan route ...'

Fry was well informed on this topic and might have gone on for hours but Sir Oscar Betts interrupted him. 'I wonder if we could retire briefly to somewhere quieter, Fry.' His accent was hard to pin down, English but not in the English rhythm. He had roughly the same build and beard as his royal pal but close up what you noticed was a coldness, a bleakness about the eyes, as if he was weighing up your price and at the same time rejecting you as not worth the money. Fry didn't particularly want to leave the ballroom but Betis explained that His Majesty's private train was leaving for Aberdeen at nine thirty and he was accompanying the King to King's Cross station. Politely stepping back, Pomeroy heard him telling Fry, 'Bradstocks' revised figures for Swordfish are eight per cent above what ...'

Mrs Fry watched them leave the ballroom together, none too pleased.

Pomeroy grimaced sympathetically. 'Business, y'know — '

'Don't tell me about business,' she said calmly, a very self-possessed little woman. 'My father died of overwork at forty-one. He left a fortune, a mere pittance by Sir Oscar Betts's standards, of course, but enough for us if only he'd lived to enjoy it. People sneer at English aristocrats for not working, but why should they work? It's up to the rest of us to achieve what they have achieved — life for its own sake.'

He shook his head, astonished that she should hit the nail so perfectly.

'Exactly, Mrs Fry. You know my father General Pomeroy's favourite line of poetry? "*Beside the ungathered rice he lay, his sickle in his hand*." "The Slave's Dream" — '

'Oh? Your father is a general?'

'Retired, of course, lives all alone with his memories of the Old South in the big house near Knoxville — ' She made a little grimace when he spoiled it all with Knoxville and he went on quickly — 'But, Mrs Fry, a little investment here and there isn't going to send your husband to an early grave. This Swordfish thing, for instance ...?'

'Oh, you know about that, do you?'

'That's what they've gone to discuss. Sir Oscar is famously astute in these matters. I only wish I could run to that kind of money myself — '

'I wonder how much of his own money Sir Oscar is putting in?' she said snappily. 'I'm only a mere woman, of course, but do you seriously think the world's waiting for huge warships that go under the water?' He shrugged, tactfully. 'Are you in business, Mr Pomeroy?'

'Why no, ma'am, I started life as a soldier — ' The fourteen-piece orchestra brought the waltz to a finale and the dancers came off the floor, Amelia making the King chuckle with some outspoken witticism. '— but I saw no future in that so I went prospecting for gold in the Yukon — '

'That's most interesting, Mr Pomeroy. Amelia, darling, I do hope you're not boring His Majesty.'

'My dear lady, one can never be bored with the company of healthy young women,' the King proclaimed just as Ellington Fairbairn's wavy red hair appeared in the ballroom. Pomeroy might have escaped among the bare-shouldered society beauties and their noticeably older male companions, but that would only postpone it; besides, he was looking forward to Nellie's reaction. The dapper little second secretary came towards them with a truly, astonishingly, remarkable figure: a very tall man, maybe six six, wearing a white cuirassier's uniform with medals and white kid boots above the knee. He had short hair plastered on top of his head and a monocle in his left eye. Suddenly the ballroom seemed like an opera stage. Reality came back as he saw who was coming along behind Fairbairn and the tall man ... Uwe Lang-Gaevernitz!

Their eyes met as Fairbairn did the honours.

'His Majesty — I believe you know Freiherr von Gutersloh.'

'I am honoured, Your Majesty.' The towering German clicked his heels and bowed forward on his toes like a toppling spruce.

King Edward's guttural accent made him sound more German than the German: 'It is always a pleasure to meet such a true friend of Great Britain, Freiherr von Gutersloh.'

Von Gutersloh clicked and bowed and vowed his sense of privilege for Mrs Fry and then Amelia. Fairbairn was moving backwards at an angle, supervising each introduction with an elegant left hand. Von Gutersloh took another sideways step on his heels to greet the last in line. Fairbairn's head turned. His eyes blinked in astonishment, his dinky little mouth fell open. Pomeroy stuck out his hand.

'John Pomeroy — pleased to meet you, sir.'

A hand for splitting logs without an axe gave him a brisk Teutonic pumping. Lang-Gaevernitz, careful not to come so far as to have his back to the King, said, 'This is a surprise, John.'

'Uwe, good to meet you again.'

Fairbairn looked on incredulously as the king told the two Germans that Mr Pomeroy was so typical of America. 'He almost knocked me down in his rush to get to the ball!' Everyone laughed heartily. Lang Gaevernitz hoped His Majesty would have good sport when the season opened tomorrow. Everyone was deeply concerned that the King should be rewarded with good sport. At Sandringham, it was recalled, they'd shot two thousand pheasants and five hundred rabbits on the first day, excellent sport.

'But not for the rabbits,' Pomeroy said.

Fairbairn swallowed. There was a moment's silence, then the King laughed and everybody else quickly joined in. The orchestra poised, people began to take the floor. Feeling he couldn't cope with all this without a breather, Pomeroy turned to Amelia. 'Miss Fry, would you care to honour me with this dance?'

She seemed a little surprised. Mrs Fry wasn't at all sure. 'Did you not promise a dance to Lord Skellingham, Amelia?'

'Why, of course, Mr Pomeroy,' Amelia said, so quickly it was plain she would do whatever mother didn't want her to do. They moved off onto the floor to Bucalossi's 'Queen of Hearts' waltz. On his toes he was pretty much her height.

'Great night for you, I guess, Miss Fry, the King of England here and all?'

'The King of England here and all?' She had a squint at his face. 'What's your first name, Mr Pomeroy?'

'John.'

'Who are you exactly?'

'I'm the man who came in with the King.'

'Come on. You seem to know lots of people but I've never heard of you. Who invited you?'

'I'm a gate-crasher, Amelia. I did it for a bet.'

She burst into laughter. He told her Naunton's ribtickler about the nervous wreck and when she stopped laughing at that, the one about the archaeologist. That took them pretty well to the end of the waltz. 'Tell me the truth,' she said, taking his arm as they went back to the royal party.

'I'm with the State Department, the embassy invited me, I hope you don't mind — '

'Shucks no, John,' she said, sounding just like an English person mimicking an American. Her mother had two young scions of the English aristocracy waiting to 'claim' her for the buffet supper. Pomeroy smiled vaguely at anyone who looked at him. Lang-Gaevernitz was talking seriously to von Gutersloh and the King. Somebody gave his sleeve a sharp tug.

'Pomeroy. What are you doing here?' Fairbairn hissed. 'How did you get past me at the door?'

'I came in with the King, didn't you know?'

'I'm going to have you thrown out of here, Pomeroy — '

'Aw, Mr Fairbairn. You wouldn't want to upset King Edward and make the Frys look foolish, would you?'

'John — ' Lang-Gaevernitz approached. Nellie Fairbairn let go of him.

'I'll see you in the morning,' he hissed.

'— ah, Ellington, going down for something to eat?' Lang-Gaevernitz took Pomeroy's arm. 'I met this young man on the

Lucania. The quality of your junior diplomats is improving, Ellington.' Uwe took his arm along the landing. 'And what do you think of smart London society? The glitter of great wealth, no? It must have been something like this in ancient Rome — '

'You mean half-naked women and all this bowing the knee? Maybe that's why Rome faded out, eh?'

'You have snobs in America — Mrs Astor, the Vanderbilts — '

'They're only copying these people, nobody takes them seriously except themselves.' He waited till they were halfway down the staircase. 'You know those crooks I played poker with?'

'That was the boat, John, you must stop all that sort of thing now — '

'One of them's *dead* now — did you see him on the train, the fat Texan? Marchbanks?' Lang-Gaevernitz stared at him. He wasn't that good an actor, it was the first he'd heard of it. 'He hung himself Saturday night, Sunday morning. I was sent by Fairbairn to handle the paperwork and there he was on a slab …' They were coming into the buffet room, now filling up with people for whom the long famine since late-afternoon 'tea' was ending not a moment too soon. Lang-Gaevernitz had a problem — Marchbanks's death had shocked him almost rigid, but he couldn't blurt it out because he was not supposed to know Marchbanks. They crossed the red carpet to a long table with around five thousand dollars' worth of light pickings. What nothing had ever prepared him for in high society was the voluptuousness of it all, grand and glittering maybe to the poor bum looking in the windows, but a very fleshy and sexual and earthy and gluttonous world once you were in it. Drink and food and ladies whose gowns would have required only an inch less material to be illegal.

'Let us find a table in a quiet corner,' Lang-Gaevernitz said, but there were no tables free now and a waiter at the long buffet table gave them silver cutlery and plates and other waiters jumped to give them anything they wished from platters of boned turkey, lobster, caviar, aspic of prawns, cold ham, cold roast beef, game pie, galantine of veal, cold roast pheasant, plovers' eggs, boar's head with truffles. From all around them came the upper-crust English voices:

'... and he said, "No gentleman has soup at luncheon!" '

'... they ate nightingales' tongues at sixty quid a time, what?'

'... how perfectly appalling — what did they taste like?'

' ... but why polish up old masters in restoration until they shine like bloody mirrors? Duveen said, "Because the rich want to see reflections of themselves when they look at works of art!" '

'... I'd hang all art dealers with their paintings, slimy buggers.'

'... according to Carnegie, all aristocrats are descended from bad men who did the dirty work of kings — '

'... we'll see if his family is around in five hundred years, what?'

'... *we're* descended from a bad woman who did dirty work for King Charles!'

'... there is only one answer to Ireland — cut it off and push it out into the bloody Atlantic Ocean!'

All the time, Lang-Gaevernitz kept glancing at him, waiting for a natural cue to ask questions, the man whose soul was weary with man's brutality to man. When von Gutersloh spotted them and waved them over, they had no option but join his group. A young Englishman with curly reddish-brown hair, smooth face and bright eyes was sounding forth in a trenchant voice with a slight lisp that only made him sound more pugnacious: 'The necessary companion of any real schemes of social progress must be reorganization of our finances by reducing expenditure — particularly upon armaments!' He had a funny way of standing with his upper half bent forward, as if poised to spring at his adversary, an older man with a face so smooth and peachlike it was almost oriental. Von Gutersloh started to introduce Pomeroy, but the two Englishmen were not about to lose their audience. The older man shook his head.

'You're wrong, Churchill. Cutting expenditure on armaments is the last thing we must do. Nobody wants war, but the best way to stop it is to make everyone firmly aware of the consequences of impinging on Britain's interests.'

'Armaments only encourage military adventurism. What we want is a smaller and cheaper army and a stop to this growth of the navy.'

'And what about our German friends? What about their naval act of three years ago?'

'Germany does not want war,' Lang-Gaevernitz said.

'You might not want war and von Gutersloh might not want war — but do you speak for the German government?' demanded Admiral Sir John Fisher, second naval lord. Pomeroy stared at him — 'I've seen your signature on a secret letter,' he almost blurted out. Churchill, he, gathered, was a Member of Parliament, all for peace and trade yet expressing his dislike for what he called 'the curse of militarism' with a vehemence that needed only the rattle of sabres. Lang-Gaevernitz finally managed to introduce them. The young Churchill grasped instantly at his nationality to fire another peace-loving broadside at Fisher. 'Two years ago there was talk of war between Britain and America, Mr Pomeroy. I said in the House of Commons, evil would be the day we embarked on that most foolish, futile and fatal of wars — and not just because my mother is American. But *if* such a fit of madness attacked our two Anglo-Saxon countries, it would not be the short, sharp, decisive conflict *some* people imagine. I shudder at the very prospect of modern warfare. Your American war between the states proved we have moved into a new and more horrific phase of armed conflict — long, immensely destructive, no dashing cavalry charges but huge armies having to be, raised by both sides, whole nations laid waste — '

'Exactly my point, Churchill,' Fisher said calmly. 'Unprepared, war does mean protracted misery and destruction. I joined Nelson's flagship, the *Victory*, at the age of thirteen, and forty-nine years in the navy convinces me it is not warmongering to advocate efficient armaments; it is a protection against war. Unprepared, we *invite* attack. People say I horrified the Hague peace conference by presenting the most dreadful and appalling picture of war ever imagined by human mind — that was my intention. I found them talking about 'civilized' war! This is what deludes people into the madness of war.' His voice was getting stronger, somewhere big guns were firing. 'War is the essence of violence. Moderation in war is imbecility. Any nation that launches an attack on us be warned — the war we wage will be Napoleonic in its audacity, Cromwellian in its thoroughness. Hit first, hit hard, keep on hitting. Oh Lord, arise and let thine enemies be scattered! Hit them between wind and high water!'

For different reasons, Fisher's broadside froze the blood of his listeners: the English because they knew he was the new voice of their country; the Germans because his warning was meant for them to relay to Berlin; and Pomeroy, the only American in the group, because Roosevelt had told him this was how men's minds were turning in Europe and he hadn't taken it too seriously in Rock Creek Park, when Europe was a faraway place he'd read about in history.

Von Gutersloh took a deep breath, way up there. 'God forbid there is any prospect of war.'

Fisher nodded, but his rounded, asiatic face was sceptical. Perhaps to prevent an argument, he turned to Pomeroy. 'It was a damned fine old hen that hatched the American eagle — I'll tell you where I heard that. After Santiago Bay, Admiral Sampson of the United States navy had dinner on the *Renown* at Bermuda — he made the finest speech I ever heard.'

'What do you think of the future of submarine warfare, sir?'

'The submarine boat and wireless telegraphy are yet to be perfected but who knows what a revolution in warfare they may bring about? It's time for me to go, gentlemen.' He smiled at Churchill. 'You're very persuasive, Winston, but what did you say — coal may be most monstrous dear but the dinner must be cooked? Remember that when you're talking about social progress ...'

They met the King and Sir Oscar Betts in the floral cavern of the hall. His Majesty made a little bow with his head to the young American who had amused him. Fry was impressed and, when he'd seen the King off, came upstairs with them, giving Lang-Gaevernitz no chance to ask about Marchbanks. Bubbling with pride at his social achievement, Fry introduced them to everyone he met, by now making a little myth about Pomeroy's brush with royalty. He found himself shaking hands with the lovely and by no means haughty Lady Hednesford among a quartet of English society fashionables.

'So, Mr Pomeroy,' she said gaily and warmly, 'you are the man who came in with the King?

'I'm also the man you sent down to your servants' entrance this morning,' he said.

She frowned. 'I don't recall ever meeting you before ...'

He got his tongue and lips in the right place for a stab at an English voice: 'Inform me when Lord Parkstone arrives.' She pulled him quickly away from the others and demanded the whole story. They both found it astonishingly, frightfully, spiffingly hilarious. They danced. She had a warm waist. Her gown fell from her white shoulders and upper chest in such a way as to continually suggest it was on the move downwards. She called him 'a discovery' and introduced him to other people, telling him the scandal when they passed on. She was very amusing about Amelia Fry. 'It's her father who's mad on getting her hitched to a title — any chinless wonder will do. They're going about it the wrong way actually. All they have to do is choose the title they want and make him an offer. Some of your American girls get the wrong idea in Paris — all these odious little Frenchmen crowding round the American heiress. An Englishman does not crowd round, he merely *accepts* a millionairess.'

'It any worse than being a jumped-up actress who grabs a lord and comes on all starchy at the front door?'

'You insolent bastard,' she murmured, holding him a little closer in the dance. 'You must call on me at teatime some afternoon very soon. I'll let you through the front door myself if that excites you.'

'Does one require to be excited for a naice kip of teeh? '

'Didn't you know — afternoon is when all the sinful lusting takes place.'

'Doesn't his lordship your husband mind?'

'A gentleman is never at home in the afternoons.'

She was like Kate, yet she was not really like Kate, too forward, but the same type, sort of ... suddenly he understood why Kate fought tooth and claw when she knew she was going through with it anyway; fighting kept it from being casual! He had Jane point out her husband, who was equally involved with some lady. 'He's a very civilized man,' she assured him. 'If he saw your bowler hat in the hall, he'd simply go back to his club.'

By now, some of the people she or Lang-Gaevernitz introduced him to had a new version of his arrival, this pushy American johnny shoving in front of the King, and being bounced off the stout royal frame. They were disappointed when he identified himself. They expected something in a string tie missing the spittoon with a squirt of 'baccy juice. With the King's departure, things grew a mite less formal. One or two gentlemen showed signs of too much champagne. Mrs Fry started saying her goodnights around the time some young bloods started slinging plovers' eggs at each other across the buffet room. (Was he imagining it, or did he detect an undertone of contempt for their American hosts among all these fashionable people?) Lang-Gaevernitz was shocked by some of the behaviour. 'Decadence will destroy European civilization just as it destroyed Rome,' he said. Just for a moment they were sitting alone at a table by the dance floor. 'This man who played cards with you, John, he hung himself you said? But that young English fellow, Viscount Holborn — '

'Depends how much credence you put on coincidence, Uwe. I find it hard to swallow, Marchbanks anyway. Hardened crooks like him don't kill themselves. I'm not too sure the police believe it either. I told them about Holborn, I didn't mention the poker game, but I think I ought to, don't you?'

Uwe's self-control was something to listen to. 'John, I warned you this was — '

'Not tired already, are we?' Jane Hednesford demanded and they were dancing again when Ambassador Fry led a vision in white onto the floor. She had black hair piled high, slim white shoulders and arms, full breasts, a white dress more like an extra skin. Alone of all the women at the reception, she had no diamonds around her throat or weighing down her ears, no jewellery of any description. Andrew Phillips Fry seemed to have lost twenty years, flushed like a boy on his first date. He came gliding around the floor with his eyes stuck on her — yes, *glided*, the old bastard must've taken ballroom-dancing lessons!

'Who is that?' he asked Jane.

'Where have you been? You don't know the famous Sophie Crediton?'

Close up, she was a little less ethereal, a fraction less flawless, and a whole lot more to do with the birds and the bees. He saw the attraction for an old warhorse like Fry — she was the kind who gave a man all her attention, laughing at his every quip, entranced by his every remark. Even as they were dancing together, she was patting his cheek and touching his nose with her fingertip, maybe even using a little foul language, a woman to free a man's imprisoned soul and make him feel like a giant.

'Didn't you know — honestly?' Jane asked. He shook his head. 'It's taken for granted in London that the Frys keep separate establishments. In a house this size they need hardly ever meet at all.'

'You mean the marriage is strictly for public display?' asked the naive American. Jane laughed in his arms. 'Gee ... you know her? *That* would be something to tell the folks back home — '

'How many millions do you have?'

'Nary a one.'

'She finds you boring already. I can introduce you to Jack Crediton, he'll take some money off you at billiards — '

'She brings her husband with her?'

'Of course. With a tame husband palely loitering in the background she's a respectable lady doing what everyone else is doing. Without a husband she's the most expensive whore in London.'

'I don't get it. What kind of man would — '

Dalrymple — he still had to remind himself he was Sir Walter Freese Tennyson — was standing in the ballroom doorway, glaring at the dancers through his monocle. He didn't see who he was looking for and turned away.

The electric shock left him numbed for a second. 'What's wrong?' Jane Hednesford demanded. No, Kate wasn't like her! ' Where are you going, John — !'

He hurried around the dance floor. Tennyson was going down the stairs. He hurried along the landing.

'Sir?'

There was too much din coming up from all parts of the big mansion. He reached the top of the stairs as Tennyson strode across the marble floor of the hall. He took the stairs two at a time — a flunkey caught hold of him.

'Careful now, sir, we don't want to — '

He walked at a running pace between the massive banks of flowers. Tennyson had taken his hat and overcoat and was out through the front door. A group of bigwigs and their matrons moved in front of them, pie-eyed gents tilting their silk hats at crazy angles, one stewed to the gills. Pomeroy swung past them and through the flunkeys handing out hats and coats. When he ran down the wide steps and looked both ways, he saw groups of drivers smoking cigarettes, no Tennyson. He ran past one group of drivers down the line of waiting carriages, looking in windows. He heard an automobile engine. Somebody called his name from behind, but he didn't look back. To get through the line of vehicles he had to duck under the heads of two matching grey horses, their warm breath on his neck.

Tennyson was in the front passenger seat of a swanky automobile heading down Park Lane. The chauffeur was wearing a big hat — a woman. 'Hey! Stop!' he shouted. Tennyson didn't look around. He started to run. The automobile slowed to take a left turn, passing under a lamp-post. It was her! He burst into a sprint. 'Kate!'

A man burst out from the line of carriages ahead of him. At first he thought they were trying to avoid each other and going the same way, but the man caught hold of him. 'I'm a police officer, sir — '

'I don't give a shit!'

He was knocking the guy aside when more men came running towards them on the outside of the line of carriages, all grabbing at him, he didn't know how many. He hit one on the mouth, two of them hugged his arms tight against his sides, a hand clamped over his mouth, a solid wall of men closed in all around him, hands on his shoulders and his neck and his arms — and then his legs. Another vehicle came down the line as they were lifting him off the ground, a four-wheel growler cab. It stopped, trapping the swaying knot of men against the stationary carriage, just enough room for the door to open. As the silent men lifted him and shoved him inside, he saw the deerstalker hat.

Somebody inside the cab caught him and shoved him down onto the seat. He started to rise. The door slammed and the cab lurched forwards, tipping him back onto the seat. A blind was pulled and a lamp turned up and Holles Holborn pointed a short-barrelled revolver at his chest.

'For you the ball is over, Cinderella,' he snapped.

20

The muffled clip-clop of horse's hooves was as regular as gallows drumbeat. The cab rocked gently as they faced each other in a light that was garishly bright above their heads and shadowy all round. Holborn's eyes were bright with a promise of revenge.

Keeping Pomeroy covered with the fat little pistol aimed right at his buffet supper, the young Englishman reached inside his black dinner jacket with his left and brought out the typed sheet Bella Busby had put in the hotel safe.

'I should have thrashed you to a pulp the other night, Pomeroy. One more rotten lie from you and I'll be happy to oblige. Where is the original of this?'

At six-foot range, the fat little pistol looked as big as a fieldgun. He had no difficulty in sounding nervous. 'Put the gun away and we can talk. In my experience guns often lead to violence.'

'You can't talk your way out of this, Pomeroy,' Holborn said in his upper-class English drawl with the permanent sneer. 'I want the original of this — tonight. Now!'

'I guess you must do at that, all this fuss.'

'No fuss,' Holborn retorted, a fraction too quickly. 'I'll ask you again, Pomeroy — where is the original?'

'It's safe.'

'Safe — or in the safe?' Holborn smirked at his own wit. 'Did you seriously imagine little Miss Busby would betray her King and country on the promise of an *American?* She told us everything — '

'*Everything?* Why, she's nothing but a brazen little hussy — Mr Brodie.'

Holborn shrugged. 'I've no doubt she told you a lot of balderdash to keep you happy. Just so long as you understand you're not up against a bunch of common thugs in Tosher

264

Delaney's.' Holborn sat back quickly against the dark leather upholstery, his right hand with the pistol resting on his thigh. 'Thinking of kicking out at me from where you're sitting? Go on, try it. If I don't kill you, the driver is an armed policeman and the doors are locked from the outside. Go on — try it.' He had the smirk of a spoiled brat, all arrogance and condescension, the kind of smirk that came with being born to power and privilege and a godgiven *duty* to rule mankind for its own good. (God being English, donchya know?)

'Okay, I'm willing to discuss a deal — '

'A *deal?* Hark to the shrewd yankee trader. How much?'

'I don't want *money* — '

'Americans *always* want money — '

'I want information — '

'The same information you were going to blackmail Tennyson for?'

'I wasn't trying to blackmail Tennyson, for chrissake!'

'You were chasing him when we collared you — '

'I met his daughter on the *Lucania,* Lady Cameron, she's a young widow — '

'I know Kate Cameron — '

'I wanted their address — '

'To invite her to a poker game?' Holborn sneered. 'Alex Cameron was one of my best friends at school, Kate's a topping girl, she wouldn't look twice at *you,* Pomeroy. Wanted their address, eh? How did Fry invite Tennyson to the ball — by magic carpet? You're a congenital liar, man — '

'The guest list! Of course!' He snapped his fingers and made a *tsk-tsk* sound at his own stupidity. 'Why didn't I think of that? Gee, thanks, Holborn — '

'You bloody smart aleck!' Holborn's chest was beginning to heave. 'Maybe there isn't an original, maybe you made all this up — '

'If you thought that, you wouldn't be risking your whole career like this, would you? Maybe I see a way to get you out of trouble, Holborn — '

'Damn you, I'm not in trouble!'

'You will be when your boss reads that statement. You call him by his initial, don't you — C? He doesn't know you got it from the Excelsior safe, does he? A secret-service officer whose brother conspired with crooks to blackmail a special envoy of the British government? That give your career a boost?'

Holborn tried bluster. 'This baloney — ' His left hand crunched through the sheet. '— this is just the kind of awful tosh Francis would write for a joke in his cups, I'll grant you that, but thanks to you and your rotten friends my brother is dead now and the joke's not funny any more!'

He shrugged. 'Pity you weren't so full of brotherly concern when it might have done Francis some good.'

Holborn's hand flexed round the fat little pistol. His face went bright red. His lips had tightened in a snarl, showing his front teeth. The cab hit a pothole and they were both jolted on their seats. From the London night beyond the blinds came blurred voices, street noises, a snatch of drunken singing: 'Come back, Paddy Reilly' ... Holborn went on glaring at him. He knew he was nearer to being shot than at any time since silent men had manhandled him into the cab. His right leg was tensed to smash his toecap up between Holborn's legs — then the stiff-necked young Englishman exploded: 'That's not true! I tried to help Francis — he was a pigheaded, self-destructive idiot! Why should his disgraceful bloody boozing and gambling ruin my life? Eh? I want the original of this or I'll kill you here and now!'

Pomeroy nodded, as if in appreciation. 'You really as dumb as you make out, Holborn? The original of that statement in your brother's handwriting is my life insurance and you know damn well I made watertight arrangements for it before I used that copy as bait. I'm here on a special assignment for the State Department, sooner I'm through, sooner I go home. You help me, I'll hand over the original to you and nobody else. I'm only concerned about protecting the interests of the United States, and we had nothing to do with blackmailing Tennyson — '

'With you and Marchbanks both in that crooked game?' Holborn said shrilly.

'Coincidence. I was only asked to play after they heard I was with the foreign service. Marchbanks was an oldtime grifter who got out of his depth. Devoy was the man — '

'Devoy works for anybody who pays him — '

'And I know who did pay him.'

Holborn snorted. 'You'll say anything to save your skin, Pomeroy.'

He smiled. 'That's so very, very true, Holborn. Times are, I *despise* myself. Well? If you're going to shoot me, get on with it — I'm getting cramp in my backside.' Holborn frowned. 'Come on — a little cooperation for our mutual benefit? President Roosevelt wants to be pals with Britain, you stood with us in the Spanish War, he sees Germany as the enemy. You can't blame me for taking precautions but I was pretty friendly with Francis, I don't want to ruin your career, gosh no — '

'Then why did you put this in the hotel safe, you bastard?' Holborn snapped: 'It was just luck I got my hands on it — '

'I knew you were the case officer for me — the right Mr Brodie?'

Holborn scowled. 'That bloody woman — I'd have her shot!'

'In all fairness, she only talked to me because you people have her half scared to death. I only had to turn the screw a little tighter — and I did promise her an entry visa into the United States — '

'Which she'd be well advised to use at the earliest!'

'—but only if she didn't tell you about our arrangement. Looks like little Miss Busby loses out all round. Do we have a deal? I'll throw in everything I know about Devoy and Marchbanks. Okay? Shake on it?'

Holborn drew back. In refusing the proffered hand, he was forced to decide about the fat little pistol. He shoved it hurriedly into his jacket pocket. 'We're never going to be *friends,* Pomeroy, I'm agreeing to your terms because I have no alternative.'

'No more tailing me, no jumping me, no searching my rooms?'

Gruffly, Holborn said, 'You have my word as an officer and a gentleman.'

His right leg was in agony from pins and needles when he moved it. 'That's good enough for me, old man — particularly when I have you by the short and curlies. That's what you say over here, isn't it?' Holborn stared at him. 'We'll get on just fine,' he said. 'You want to know who was paying Devoy and Marchbanks? Herr Uwe Lang-Gaevernitz, so-called cultural attache´ — bet you never guessed he's Germany's top man in London!'

Holborn sniffed. 'We've known for some time, actually.'

'If you say so. Anyhow, now you can have him shot as a spy — '

'And have Berlin shoot our spies? We *watch* them, we don't *shoot* them.' Holborn thought of something and in a flash the anger was back in his eyes and his chest was rising. 'Are you claiming Francis knew about the Germans?' he demanded.

'No, he thought it was strictly for the money.'

Holborn snorted. 'He wouldn't have conspired against his own country, ridiculous idea.'

'Why was Tennyson using a fake name anyhow?'

'I dunno,' Holborn said airily.

'Jesus, I thought I was a poor liar, Holborn.'

'He wasn't on an official mission, he was sent by Sir John Fisher — oh God, if they knew I was telling you this .. .'

Holborn was only a big schoolboy with a moustache — he still had a spot or two under the jawline — but his upper-class English voice carried the same intimations of power and history as Theodore Roosevelt's highpitched Harvard drawl and just as in Rock Creek Park, the same eerie fascination began to grip him, the same sensation of having been invited to step behind a curtain where a few men of power were deciding history in secret.

Jackie Fisher, the British admiral with the asiatic face, led the movement for rearmament and modernization of the Royal Navy in British ruling circles. As Pomeroy had just heard him saying in the Fry mansion, Fisher shared Roosevelt's philosophy — nobody wages war on you if you carry a big enough stick. The King, who disliked his nephew the German Kaiser, was backing Fisher against diehards who wanted the navy to stay faithful to Nelson, and against the weak-kneed and the naive who didn't want bigger and better armaments in case the weapons themselves would lead to war. Fisher would have been a handful for any government even without the King's support; his unorthodoxy was such that he once suggested the Royal Navy should free the Jewish Captain Dreyfus from Devil's Island and let him ashore in France to embarrass the French government; most people believed he was joking. Now, according to Holborn, he was playing 'a deep game', getting the Royal Navy ready for war ahead of official government approval. He had sent Tennyson in secret to the United States to arrange oil supplies for the British fleet in the event of war with Germany. Holborn shuddered.

'If Tennyson's mission became public knowledge, the political storm would be *cataclysmic.* The King would be seriously embarrassed, the Conservative government would probably fall, we'd have the damned lily-livered Liberals in power — I'd have had that little rascal Lloyd George shot as a traitor during the Boer War! Abroad, the repercussions would be disastrous — Kaiser Wilhelm would assume we're actively preparing for war with American support! The French and the Russians — '

'I think I get the drift — Tennyson plays poker and the world goes up in flames? You keep files on American diplomats?'

'We hear things — '

'What do you hear about a possible German informant in our embassy?'

Holborn said that Berlin seemed well informed about American activities and affairs in London. 'We weren't sure if it was official policy or some pro-German individual. Fry's an Anglophile, so's Fairbairn, we don't know much about the junior staff — '

'What do you have on Fry's relations with Lady Crediton?'

'Sophie Crediton? She's a spy, of course — '

'She's a *spy?* Who for?'

'Our dear Gretchen, naturally — she was born in Berlin, still has relations there. Her interest in your ambassador is purely mercenary — '

'How you can be sure?'

'Does Fry know anything worth a spy's trouble?' Holborn retorted, always the little dig at anything American from these haughty milords except when they were marrying American heiresses ...

'I mean, no danger of a public scandal — a divorce or such?'

Holborn grimaced dismissively. 'She's a very shrewd woman at a certain level. Fry doesn't know he shares her with two other rich men. Frankly, he's just silly enough to believe she loves him — no fool like an old fool — but she's very discreet.'

'What about her husband?'

'Old title, no money. He supplies respectability; she pays his tailor and his bookmaker and provides spending money. Jack Crediton won't be rocking the boat, my word on it!'

'Dawson City didn't know the meaning of respectable. Sir Oscar Betts?'

Holborn hissed air through his teeth, exasperation at being pumped so directly when the local style was the half-hint and the muttered clue over a two-hour luncheon. 'He was born Oskar Beitz in the Warsaw ghetto they say, worth anything up to two hundred million, has interests in lord knows how many countries — one of the King's more dubious friends, which is saying a lot — he's given his basic allegiance to Great Britain, as much as these cosmopolitans are loyal to any country. Personally, I'd send the whole damned lot of 'em packing back to their stinking ghettoes — '

'*Swordfish* mean anything to you — a warship of some kind?' Holborn shook his head. 'Bradstocks?'

The shipbuilders? They have a big yard near Shoreham in Sussex. You can look up Sussex in an atlas.'

'One last favour, old man, if you could drop me back at the Fry residence?' Holborn called out to the driver and the cab did a tight turn. They stared at each other in that gloomy sealed compartment.

Holborn seemed to have accepted the situation. 'Mutual co-operation can't do any harm,' he growled.

'Say — now we're kind of unofficial partners, you think we could use first names? On the boat it was Francis and John — '

'No wonder he jumped overboard,' Holborn drawled icily.

Was that a joke?

'You'll ask around about *Swordfish?*'

'I'm not working for you, dammit!'

'Come on, a couple of questions here and there? Shall I ring you tomorrow at Westminster 121?'

'I'll ring you, I'll use the name Brodie.' Holborn frowned. A worrying thought brought a hint of panic to his voice. 'What if something happens to you?' he demanded. The cab pulled in and came to a halt. 'If that statement falls into the wrong hands, I'm sunk!'

The cab lurched with the weight of the driver getting off. They heard him walking round behind, then he called out, 'Captain Holborn?'

Holborn reached to turn the lamp down, then raised the blind. Pomeroy saw the brilliantly illuminated frontage of the Fry mansion. Some sign from Holborn informed the driver it was all right to unlock the door.

'I've taken good care of the original,' he assured Holborn. 'Anyhow, nothing's going to happen to me.'

'I wouldn't count on it, Pomeroy,' Holborn said almost vindictively. 'I very nearly blew your brains out twenty minutes ago — God knows what the German secret service and Charles Devoy have in mind for you!'

He was collecting his things in the hall when Fry came down the great staircase with a small party that included Sophie Crediton, a couple of seal-smooth Englishmen and Amelia.

'We missed you, Mr Pomeroy,' Fry boomed.

'I must thank you, ambassador, a really swell evening. Miss Fry — '

'Who is this handsome man I haven't been introduced to?' Sophie Crediton demanded. She wasn't really interested in him, she just had to be the centre of attraction at all times. Her eyes were bored with him before they'd hardly looked at him.

Amelia seemed quite struck by him in a sisterly kind of way. He thought he was going to get away with it, then Fry took him by the elbow. 'You didn't tell us what you're doing in London, John.'

Oh well, what the hell.

272

'Why, sir, I'm a third secretary at the embassy.'

'Oh, how interesting. Which embassy?'

'The American embassy, sir.'

Fry took a couple of steps before he looked around, beginning to frown.

21

'You did it for a *bet?* ' Fairbairn squeaked. 'A bet with whom, may I ask?'

He did the honourable thing and didn't look at Sleath. Loose, however, gave the game away by going bright red. Fairbairn took a deep, deep breath. It made him look like a pigeon that can blow up its chest.

'I'm sorry, Mr Fairbairn,' Sleath mumbled.

'I'm sorry too, Mr Fairbairn,' Pomeroy said contritely. The lizard's-tail trick — what the swooping hawk grabs isn't the lizard but its tail. The lizard sheds its tail and runs. If you're going to commit a major offence, chuck in a minor offence you can admit to and keep them happy.

'I would fire you both,' Fairbairn said. The phone rang on Spence's desk. 'The ambassador, however, takes the view that young Americans should show what he is pleased to call the get-up-and-go spirit. In future, all embassy staff will be officially invited to receptions . . .'

'For you, Pomeroy,' Spence grunted, letting the mouthpiece clatter on the desk.

Sleath was slapping him on the back as he heard the voice of culture: 'John? Uwe. Can we meet? It is rather urgent . . .'

He met Lang-Gaevernitz by the lake in St James's Park at a quarter past one. It was damp and raw, with a misty grey sky. Ducks were making a helluva din. Lang-Gaevernitz looked as fresh and pink and troubled of soul as ever.

'I had to telephone you, John. I hope it didn't cause any trouble for you.'

'No. What's wrong, Uwe?'

'John, I don't know how to ... shall we walk? John, I ... I have betrayed our friendship. I want to apologize — and warn you.'

'Sounds very dramatic, Uwe.'

'I give you my word, I knew nothing of this. Those crooks you played cards with — they were working for Wilhelmstrasse!'

'Come again?'

'I'm sorry, the German Foreign Office. More exactly, the political department of our secret service. They didn't tell me about it, naturally, I am only a cultural attache.'

'Blackmailing the Englishman Dalrymple?'

'His real name is Tennyson — I learned this today. I asked one of our people if he knew anything about these men. I was worried about you, John. Tennyson was an envoy for the British government, our secret service wanted to compromise him. I shudder to think of what these maniacs might do if — however, John, I am only concerned about our friendship. Do you know that Marchbanks was murdered by Devoy?'

'The police said — '

'Yes yes, he hung himself. I don't even like talking about it, but it's ingenious. A blow to the throat, the victim is helpless, he counts on the rope that hangs the victim concealing the mark of the original blow. Almost a perfect murder. He's out of their control, John!'

'Devoy?'

'You swear you will never talk about this to another living person?'

'Yeah, sure — '

'Devoy is what these people call a freelance agent. Mainly he works for the International Secret Service Bureau in Brussels, a semi-private espionage agency that sells information to anyone who will buy it. They have no loyalties, no scruples. I hold our own espionage people in contempt, but these are truly creatures of the shadows, mercenaries, jackals, traitors to all countries. I shall put in a very strong protest to Berlin about this whole matter. I am sure His Imperial Highness Kaiser Wilhelm would not countenance the use of such methods in the name of Germany. You must be very careful, John.'

'Why would he murder Marchbanks?'

'Money, I am told. Devoy has now informed our people they will have to pay a great deal more for him to compromise Tennyson or he will go to the British secret service.'

'That'll get him hung, won't it?'

Lang-Gaevernitz sighed patiently. 'These people deal in secrets and in people's lives where Armenians deal in carpets. In many ways they are above national laws. John — if Devoy contacts you, please telephone me immediately.' They were coming within sight of Buckingham Palace at the western end of the lake.

'I don't see how I come into all this, Uwe, all I did was play cards with them — '

'You told me yourself, you cheated, you knew they were crooks.' The German waited until three typewriter girls walking in their luncheon hour had passed. 'He may have some proposition for you, John — but don't trust him! A man like Devoy would not hesitate to kill you to protect himself. I wish I had never given you the money ...' They came round the end of the lake and started back along the path on the other side, towards the skyline of Horse Guards Parade and Whitehall. To their left, mounted Life Guards with plumed helmets and blue tunics were riding along The Mall, the wide avenue running from Buckingham Palace to Trafalgar Square. Uwe was still apologizing as they came along the other side of the lake. 'How was I to know my own colleagues were involved in such a disgraceful affair? This only proves that men like you and I must unite against the brutes, John. As the famous Englishman Dr Johnson said, patriotism is the last refuge of the scoundrel. Nationality is an accident of birth, friendship is a declaration of independence — don't you agree, John?'

'I never heard an American play Liszt like you, Uwe.' He said this with sincerity and Uwe knew what he meant, which was more than he did. Through all this bullshit he was listening for the point of it all, the real reason for warning him about Devoy.

Approaching the Whitehall skyline, which had a look of India and took the imagination to far corners of the British Empire, Uwe went on about the struggle between progress and barbarism, the future of the human rate depending upon men of culture and intellect uniting against intellectual and moral degeneracy, engaging in a free exchange of ideas and *information* as their only defence against the neanderthals. Uwe had taken his elbow, a gloved hand on several layers of cloth, a touch rather than a grip but a gesture of surprising intimacy. When he came to the point, it was in the voice of a friend and fellow conspirator. 'We must hope my people get hold of this creature Devoy before he can do any damage but, in case they do not, you must be prepared for him, John ... if he suspects you are a threat to him, he will kill you without hesitation. He is very likely to make you a proposition. Say yes, agree to anything — above all, don't make him suspicious. At the same time, telephone me at the German embassy in Carlton House Terrace — telephone me immediately. If your life is not at stake, then your career most certainly is!'

'My career?' he said anxiously.

'You took part in a crooked card game and you cheated. The British secret service would believe *you* were going to blackmail Tennyson. How could you prove otherwise? Would the State Department protect you? To prove your innocence you would have to admit to cheating! But don't worry, John — I am your friend and I will do everything in my power to help you because you cannot ask your own people for help, can you? If Devoy contacts you — '

'You really think he's going to, don't you?' he asked, licking his lower lip.

Uwe squeezed his elbow. 'Do *everything* he says, John, don't try to out-smart him, don't call to anyone for help but me — think of him as a dangerous escaped maniac you are humouring until help comes …'

The big ring glinted on his knuckled fist as he rubbed at his jawbone. Devoy was wearing black, with a starched white shirt and collar. In the crowded hotel bar full of businessmen and out-of-town salesmen and seekers after the fleshpots, he looked like a Calvinist studying a den of iniquity.

'What will you have, Pomeroy? We can sit over there by the wall.'

'Scotch whisky, neat.'

22

They sat facing each other. Devoy touched at his nose showing enough white linen to hide a piano. His eyes patrolled the room. Pomeroy thought he was making up his mind about something, but he'd already made it up.

'Let's not waste any time over Marchbanks. He was a con man and a cardsharp — he chloroformed you and stole the money you cheated us out of. He was a sexual pervert — I made a mistake getting involved with him.'

Pomeroy looked surprised. 'You don't beat about the bush, Devoy.'

'I don't have time. We both know the score. You remember Dalrymple?'

'Tennyson, you mean,' Pomeroy said slyly.

'Of course. Holborn must have told you. He was another mistake.'

'Holborn told me some of it — Lang-Gaevernitz told me the rest this afternoon.'

Even that didn't shake him. 'You've got a good face for this business, Pomeroy. You look too naive and clean-cut to know what time of day it is. Where did you learn to handle a deck of cards?'

'The Yukon mainly. I used to do conjuring tricks as a kid.'

'All I'm interested in is whether you want to make some money. I don't care what relationship you have with Uwe. I don't mind doing business with the Germans if they pay enough.'

'What business?'

'The thing Marchbanks and I were working on.'

'Blackmailing Tennyson? You seem to forget — I'm a diplomat. Sure, I'm a little tricky around a card table but — '

'Cheating at cards is crookery, what's the difference? As a respectable diplomat, your word would be almost as good as

Holborn's. The threat would be enough for Tennyson, bloody snob. He's very close to Sir John Fisher. I know three countries would pay big money for anything we get out of him — long-term British naval strategy, new warship designs, armour specifications, you know the sort of thing.'

'Devoy, I'm with the American foreign service — '

'We'll sell the stuff to America then, I couldn't care less. That way you'd only be doing your job, wouldn't you?'

'Let me get this straight, Devoy — you're suggesting we team up to put the bite on Tennyson? I have to say he was cheating at cards? Whatever we gouge out of him we sell to any country that'll buy it?' Devoy nodded. 'Aren't you taking a big chance telling me all this?'

'There's probably a flat-footed London bobby out on the street — why don't you run out and tell him? I'm conspiring to blackmail an important government official. Go on, I'll wait here ... if they don't frog-march you off for being drunk.'

He acknowleged Devoy's cleverness with a little grimace. 'Well, I dunno ... what kind of money are we talking about?'

'The Germans paid us two thousand pounds as a retainer and they put up the boat tickets. We were to get one thousand pounds a month as long as we had Tennyson feeding us reasonable material. I'm sure we can double that at the very least, but I'd rather sell it bit by bit to the highest bidder.'

'Working through Brussels maybe?'

Devoy sighed impatiently. 'Pomeroy, you don't seem to understand. All these little aces you keep bringing down your sleeve, I'm way beyond that. I don't care what Uwe told you or how much you know. Of course I work for the ISS Bureau, I'll work for anybody. Are you interested or not?'

'Well, I'd be a liar if I said I wasn't interested in that kind of dough but ...'

'I'm hungry. We'll go to Simpson's in the Strand. I hate this stinking country, but I do like the roast beef of old England. Which hotel are you at by the way?'

'Didn't I say I was staying with friends?' Devoy didn't smile; he snorted, but it sounded like a smile.

The gentlemen's dining room at Simpson's famous old English tavern a hundred yards or so up the Strand from the Excelsior had a red carpet, tables in the middle and tables along one wall with upholstered partitions. The frock-coated majordomo called Devoy Mr Stewart. A head waiter also in a frock coat took their order. Chefs in floppy white hats and long white coats cut slices off the roasts on stands they wheeled about the long room. Under a high fancy ceiling, with an oil painting of voluptuous ladies over a big fireplace, it all seemed pretty luxurious.

'You ever come here with Marchbanks?' Pomeroy asked.

'I despised Marchbanks, just a cheap crook. That awful voice of his. We once had lunch in Brown's Hotel and he asked the head waiter if the meat was fresh! Why are you so interested in him?'

'I dunno . . .' A chef was sharpening his carving knife at the next table. Steel flashed and scraped on the whetstone. A jolly chef, with a happy red face. 'You know they sawed the top off his head to take his brain out and his heart? Why would he hang himself, you think?'

'Taking money off small-town charlies was his limit. I didn't want to use him, but the Germans are always in such a bloody hurry and it was a good chance to get at Tennyson. Next time I'll deal with Koenigergratzerstrasse. Uwe's lot are under the Kaiser's thumb.'

'What's Koenig whatever you said?'

'Number 70 Koenigergratzerstrasse is the intelligence department of the Imperial German Navy. The Kaiser doesn't interfere so much with them. I've done business with Captain von

Tappken and von Richter before — I did a job for them on the French Riviera with an agent called Graves. They gave us twenty thousand reichsmarks for fourteen days' work.' He took the last spoonful of his thick leek soup and wiped at his lips with his napkin. His tone didn't change. 'I could probably get you five thousand dollars for the *Swordfish* specifications.'

'How would I get those?'

'Ambassador Fry must have a set of specifications; he's putting money into it, isn't he?' Pomeroy frowned and for some reason Devoy took this as a danger signal and went on quickly. 'Mind you, the Krauts are hard bastards ...'

Eating roast beef with Devoy was the beginning of an education in the European secret-service world. The Germans were the most efficient by far, and the most ruthless, particularly to their own agents. Former naval Lieutenant von Zastrov did nothing worse than flirt with a female Russian agent. As an ex-officer, he was entitled to have his case heard by a tribunal, but that might lead to complications. 'So they got another agent to pick a quarrel with von Zastrov and challenge him to a duel. Unfortunately, von Zastrov killed him.'

'Rough justice, eh?'

'They simply sent another agent to pick a quarrel with him. The second one got him.'

'All over a little flirtation? Hell's teeth!'

'He knew too many secrets for them to take a chance.'

For all his previous urgency, Devoy wasn't rushing through dinner and ordered a second bottle of Niersteiner Pettenthal, the 1900 vintage. 'Red wine with meat is a convention, I despise all conventions. Sidney Reilly taught me the way things are — no, you wouldn't know him, works for the British secret service, actually a yid called Sigmund Rosenblum from Odessa, the most famous agent of them all. They sent him into Russia in ninety-seven to see if the Russians had discovered oil at Baku. Instead he got them an option to buy the whole Persian oil concession from a man called D'Arcy, for around twenty thousand pounds, I think. They said it was too expensive! Now there's a character — he fell in love with the young wife of a Church of England vicar, so he simply poisoned the reverend gentleman! They sent him to China — he stole the complete plans of the Russian naval base at Port Arthur. The Russians try very hard but …' On and on went the stories. Devoy ordered a Kirschwasser liqueur and a Henry Clay corona imperial.

'Money — I take out expenses first then we'll split fifty-fifty,' he said expansively. 'I don't care — anyway, I can't do it without you.'

'You've double-crossed the Germans — isn't that dangerous? All these people they've killed — '

'They won't touch me as long as they think they've a chance of getting at Tennyson. They won't mind paying more. And they won't know anything about you.'

'What if Tennyson won't play ball and goes straight to the British secret service?'

'Men like him don't think like you and me. Cheating at cards — worst sin in the world. Social death. But — slaughter a few thousand Fuzzy-Wuzzies, wage war to make the Chinese buy British opium, sell little girls of six to rich perverts, starve the poor to death — '

'You really hate 'em, huh?'

'My mother was from a respectable French family. She fell in love with the son of one of England's most powerful and aristocratic families, you'd be staggered if I told you his name. They were forcibly parted and she was sent to Australia. I'm illegitimate as a result. Waiter — another Kirschwasser.'

'Coffee for me.'

Gray did say there was something wrong about the kind of men and women who became spies by choice, some type of mental quirk or sickness. Devoy's fantasy of being some aristocrat's bastard didn't come across as a tall tale but as a hint of some deeper malignancy. Anyway, he'd heard enough. Casually he said, 'Where are you planning to string me up, Devoy?'

'Is that an American expression? I don't know it,' he said calmly. He lifted the delicate liqueur glass toward his pursed lips.

'That young pathologist who cut up old Jesse? He found the injury where you smashed him across the throat. Almost the perfect murder. The police are going for suicide — I didn't tell them you and Marchbanks were partners in a blackmail scheme. I could, though.'

The brimful glass didn't even tremble. Devoy's lips wiped each other.

'Have you had too much to drink?'

'Tennyson's honour is such he'd betray his own country to beat a false accusation of cheating at cards? Crap. The Germans knew damn well he'd go straight to the British secret service. There is no money in selling secrets but there is scandal. Tennyson would involve Sir John Fisher. That's what the Germans want, discredit Fisher to stop him modernizing the Royal Navy. You need me to make the scandal now Holborn's dead. Afterward — what do you use, Devoy — a stick? Lead piping? Your hand maybe?'

Devoy shrugged. 'You're in it now anyway Pomeroy — '

'Uh uh.' He brought out a white envelope. How's this for a little ace?

Devoy opened the envelope and unfolded a copy of Francis Holborn's statement. He read it twice without looking up. He brought out his big white handkerchief and wiped at his nose and mouth. 'You come near me one more time, Devoy, and the original of that goes to the British. You'll be hung for treason — if they bother with a trial. Think about it while I'm in the john.'

He took his time and when he came back Devoy was gone, leaving him with the check. The majordomo said Mr Stewart was a regular patron, when he was in England between trips abroad connected with his financial interests.

'Cab, sir?' asked the doorman. 'No. I'll walk.' He went left in the direction of Trafalgar Square. It was cold and raw, few people on the pavement. He pulled up his collar and stuck his hands in the pockets of his short overcoat. It was just beginning to worry him that Devoy might have panicked when a four-wheel growler cab overtook him, then stopped a few yards ahead and Devoy got out, holding the door open. 'Get in, Pomeroy.' The driver jumped down and came round behind him, with another man getting out of the cab on the other side. He went from walking to a sprint in three strides, hitting Devoy aside with his shoulder and getting five yards ahead before he heard running feet behind. He ran across the Adam Street opening on his left, leaving them farther behind until he stumbled and ran on with a slight limp. They didn't shout, they just kept running. He came past the Excelsior entrance, looking away in case Hoare was sheltering under the awning, then past the cab forecourt of Charing Cross Station. He looked over his shoulder. They were catching up fast. He came to the wooden barricades round the tunnel works for the new underground railway. Before they reached him, he jumped up on piled bags of cement and swung his leg over the barricade. A dim light from the high windows of the railway hotel showed him piled earth, cement bags in stacks, lengths of metal track, the massive timbers shoring the tunnel shaft.

The sloping shaft had timbered stairs running down parallel with narrow bogey tracks. It was lit every few yards by safety lamps. He took the wide wooden steps two at a time. They ended on what was to be the platform of the subway station. He ran to the end of the raised platform, where the tunnel started. They came running down the wooden stairs.

'That's a dead end, Mr Pomeroy,' came a mocking voice.

285

He jumped down onto a bed of stones supporting bullhead rails all the way from the Carnegie Steel Works in Pittsburgh and ran into the round tunnel. Oil lamps strung up every twenty yards or so threw a dim light that kept him between the metal rails, then his feet went over a drop and he was running on curved iron, along the big pipe under London's streets, heavy iron that rang with his running steps and then echoed to its own ringing tone. When he looked back, he couldn't see them in the dim light but he heard the following echoes.

He ran maybe two or three hundred yards, past the timbers shoring another, vertical shaft, running on iron towards a faintly brighter glow of oil lamps. They were strung up on the machinery of the Greathead Shield and Price Excavator being used to cut through the London clay. The iron tunnel stopped before a stretch of muddy clay churned up by workmen's boots.

He stood on the tip of the last section of iron tunnel and waited for their shapes to come into focus and their faces to come into the light. Two of them, shapeless and unrecognizable in the tunnel gloom. One stopped thirty feet back, the other came forward to within ten or twelve feet. He wasn't Devoy but his face was vaguely familiar.

'Not remember me, Mr Pomeroy?' The guy sounded amused. 'Last time I served you with coffee during the poker game on the *Lucania.'* It was George the steward, the one Marchbanks said he had bribed for the use of a stateroom. .

'Where's Devoy?' he demanded. He craned to look past George the steward at the second man. 'Devoy?' he called. The second man took a few steps nearer — it was the cab driver. 'I want to speak to Devoy.'

George the steward took a couple of steps nearer. 'Mr Devoy doesn't like to get his shoes dirty.'

He accepted defeat with soldierly dignity, standing stiffly with his arms down his sides. 'All right, I'll give you the original of Holborn's statement — '

'It doesn't matter.'

'Look, I want to speak to Devoy!'

'Naturally, you've made sure the original will reach the authorities if something happens to you?'

'You bet I have!'

George the steward unbuttoned his fur-collared shooting coat. The cab driver had a bad cold and kept sniffing. 'Mr Devoy won't be here to deny Holborn's drunken fantasy and you won't be here to substantiate it you have nothing to bargain with.'

His mouth fell open. 'Now just hold on a minute here, I don't have any quarrel with you fellows — '

'I heard you were upset about Jesse Marchbanks.' George the steward pulled out a shiny baton and held it horizontally level with his throat, making little jabbing motions at his adam's apple. 'It's a London bobby's truncheon — you were curious, I believe.' George the steward had. his chin up, contemplatively stroking his exposed throat with the shiny, rounded stick. The sniffing cab driver was getttng nearer. Pomeroy swallowed noisily. 'You can't fake my suicide down here!' he protested.

'You committed suicide when you played the wrong cards, Pomeroy.

'You're not seriously thinking of killing me, are you?' He tried to laugh. 'I was discussing business with Devoy ten minutes ago — you want money? I have plenty money — ten thousand pounds? You name your price. For chrissake listen to me — I'll give you anything you want!'

'This is what we want, Pomeroy. You meddled in our business. It's been decided you're a nuisance. Just think — you'll be down here, underground trains thundering through this tunnel every five minutes, millions of clerks and shopgirls passing over your grave every year — '

'Why kill me?' he pleaded. Then he tried bluster. 'You're in enough goddam trouble — Devoy has double-crossed the Germans!

George the steward smiled. 'We are the Germans, Pomeroy.'

He frowned, then seized at this straw. 'Uwe! Ask Uwe Lang-Gaevernitz! He wouldn't let you kill me!'

George the steward was even more amused by that. 'Your dear friend Uwe? I knew Americans were naive but ... that's very funny.'

'Please don't kill me,' he pleaded.

The cab driver stopped shuffling. George the steward took a step forward.

Pomeroy raised his right arm until the Smith and Wesson was at shoulder level and shot George the steward in the chest. He fell backwards. The cab driver ducked his head and started to twist round. George shot him in the side. A monstrous booming echo took his breath away. George the steward didn't move. The cab driver was trying to run away on hands and knees, his shoes scrabbling against iron.

He walked after him and shot him through the back of the neck.

23

Wednesday, October 14, 1903, a date on the calendar, a day like any other day, except that he was in it and they were not. Fog started coming down in the early afternoon. At first he thought a building was on fire when he saw a billowing cloud moving down Victoria Street. Nobody raised an alarm, nobody shouted, nobody stopped to point. It felt like a dream. He was tired. Nobody looked at him and nobody bumped into him, although the people in the dream looked solid enough to be real. Just a date on the calendar, a day like any other day . . . a routine miracle. Nobody pointed him out for having killed a man called George and another man whose name he didn't know.

Spence came back from Tottenham Court Road police station just after three and reported that the two arrested bombers had no proof of their claim to be American citizens, which would save them from being hanged for treason against the British crown. This gave him the beginning of an idea to stop Fry making his speech that night at the Imperial League banquet.

'They say they were taken to Boston as children and don't recall when or where their parents became citizens,' Spence said. 'They've obviously been to Boston, but they're lying to save themselves from the hangman. Accents thick as the bog they were spawned in. The police say we don't have to take any action.'

'We'd better hope they're lying,' Pomeroy said. 'Us helping the British hang two Americans might be a little hard to understand back home.'

Spence was annoyed at his interference but Nellie Fairbairn pouted his lips and made little noises with his teeth. 'Good thinking, John. If there's one chance in a million they're Americans we can't afford to get egg on our faces. Mr Spence, send a cable to the Department of Immigration and have them check the names.' Sleath winked at him behind Spence's back and said, 'Did you notice — he called you John?'

Spence hated his guts by then. 'The little faggot has taken a shine to you, Pomeroy. Flattered?'

'Jealous?' he murmured in reply.

Spence went very red. Sleath was now his pal and when Spence was in with Fairbairn he asked him about the guest list for Amelia's reception. 'There's a lady I might want to look up …' There was no Tennyson on the list. Maybe he'd only come to catch Sir John Fisher.

'Fry's spending the weekend at Betts's country place in Sussex,' Sleath said slyly. 'Haven't you been invited?'

'No, but if you want another little bet …'

The fog was a lot thicker when he came out of the embassy and headed along Victoria Street. Holborn had called the tail off but he found himself wishing for Deerstalker; at least somebody had been looking after him.

Where the hell was Devoy? At the desk he asked for Miss Busby. 'She's left the hotel's employment, sir: the desk clerk told him, 'Her mother's fallen ill in Scotland and she'll have to do the nursing. I don't imagine she'll be back.'

'Oh. She put something in the safe for me — here's the ticket.'

It was back in the safe, the envelope with the carbon copy inside. What could these people not do? In the elevator he asked Frank the one-armed veteran to send Naunton up to his room. Frank raised an eyebrow. 'Nothing *dodgy* going on between you two, is there?'

'Say that again and I'll use your stump to stir my tea.'

'Only kidding, Hiram.'

'You keep calling me Hiram and I'll move to a proper hotel. How come you couldn't handle a few Dutch farmers anyway?'

The elevator stopped. Frank Smythe didn't open the gate for a moment. 'You want to know the truth, John? Why I'm a socialist? This country's no good for the common man; it's run by rich idiots and the worst of them get to the top in the army. They just led us to the slaughter, the Crimea all over again. I only lost an arm, most of my mates are fucking dead because of that fool General Redvers Buller. I hope he never gets in this lift. I'll kill him with my bare teeth, the bastard!'

Frank promised to warn him immediately if a man answering Devoy's description turned up in the hotel.

Naunton and he left the hotel separately, then met by the public telephone box inside Charing Cross railway station. There was just enough room for both of them. He showed the boy a piece of paper.

'Say this in an Irish voice, Naunton.'

The boy screwed up his face, twisted his mouth, cocked his head to one side: 'Dis is de Fenian Brudderhood, dere is a bomb goin' off dis evenin' at your banquet — ' His eyes widened in horror. 'Is this true?'

'It's a practical joke, Naunton. You ask the exchange girl for the number — London Wall 5916. It's the City Livery Companies' Hall. When they answer, say that stuff twice, don't get into conversation, don't stop for anything … shit, have you got any pennies?'

Through murky glass he watched the station crowds for a dark man with deepset eyes and a ramrod back.

The fog had turned into what Naunton called a pea-souper when they separated again outside the station. Thick yellow fog caught in his throat and blanked out the station before he'd crossed the cab forecourt. People loomed out of the yellow fog and each time he held his breath until he was sure it wasn't Devoy. Where you could see the fog against streetlights, it was like snow you couldn't touch. Men walked at the heads of the horses pulling buses. Outside the Excelsior, people going to the Alhambra music hall were arguing whether it was safe to set out walking. He called the Fry residence from the desk telephone. A maid answered, then Griffiths the butler came on.

'Pomeroy from the embassy here, Griffiths. I don't know how bad the fog is up there in Mayfair but nothing's moving in the Strand. I thought the ambassador better know — his banquet tonight?'

'It's been called off because of the fog, Mr Pomeroy, but I'll inform His Excellency you called, I'm sure he'll be most grateful.'

Did they call it off because of the fog or the anonymous bomb warning? We'll never know, Gray, but I'm making the credit anyway. Not for the fog …

He was in bed by eight, intending to sleep. Fog muffled all sounds, up there on the rooftops. Like being in the sky. Down there in the tunnel there wouldn't be any fog …

Four shots did it.

He'd had to drag them feet first off the lip onto muddy clay that was up past his ankles. He was sweating like a pig by the time he shovelled enough clay from under the iron curve to push the bodies out of sight and shovel clay over them again. Next day they'd pour concrete on the outside of the iron tunnel, stabilizing it against the wet London clay, and they'd be buried for ever. He'd come back into the hotel by the kitchen entrance and up the dark stairs. He'd washed the clay off his shoes and socks and pants in the bath; they could be dumped in an ashcan without a trace of where they'd been. A competent, professional murder, justified by self-defence ... except that he'd led those two men down into the tunnel that would be their tomb through all the years when the city millions were whisked through an iron pipe under London's streets to their cosy homes in the suburbs.

They were killers, Gray said. Remember Marchbanks on the slab. That's not what's bothering me, Gray. I didn't get to kill Devoy, that's what's bothering me. Now I think he's waiting out there to kill me!

He took a cab to the embassy next morning. The fog was patchier. Miss Willoughby said a woman called Lily had telephoned him and left a message.

'You wanted the address of somebody called Tennyson. It 's 13 Onslow Square South Kensington — oh, going out again are you?'

'Tell Mr Fairbairn I have a toothache.'

The cabbie wasn't finding number 13 quick enough so he paid him off and started looking up the front steps of the big houses. When he found 7 and 8 in sequence, he started to hurry, just in time to see the same red and gold automobile she'd been driving Monday night pull away from the curb. She was wearing a stiff straw hat held to her head by a band of white silk.

'Kate!'

She didn't look round.

24

He ran to the corner, already feeling the smile on his face. She was going quite fast — surely she was exceeding their twelve-mile-per-hour limit?

'Kate?'

She turned the red and gold Siddeley right into Fulham Road. She couldn't hear for her hatband!

He got in the middle of the road and started to sprint. His wide-awake hat fell off. He held it against his chest and ran in earnest this time. Coming around the corner in Fulham Road, he skidded to a stop before he crashed into a grey horse pulling a cab, ignored the cabbie's cheerful cockney invitation to have his block knocked off and tried running on the pavement, until all the dodging he had to do sent him back into the street again. Some gal, eh, driving that speed with the bobbies coming down on automobiles at every chance?

She slowed down behind a bus. Hat flapping in his right hand, he took a breath for the final spurt — and she overtook the bus and was out of sight!

He ran. A man walked out in front of the horses and he had to grab him first before he could shove him aside.

'Ain't you got eyes in yer head, mate?'

She was turning left. He felt like throwing the goddam hat away but no, he'd catch up with her and then he would have lost a good hat for nothing.

Beaufort Street had less traffic, nothing between him and the Siddeley.

'Kate!'

She didn't look around — she accelerated! The automobile began to leave him behind. Go back and wait for her? The hell with that, she might be gone all day. Run, man, run!

There was still enough trace of fog around to rasp in his throat. She was mad, she was the only woman on earth he'd do this for, just the thought of her being a woman driver made her seem even more wonderful. A crazy eccentric English lady! She was slowing down at a street crossing.

'Kate!' His chest was tight. His left shoulder was aching where the bouncer had hit him, his right shin was hurting. 'Kate!'

He was only twenty yards' behind at most when she shot across Cheyne Walk onto Battersea Bridge over the river Thames. How fast can a man run compared to a six-horsepower, single-cylinder engine? On the bridge, London opened out, misty and grey, cold air off the river. His throat was in pain now, his head was aching. What happened to your breathing system, Pomeroy? Let me catch up to her, I'll never use a rude word again …

'Kate!'

Inexorably, the swanky automobile pulled farther and farther ahead of him and he began to slow down — no, goddammit, that isn't the American way! All along Battersea Bridge Road he pounded after her, aching in the legs, chest ready to cave in under the pressure — and she slammed to a halt just in time to avoid smashing into a big brown horse pulling a coal cart.

When he got there, the coal man was striding back and forth in front of the Siddeley, smacking at the gold bonnet and front lamp with his dirty cap.

'You bleedin' toffs! You fink you own the bleedin' roads, do yer? You fink you can scare the 'orses to death an' git away wiv it? I'll 'ave the bleedin' law on yer, I don't give a stuff who you fink you are!'

Pomeroy got both hands on the black leather upholstery of the rear seat and let his head hang down. No point in taking on a gorilla like that without some air in his lungs. Through the rasping sounds from his mouth and throat he heard that voice like roses, *her* voice: 'Shouting abuse at me will not achieve social justice. Your horse doesn't look in the least frightened —

in fact, it looks decidedly hungry to me, my good man. I hope you feed it properly. Now, will you stand clear? Thank you.'

He managed to drag himself into the front passenger seat before she took the brake off. The big hat turned. Her eyes narrowed, her lips tightened.

'It was you doing all that shouting, was it?'

'Why didn't you look around?' he gasped.

'Don't be silly — ' the motorcar started forward with a severe jolt — 'if I look around, I always crash into a lamp-post!'

Kate did what she called 'good works'. She treated him to a lecture on the drive through shabby South London. Two thousand homeless people 'slept rough' every night in London. At the age of seventy-five, one in three of the population was a pauper. The life expectancy for a male infant at birth in rich Hampstead was fifty years; in poor Southwark, thirty-six years. The average annual pay of a working man was fifty pounds a year, but the minimum living wage for a family was sixty pounds. People were literally dying of starvation and the workhouses were full of men, women and children being kept alive on broth and suet dumplings. She was on her way to a school in Lambeth where few of the children ever got any breakfast. She and her sympathizers in the movement for social justice had counted 125,000 London schoolchildren suffering from malnutrition.

'Come in and see for yourself,' she said snappily outside the school. 'No — on second thoughts, watch the car, they'll steal the wheels and the lamps in this area.'

He watched her walk across the stone yard they called the playground. Was that eccentric woman the lovely creature he'd held naked in a deluxe stateroom on a great ocean liner?

On the way back, when he was breathing something close to normal again, she tried to fend off any personal stuff with another lecture on the disgusting selfishness of the rich, the total indifference to human suffering that had turned her into an ardent socialist.

'I saw you Monday night,' he said. 'I was at the Frys' reception, your father didn't give me a chance to — '

'He said he saw you.'

'You *knew* I was there? But you just drove off — '

'I told you on the boat — all *that* is finished.' She looked sideways at him, the Siddeley immediately veered into the kerb. He closed his eyes against a crash. 'It's perfectly all right. I've been driving for a month without any mishap. Anyway, I'm glad you've found your way into smart society — do you realize those pompous snobs spend enough in one evening to feed a thousand hungry families for a whole year?'

'I'm not Robin Hood — '

'Is that all you can do, make jokes about it?'

'What are the thousand hungry families doing about it?'

Anger rising, she hurtled the Siddeley round the corner into Onslow Square. Two grey-uniformed nannies pushing perambulators veered away from the kerb in case the automobile took to the sidewalk. 'Don't worry, their time's coming and you'll have to choose sides.'

'I'm not even English for chrissake!'

'Being American absolves one from all moral responsibility, does it?'

'Your father's doing all right, what's his moral responsibility?'

She slammed on the brakes without slowing down. He pitched forward out of his seat, narrowly avoiding a head-first dive through the windshield. 'For God sakes — !'

The Siddeley was still shuddering when she switched off the engine. They were in the middle of the street. She turned to glare at him. 'I am deeply ashamed of the fact that my father works for that warmongering brute Jackie Fisher. This country will have a revolution very soon, mark my words. Once women get the vote there will be changes, I promise you. We'll burn the Union Jack on Jackie Fisher's doorstep! We won't waste money on bigger warships and bigger guns to rule the world. The biggest empire in history and it can't feed its own little children? Do you know that within a five minutes' walk of the Houses of Parliament families live in squalor, no running water, no shoes for the children, no — '

'I say — I hate to bother you ...' They looked around. A pink-faced gentleman was leaning out of a carriage whose coachman couldn't drive his two matching bays past the Siddeley. The gentleman recognized Kate. 'Oh, it's you, my dear, *do* forgive me.'

Pomeroy got out and pushed the Siddeley into the kerb, which seemed quicker than using the starting handle, once he managed to interrupt them and got Kate to take the brake off. The carriage passed on, the gentleman raising his hat to her. She got out quickly before Pomeroy could help her down.

'Who's your friend?'

'Bobby Hednesford. Bit of a fool but quite goodhearted, married an actress.' She came around the front of the Siddeley and met him on the pavement. 'I hope you enjoyed the ride. Goodbye, John.'

'Aren't you asking me in for a cup of tea?'

'No.'

'Aw, Kate — '

'Goodbye, John. I mean it.'

Watching her go up the steps to her front door, he felt he was seeing the last moments of a beautiful young woman before she turned into a charity committee matron, but what could he do about it?

Looking for a cab, he remembered Devoy. The back of his neck instantly developed a twitch. He looked over his shoulder. The ominous figures of the two grey-uniformed nannies pushing big black perambulators looked to be stalking him along the sedate Kensington sidewalk. Where the hell had all the cabs gone?

Scared of Devoy? No, scared of dying.

Ever since he'd come up out of the underground diggings into the foggy Strand and found no sign of Devoy, he'd been telling himself Devoy had taken it on the lam, realizing he was up against a Skagway graduate.

The back of his neck was not convinced.

We are the Germans, Pomeroy ...
Your dear friend Uwe? I knew Americans were naive but ...

Devoy wasn't dumb enough to commit suicide by reneging on a deal with the German secret service. They'd cooked up that yarn to keep Lang-Gaevernitz in the clear whichever way it went. Just as Devoy wasn't dumb enough to be lured down into the iron tunnel. They'd both set out that night with a view to killing each other. That made it spooky, knowing one of them was living on borrowed time.

A hansom cab came along, not a moment too soon. 'A hundred and twenty-three Victoria Street, fast as you can,' he snapped. He didn't wait to discuss it. The hackie flicked his whip, the cab lurched away from the kerb; he began to feel like the fish in the barrel — all this goddam glass! Francis Holborn's confession and his testimony put Devoy straight on course for the hangman's noose. Once Devoy realized what'd happened to George the steward and the cab driver, he had but two choices: run away or kill him. Devoy was a sonofabitch and a cold-blooded murderer and a traitor but he wasn't the type to run away.

It crossed his mind that the cabbie might be Devoy in disguise, and then he knew he had to do something about it or he'd be too spooked to get through the day.

Paying off the cab outside the embassy, he had a sudden attack of sheer goddam brilliance; dump the whole damn mess right back in Uwe's lap!

He hurried inside. He could come clean with Uwe — almost — tell Uwe how scared he was of Devoy, ask Uwe if he should go to Scotland Yard for help; self-defence would cover him for killing George the steward and the cab driver if diplomatic immunity wouldn't. Uwe wouldn't let it go that far. Faced with the choice of having him or Devoy killed, Uwe would see that Devoy was a liability, the one link between the Germans and the blackmail attempt on Tennyson.

(All those reichsmarks spent for what? One man drowned in the Atlantic Ocean. One man hung up in a London hotel room. Two men shot dead in a deep iron tunnel.)

Uwe would see that killing an American diplomat was too risky; no single scheme was worth the possible exposure of your network. Devoy was a freelance, strictly expendable; Uwe hated the brutes — now he could set them to work killing each other. Francis's statement didn't mention the Germans — he and Uwe could stay on terms, just like Gray wanted; Tennyson's mission would be kept secret and the neutral United States wouldn't be required to explain why American oil companies were fixing to fuel the British navy in a war against Germany; Theodore Roosevelt could carry on as the great peacemaker for a little while longer …

Brilliant!

He asked Miss Willoughby to get him the German embassy and took the call on Sleath's line. They said Herr Lang-Gaevernitz had unfortunately been called back to Berlin because his mother was ill.

Jane Hednesford telephoned inviting him to tea the following Tuesday at four. Not by so much as the merest pause or inflexion did her ladyship even hint that she had more than tea in mind. Like everything else in this goddam country, it was all utterly and totally *correct* — on the surface. Mr Brodie called a few minutes later. It came through on Spence's line. He stood by Spence's desk to take the call. Spence could have done the polite thing but he sat still and listened.

Holborn sounded as if he'd enjoyed a good lunch. (The English were always more amenable in the afternoons, he was to learn.) 'You wanted to know about *Swordfish,* old boy.'

'Can we meet?'

Uwe's mother wasn't ill, Uwe had cleared out of London because Devoy was out of control. Holborn was saying he was just off to Dorset for the weekend, they must meet soon for lunch.

'Anyway, it's nothing for you to worry about it, they have unofficial blessings from on high — '

'Blessings for what?'

'Putting *Swordfish* into production, of course. Betts is going to build six of the brutes at Bradstocks. Your man Fry's joining the consortium. They'll sell 'em to the navy when Fisher becomes First Sea Lord. It's to save them having a row about armaments expenditure in Parliament, all these weak-kneed Liberal johnnies would trot out their usual bilge about warmongering and — '

'Brutes? What kind of brutes?' He saw Spence listening while pretending to be copying out a memorandum. Spence seemed very alert for a guy who normally suffered from vertical fatigue. Was he the German spy in their midst?

'Submarine boats, supposed to be years ahead of their time,' Holborn was saying. 'They're running a trial for the moneybags at Bradstocks on Saturday and then the consortium contract will be signed and sealed. Your man Fry's going in for quarter of a million, that should keep him pally with the King, what? By the way, we decided to have a little chat with your friend Devoy but he's.flown the coop. Hasn't been in touch with you, has he?'

'He called here a couple of times when I was out. Where were you looking for him?'

'He was staying at the Cecil. He took a cab to Victoria station, thereafter the trail peters out. Let us know if he surfaces in your direction, there's a good chap.'

'I'll do that, old boy.'

When he put down the phone, Spence sneered: 'Old boy now, huh?'

'It's called diplomacy, Mitch, you should try it some time.' He had a little bout of coughing. 'This throat gets any worse could be I'll have to stay in bed tomorrow.'

He left the embassy the rear way and after dinner in the Excelsior stuck to his room with the door locked. The idea of Uwe Lang-Gaevernitz running home to a sick mother was fairly amusing. On second thoughts, Devoy wasn't out of control, he couldn't see Uwe running away from a mess; the fastidious Uwe had merely stepped into the next room while his brutes did his dirty work.

Getting out of London for the weekend seemed the healthy thing to do.

He kept his hansom waiting a few yards along until the gaunt figure of Sir Walter Tennyson came down the steps of his smart Kensington House and got into his official carriage. Bright-red cheeks went even brighter when Letitia saw who was at the door. He raised his bowler. 'Good morning, Letitia, we met on the *Lucania* — John Pomeroy? Is your mistress afoot yet?'

Letitia giggled. Such a well-developed girl, too, and such thick, black shiny hair. 'I'll see if Lady Cameron is seeing anyone this morning,' she said in her yokel's burr, leaving him in the hall. He admIred a mounted tiger's head, a stag's head with antlers, another tiger, a painting of a stag, a candlestick made from the leg of a deer, a hoof mounted on a plinth, a silver bracket where the knee should have been, a hollowed elephant's foot for standing umbrellas in, a painting of Queen Victoria side-saddle on a horse. He reached up to touch the fangs of a tiger.

'What are you doing here may I ask?'

Kate was on the landing, framed against a stained-glass window that turned grey morning light into soft reds and blues. He couldn't see her face but he knew the tone of voice — she was mad enough to add his head to the collection.

He took the carpeted stairs two at a time and came thudding down on his left knee before her, bowler hat held against his chest.

'A humble varlet at your service, ma'am.'

Letitia giggled from the top of the stairs.

'Get up and get out,' Kate hissed …

'Gadzooks and oddbodkins, milady — I come to offer my services in a noble cause, dost I not?'

He waited till Letitia had left them in the breakfast room with enough buttered toast to feed a family of four for a fortnight before he told her about a brute called *Swordfish*.

25

They crossed the Thames by the same Battersea Bridge he'd run across the day before, and then through grimy Battersea and unfashionable Clapham to Wimbledon, where the great sprawl of London began to thin out. Her lovely profile under her big driving hat gave him a touch of conscience.

'You quite sure you want to go through with this, Kate?'

'Stop talking; I can't listen to you and drive at the same time.'

She had a funny way of sitting forward on her black leather bucket seat, crouched over the wheel and peering through the angled windshield as if she was trying to find the road in the dark. Coming through Epsom, it began to look more like countryside; she stalled the automobile a couple of times when they met smart girls in velvet riding hats trying to control frisky mounts; the starting handle had a kick that almost put his arm out of joint.

'They still think one should have a man with a red flag in front,' Kate said airily. 'Progress isn't popular in this country, y'know ... Say something, for goodness sake.'

'You told me not to talk.'

'It helps my concentration.'

'Back there you said it spoiled your concentration.'

'We're out of London now, isn't the air nice?'

'There's a lot of it ... mainly up the legs of my pants.'

'I don't want to hear about your underwear.'

'Sorry — trousers.'

'Pull my rug around your legs.'

'Well ... if you're sure it won't cause talk.'

'We're going to destroy a bloody great submarine boat and you're worried people will see us sharing a rug?'

'We're not going to destroy it; we're going to put it out of action.'

'We haven't reached Dorking yet and you're getting cold feet!'

'No, cold legs.'

'How else can we put it out of action without destroying it? What's the point of putting the bloody thing out of action; we *must* destroy it! We 'should've brought some dynamite. You were right, all I've ever done is talk talk talk, that's all women ever do. Well, I'm sick of complaining and whining and pleading — there's only one way to stop Sir Oscar bloody Betts and his kind dragging us into war for profit and that's by *hitting* the buggers!'

'I wish you wouldn't use words like that — '

'I'm sorry, it slipped out. What's your plan for when we get to Shoreham, John? I'd better go faster or we never will get there.'

'No, you're doing fine.'

'The makers say she'll do over fifty, I've always wanted to see just how fast — '

'We have plenty of time! You want to let me take the wheel for a spell?'

'No, I'm used to our roads.'

'For chrissake, you want to kill us both?'

'Honestly, I think you're a bit of a coward.'

Terrified of her reckless driving, turning to ice in a steady blast of cold air through the open automobile, he saw the famed English countryside in a less than rapturous frame of mind as she drove them south through the county of Surrey into the southernmost county of Sussex. She enjoyed his nervousness and laughed every time she stalled the Siddeley and he had to get out and swing the handle. She thought he was losing his nerve and tried to inspire him with fresh confidence for their audacious blow at the men who made money from war. She thought her lectures on militarism had converted him to her righteous cause; the truth was he had to get tomorrow's sea trials postponed or Fry would be signing contracts to invest in a whole fleet of British submarine boats and Gray would have an excuse to renege on his twenty thousand dollars. (Ask the Indians if anybody in Washington had ever honoured an agreement.) Apart from being the only person he knew with an automobIle, she was so eccentric no rural cop was ever going to suspect her of being a dangerous saboteur. Eccentricity, the more flagrant the better, was the cover you needed in England; people in country villages smiled politely at the smart lady and her bowler-hatted companion whose noisy contraption had frightened the geese. Toiling labourers in fields waved their caps and shouted rude dialect. Kate waved back at them untIl he begged her to keep both hands on the goddam wheel. They reached Shoreham on the coast late in the afternoon, having stopped for a good lunch at Horsham — as she said, an army marches on its stomach.

Bradstocks shipbuilding yard was just out of town. The road went past the main office building, which looked like a farmhouse with modern extensions, and then turned away from the sea, where a field with brown cows bordered the fence around the waterline sheds.

'It's bigger than I thought,' he said, when they stopped a half-mile up a narrow lane at a break in the hedge. She rummaged In her gladstone bag and produced a pair of binoculars. Absentmindedly, he held out his hand — but she was using them. ' That new shed at the other end looks like the one. You see any guards?'

"They'll have a night watchman.'

'The most advanced underwater boat in the world and you think they'll have a night watchman? They'll have guards with guns.'

'Don't be silly, this isn't America. Turn your back.' She shoved the glasses at him. 'I want to get my walking boots on.'

He re-focused the fieldglasses and scanned the shipyard and its big sheds. He saw workmen in overalls but no guards. The yard was surrounded by a barbed-wire fence. He lowered the glasses. She had her skirt up to her knees.

'Turn your back,' she growled.

'Sorry. Say, do you think — '

'Hold the rug, will you?'

'How can I hold the rug with my back turned?'

'Close your eyes then.'

'Sure.'

'Is anybody coming?'

'You said to keep my eyes closed.'

'Open them, but don't look.'

'Jeez, I've seen you with nothing on — '

'Only a rotter would talk about it in broad daylight.'

A red sun sank slowly across a grey October sky. They took turns of the glasses to watch the shipyard. 'What if we get caught breaking in?' she asked.

'I have that figured. I got an anonymous warning the Irish Fenians plan to assassinate Ambassador Fry because he won't help those two bombers. I had to get down here in a hurry, you offered me a lift, I wanted to check the security arrangements without tipping anybody off.'

She grimaced. 'Not bad ... what if we get caught destroying their precious submarine boat?'

'I told you, we're only putting it out of action!' Behind her back, he slipped the Smith and Wesson under the leather upholstery; she was right, this wasn't the States, the pistol would take a lot of explaining if they were caught. 'I guess we just have to run like hell.'

They waited till dark and walked down the country lane carrying one of the Siddeley's brass oil lamps and a spare can of gasoline. They climbed a five-barred wooden gate into the field of cows and went across wet grass to the barbed-wire fence.

There was no fog here by the sea and they made their way along the fence in moonlight through scudding clouds. Soon they heard the soft whisper of little waves. The barbed-wire fence ended where grass met sand. Nobody had thought intruders might risk wet feet; maybe the fence was only to keep the cows out. They were inside the fence and heading towards the dark sheds when a dog barked, not too far away. They froze, his hand gripping her shoulder. The moon appeared above a mountain range of white clouds. The dog barked again, then stopped abruptly. He thought he heard somebody calling out, a man's voice. 'It can't have heard us or we'd be ripped to shreds by now,' she whispered.

'Sshh.' He strained to listen. For a moment he heard only the faint whisper of a breeze off the sea, then an engine, deep and powerful, roared to life. 'Guard dogs,' he muttered, 'I should've brung my pistol — '

'Shoot hard-working dogs who never did us any harm?'

'You said we'd be ripped to shreds!'

'That was only to cheer you up.'

The first shed was dark and silent. From the corner, they saw chinks of light in the walls of the new shed, at the far end of the yard. They moved quickly across an open space to the next dark building, Kate in front. In the dark shadow of the shed, Kate had to turn up the lamp to find a way past stacked wood and piled sand and heaps of rusty metal. When she stopped without warning, he bumped into her.

'I stood on something soft,' she hissed.

A faint pool of light fell on thick brown hairs tinged with black. The light gleamed off dark red blood oozing over the hairs between the dog's ears. It was a German shepherd — Kate called it an Alsatian. The blood was coming from a savage wound in its flat skull. Kate's fingers dug into his arm.

'I'm sorry, John — '

'You going to faint?'

'— they do have guards, I saw one through the binoculars — '

'Ye gods! Why didn't you tell me?'

'Ssshhh. You wouldn't have let me come. Anyway, he didn't look very alert — '

'Give me the lamp — '

'I said I'm sorry — what is it?'

' The lamp — ' Alerted by his tone, she turned with the lamp before he could get hold of it. What he'd seen, just beyond the dog's head, was a man's boot, toe up ...

The nightwatchman had been dragged among grass and weeds growing thickly round a big rusting boiler. He was in his fifties, grey hair, red face half buried in green shoots. His cheek was warm. He'd been strangled with a length of white rope still crossed at the back of his neck.

I could get you five thousand dollars for the Swordfish *specifications ...*

A man who could kill a big guard dog with one savage hammer blow, strangle an alerted guard before he could raise a shout. All in silence, in the dark ... manic ferocity on tap ...

Took a cab to Victoria Station, thereafter the trail peters out...

He guided Kate in against the shed wall. 'What London railway station brings you here?' he whispered.

'I came by motor vehicle actually ... '

Before she giggled out loud, he slapped her smartly and clamped his hand over her mouth. He put his lips close to her ear. 'We could both end up dead here. One more sound and I'll knock you cold. Just nod Victoria station?' She nodded yes.

Devoy, it had to be Devoy, too much of a coincidence to. be anybody else. Devoy was on the run now; getting hold of the

Swordfish specifications might be his one chance of placating his German masters and of getting out of England. Tentatively, he eased his grip on her mouth. 'Sorry,' she whispered stiffly, hysteria under control. He took her arm.

'Come on, I have to get you out of here.'

She pulled back. 'What about you?'

'I can take better care of myself without you to worry about — '

'Leave me on my own? No thanks!' she hissed, grabbing hold of him with both hands. She wasn't about to let go and he wasn't about to give up. He decided against running back to the automobile for the pistol. It would take too long and gunshots would only draw a crowd, even if he managed to loose off a shot once Devoy's big hands found his throat in the dark ...

26

Kate was brave, Kate was impatient. He made her wait. These upperclass English seemed keen on noble causes worth dying for, stupid bastards.

They were under a big yacht hull on a timber cradle. Between them and the long, low shed was open ground lit by gas mantles on the shed wall. His eyes scanned slowly for any movement in that deathly orange light. There would be no second chance with Devoy.

When he nudged her, they sprinted across the open ground and ducked into the shadows under an iron staircase. Inside the shed they were boosting the powerful engine; the corrugated-iron wall was vibrating — so was the ground under his feet. He positioned one eye, against a crack in the metal sheeting but got no more than an impression of space and light. Every time he blinked he saw old Jesse laying there with the top of his skull open in a flap .

Climbing the first flight of iron stairs, they were exposed to the full glare of the gas mantles, then they were above the orange light. The rest of the yard was in darkness. At one end of the long shed was the main office building, its windows dark; looking the other way, he saw a dagger of moonlight rippling on water. His guess was that the watchman had intercepted Devoy making for the main office building where the specifications would be kept.

The staircase ended about forty feet up at a door under the overhang of the shed roof. They stood for a moment on the iron grating, watching for any movement below. Again she was nudging him to get on with it. He tried the door handle.

Noise and light and warm air smelling of oil and salt water flooded past their faces as they stepped inside onto a maintenance inspection gantry which ran under the sloping roof in both directions, with suspended catwalks leading to the heavy superstructure of an overhead crane running the whole length of the shed. Then they came to the handrail and looked out over a vast arena.

At one end, the big new modern shed had sliding doors open a few feet; at the other, a vast tarpaulin curtain to keep out wind and rain off the sea. The black submarine boat was in one of two dry basins sunk in a vast concrete floor. From up here, it looked like a cigar tapered at both ends, or a fat porker trapped in a narrow slaughterhouse pen. At the deep end of the sunken basin, where big angled doors kept out the sea, a small spume of water from an inlet valve was making a tiny puddle. The roar of the engine came up at them like a hurricane blast.

They could see three men, two painters, one floor-sweeper. The painters were moving about on the black hull, probably touching up dirty marks; they looked to be nearly finished and had their pots and stuff assembled on a mobile gangway between the edge of the sunken basin and the black hull. The third man was sweeping slowly with a wide brush from the big sliding doors towards a row of flat-roofed offices and storerooms lining the opposite wall of the submarine-boat construction shed.

Pomeroy leaned out over the handrail. Directly below were stacks of metal plates, lengths of piping and tubes, wooden beams, big wooden crates, drums of coiled copper wire, barrels of paint: what looked enough material for a whole fleet of underwater warships. He had just spotted the safety hoops of a vertical ladder from the platform down to the shed floor when Kate nudged him.

A man in shirt sleeves carrying a roll of white paper under his arm was crossing the big concrete floor from the row of office cabins towards the sunken pens. He said something to the sweeper, gesticulating authoritatively, then walked on. The sweeper leaned on his brush, staring after the man in shirt sleeves, his resentment obvious even from this height and angle.

This shirt-sleeved man followed a meticulous path of straight lines and right angles to reach the gangway. He crossed over to the black hull of the submarine boat. He called out to the painters and pointed to the pots cluttering up the gangway, obviously telling them to clear up their mess. Then he climbed the ladder on the outside of the submarine boat's stumpy tower and disappeared down through a small, round hatchway. A moment later, the roar of the engine subsided to a steady, high-pitched hum. The painters were carrying their pots off the submarine boat.

Pomeroy picked up the petrol can. 'Give me the matches.'

She frowned. 'What for?'

'To light a fire, of course.'

They're going home now, John — '

'But the guard won't be here to lock up, so they'll go looking for him and this place will be swarming with cops — the matches!'

She was shocked. 'John — they're only working men — no, I simply refuse to let you do anything so terrible.' She folded her arms and stood there defiantly. It suddenly dawned on him: she thought he intended to burn down this whole shed with the workers still in it.

'We have to get them out of here,' he explained, holding onto his temper. 'I'll start a fire at the other end of the yard — the matches, would you give me the goddam matches?'

'I don't have them,' she said apologetically.

'I gave them to you.'

'No, you didn't — oh yes, you did.'

He grabbed the box of Vestas. 'You stay here — '

She reached the door ahead of him. 'You're not leaving me here on my own!'

313

'You're safe up here,' he said grimly, 'You stay here and you don't make a sound, you hear? Devoy wants the specifications real bad; he could be hiding down there already. You stay here and keep a lookout for him.'

She shuddered. 'I wish I'd never come.'

He hurried down the iron staircase and across the open ground in that garish orange light, heading for the side of the yard nearest .the road. Eyes adjusting again to moonlight, he saw a biggish hut standing apart, about fifty yards beyond the office building but still in sight of the front of the long shed. He sloshed a little gasoline against the wooden doors and didn't see the sign FUEL STORE — NO NAKED LIGHTS until he d thrown the flaring Vesta.

Halfway back to the long shed, a flicker of light began to play on the brick wall of the office building. He reached the corner of the long shed and waited. Nobody came to the big doors. He groped around on the ground until he found some stones. He stepped out a yard or so and hurled them at the narrow gap in the tall doors, then Jumped back against the wall. A shadow broke the shaft of light.

'That you, Fred?' came a man's voice.

The fuel store went up with a soft roar. A twisting spire of white flame pierced the night sky like an arrowhead, followed by a surging column of red flames and black smoke.

'Hoy — the oil shed's on fire!'

He watched them running past, first the sweeper, then one of the painters, then the shirt-sleeved man, and the other painter and three men in brown mechanics overalls. 'I'll send for the fire brigade, the shirt-sleeved man shouted, splitting off and running to the office building.

Pomeroy gave it a couple of seconds, then sprinted for the narrow gap in the big doors. There was no one coming across the big concrete floors.

He closed the tall door easily on its castor wheels, and slammed down the iron retaining bar.

Petrol slurped about in the can as he sprinted to the row of offices. Under the glare of electric lamps, it felt as if he had at last discovered that vast hobgoblins' cavern he'd always known was out there in the night somewhere. Only one office was lit, the door ajar. A man's coat and hat and jacket hung from a small hatstand. There was a small coal fire and a rolltop desk with crammed pigeonholes. A door on the other side opened into a corridor running against the outside wall of the shed.

Pinned along one asbestos wall were draughtsman's blue tracings of the submarine boat, full length and sectioned diagrams, the specifications printed in copperplate lettering, with separate sheets for the engines. He began to pull the flimsy sheets off the wall . . .

Hurrying across the concrete floor, he shielded his eyes against the down-glare of the lamps. 'Kate?' he shouted towards the shadows under the roof.

She was almost at the bottom of the wall ladder. 'They've all gone,' she said. He was already striding towards the sunken pens. He climbed up onto the concrete ramp. Kate. pulled herself up beside him.

'Good God...'

It stood on a cradle of angled timber supports in the deep concrete basin: *Swordfish,* the most advanced underwater warship ever devised by man. The sloping concrete basin, the massive wooden lock gates, the huge tarpaulin curtains blocking out the night sky, all made it seem like a titanic stage setting. They stared in awe ... *Swordfish.* It was painted a dull black that didn't glisten in the electric light, looking like a great whale now they were level with the propeller under the tapered stern, bulging massively in the middle where the tower was, maybe 120 feet long, a mounted gun at each end, big guns tightly cased against water penetration ... *Swordfish* ... a big black machine for taking war down into the ocean depths. In face of the monster, madness became logic. She ran behind him to the lock gates. The handle of the inlet valve on this side turned at .a touch. Water started gushing into the basin far below. 'Get them both open,' he snapped. She frowned, realizing she'd have to walk along the top of the lock gates to reach the other valve. It was a long way down to the floor of the concrete basin. 'For chrissake, move!'

He ran back and crossed the wooden gangway and climbed to the top of the tower, where raised sides formed a little bridge. He hesitated a moment, scanning the huge shed, sure he was being watched, seeing nobody but Kate energetically turning the inlet valve handle. He stepped into the small square hatchway and climbed down, holding the gasoline can in his left hand. He stepped off into a shadowy light coming off the floor of the small, cramped control room. The engineers had been working by the light of electric bulbs in wire frames on the end of extension cables. He picked one up and saw diagrams and printed material on a sloping table, simple stuff to satisfy the moneybags who were going to give the world six of these monsters ...

... *an electric motor will power the* Swordfish *while submerged; the heavy diesel comes into use on the surface, giving* Swordfish *a speed of up to 10 knots underwater and 22 knots on the surface .*

... the most advanced system of gyroscopes now available will keep Swordfish stable in all conditions and at all depths ...

... apart from three-inch guns mounted on the hull, Swordfish can carry up to 40 high-explosive mines, capable of underwater release, and 8 Whitehead torpedoes, Mark IV, with a range of 3,000 yards and a top speed of 26 knots ...

The diagrams took him aft to the engine room along a narrow passageway festooned with twisting pipes and electrical wiring in flowing bundles. A roaring hum made the small engine room seem like the heart of a living creature. The engineers were testing the 400-horsepower diesel; he moved the brass handle slowly across the clock face panels. The roaring hum swelled to a deep thunder, the vibrations from the soles of his feet made his teeth dance, then the whole boat shuddered as the brass handle stopped at FULL SPEED AHEAD.

He went back through the control room. The forward passage brought him to the crew's quarters — hammocks slung in a narrow space between the sloping bulkhead and huge black torpedoes. He rolled a hammock into a bundle, poured a little petrol on it, shoved the canvas bundle under a wooden locker and struck a match . The hammock began to burn. He retreated, sloshing petrol in the narrow passageway, partially closing the . hatch door to the forward compartment as he stepped into the gloomy control room.

Easing his way towards the ladder at the foot of the tower, he was suddenly hit in the back. A brutal hand seized him by the hair and he was rammed to his knees against a metal column. The big hand dragged his face to the side and the nozzle of a silver-plated pistol was rammed into his cheek. A knee jabbed brutally into his spine.

'Likewise, Devoy,' he drawled.

Being a smart-ass earned him a kick in the kidneys.

27

The big hand jerked on his hair.

'Get off your knees, Pomeroy, God doesn't like you any more'

He staggered to his feet before his hair was torn out by the roots, The big hand released its agonizing grip and searched him roughly and intimately,

'No gun, Pomeroy? And you killed my friend George?' The big hand seized his ear and twisted it, forcing him to turn, 'You must be very dangerous.'

In the patchy light from the engineers' electric bulbs on the floor, Devoy's deepset eyes were like sockets in a skull. His black hair glistened as if he'd just risen from his dressing table, He was wearing a hunting jacket with leather shoulders,

'Who are you working for?' he demanded,

'I told you, I'm an American diplomat — '

Devoy slashed the pistol barrel across his cheek without even thinking about it, then jabbed the nozzle under his jaw-bone, forcing his head up.

'You took the specifications from the office, didn't you?'

'No, I was looking for them down here.'

'They had a full set of specifications pinned on the deputy manager's wall, I saw them earlier today when I was here on behalf of the Royal Belgian Navy, That's how it's done, Pomeroy, I could have taught you a lot.'

Devoy's knee jabbed up into his testicles, His mouth opened to yelp Devoy's left fist rammed into his stomach, He started to double forward Devoy's left hand closed on his hair again and he was dragged across the control room and shoved against the wall near the engine-room passage, Devoy moved the nozzle of the pistol onto his ear. 'Pick up that light, Pomeroy.'

He stooped slowly, felt for the bulb in its mesh guard, and straightened up, Devoy took it and hung it over a pipe, This close, the naked electric light was dazzling.

Devoy came closer, chest and stomach touching him, little saliva bubbles in the corners of the mouth, eyes like creatures lurking in dark caves, tight lips open over white teeth wet with froth, His voice was hot and thick, 'You got greedy when I told you how much they were worth, didn't you?'

'I don 't need the money, Devoy — '

Devoy's left hand came to pinch his cheek, That same big gold ring from the poker game caught the light and golden rays shimmered mistily in his eyes, Devoy's finger and thumb tweaked his cheek; the obscene intimacy of it was a lot worse than the pain.

'Where are the specifications, Pomeroy?'

That was when he heard the high-pitched drawl: *By Godfrey, it does my heart good, a fine young fellow like you dedicating himself in the ultra-American spirit of patriotism!*

Devoy moved even tighter against him and started wiping his face with the nozzle and sharp foresight of the pistol, dragging the barrel back and forth across his cheekbones and teeth and nose.

'George wanted to throw you overboard on the *Lucania,* Pomeroy, I stopped him. You ruined a set-up that took months to organize but I let you live. Aren't you curious?' He stared into the deepset eyes. 'Then you killed George and Silkman. George was my best friend.' Devoy's eyes glittered in their shadowy caverns and taunted him with how easily a finger would flex and send a bullet shattering through brittle face bone, ploughing through soft brain, battering out through hard skull. The engine roar had taken on a slightly new tone. Devoy tapped the bridge of his nose with the pistol, delicate little taps. Devoy's tongue pink and purple peeked out between his wet wolf's teeth.

Weakness always invites attack came the high-pitched drawl.

'Why was that girl letting water in?' Devoy demanded.

He felt his stomach sink. He'd been hoping Kate had seen him and run. 'She wants to destroy all weapons of war,' he said. 'What did you do to her?'

'I shouldn't waste your precious time worrying about her, Pomeroy.'

'Maybe I know how to get hold of the specifications, Devoy, my ambassador is investing in this boat —'

'Ready to do a deal now, Pomeroy?' Devoy pushed the nozzle of the pistol between his lips and forced them open. 'I'll have to get out of England because you interfered, Pomeroy.' He was forcing the pistol between his teeth, then changed his mind and proffered the nozzle to his lips.

'Kiss it.'

Pomeroy frowned, not understanding. Devoy rapped his front teeth with the barrel, shoved the nozzle against the nose.

'Kiss the gun, Pomeroy.'

As roguishly as he could muster with a pistol picking his nose, Pomeroy smiled and said, 'You sure the gun's all you want me to kiss, Charles?'

Devoy frowned. His dark cheeks flushed. His tongue licked his lips clear of froth. His perversion required a ritual of humiliation by terror and then the surrender of a male victim to the ultimate gratification of death. Devoy's hand felt for his hair. Such was the overweening arrogance of the man, so entranced was he with the artistry of his own sadism, he had his forefinger resting across the trigger guard when he jabbed the pistol at his mouth. At this range he saw Devoy's tongue and teeth and lips perform their different functions to produce the hissed words: 'Kiss the gun, Pomeroy!'

'Sure — anything you say!'

His lips pursed to kiss the pistol, then he snapped like a dog and got Devoy's thumb and a finger and the chamber between his teeth and bit hard on bone and metal until something cracked.

Devoy barked with pain and jerked his hand away. The silver-plated pistol flew out of his hand and clattered across the floor under some pipes against the bulkhead. The narrow space forced them together shoulders and hips in a frantic scramble to reach it first. He elbowed Devoy in the belly and got ahead — Devoy grabbed him by the shoulders and tried to run him headfirst into the bulkhead. He stiffened his legs and rammed himself backwards at Devoy, battering at Devoy's face with his left elbow. Devoy held onto his jacket and the left sleeve ripped away from the shoulder. They came together in a rush, punching and gouging and kneeing. The moment Devoy's arms closed on his ribcage for the bear-hug, he knew he was a dead man if it came to a trial of strength. He butted Devoy three or four times on the nose and thumbed at his eyes. Devoy the sadistic bully didn't squeal for mercy — he lowered his head and rushed him bull-like back across the control room. He was kicking and punching and trying to tear Devoy's ears off but Devoy rammed him against the wall and tried to hold him there for a punch into his lower belly. He got his hands on Devoy's shoulders and jerked his knees up into Devoy's face. Devoy had to straighten up — he ducked and charged headfirst into Devoy's belly. He almost got Devoy off his feet as he staggered upright, but Devoy caught hold of a vertical pillar and threatened to get a leg-lock round his waist. He let himself slip down to his knees and scrambled away. Just for a moment there was room to throw a punch and he got in two lefts at Devoy's eyes and was getting set to batter Devoy senseless when Devoy hit him low in the belly with a right that would have broken him like a dry stick if they'd been standing a few inches closer. He dodged behind a narrow upright beam.

'The boat's on fire, Devoy!' he shouted.

Devoy came at him quickly, feinting in either direction, trying to panic him out from behind the beam. He fended Devoy off with two left jabs right on the button and got back behind the beam. Under the hanging light, Devoy's face was bruised. There was blood round his mouth. His oiled hair was askew. But his eyes were smiling and Pomeroy realized Devoy was crazy to kill him. He ducked away, trying to reach the ladder at the foot of the tower — Devoy got in front of him. His hip hit on something solid and a wave of pain made him wince. Devoy came towards him, not in a fighter's crouch but standing erect, shoulders square, hands in front of him as if ready to meet in prayer.

Pomeroy felt nothing behind him and stepped back into the engine-room passage. Devoy now had a chance for a dive at the gun on the floor under the pipes but the bastard wouldn't take it. Arrogance won out. The great Devoy didn't need to scamble on his hands and knees for a little gun; he could do his own killing. Pomeroy backed along the passageway. Devoy stooped and picked up one of the lights on a cable. He held it up like a candle. His broad shoulders filled the hatchway.

'The boat's on fire!'

Devoy shook his head. The boat lurched heavily. Devoy seemed to shrug, it was difficult to see exactly through the dazzle of the electric lightbulb. *Swordfish* lurched again. Devoy came forward, shouting something that was lost against the engine roar.

Pomeroy let him get within three or four feet, then grabbed a narrow overhead pipe, jack-knifed his body and catapulted himself feet first at Devoy's face.

It was his one chance of getting out and, when he felt his heels connect, he started kicking both legs like demented pistons, at the same time swinging himself hand over hand along the pipe like a monkey. Devoy staggered backwards but

322

wouldn't fall, as if his broad shoulders were jammed. He went on kicking and then he felt Devoy under him and he stamped and kicked downwards and pulled himself another few inches along the pipe and vaulted forward.

He almost toppled back on his heels when he landed. Devoy was on the floor, struggling to turn and rise. He clutched at some wires and got away from Devoy's big hands, going through the hatchway so fast he banged his head but didn't stop to rub the bruise. The pistol! He grabbed the light hanging from a pipe — and saw smoke coming from the forward compartment!

He threw down the light and hit the bottom rungs of the ladder and started up inside the tower towards a square patch of dazzling electric sky. The boat was rolling. Don't let him find the gun till my ass is clear, oh Lord!

As he pulled himself up out of the hatch, *Swordfish* lurched dramatically off her cradle of timbers. A huge wave smashed against the side of the concrete basin and came crashing back against the black hull. The submarine boat rose in the air and he saw Kate spread-eagled on concrete near the other inlet valve. The wooden gangway slewed off the black hull into churning water. The propeller bit water and *Swordfish* began to slide forward. He held onto the side and leaned to look over the rim of the hatch — Devoy was halfway up the ladder with the silver pistol shining in his right hand!

The hatch cover didn't have a bolt on the outside — he slammed it down anyway to delay Devoy a couple of seconds and clambered over the side of the conning tower at the front, the direct route to Kate. He dropped onto a narrow walkway of wooden slats with a handrail as the wooden gangway rose on a crest of water before being crushed to splinters between the black hull and the side of the basin.

Swivelling on her prow against the lock gates, *Swordfish* was swinging massively from side to side in the basin. Water was hurling from end to end in big waves and deep troughs, which crashed into each other and sent huge spumes high in the air. He ran along the wooden slats. Ahead of him, the massive lock-gate timbers were shaking visibly as the powerful diesel engine pushed the submarine boat forward at maximum power. On the wooden slats he was about level with the edge of the basin but to jump he had to get onto the hull itself, with water surging over it in great spasms. As he clambered over the hand-rail, he looked back — Devoy was standing on the tower aiming at him. The hull hit a wall of water coming off the side of the basin and seemed to climb into the air. He took two or three running steps on wet iron and jumped. When he landed and pitched forward on hands and knees, the weight of water rushing back into the basin very nearly took him with it, then he was running for Kate, dodging from side to side.

Kate started to move! He was sprinting diagonally towards her when she rolled over on her back, one knee raised to show her white pantaloons.

'Kate!' he bawled. She started to sit up, rubbing her eyes. A sudden pain made her hold her head. 'Kate! Get up — move!' he was roaring as he reached her and grabbed hold of her arms. She started to complain he heard a pistol shot and a bullet whanged off concrete inches from her boots.

Pomeroy started to drag her into the meagre shelter of the inlet-valve mechanism — a metal pillar and a handle — Devoy fired again and a bullet screamed off the metal pillar. He threw himself on top of her, trying to get down behind five or six inches of raised concrete.

On the tower of the rolling submarine boat, Devoy was taking careful aim with both hands holding the silver pistol when a ball of fire erupted up from the interior of *Swordfish,* Devoy right bang in the middle of it.

The flames went spinning on up towards the roof. Devoy spun wildly in circles trying to beat out flames silhouetting his arms and shoulders; black smoke and fiery particles roared up out of the conning tower in a sheer column.

Pomeroy picked Kate up and got her over his right shoulder, then ran through three inches of cascading water and went along the top of the lock gates on his toes — too big a risk any other way of running into shipyard workers. He ran with her across the huge concrete floor to the foot of the wall ladder up to the maintenance gantry. She was struggling violently to get off his shoulder by then, indignant he should treat her as a helpless female.

As he climbed the iron rungs, he looked over his shoulder. Devoy was beating wildly at his burning shoulders and arms when the massive lock gates finally gave way. The water inside the basin was level with the outside channel — the gates gave a last shudder and slowly parted. Black *Swordfish* bounced a little in her narrow pen and the monstrous tube began to slide forward, scraping through the gates, flames and oil smoke and greasy black flakes shooting up out of the conning tower. Men were already running towards the basin from the offices.

Devoy saw too late that *Swordfish* was moving out of the basin — he was stumbling jerkily, still burning, trying to get down the outside ladder, when the conning tower crashed into the great tarpaulin curtain. It came billowing down and crushed Devoy flat and enveloped the tower like a shroud. A huge backwave rushed to fill the concrete basin and came smashing across the ramp, knocking men off their feet. They were up on the platform under the roof as *Swordfish* moved out into the black sea and a spot of flame suddenly burned red through the tarpaulin. . . They hurried down the outside stairs and had only to hide in the shadows once to avoid running men. That was when his tongue identified the source of a sharp pain every time he breathed in cold air — he'd broken a corner off a front tooth,

lower, biting Devoy's hand with the gun. His stomach sank —
those goddam dentists!.

They were climbing the wooden gate out of the held of wet
grass when *Swordfish* appeared beyond the flames and buildings, heading out to sea in a blazing shroud of tarpaulin. The
shooting column of flames and smoke made the conning tower
look like the mouth of hell. He wanted only to run but Kate
stood up on the old-fashioned farmgate to watch and the first
explosion thundered across sea and land, turning night into
fiery day, setting dark water on fire, volcanic explosions that
sounded like the war machine's promise of vengeance to
come...

'I'm going behind this hedge for a call of nature, don't look.'

He shivered in the cold air of the English countryside at
dawn.

'Do people live out here by *choice?*'

'Do you good, you lounge lizard. What a shame we'll, never
be able to tell anybody, isn't it?' she said through the hedge.
'I've never felt so excited in my whole life. We must have cost
Sir Oscar bloody Betts millions!'

'You can bet he's well insured — probably with another of
his own companies.'

'I'd still like to see their faces.' He got down and went
around to the other side of the automobile in case she could see
through the hedge. He pulled out the flattened roll of specifications from his trouser leg and shoved it under the back seat.
Destroying the *Swordfish* prototype would only delay things
but it would give Uncle Sam time to get in the game. 'Pity it
isn't spring,' she was saying, 'you'd love the countryside when
the flowers are coming out . . . John? Where are you?'

'Right here, matter of fact — '

She slapped down her skirt. 'Sneaking a look like some horrid little schoolboy?' she sneered, then her eyes narrowed. 'Why are you carrying that rug? If you think — '

He shook out the rug and got hold of her hands and fell back, pulling her down on top before she started to fight back. 'Hey — you said it excited you —'

'I told you — that's all finished! Let go of me!'

'Promise not to scratch my eyes out …?'

A knee jabbed into his groin. Leather boots hacked at his shins and ankles. 'It's the man who's supposed to be rough!'

She got her left hand free and landed a solid slap on his ear. 'You bastard! Just because you are stronger than me —'

He jerked his head, side to side, avoiding her slaps. 'I love you Kate —'

'You'll be bloody sorry —'

He let go of her wrist and raised his hands.

'Okay okay, I surrender, you win —'

Her right hand landed a smack on his cheek. Head ringing, he tried to roll off the rug but she got her full weight on his legs and pinned him down by the wrists.

'Surrender? Oh no — you are not getting away with it that easily you bastard.'

ASK THE INDIANS IF WASHINGTON
EVER KEPT ITS WORD ...

It took Gray a week to reply to his cable. Pomeroy decoded it sitting by the coal fire in his little room up there on the London rooftops, his copy of *Oliver Twist* on his lap. It had rained all day, now they were talking about frost. It took a lot of jumping from page to page to turn the lines of numerals into words — Dickens wasn't too interested in submarine boats and German secret-service masterminds. The message came clear halfway through but he went on to the end:

Good work so for. Plans most useful. Frying trouble not satis-factorily resolved. Who is giving secrets from workhouse? Exploit friendship with long friend. Report on blackmail regards frying.

Frying was Ambassador Fry — taken from Fagin cooking the sausages the night Oliver came down Saffron Hill with the Dodger. The workhouse was the embassy. Long friend — Lang-Gaevernitz, now back on the glittering Mayfair social scene and not betraying by so much as a blink of an eyelid his total innocence of the sabotage perpetrated on the secret submarine *Swordfish* by a freelance agent called Devoy acting, it was presumed, for a rival manufacturer of warships.

Without Gray's say-so he couldn't pick up his money, so there was not a lot of profit in cursing Gray for a cold-blooded, two-timing sonofabitch.

I didn't think you'd let me come home so easily anyhow, Gray you bastard, but that's okay. I'd like to tell you about Kate and Jane Hednesford but I don't think the right word's in *Oliver Twist*. Oh well, what the hell, if I'm here anyway I might as well ask for more . . .

Lightning Source UK Ltd.
Milton Keynes UK
UKOW06f0045290616

277303UK00001B/24/P

9 781908 390356